W9-BWB-057

A VENOM DARK AND SWEET

JUDY I. LIN

FEIWEL AND FRIENDS
New York

A Feiwel and Friends Book
An imprint of Macmillan Publishing Group, LLC
120 Broadway, New York, NY 10271 • fiercereads.com

Our books may be purchased in bulk for promotional, educational, or business use. Please contact your local bookseller or the Macmillan Corporate and Premium Sales Department at (800) 221-7945 ext. 5442 or by email at MacmillanSpecialMarkets@macmillan.com.

Library of Congress Control Number: 2022901732

First edition, 2022
Book design by Michelle Gengaro-Kokmen
Feiwel and Friends logo designed by Filomena Tuosto
Printed in the United States of America

ISBN 978-1-250-76710-3 (hardcover)
1 3 5 7 9 10 8 6 4 2

ISBN 978-1-250-88899-0 (special edition)
1 3 5 7 9 10 8 6 4 2

To my husband: Your love helped me through the most challenging times.

Chapter One

Kang 康

When he was a young boy, Kang dreamed of returning to the palace.

An envoy would arrive at Lùzhou, a spill of color against the gray skies and black rocks. Musicians playing something bright and cheery, banners fluttering in the wind. A palanquin would deposit a blue-robed court official to stand on the sandy beach where these daydreams often played out before him, and they would unfurl an embroidered scroll—a decree from the emperor. His family would be asked to return to Jia, their positions restored, and he would return to his life among the palace children.

But no envoy came, and those childhood dreams faded away. Only now, waiting before the grand gate to the palace, did those memories return to him. Cutting into him like those northerly winds once did, filling his nose with the scent of salt. He knows the truth, though: The home he knew as a child was no longer. No dowager empress asking the kitchen to bring them another plate of sweets. No emperor uncle demonstrating calligraphy on a stretched canvas. No princess reciting yet another treatise on negotiation before their tutor. He came back under a rain of arrows, bringing with him nothing but lies and destruction. No matter how much he wants to pretend otherwise, he had a hand in everything that will happen after this.

His horse nickers softly, jostling the one beside him. The animal senses the change in the air, the shift in the wind. He thought a coup would be bloodier. Blood and fire, from the stories told by the teachers and his own fragmented recollections of ten years before. Instead, he saw the soldiers of the army stream into Jia's crevices like water into a dry riverbed. The capital of Dàxī drank them in throughout the night, as the sky turned pale and a new dawn settled over the sleeping city.

The gate opens before him. Kang enters, flanked by his father's men. Rows of soldiers stand at attention, clad in the black uniform of the city guard. A path had been left for them, and the soldiers bow when they pass. There is no sound of battle up ahead, no defiant clash of steel. There is only that weight of expectation, of coming change.

When he met his father at the teahouse, the general was all smiles, face reddened by wine. His father clapped him on the back, told him that he had done his part. Like a good son, a good soldier. Although he wants to enjoy the warmth of his father's approval, Kang still feels a sense of unease at the back of his mind, like an itch he is unable to scratch. Zhen's voice whispers to him: *All these schemes coming to fruition, but at what cost?* He thought she meant their fraud of a betrothal, but she laughed in his face when he said so.

One of the foot soldiers steps forward to take the reins of his horse, and Kang dismounts. An official greets him with a slight bow, dressed in the black and green of the Ministry of Justice, introducing himself as the Governor of Sù, Wang Li. They slip in through a side door and ascend the narrow stairwell hidden in the high wall beside the Courtyard of Promising Future.

"The General of Kǎiláng!" a herald announces in the distance, and the resulting cry is thunderous, echoing through the stone passage.

"I want to extend a personal welcome to you, my prince." The governor is all smiles at the top of the stairs, gesturing for him to continue forward. "Welcome back to Jia."

The sound of that title makes Kang's skin crawl. *Prince.*

But the thought is chased away by what awaits him in the courtyard below. From this vantage point, he sees the court officials clustered in the space before the stairs that lead up to the Hall of Eternal Light, surrounded by the red of the palace guard and the black of the city guard. Some of them appear bewildered, while others have already fallen prostrate on the ground in their eagerness to show deference to the soon-to-be emperor. To Kang's left, the long wall is lined with archers, and he sees similar bobbing shadows along the length of the far wall. Their presence obvious to those below, a reminder of the general's power.

The general stands at the top of the stairs, adorned in full battle armor. He gleams black and gold from the curved prongs of his helmet to the shine of his boots. Chancellor Zhou stands to his right, dressed in formal court garb. There is no question who will rule and who helped him onto the throne.

Kang's father raises his arms, and the roar of the soldiers falls silent. They drop to one knee in a salute, a coordinated wave. The remaining stragglers of the court still standing kneel as well, following the lead of their peers. But Kang commits those faces to memory, just as he knows the chancellor is also taking note. The ones who bowed first, and the ones who hesitated.

The general's arms return to his sides as the herald steps forward again. "Rise to hear the words of the regent, soon to ascend to the throne of our great empire."

The soldiers stand once again at attention with a thud of their spears, shaking the walls of the courtyard. The officials stagger to their feet.

"For some of you, it may be a surprise to see that I have returned," the General of Kǎiláng's voice rings out over the crowd. "I had willingly gone into exile so many years ago, wishing to see the glory of our great empire continue without internal strife. We cannot stand strong when we are fighting from within. I thought I would give my brother a chance, and instead, he sought to bring Dàxī to ruin."

Father was always one for rousing speeches, known for his ability to stir up the blood of those who follow him, to encourage them to fight on his behalf.

"With all his own ambitions, he never thought one of his own would turn on him. The princess he raised poisoned her own father and attempted to remove those of the court who would stand in her way of consolidating power. I have been entrusted now with restoring honor to the Li name and securing justice for my brother's death."

The general's impassioned speech seems to have thrown a hornet's nest into the midst of the court, for they can no longer hold still and keep silent; they whisper and mutter among themselves at this revelation. Kang senses attention on him, and he struggles to keep his face impassive, even though his unease grows.

A girl told him about the components of the poison and its origins in Lǜzhou. A princess tried to hide the news of her father's passing from the rest of the people. He has glimpsed only a small part of his father's deeply laid plans, and the general has refused to respond to his questions about the origins of the poison.

He meets the chancellor's eyes, and the man gives him a small smile before turning back to the courtyard.

The doubt crawls deeper under Kang's skin. Does it matter if his father released the poison? The emperor is no longer, the princess is gone, the throne is empty and waiting for the one who will ascend it. But inside, the question still burns: *Was it his father who gave the order?*

"I will bring peace and prosperity back to Dàxī. I will root out the traitors, the corrupt," the general announces with great fervor. "Starting with the palace. The traitorous princess and her pet shénnóng-tú have escaped the palace, but they will not remain free for long. The Ministry of Justice will bring them back."

Chancellor Zhou steps forward and proclaims, "So wills the emperor-regent of Dàxī!"

"So wills the emperor-regent!" his subjects echo, and they kneel once again to receive his divine command.

His head bowed, face hidden from suspicious eyes, Kang feels his lips curve into a smile.

She's alive.

Chapter Two

Ning 寧

Mother said the world grew from darkness. From that great primordial nothing came awareness, and the first gods awoke from their slumber. The Great Goddess emerged, splitting the darkness open like an egg. With her brother, they separated the heaven and the earth.

Never forget, she told us. *The world began with a dream. Our lives are the same. Keep dreaming, my daughters. The world is greater than you know.*

Sunlight streams through the canopy of green overhead, leaves rustling slightly in the breeze. The air smells like a pleasant summer day, but I'm caught somewhere between sleep and wakefulness. I feel like I've forgotten something important, just out of reach. My body is jostled by movement underneath me, and I sit up too quickly, head spinning.

Trees fly past my eyes. My hands brush against rough fabric, a blanket that slid off me when I moved. I turn and realize I'm sitting in a wagon. My sister sits across from me, eyes closed, mouth moving. I know that expression: She's working through a particularly difficult puzzle in her mind. Some sort of embroidery pattern, or accounting for ingredients in Father's storeroom. But then her eyes snap open and meet mine. She scuttles over to sit beside me.

"You're awake," Shu says with relief, and then before I can stop her, she calls out to the two figures sitting at the front of the wagon, "She's awake!"

I can't help myself. I grab her arm to make sure she is real. I need to know I'm not still dreaming, sleeping on a boat floating down the Jade River, still trying to find my way back home. Or worse, curled up on the floor of the palace dungeons, awaiting the morning of my execution. Those uneasy thoughts chase away the heat of the day, leaving only a chill in its wake. Shu looks down at my hand, and then she places hers over mine.

She opens her mouth to say something, but before she speaks, the wagon jerks to a stop, throwing us forward. One of the figures swings over the front of the wagon and lands next to us, the brim of their wide hat casting their face in shadow. It is only when they look up that I recognize the face—her striking features, revered by poets in their flowery texts, which are now familiar to me. Someone whom I may even dare call a friend.

Zhen, the princess of Dàxī, is dressed in a plain brown tunic, her hair tied back in a long braid. Behind her is the driver, someone I recognize as well—Ruyi, her handmaiden, dressed in an identical brown outfit. They look like farmers returning from a day in the fields.

Ruyi gives me a quick nod of acknowledgment before turning back to urge the horse forward again with a click of her tongue.

"How are you feeling?" Zhen asks. Shu also looks at me with great intensity, and my sense of dread deepens.

I shake my head, still a little dizzy, trying to remember. "You'll have to tell me what happened."

Images then appear unbidden before me. The imposing face of the chancellor, sentencing me to death. The vivid petals of the peony bloom on Shu's embroidery. Chasing my sister through dark woods. My father, weeping over her body. The descending form of the Gold Serpent and the flash of its vicious fangs . . . its bloodred eyes.

A sudden pain pricks the center of my brow, and I gasp, doubling over.

Agony spreads like wildfire through my body, obliterating all other thoughts. Dimly, I feel hands on me, helping me to lie down as the pain crashes over me again and again. I drift through it for a while. It could be minutes or hours, I do not know. Until finally, bit by bit, the pain eases. Until I can slowly find my way back to myself and push back to sitting again.

"Here. Drink some water." A flask is thrust into my hands, and I pour the cool water into my mouth.

"You were asleep for three days and three nights." Shu passes me a handkerchief to wipe my face, radiating concern. "Your fever was high, and Father tried to draw out the infection as best as he could. Some probably still lingers . . ."

I pulled Shu out of the darkness only to fall into it, and I remember nothing of what happened after.

"Father . . . where is he?" We set aside our differences in order to save Shu, together. But I have much more to ask him. About him and Mother in the palace. About what he gave up to start a new life in Xīnyì. All that I never understood until I went to Jia.

Shu seems reluctant to speak. "After you lost consciousness, Father sent word to the village that I had taken a turn for the worse and could not make his daily rounds. Captain Wu came to check on me, and also to provide a warning."

Our father once saved the captain's life after a bad fall. Captain Wu has always been kind to us, trying to sneak us extra rations even though Father would usually refuse them.

"He warned us soldiers would come soon from Nánjiāng to search for you, by order of the governor. Father permitted him to search our house while I hid in the bed with you." Shu's lips quiver with the memory. I reach out and grasp my sister's hand, knowing it must have been terrifying to experience.

"Your father came to find us later," Zhen tells me. "Told us we should be on our way. Provided us with the clothes and the wagon and said he would send them in the opposite direction if the soldiers came."

"Why isn't he with us?" I demand. "He'll be in danger!"

Zhen exchanges a look with Shu. That familiarity sends a jolt of irritation through me. There is something they know that I do not. What is it they feel they have to hide?

"He didn't want to," Zhen tells me finally. "He said he still has patients under his care."

Of course. His patients. His obligations.

"I tried to persuade him to come," Shu says, but instead of reassuring me, it only irritates me further. How she always tries to see the best in people, even when they continue to disappoint us. She should not be the target of my anger, yet—

"Village up ahead!" Ruyi calls from the front of the wagon, disrupting the tension.

Zhen climbs back to the front while Shu looks ahead with interest, leaving me alone with my questions and my dark thoughts.

The slanting afternoon sunlight does not shine on a bustling village. Instead, only a scattering of chickens runs across our path when we enter the gates. We pass mud-brick houses built around small courtyards, separated from the main road by low wooden fences. One woman hangs her washing on a line, and Ruyi goes over to talk to her, returning with the location of an inn. Looking back from the wagon, I see her stare after us, only turning away when she notices me watching.

Ruyi leads the horse down another road and pulls into a wide courtyard with an opened gate. The plaque hung on the wall only indicates it is an inn, without an official name for the establishment. An elderly man comes out to greet us with a smile and takes the reins of the horse from Ruyi's hands.

I slide off the back of the wagon, but my legs almost buckle under my weight. I steady myself against the side. If I have been asleep for three days and three nights, it would explain my overall weakness . . . and my growling stomach. Zhen chatters cheerfully with the elderly woman who comes out to welcome us with a platter of sweets. I hear her weave a tale about how we are pilgrims heading up to Yěliŭ to pay our respects to the Emerald Tortoise of the West.

I recognize now we are at Xìngyuán, a village before the mountain pass that leads to Yěliŭ. We are two days' journey north of my home, a place I have never been. Zhen must be following the directions in Wenyi's letter, as she had originally planned. She will ask for aid. I am grateful to her for helping me get to my village, diverting her plans so that I could save Shu. She did not leave us behind, even though she easily could have.

"Let me look at your wound." Ruyi comes up behind me and steadies me, noticing how I can barely walk. "We'll need to change the poultice again."

When she mentions the poultice, my arm begins to ache, almost as a reminder. I limp over to the door Zhen and Shu have already gone through. Inside is a large room with several wooden tables and benches. Ruyi assists me to sit down heavily on one bench.

"I'll bring some tea over to you, kind patrons." The elderly woman ducks her head, and Ruyi follows her through the other door on the far wall.

I stare down at the bandage, remembering the serpent tearing his fangs into my arm, and the horror of returning to my body with those marks still on my skin. I'm filled with a strange desire to see what they look like now.

Shu hovers close to me, trying to be helpful, but I sense her anxiety.

"You don't have to see this. Ruyi will help me," I tell her, knowing she is uncomfortable with the sight of blood.

She tries to protest, but Zhen calls out for her help, and she leaves me with a reluctant glance.

When Ruyi returns with a large bowl of steaming water and some clean cloths, I had already used what remained of the fabric to clear away the poultice remnants to see the wounds directly.

Part of my arm is pink and swollen, warm to the touch. There are two gashes where the fangs punctured my skin and pulled away when I fell out of the tree in the world of the Shift and back into my own body. I once believed, as I told Steward Yang, that I was not aware of any magic that could send a person through time and space.

These marks tell a different story. There are darker magics out there than we know.

Ruyi helps me clean the wounds. I grit my teeth at the sharp, stinging pain. She pulls out the herbs soaking in a separate bowl and packs them onto my arm. The pungent scent they release is medicinal and familiar—it reminds me of my father. I swallow down my sadness and tell myself that *he* chose to stay behind.

After the poultice has been applied and the wrap secured, the warmth of it eases the ache slightly. I open and close my hand, feel the skin pull and stretch. We are done just in time for our hosts to welcome us to eat dinner in the back garden, where we are surrounded by beautiful roses in varying hues, growing on the fence and the trellis overhead. Pale white with edges of the lightest pink, bright yellow blooms the size of my fist, and peach-colored climbing roses with many small, delicate flowers. The fragrance complements our meal as we eat bowls of spicy noodles tossed in chili sauce, topped with crunchy pork intestines and bean sprouts. The noodles are accompanied by small dishes of pickled cabbage and radish. We also share a plate of zhéěrgēn, a white tuber softened in oil, its sweetness a delicious contrast to the salty, cured sausage it is stir-fried with. The dishes of this village are considerably spicier than what I am used to, which is no surprise as this region borders Huá prefecture, well known for their love of chilis. Ho-yi and Ho-buo, the friendly innkeepers, keep our cups filled with chrysanthemum tea and refuse to be referred to by more respectful titles due to our elders.

With our stomachs satiated, we retire to our respective rooms early, knowing the journey to ascend the mountain to Yěliŭ will take us most of the next day. Ho-buo offers to help us trade our wagon and horse for two sturdy ponies to carry our provisions up the mountain.

Shu helps me tighten the wrappings on my arm to make sure

it will not slip off overnight, but she frowns at my arm, as if it has insulted her somehow.

"Something wrong?" I ask gently.

She tugs on the wrappings one final time, making sure it's secure, but does not meet my eyes. "I . . . I don't like that you got hurt because of me," she whispers.

My heart constricts at her expression. My softhearted sister, always willing to help, never wanting to see anyone in pain. I should have known she would fret. We have yet to discuss what happened before I came back, and what's happened since. But I don't know if I'm ready to speak of it.

"I'm back now." I shrug, attempting to keep my voice light. "And *you're* back, which is all I care about."

She sighs. "I hate that I wasn't able to help you, that I couldn't even really help Father when he treated you." I recognize her helplessness because I've felt it myself. It grieves me that I could not protect her from it.

"If it wasn't for your embroidery, I wouldn't have figured out the antidote," I remind her. "Clever girl." I try to ruffle her hair, like I used to do to annoy her when we were younger. She dodges my fingers, smiling a little at least.

I blow out the candle, and we sleep, setting those worries aside for the night. But instead of soothing dreams and happy memories, I dream of red eyes watching me in the dark.

Chapter Three

Kang 康

When his mother died, Kang thought he would lose his father, too. For three days and three nights, the general kept vigil in the room where his wife's body was kept, refusing to leave even when her family tried to encourage him to eat or rest. They asked Kang to speak to his father on their behalf, but it was futile. He would speak to no one. Kang could only kneel by the door and listen to the sound of his father weeping or raging on the other side. On the fourth morning of the vigil, a letter came from the capital marked for the general's eyes only, and it was slipped under the door.

The general came out soon after, took a boat and enough supplies for a week, and disappeared. He said nothing of where he was going or when he was coming back. Kang performed the rest of the funeral rites alone. The prayers. The endless ceremonies, processions through the village. Receiving the tributes from his mother's people, his father's soldiers. He watched as the flames of his mother's funeral pyre lit up the night, and he carried her bones down the cliffs to be offered to the sea.

Kang almost convinced himself that his father went on a journey to die. Then the sail of the boat appeared on the horizon almost one hundred days after his mother was laid to rest. He received his father on the shores under the Emerald Cliffs, still wearing his mourning white. His father looked gaunt, browned from the sun, but his eyes shone with a desperate fervor. Kang found out about the contents of the letter, about the hunting accident that wasn't quite a hunting accident, and the emperor's hand in his mother's death.

It was then he understood his father's renewed purpose.

Vengeance.

Two days after the general marched on the capital with his forces, Kang is summoned to his father's council chamber. Waiting for admittance to the inner palace, Kang thinks fleetingly how everything looks the same and yet everything has changed. The guards posted to his residence have been replaced by his father's private guard, familiar but not friendly faces. The officials who hurried past him in the halls not even a week ago now acknowledge him with a nod or even a reverent bow. The servants seem unsure as well of how to greet him and tend to avoid him instead, taking a different path if they see him coming from a distance. But those who serve him now serve with deference and a hint of fear, for the Ministry of Justice has begun its sweep through the wings of the palace after the general's proclamation, rooting out those suspected to be in allegiance with the plot that resulted in the escape of the princess.

Other than the time he was brought to the princess's private gardens as a prisoner through the secret tunnels, this is the first he has seen of the inner palace in years. Not much has changed from what he remembered of the painted hallways, but inside the council chamber, the walls are bare. All decorations of the former emperor removed, waiting for the new ruler to determine what he will find pleasing to his eye. There is only his father, seated at the redwood desk, and the chancellor to his left, sipping a cup of tea.

"Father." Kang bows. "Chancellor."

His father gestures for him to sit in the empty seat across from the chancellor, while the chancellor gives him a nod in greeting.

Kang sits down in the hard wooden chair as a servant comes by with a tray of delicacies and tea. He had hoped for a private audience with his father, but it looks like there is another purpose to this meeting. Something beyond family matters.

After his father returned from his journey over the sea, he never spoke to Kang further about his mother's death. Never discussed his plans. In public, he always treated Kang as one of his soldiers, refused to show any preferential treatment, and Kang was grateful for it. But in their own residences, his father grew reclusive.

He remembers when the chancellor first appeared in Lǜzhou, disguised as a merchant on a smaller vessel. They spoke late into the night, meetings Kang wasn't privy to, until Kang forced himself into his father's study. A place forbidden to him before. He spoke passionately then, about no longer being dismissed as a child, about being treated as a capable soldier. He used terms his father would understand, even if Kang would not admit to the undercurrent of fear that ran through it all: He did not want to lose his father, too.

It was the chancellor who spoke up for him, who persuaded the general to send him on the task to infiltrate the capital.

"Our plans have come to pass as predicted." The general sets his brush down on the stand, disrupting Kang's memories. He moves the missive over to the right for the ink to dry. Kang sees only a few characters from this perspective. Something about granaries and Ānhé.

"It could not have gone more smoothly," Chancellor Zhou comments, setting his cup down beside him. "We've sustained minimal losses in our numbers. Now it is only the support of the court we must gain to ensure your ascension is successful."

Kang should be grateful to the chancellor for appealing to his father many months ago, allowing him to participate in the mission. Yet he has seen how easily the chancellor turned on the princess, heard the rumors about how *No one ascends the throne without the chancellor's approval.* To survive the ascension of two emperors, now approaching the third . . . Chancellor Zhou is not a simple man, and the more Kang learns of him, the more his suspicions deepen.

"The Ministries of War and Justice have always deferred to those with greater numbers," the general says. "I have the conscripts from Lǜzhou, my loyal battalions in the area, commanders willing to lead, carrying my banner. Along with the reserves from Governor Wang, I believe we control at least half the military force of Dàxī, and others may be persuaded when they are offered incentives. It is the Ministry of Rites, the astronomers, those involved in the governance of the empire, that I have to convince." Kang's father speaks of his numbers with confidence, and it is only when mentioning the court that his brows furrow.

"Minister Song loves his symbols, a grand purpose." The chancellor smirks. "I believe my proposed plan will bring Your Highness what you desire, the acceptance of all the ministries."

From his hand comes the sound of clinking stones. Kang's eyes are drawn to two orbs as they are manipulated in Chancellor Zhou's right palm. They are a deep, rich green, a sign of high-quality jade. These trinkets were popular when he was young, made of various precious, polished stones. Said to assist with concentration, but they have fallen out of fashion in recent years.

"Yes, I have reviewed your plan." Kang's father does not seem as convinced.

"We must act swiftly," the chancellor states. "A quick reckoning for those who opposed you, to demonstrate that you will not hesitate to use the forces at your command. But . . ." His eyes slide to Kang, and he bows his head. A quick flare of annoyance twitches within Kang, even as he struggles to hide it. The obvious attempt at politeness, an old court official playing the part. It's nothing he hasn't seen before. The army commanders have their own posturing; the court officials use subtle gestures and veiled words. In the end, they are all the same, shuffling pieces on the board to ensure they have the most power.

"There is a reason I invited you to join me at this council," the general says, speaking directly to his son. Kang feels the weight of it, the importance of what is about to be bestowed upon him. "Your mother always wanted to give you time to grow into your own person, before you have to take the responsibilities of upholding the Li family and the Li name. But now it is time for you to claim your place."

"I have followed your instructions, Father," Kang says softly, meaning every word. "I came to the palace in your behalf."

"And you completed your task as I expected." His father bestows a smile on him. To Kang, this is high praise. To have completed a job, to have the acknowledgment he so desperately wanted.

"There was a purpose for your presence in the palace before my arrival," the general continues. "It was not only as a distraction, as I initially proposed to you, to ensure those in the court looked the other way while I executed my plans. It was also to prepare the court for the role you are to play, to plant those seeds of legitimacy."

The warmth of the praise disappears as quickly as it came, replaced with a sudden chill. His father's hesitation has a different meaning than that of the chancellor's. He knows it will not be something pleasant. "What do you need me to do?" Kang asks.

"You will be named prince after I ascend, for a ruler with a suitable heir is one that offers greater stability. The natural order of things to come to pass. You have never expressed any sort of ambition for this role, and so I have to ask. Do you accept this?"

Here it is. The question that always loomed over their heads in Lǜzhou. The question all the advisers skirted around, the question his mother never wanted to answer, for Kang would never dare to ask his father directly regarding his ambitions for the throne. And the first instinct, the first expectation is always to follow. To obey without question, and yet . . . Kang is unable to do that. He has to ask. He has to know.

Kang leaves his chair and kneels on the floor, bowing his head, knowing this question could cost him everything. He has gone over various ways to say this time and time again. He defended his father to Ning, even when she gave him the terrible knowledge of the poison's origins. At this point, the throne is within reach, and there should no longer be any reason for his father to obscure the truth from him.

"Father, if you will permit me to ask a question that has been nagging at me all this time in the capital . . . I beg that you hear it, and you grant me an answer."

The chancellor makes an offended noise, but Kang does not care of him. He only cares for his father's response. That has always been what mattered to him. His acceptance. Worth more than any amount of gold.

"Speak."

"About the poison . . . the poison tea bricks that were distributed among the realm last year," Kang says. He always feels a step behind, only recently admitted to the councils, and yet, still apart from them. From the trusted inner circle. "I heard rumors the physicians and shénnóng-shī separated the components of the poison, and one of the components is yellow kūnbù. From Lǜzhou."

"What do you want to know?" His father's voice is flat. He doesn't seem perturbed by this, only curious.

"I wish to know why . . . Why did you poison the tea?" Kang chooses his words carefully, because he is mindful of his mother's shared wisdom. She always told him choosing the right words is winning half the battle, in what is said and unsaid, known and unknown. Sometimes it is better to push forward than to step back.

Kang forces his gaze to remain steady as his father searches his face. He has learned quickly over the past few weeks how to swallow his own sadness, his own anger. How to imagine himself to be like the tides, never faltering.

"I warned you of this!" The chancellor slaps his hand on the table beside him, the noise as loud as a thunderbolt. He shoots to his feet, standing beside Kang, also bowing for the attention of the general. "He has spent too much time in the presence of the princess and that shénnóng-tú. They have whispered suspicions that would cloud his judgment, affect his loyalty."

The chill is replaced by ice shooting through his body. Doubt, eating away at him. While he was struggling with his own doubts, it seems others were wary of the same. The chancellor is preparing to secure his place in the court. If he wins his father's loyalty, places everyone else around him under suspicion, even the general's own family . . .

"Father, I beg for you not to—"

"Sit down, both of you," the general says forcefully, interrupting his plea. "Enough of this.

"Soon you will understand the ways of the world and how we must use the weapons we have at our disposal," the general finally says after they have returned to their seats. "I have depended on the sword for too long, believed that loyalty and family ties would be enough to save those I care for. But even the distance was not enough. My brother was not content with my success in carving out a life on rocky Lǜzhou. He wanted to see me suffer, and now, I have brought the suffering to his own door." The quiet intensity in his eyes is unsettling, and for a moment, Kang is afraid. Chancellor Zhou nods beside him.

"You have to thank the chancellor directly for bringing this to my attention many months ago. We would never have known the truth about your mother's death if it were not for him."

Ah. The origin of the plot. How cleverly the assassination was performed, an infiltrated spy among his mother's people. The emperor's knife in the dark. What was the chancellor's price for sharing this information?

"It is only my duty, Highness." The chancellor smiles then. The clinking of the stones is back, rotating in his hand as if in meditation. "No thanks required."

He then looks over at Kang, and Kang understands the explicit warning: *Watch yourself.*

"Poison is a tool," his father says gravely, staring into the distance, as if pondering the lines of an ancient text. "Like the use of the sword, the horse, the arrow. It can create utmost devastation, but it can also be used to weaken our enemies, slowly and discreetly."

"Even if those enemies are Dàxī's innocents?" Kang asks. Hundreds, maybe thousands, dead. All commoners, afraid.

"Would you lose one in order to save many? What about a hundred lives for a thousand lives? The lives of everyone in Dàxī?" his father counters.

Kang does not know how to respond.

He only knows it was the loss of one person that set this entire plan in motion. It was the death of Kang's mother that sent one rock tumbling, and now an avalanche will follow, with devastating results.

His father's face softens. "I always forget; you did have your mother's sympathy for the common people."

After assuring his father and the chancellor he would play the part, Kang is dismissed. With his hands still on the doors, he hears his name. He pauses, listening through the gap.

"Do you believe he will do as he should?" The chancellor, still questioning. Kang feels his mouth clench into a thin line. He will have to be careful.

"I believe he will see in the end all I have done for the empire." His father suddenly looks tired, resting his head on one hand. "All I have done for *him*."

"I hope you are right," the chancellor says, rising to take his leave.

It may be a strange trick of the light, but when the chancellor turned, Kang could swear his eyes glinted red in the lantern light.

Chapter Four

Ning 寧

In the morning we load up two ponies with help from Ho-yi and Ho-buo. I notice sets of painted clay teapots and teacups on shelves in the main room, and I am reminded of my mother's ruined shénnóng-shī box. All her tools, destroyed. Despite my bitterness, I am the keeper of her legacy, and I'll continue in her memory. Because memory is all I have.

"I painted those myself," Ho-yi says to me when she sees me pick one up, a finger brushing over the roses crafted with such a delicate hand. I buy a set from her and also a pack of dried chrysanthemums. The weight of the cups in my bag reassures me, and I didn't realize until then how naked I felt without the tools for my magic.

Before we leave, Ho-yi gives us an extra sack of food and waves off Zhen's offers of more payment in exchange, stating these supplies would go bad if we didn't take them.

"It's been a difficult year," she explains. "Not many pilgrims are coming through the pass, not like previous years."

"If only you'd traveled through here even two years ago!" Ho-buo exclaims. "The entire village would be bustling with people throughout the summer months. Food and market stalls, decorations strung up on every street."

"Has your village encountered the poisoned tea bricks as well?" Ruyi asks.

They both shake their heads. "We've been spared that, thankfully," Ho-yi says. "We had one poisoned brick, but it was found before it was distributed."

"What plagues us are the bandits." Ho-buo grimaces. "They've been menacing the roads around us, and they've been worse this past winter. Be careful."

We start up the well-tread path early enough in the morning that the treetops are still misted with fog. I've made treks into the mountains near Xīnyì previously with my parents, but those seem more like hills compared with these peaks.

The forest is busy with activity. Something darts away from us in the dense shrubbery, frightened by the noise of our footsteps. The drone of insects and the sound of birds calling to one another fill the air.

Ruyi takes Shu up ahead with the first pony while Zhen stays back, taking the reins of the second from me. I can tell from her expression that she wants to talk, and I wait for her to begin as we start our ascent up the side of the mountain.

"We must speak of the contents of Wenyi's letter," Zhen says. "We've had little time for you to provide me with your counsel."

I glance at her, surprised. The princess appears troubled as she leads the pony along the path. It is unsettling that she would show this level of concern, so different from her usual impassive demeanor.

"What did it say?"

"His family resides close to the Clearwater River. Over the past year there has been a rise in the numbers of a rebel group who call themselves the Blackwater Battalion." A clever play on words, I have to admit. The Clearwater is the river that divides the province of Yún from the Lǜzhou peninsula. "There are suspicions this is the return of the general's own troops, that some of the members were former leaders in his ranks."

The General of Kǎiláng. The one I briefly encountered in the teahouse, whose presence terrifies me even when I think back to it now. He is Kang's father, and it is a truth my mind finds difficult to align. The boy whose thoughts I felt as if they were my own, who I believed was innocent in the schemes until he broke my trust. He hid so much from me, out of reach of my magic. He should be one of the targets of my anger, and yet . . .

"Ning?" Zhen interrupts my wandering thoughts, and I realize I let the silence continue longer than appropriate.

"I'm sorry, please continue." I shake my head. What is the use of remembering him? He is on the other end of the empire, out of reach, and I am walking beside his enemy, the greatest threat to his father's ambitions.

"The local magistrate is suspected of charging citizens with petty crimes and sending them to Lǜzhou to serve time, but they never make it to the salt farms. They are conscripted into the Blackwater instead, forced to terrorize the countryside while pretending they are keeping the peace."

"These are grave accusations," I say. Even with my limited knowledge of politics, I know this is a level of corruption that could be achieved only with deep connections and resources. We know the corruption has crossed the empire from Lǜzhou to Sù, evident with the governor's involvement—I wonder if there is any corner of Dàxī to which the general has not extended his influence, if they all are a continuation of his plan. His final, grand ascension to the throne.

"It is treason," Zhen says. "But this is not the worst of what he has been accused of. Those able to escape the grasp of the Blackwater return home . . . changed. As time passes, they slowly begin to lose their hold on what is real."

"I'm . . . not sure I understand," I say.

"Apparently, the changes are slight at first," she tells me. "But they slowly begin to succumb to what Wenyi suspected is another type of poison. They grow confused, stop recognizing their families and friends, and begin to hurt themselves or others around them."

I shudder. What terrible power, to send your enemies to madness.

"Why would they want to hurt commoners?" I ask. "They don't have the power to oppose them."

"Fear. Fear is their weapon." Zhen frowns. "Now, instead of raiding the settlements along the river for provisions, bandits are supplied and outfitted by the Blackwater, and they are afraid that if they refuse, the Blackwater will conscript or murder their loved ones. Some of the villages and towns have even welcomed them, announced their loyalties to this rogue battalion. They believe they offer better protection than the imperial forces."

She shakes her head. "Enough about the politics of that region. What I want to know is, are you aware of this sort of poison? Or is it a type of magic . . . like what you did with the bird?"

I understand what she is asking of me. She remembers what happened with Peng-ge, whom I forced to drink poisoned water when I distorted his reality, causing him to believe he was dying of thirst. It went against my very nature and Shénnóng's teachings, and yet I saw no other way to conquer that task. But I feel no regret, because it allowed me to pass that round of the competition.

It is a line I may one day have to cross again—to use my magic against not only a bird but also a human enemy if my life or Shu's is at stake.

"I was able to influence the bird because it is a simple creature," I tell her. "A simple creature that had simple needs, and I appealed to its basic nature. The need for food, shelter, and water. I was also not far from it, allowing me to establish that link through the Shift. To have that sort of influence across a great distance, to control the minds of so many at once . . ."

"I see," Zhen says, and her disappointment causes a twinge of annoyance to spark inside me, just for a brief moment. It was not such a pretty solution in the context of a court-sanctioned competition, and yet these not-so-pretty uses of Shénnóng magic still had their purpose. The hypocrisy of it burns a little, but then I remind myself it was not the princess who rebuked the use of this magic—it was some of the other judges who exhibited their distaste for such methods.

Anger would not help us right now. I need to remain clear-headed for the days ahead.

"What I understand of the magic is limited," I continue. "I've never received formal training, and my sister had only just started her apprenticeship when she fell ill. But you saw for yourself the three-headed snake I pulled out of Ruyi. Different magics could exist, ones I have never encountered before. Ones my mother may have never seen, either."

Zhen grimaces at the memory.

"Your arm . . . ," she asks, as if she does not want to know the answer to the question, "What happened to it?"

I tell her about what occurred when I followed my sister into the Shift, about the serpent in the woods, and the impossibility of a creature in that other world hurting my physical body. Creatures that should not exist, yet they are coming to life before us.

She considers it all, then finally says, "It's troubling, these signs and rumors. The appearances of these abominations. I hope Yěliŭ will provide us with the answers we are looking for."

I take my turn leading the pony over the next stretch of the road as we continue our slow trek up the mountain, making steady pace through the forest. The path narrows the deeper we get into the woods, the trees growing thicker. While the others keep a steady stream of conversation going, I keep returning to the troubling information Zhen shared.

New magics. New things to fear.

"Look at this," Ruyi calls from up ahead. She stands before a broken pillar, its base covered with moss, but the difference in color on top indicates the damage was done recently. At our feet are pieces of a shattered stone tiger. These are guardian statues, seen as representations of the watchful eyes of the gods. The desecration of them is troubling. Someone does not fear retribution from the heavens.

"It's one thing to read reports about the unrest." Zhen looks down at the tiger missing half its face, its ferocious snarl diminished. "But Dàxī has changed since my father's last tour. I see it clearly now."

She meets my eyes, and I know she is thinking of my previous warning: *There is a difference between living the suffering and reading about it.*

A fallen tree lies across our path and we have to navigate around it through the thick brush, cutting down the undergrowth to lead the ponies through. As we continue our trek, we consume handfuls of nuts and soft white buns for energy as our calves begin to ache from the steady climb. Although Ruyi does not hurry us, I sense her eagerness to put as much distance between us and my village as possible. Hours later, with the sun approaching the horizon and the light beginning to fade, the path widens again under our feet.

The dirt changes into a road paved with stone as the trees thin out. We continue toward a bridge spanning a small ravine. The stone tigers that sit on either side of the bridge are unharmed, but signs of destruction are evident here, too. There are flags trampled on the ground, covered in boot prints. Ruyi crouches in front of one of them, reading signs undecipherable to my untrained eyes.

"They brought horses, wagons." She points out patterns on the fabric. Wheel marks and creases. "But they didn't bring regular supplies. They brought something heavy . . . Something's wrong."

"Should we continue?" Zhen asks.

Ruyi nods. "Stay close, and be careful."

We make our way across the stone bridge, the forest suddenly quiet around us. The great stone gates, the height of three men, stand open, but when we draw closer, I see a crack along one side. As if an explosion happened here.

A sword is drawn to my right, then another. Ruyi and Zhen stand with their weapons in hand, keeping them ready. Shu and I take control of the ponies. I step closer to her, not knowing what we will find.

We pass through the gates and into the courtyard, taking in the destruction before us. My pony snorts and paws at the ground. I smell the strong stench of lingering smoke.

"I don't like this," Shu mumbles to herself. I reach for her hand and grasp it, offering her what comfort I can, even though the fear continues to slither and grow inside me, trying to take hold.

I could tell the structures of Yěliŭ were quite majestic once. The buildings are made of gray stone, with sloping roofs of black tile. It must have taken a lot of effort to haul these materials up the mountain. The lake at the center around which the buildings are gathered is a dark, murky blue. A bridge of many turns crosses the surface, a zigzag path meant for reflection, suitable for an academy of learning.

There are also groves of bamboo growing up from round stone bases. They rise from the earth, topped with green and yellow leaves. But looking around, we see many of them have fallen or have been cut down. Approaching one such grove, I notice something lying across the stone tiles. But instead of another ripped flag as I expected, I recoil in horror.

It's a body.

"Shu, don't look!" I yell, and throw up my arm to cover her eyes.

Up ahead, Ruyi turns to meet my gaze, her expression mirroring my own. She stands over another corpse. I notice them everywhere. All over the courtyard.

We've walked into a massacre.

Chapter Five

Ning 寧

"Don't look," I whisper again to Shu. Her hand tightens on mine.

"Can you hold on to the reins?" I ask her. She nods, eyes shut, and I pass her the lead to my pony. "I'll be right back."

"Don't . . . don't go too far," she says, voice quivering.

"I won't."

I approach the first body. Using my foot, I gingerly roll the man over from his side to his back. His throat is slashed, a deep red wound. His eyes stare up at the sky, unseeing. He is dressed in scholar's robes, a long black tunic with a white sash, its edges stained with blood. At his side is a familiar pendant, one I recognize as the same symbol that never left Wenyi's side.

So many bodies are scattered across the stones like refuse. None of them had weapons, not fallen at their feet or within reach. They were cut down, defenseless, where they stood. Their arms bloodied from trying to defend themselves.

"This is murder," I say to myself, but it comes out louder than expected, ringing in the air.

"We don't know who may still be here." Ruyi approaches with Zhen; they both look grim. "We should get out of the open."

The two women flank us with their swords drawn. Shu and I

hurry the ponies forward; they are eager to be led away from the stench of smoke and blood, tugging at their reins.

"The smaller structure." Zhen points in the direction of a building away from the main path, surrounded by a grove of trees. We hurry along the low fence, searching for anything that may still lurk in the shadows. I wish I could brew a cup of tea to heighten my awareness for danger, to sharpen my senses with goji and chrysanthemum. I'm painfully reminded again of the difficulties of using my magic, my limitations without my tools.

Tying the ponies to a post, we make our way to a set of stone doors at the center of the building. The doors are carved with elaborate figures of armored warriors wielding curved daos on rearing horses, their hooves touching at the point where the two sides meet.

It takes Ruyi and Zhen straining side by side to push open even one of the heavy doors. It slides against the ground to reveal a cavernous space. The ceilings seem too low, the walls too dark. Two imposing pillars stand in the middle, encircled by dragons carved out of rock, both with bulging, fearsome eyes. One leers from above; the other peers from below.

In the center of the room is a giant bronze censer. Ruyi uses the tip of a stick to stir the ashes, looking for embers.

"It's cold," she says. "It's been at least a day since they died. The zhīcáng-sī would never permit the fires to go out."

The zhīcáng-sī of Yěliŭ are their elders, their Keepers of Secrets, just as the shénnóng-shī are the masters of tea. They revere the Tortoise of Wisdom, Bìxì, upon whose back the empire is built, providing their divine guidance. This is the first temple I have ever visited—the White Lady is worshipped in the trees, and her messages are heard on the wind, rather than contained within formal temples. Shénnóng was a wandering god, only returning to civilization when he had further knowledge to impart—Hánxiá records his teachings but was not where he was worshipped. His texts urge his followers to explore, to experience.

Along the far wall, set into an alcove, are three statues. The philosopher Mengzhi, a book in hand, contemplating questions about governance and moral nature. General Tang stands with his arms clasped behind him, his sword sheathed at his side. He was a famed soldier who once persuaded a city to lay down their weapons and join his cause with only the power of his words. Positioned between them is a representation of the Great Tortoise, bearing a stela on their back carved with the six virtues: harmony, honesty, humility, wisdom, compassion, and dedication.

Above our heads is an opening in the roof of the temple so that when the sun rises and sets, it illuminates each of the characters on the stela in turn. At present, compassion is catching the light.

The competition was supposed to pay respect to those six virtues, but instead, it exposed treacheries in the court. I remember the chancellor's speech, with his empty words and manipulations. I feel sick at the thought that I used to believe in his lies.

"No!"

The scream echoes across the temple, sending my pulse racing. Zhen kneels in the corner, weeping. My eyes search for an assailant, certain it was a cry of pain, but then I see an outstretched hand before her. A foot. A body clad in armor, and then another—four in all. They fell on the steps on which those who would pay homage to the gods would kneel. These are not scholars, like the bodies outside. These are soldiers who will use their weapons no more, having died protecting the man in the corner within their circle of protection. Their mission failed.

So many dead, a stark reminder of the fate that awaits us if we are captured by the general, and the dangerous road ahead.

"Duke Liang," Zhen says, struggling to stand on shaky legs. She wipes away her tears with her sleeve.

"You are certain?" Ruyi asks, standing beside her, offering her support. Zhen nods, then turns to rest her cheek against her handmaiden's shoulder. Ruyi's arm encircles her, weariness evident on both their faces.

"I remember him from Father's private councils," the princess whispers. "But it's been years since he left as Adviser of Yĕliŭ."

A grinding sound fills the temple. I spin around, suddenly afraid. Where is Shu? I see her on the other side of the room, staring at a portion of the wall behind the statue of the philosopher. It's moving, a panel sliding open.

"Back away!" I yell, ready to defend her against whatever might come out.

Ruyi is faster than me, already there with her weapon drawn, sword glinting in the dim light. "Did you touch something?"

Shu shakes her head. "No, it moved on its own."

"Please . . . don't hurt us . . . ," a young voice pleads from the shadows. Two slight figures step out from the hidden room, into the light that encircles the tortoise. A boy who appears to be a few years younger than Shu, around ten years of age, and then a girl, who is even younger, perhaps only six or seven. They look slightly gray, their complexions haggard, covered in a layer of dust and grime.

"I told you I recognized her!" The girl darts out from behind the boy, slipping out of his grasp.

"Fei, no!" the boy cries out.

The girl throws herself down in front of Zhen, touching her

forehead to the ground. "Please, Princess!" she begs. "You have to help us!"

The boy tumbles over the steps in his haste and almost lands on his head. He tries to pull the girl up and away.

"It *is* her," the little girl insists with a hiss, refusing to budge. "You should bow, too."

"Who are you?" Zhen asks in a commanding tone.

The boy hesitates. The girl ducks her head again and then stands. The pair of them, one hopeful, one defiant. He looks like he is ready to defend her with his bare hands, even if the odds are not in his favor.

"We're part of the Yěliŭ orphanage," he says, jutting out his chin. "The elders took us in when we lost our families."

"We mean you no harm," Zhen says, voice softer now. "Tell us what happened here."

The children glance at each other and then the boy speaks up again. "Duke Liang received a message last week, news of unrest to the east. He closed the academy and sent the students home. Only the monks remained, and the two of us. We had nowhere else to go."

Zhen frowns, unhappy with his answer. "What about the guards? There should have been at least a company of soldiers here."

"The duke sent half of them away with the commander up north."

"The commander?" Ruyi asks.

The boy swallows before continuing. "Commander Fan."

"Why would he leave Yěliŭ defenseless?" The princess crosses her arms, puzzled.

"They argued for some time before he left. I heard it outside when I was sweeping the walk." The boy's lips quiver, his fierce composure faltering. "It wasn't long after that when the other soldiers came. The duke made us hide in the back of the temple."

"Are there more of you in the room?" Ruyi asks.

The girl suddenly jolts. "You have to come with us! You have to help Elder Tai!"

"Show us," Zhen says with a sweep of her sleeves.

"Let me go first." Ruyi steps forward, keenly aware of the dangers that could lurk behind those walls. She disappears through the doorway, and then after a few moments, she calls my name from within.

"Stay here," I tell Shu, wanting to keep her out of any potential danger. Her expression falls, and I remember what she said the other night about her feeling of helplessness.

"Can you stand guard?" I ask her. "Keep an eye on the children, and call for us if you notice anything out of sorts, if you hear anyone approaching."

Shu nods and stands a little straighter, happy to be given a task.

I step into the hidden chamber, and my nose is immediately assaulted by a heavy stench. The smell of decay. Something or someone has died in here.

My eyes adjust to the light, although it is quickly fading at this time of day.

Ruyi is crouched in the far corner, and she beckons me closer.

"Is it her?" I ask, covering my nose with my sleeve, although the scent of rot still permeates.

"No, there are two dead over there." Ruyi gestures over to the wall, where I see two bodies clad in armor. "This one is still alive, but barely."

A woman rests on a stone platform that has been fashioned into a bed. I see the children have tried to make her comfortable by tucking mats beneath her and wrapping her in cloaks. I note the gray pallor to her skin and the shallow rise and fall of her chest. Her eyes are closed, her mouth moving as if in prayer, but no sound comes out.

"Can you hear me?" Ruyi places a hand on her arm. The woman shudders at the touch, pulling away. A scraping sound follows. One of the cloaks slips, revealing what is underneath.

I gasp. Her wrists are bound in chains, connected to rings on the wall. She moans to herself, rolling onto her side.

I have to know what happened to her. I ask for Ruyi's help in removing the cloaks so I can better see what I'm dealing with. Ruyi lights the torches in the wall sconces to combat the fading light. I go through the steps of Father's assessments. Checking her temperature—slightly cool. Reading her pulse—fluttering, weak to the touch. I pull her mouth open and check her tongue, examine the white ring around her cracked lips.

All signs point to poison; I'm certain of it. The same one distributed through the empire's caravans.

The same one that killed my mother.

Chapter Six

Kang 康

The general calls for a gathering of the court five days after his march on the palace. The officials are dressed in all their finery, standing once again in the Courtyard of Promising Future as the hot sun beats down on their heads. They dab away the sweat on their brows with their handkerchiefs, and those with greater foresight have brought paper fans to cool themselves.

For the past few days, Kang's father has met with advisers and officials late into the evenings, poring over scrolls on governance and government records. There has been no further mention of what they discussed in the private meeting with the chancellor. Kang was given the task of assisting with the training of the palace guard recruits, but he still feels out of place, knowing of the coming change to his status. The other commanders keep their distance, varying between overly deferential and subtly hostile, while the officials—probably spurred on by the chancellor—have begun to send gifts to his residence. Kang has yet to accept an offer of meeting, but he knows soon it will be time to step into that role.

He wishes he could go into the city. Pretend he is one of many, lose himself in the crowds, and clear his head. But he is not permitted to leave the palace grounds. Sometimes the memory of that afternoon in the market returns to him. When he pretended for a moment he was only a scholar's son making the acquaintance of a stranger, but the memory doesn't last long. Inevitably, it all leads to the same image that has been burned inside his mind: Ning, looking at him with a shattered expression in the Hall of Eternal Light.

The herald announces the arrival of the general, the emperor-regent. Kang's father is the very picture of vigor—he knows his father has chosen his appearance carefully, wearing a full set of ceremonial armor to remind the officials of his background and of the power he wields. He gleams in the light, shining gold. Almost too bright to look at directly, rivaling the sun itself. Kang finds himself standing at attention, his body reacting automatically to the arrival of someone of higher rank. This is what he should remember. His purpose: awaiting orders, maintaining discipline, just like the soldiers who line the walls of the courtyard, spears standing upright at their sides, the glint of their sharp tips a reminder of their vicious potential.

"I promised you justice," the general booms, addressing the court as he would his own soldiers. "The ministry has found those guilty of aiding the former princess and her coconspirators. They will be punished before you, a reminder that Dàxī will not be cowed by those who seek to disrupt the coming peace."

The court officials murmur among themselves, looking at one another uneasily.

From the gate, a tall man appears, wielding a long axe. The executioner. Behind him is one figure bound by chains, led forth by palace guards.

The general means to set an example for his rule, that much is clear. So all will know he has the means to carry forth any threat. *A victor does not hesitate*, his father always told him. His mother, though, was more skilled at diplomacy. Father called her the opposite edge of his blade. One embodying strength, the other mercy.

Now Kang and all of Dàxī would see how his father wields his rule—with only one cutting edge.

Kang keeps his attention on the officials, noting their reactions, as the executioner grinds his axe against a stone. Some wince, while others appear impassive, but they all look uncomfortable with this display.

"Hu Zixuan," the herald reads out the name of the man, who is pushed to kneel before the emperor-regent. "You have disgraced your honorable position as a palace guard. You have assisted with the princess's escape from the city and will be sentenced to death by beheading."

The man only looks up at the emperor-regent with a blank expression. He does not show any emotion, no fear or sadness or anger. It is a different type of fervent belief. The willingness to give up his life for his cause, with no regrets. Kang feels a sharp pang of admiration for the devotion the man exhibits.

He forces himself to remember his promise. He will be the worthy heir his father needs at this time, though he may disagree with some of his methods.

The blade falls. Kang does not flinch, even as some of the court officials cover their faces to hide their shock, their disgust. The reckoning his father promised has begun.

That evening, the heads of the ministries are called to a small council with the emperor. Kang sits at his father's right hand, in an honored position across from the chancellor. He is stiff and uncomfortable in his new purple robe, the color befitting a member of the royal family. Behind his father is a small screen, where the poison taster and a court physician sit, hidden from view. They are tasked with testing anything that may pass through the emperor-regent's lips.

The new head of the Department of the Palace, eager to prove himself, reassured the general every precaution was put in place. The backgrounds of each and every member of the staff in the kitchens, the servants of the inner palace, the families of the court physicians, have been checked. But who knows which servant may be a loyalist to the Benevolent Emperor? And which official may still harbor the desire to see the princess return to her former position?

Kang stares at the four ministers in turn, wishing he could delve into their minds, like the powers of the shénnóng-shī. But the new court shénnóng-shī has yet to be instated after the deaths at the celebration banquet, and the ministers are waiting for a decision as to whether the role will remain in the new court. Kang told Ning the truth when they spoke at Língyǎ Monastery. No shénnóng-shī ever visited Lǜzhou, for what use does an isle of exiles and bandits have for diviners and soothsayers?

After a meal of roast goose and cabbage, washed down with plum wine, the plates are cleared, and Kang finds himself still nervous, even with his attempts to soothe his stomach with alcohol. For since that meeting with his father and the chancellor, he has been dreading the forthcoming announcement. *A suitable heir.*

He stares down at the embroidered sleeves of his robe. Purple with threads of silver and blue, rippling patterns depicting the movement of waves. The pattern moves and shifts before him, and Kang feels his head spin slightly. He's had too much wine.

The chancellor claps, and the music stills, the room falling quiet. The musicians exit, as do the servants and poison tasters, leaving the council to continue.

"I have gathered you all today to discuss the future of the empire. How we can move forward to ensure a swift and unopposed ascension," Chancellor Zhou addresses the ministers.

Minister Hu is the first to speak. "The Ministry of Justice is eager to report that our investigation into the palace staff continues." He reminds Kang of a nervous, pecking bird, always looking over his shoulder. "Tomorrow at court, five more servants will face the emperor-regent's judgment."

"More executions?" Minister Song's nostrils flare, his expression one of distaste.

"I would not expect a scholar-official to understand how discipline is to be maintained among the populace," the Minister of War growls.

"And I would not expect a brute to understand the complexities of governance," the Minister of Rites snaps back, unaffected by the criticism.

"You—"

"*Enough*," the general silences them with a word. His cheeks are flushed, but his eyes are clear. "I have consulted the *Book of Rites* with the guidance of the minister and his various departments. The northern floods and the peasant unrest are in our favor. The people have already been questioning whether the princess was fit to rule. We will only prove she is unworthy when we provide them with signs of unification, a return to the former glory of Dàxī. Starting with a plan for succession, the pronouncement of my son as my heir."

A ceremony the princess never experienced before her father

fell ill, bringing with it questions about her legitimacy to ascend the throne.

None of the ministers disagree, and something inside Kang churns. Is it relief he was not denounced as unworthy? Or is it dread? He isn't sure.

"And then to follow, the support of the monasteries and the academies."

Minister Song raises an eyebrow. "You have support from the pillars of the empire?" Kang could tell this surprises the usually stoic minister, for the monasteries and academies of the gods are supposed to be separate from the politics of the court. They are to educate and to advise, but never to interfere. Only in dire times would they contribute to a cause, just as when they supported the first emperor in the founding of Dàxī.

"Bring them in," the chancellor calls out.

From the door to the side of the chamber, three figures stride in. They are each dressed in loose tunics and pants. Metal cuffs gleam from their wrists, etched with designs. These patterns extend up and over the brown skin of their arms. Not the blue-black of the tattoos on his father's face, but instead, a network of scars—their training involved hardening their skin, binding with ropes or beating with sticks. These are Wǔlín warriors.

Kang was honored to face off against one of these revered warriors during the third round of the competition, then was ashamed when he realized he was negatively influenced by the magic of one of the shénnóng-tú. He felt as if he betrayed his teacher.

Those memories rush back to him. When he was twelve years old and still angry about his new life. When he felt as if everyone looked at him and whispered. The skills he excelled at, sword fighting and horse riding, meant nothing in this new world. He was clumsy at pulling in nets, even worse at boat building. When he almost died under a rogue wave while trying to prove himself to the other children, the wŭlín-shī who pulled him out of the water told him that to continue to rush in with sheer will and desperation was going to get him killed. If Kang was interested, he would instruct him on how to channel that will. Use it to better serve the gods. With his father's permission, Kang trained with him.

Teacher Qi was a fearsome fighter, a vision to behold. He could fight off ten of the general's soldiers easily, with the power of his body and harnessed energy. Under his tutelage, Kang learned how to flow like water instead of fighting against it. He learned how to control his breath, how to slow down his heart, how to manipulate every part of his body using the power of his mind. He taught him about Wŭlín's tenets. Protect the people of Dàxī. Follow what is true, what is right, what is just.

One day he woke up and his teacher was gone, and it wasn't until years later that he discovered his father banished him for suggesting that Kang follow him to Wŭlín. To don the cuffs and serve the Black Tiger.

The wŭlín-shī stand in the middle of the room and bow to the general, before taking their place behind him. Legendary warriors, here to serve the empire in a time of need.

"I requested assistance from Wŭlín, and they were willing to lend aid to support my cause. An empty throne creates a dangerous whirlpool that could destroy the empire. The summer solstice approaches, the rites must be performed, or else Dàxī could fall prey to other evils without the protection of the gods."

The ministers look at one another uneasily. The emperor's essence is said to directly feed into the life force of the realm. It was why, when the former emperor was so ill, it was suspected that all of it tied into the unnatural occurrences plaguing the kingdom—the storms, the earthquakes. The gods were displeased.

"In one month's time, it must be decided. The fate of the empire is at stake," the chancellor pronounces.

"What if the princess returns and challenges your claim to the throne?" Minister Song asks.

"The shénnóng-shī of Hánxiá will gather in the coming days at the palace for the rite to instate the next court shénnóng-shī. My envoys are already at Yěliŭ," the general continues, unperturbed by these dire omens and possible challengers. "Soon we will hear their answer. If I have the support of the army and the support of the gods, will the Ministries of Rites and Finance be willing to prepare for my ascension? Even if the princess were to make a claim?"

"The Ministry of Finance will support the emperor who is the final choice of the court. The treasury would spare no expense at the ceremony." The Minister of Finance, the matronly Minister Liu, is already taking notes, recording numbers, the imaginary abacus clicking under her fingers. "It will be a grand affair like the empire has not seen since the wedding of the Ascended Emperor and the dowager empress."

After a pause, Minister Song nods. He stands and bows. "If you can show support from Hánxiá and Yěliŭ, Your Highness, I am certain the court will follow. Even a princess cannot defy the gods."

Chapter Seven

Ning 寧

I'm choking on a sudden wave of emotion. The face of Elder Tai blurs before me. I'm furious at this poison's reappearance, furious it is on its way to taking another life. The poison's origins was revealed by the chancellor's gleeful revelation, confirmed by the timeline in Wenyi's letter . . . It all points to Kang's father. It all points to Kang.

I cannot forget it. I've been so eager to make excuses for him because of our previous connection. But this is the result of their play for power, and I hate these despicable methods. I hate those who would use them for their own gain.

"Can you bring the boy?" I ask Ruyi, my voice shaking. She gives me a questioning glance, but I stare back. "Get him. Please."

She obeys, and I use that moment to collect myself. Force my trembling hands to still.

I cannot let my anger overwhelm me, and I don't want Shu to see me like this. I cannot affect her recovery, especially when I know she is experiencing the same helplessness and frustration that I am feeling.

Zhen is the one who returns with the boy.

"What's your name?" I ask him. The boy senses my anger and keeps his distance.

"Hongbo," he says, sullen, after Zhen gives him a small push forward.

"How long has she been like this?" I say, more gently this time.

"She's been ill for a while now," he replies, still wary. "Since one of the last snowfalls of the season."

"Do you know what made her sick?"

"It was the tea, the governor said," the boy tells me. "Came by and took all our tea bricks away. Had the commander grumbling for weeks because they promised to send a new batch, but none came."

I ponder over this. So Governor Wang passed through here, too. Our poison tea was mixed in with the Mid-Autumn Festival batch, and this next allotment must have been for Dōngzhì, the Winter Festival of year's end. But Zhen didn't mention it with the reports, so the news may have never made it to the capital.

"She's another reason why Duke Liang stayed." Hongbo continues to defend the duke; it seems he was well liked by all. "He would never leave anyone behind."

"Did they carry her in here? Those soldiers?" Zhen points to the bodies. He nods.

I turn back to the boy. "What happened to them? Was it the tea as well?"

Hongbo stares back at me, frowning.

"What happened to them?!" I demand, and his face scrunches up. He starts crying, and Zhen puts her arm around his shoulders.

"You're not in trouble," she says as he buries his face in her side. She gives me a tiny shake of her head, warning me not to push him too far. Even though I know I shouldn't direct my frustrations at a helpless boy, I'm not certain I can maintain my composure much longer.

Before I say something else that will cause the boy to cry even more, I turn to kneel by the dead soldiers instead. Focus. Look at the details. I am not afraid of death. It is a sight a physician's apprentice grows accustomed to, for we often assist with funeral rites.

It doesn't take long to determine the cause of death. One of them has two arrows in his leg, the other an arrow in his back, dark blood already dried. Parting the fabric so I can look at their skin, I note the dark tendrils spreading up their limbs. I open their mouths and see their blackened tongues. Pulling their eyelids back, the same black tendrils are also present in the whites of their eyes.

"Why did they chain her to the wall if she was so sick?" I ask Hongbo, taking care to keep my voice quiet. Unthreatening.

"The soldiers did that," the boy says with a slight whimper. "They fastened her to the wall because she clawed the door bloody trying to get out."

Like how Shu was bound when I found her, when Father told me she had a tendency to feverishly wander in the night.

"This looks familiar." Zhen crouches down next to me. She does not seem uncomfortable with death, either. She eases an arrow out of the flesh of one of the soldiers.

She catches the expression on my face and smirks. "What? I've bandaged up Ruyi enough times to not be squeamish about the sight of blood."

I snort, my anger easing slightly.

Zhen turns the arrow in her hand, her expression turning serious again. "The arrowhead design, the wood used in the shaft . . . it's the same kind of arrow that almost killed Ruyi." By the way her hand tightens around it, I know she could just as easily snap the necks of the people who would hurt the woman she loves.

If I help Elder Tai, then she may have the answers we are looking for: the identities of those responsible for this massacre. I return to Elder Tai's side and touch her wrist, reading her pulse. They must have had a physician on the grounds who kept her symptoms in check with medicine. Without that careful attention, she is fading quickly, her pulse sluggish, her breathing labored. She does not have much time left.

"Can you save her?" Zhen asks.

"I don't know," I tell her. I have no pretty words to offer, no promises. I have only my magic. "I can try."

"That's all we can do." She nods, then looks over at Hongbo, who is biting his lip. "You want us to help Elder Tai, right?"

"Yes," he says without hesitation.

"She is your best chance at saving her." Zhen thrusts her thumb in my direction. "Can you help her find what she needs?"

He gives me a tight nod but still regards me with suspicion. I suppose that will be good enough for what I need him to do.

Ruyi accompanies me and Hongbo to the kitchens. Whenever I catch movement out of the corner of my eye, I immediately think it's assassins looking to ambush us. But it is only shadows.

The torchlight reveals a small apothecary attached to the kitchen storerooms. It is well stocked, which does not surprise me, being so high in the mountains and away from common trade routes. I don't have a medicine chest with compartments as my father does, but I do grab an assortment of herbs, wrapping each in paper, the lightest way to carry them. Thankfully, I find lí lú and licorice in their respective drawers, but after sweeping through the shelves twice, I'm still missing one component: the pearl powder that seems to strengthen my magic. Without it, I may not be able to pull her out, yet if I do not try, we will have to leave her to die.

When we return to the temple, I bow my head before Bìxì, palms pressed together in prayer, hoping they will look kindly on us when they recognize I am trying to save one of their followers. I ask them to remember the monk named Wenyi, one of their dedicants before he left the ranks and became a shénnóng-tú.

Thinking of him now, I wonder what set him on this peculiar journey. I wish I could have asked him about it, gotten to know him a bit better. How he went from Ràohé to Yěliŭ, from Bìxì to Shénnóng, and then to a magic competition in the palace. But I will never get the chance. I feel a trickle of sadness, and it chases away the remaining warmth of my anger.

While we were gone, Zhen, Shu, and Fei reignited the fire in the brazier. I don't think Bìxì would begrudge the use of their sacred fire to save one of their zhīcáng-sī. I set the kettle I took from the kitchen close to the fire for the water to boil, and I enter the other room to prepare for what I need to do.

Ruyi and Zhen have carried away the bodies of the soldiers, but the stench still lingers. I place the clay pot and cups from Ho-yi on a woven mat on the floor next to the elder. The feel of the cups is rough, catching against the calluses on my fingers, but they are familiar to me, like the ones my mother used to make.

I have pilfered tools from the Yěliŭ kitchens as well with a twinge of guilt, even though no one is left to miss them. I scoop out the high summer tea and put it in the pot. These are not the most tender buds that offer the brightest flavors, nor the autumn teas that offer a depth to the drink; summer teas are strong and have a tendency to be bitter. I need its potency, because without a dān or a previous connection to Elder Tai, I need all the strength I can muster to see this through.

Following my instructions, Ruyi brings me the water bubbling away in the kettle, and I pour it into the pot. The scent of the tea rises though the air, joining the smell of fire from the torches and the small incense censer I have burning above the elder's head—benzoin, for calm and focus.

When the tea is poured into the cup, my magic unravels, seeping into the strands of lí lú and slices of licorice root. I take a sip of the golden liquid, allow it to send a burning path down my throat. Zhen tips the older woman's head back, and I pour a trickle down her throat. The princess is a comfort to me at this point, offering her steady hands and calming presence; we have done such work together before.

Mist falls over the room, obscuring my vision. I part the veil, like brushing aside a bead curtain, and find my way into the Shift. Each time it is easier, and yet each time it still feels like I have to let go of a part of myself. To trust that the magic will catch me, as Lian described it. The space between wakefulness and dreaming. When I see if the gods will respond.

There is always that slight hesitation, that whisper of fear at the back of my mind, if one day nothing will answer. But Shénnóng hears me, and I find myself standing on a road in a town I do not recognize. Fog curls around my ankles and obscures the way ahead so that I can see only twenty paces in front of me.

The walls on either side are high. There is a gate to my right, with shuttered doors. A faded, peeling new-year banner is stuck to the wood. Approaching, I press my hand against its surface, and my hand disappears. All I feel is a slight chill, and I snatch my hand back.

This is not the way to proceed.

I move forward along the road, trying to see what lies ahead. There's a smell in the air, slightly stinging the back of my throat. As if someone is burning a bonfire in the distance. I pass other gates, but the farther I walk, the walls grow dirtier, smeared with some sort of black substance. The doors are no longer whole—many of them are broken, but I see only swirling darkness through the gaps. I know better than to step inside.

The strands of magic inside me pull me forward. Our shared cup tethers me to the person waiting on the other side. The road ends before a grand gate, held up by pillars wider than a person's body. Looking through the opened doors, I see a large courtyard. It must have been spectacular once, filled with shrubs and flowers, but all the plants are wilted or dead. Weeds reach up between cracked paving stones.

I crane my head up like a small child to see the plaque at the top of the gate: TAI SHAN ZHUANG. The Tai family must have been a wealthy household to maintain a residence like this.

I walk down the path and stop before a tree in the middle of the garden, its trunk split. It is hollow in the center, its ends scorched as if burned. I carefully climb over it to pass, and the wood groans under my weight. Heaving myself over the other side, I see the opposite end of the courtyard. The path curves, and there is a pond up ahead, a pavilion with black pillars and a curved, red-tiled roof at its bank. I once again wish I could have seen this place at the height of its splendor instead of its current neglected state. There is the shape of a house in the distance, obscured by mist.

I notice then a figure sitting on the edge of the pavilion, trailing her fingers in the water. She is where the magic leads me. She does not acknowledge me as I approach and ascend the pavilion steps. From her side profile, she appears about the same age as Zhen. She is dressed in a delicately embroidered outfit, a blush pink as soft as the petals of a rose, with a pink skirt of a deeper hue. Her hair is pulled back in a fashion suitable for a nobleman's daughter, secured into place with a single silver pin. She is the only thing that shines in this dark place, surrounded by decay and ruin.

When I stand before her, she finally turns and looks up at me with sad, tired eyes. She looks nothing like the woman I saw curled up on the floor. She looks as if she has her entire life ahead of her, to do as her heart pleases.

"Elder Tai," I say, bowing my head in acknowledgment.

She inclines her head as well. "What are you doing here? You don't belong to this place."

"You do not belong here, either," I tell her. "You've been poisoned." I do not know how much time she has left, and if she leaves with me willingly, there is a greater chance I can still bring her back to her body.

Her brows furrow with slight confusion, then she looks longingly toward the residence in the distance. "I haven't been back to these gardens in years and years."

She waves her hand in the air, and something shifts. I see the fog lift slightly from this place. The pond is suddenly clear, filled with orange and white fish circling one another under the surface. The trees are lush and green, the orange blooms of osmanthus flowers brilliant against the leaves.

"There are people waiting back in Yěliŭ for you." I lean forward, pleading with her to listen. "Children you are still responsible for."

I offer her my hand, hoping that she will take it, that the connection will allow me to pull her through and break free of this enchantment. Then the ingredients of the antidote can work, to stabilize her fever and calm her racing heart.

"Ah, yes . . . the young Fei and the headstrong Hongbo." Some clarity returns to her eyes, a memory of the person she was and the life she has already lived, before this place took her away. "I heard their voices, but I thought I was dreaming."

A sudden wind picks up, sending her hair flying behind her. I shiver. A strange whistle comes from the direction of the gate, like the piercing sound of a bamboo flute played too sharply.

"Listen . . . ," she whispers, and she grows unfocused again, looking up at the sky dreamily. "I hear its call."

"The flute?" Unbidden, I blurt out, "Don't listen."

It's not safe. There is danger held in that discordant tone.

"But it sounds so sweet . . ." Her expression returns to a dreamy, placid smile. The whistle sounds again, this time more insistent, harsh. A sharp pain burns down my arm, and I hiss. I look down to see my arm glowing with a peculiar, pulsing light.

"Come with me, please," I beg her. Something is coming. What or who, I do not know, only that we have to flee. To leave here before it comes.

Elder Tai looks at me again and sighs, as if burdened by the weight of her memories. "My home burned years ago. None of this is left."

She reaches for me then, and when our hands connect, I feel the bridge built by the tea, the magic straining to meet her. The wind howls around us in protest. I throw my arm up to protect my eyes from the sudden gale, the stinging dust that peppers my skin. A sense of hopelessness fills me, reminding me of the storms that whipped up the dried dirt around the cracked creek bed the year we had the drought. When we were thirsty all the time.

Around us, the pavilion begins to crumble.

"Come on!" I yell, pulling her to her feet. We escape the pavilion just as the roof caves in. The grand house in the distance collapses on itself. The trees and shrubs around us tremble, as if afraid of what is to come.

I try to run, but her hand falls away from mine. I turn, only to see that she is not quite as real as she once appeared. She is slightly translucent, her once vibrant outfit now gray.

"It's too late," she says to me.

I lunge at her, trying to imagine my magic as a golden net, pulling her back in. But my arms fall through her. She grows fainter every moment, pieces of her disintegrating into ash, swept away by the wind.

Elder Tai tries to speak, holding my gaze. "He wants to claim what he always thought was his. What was taken from him the first time . . . stop him . . . too late . . ."

She's swept out of my arms, disappearing into a swirl of dust. The storm surrounds me, a violent vortex. I stand in the center. Looking up, the serpent leers above me, flashing its fangs. It is as giant as I remembered from Shu's dream. The red points of its eyes burn into my mind, as if it is capable of reading my every dark thought and reveling in them.

Pain shoots up my arm and pierces my skull, as if someone

took a dagger and plunged it into my forehead. At the seat of my soul.

I scream and drop to my knees, falling through the Shift and back into my body.

Back into reality, where I know with certainty that I've failed.

Chapter Eight

Ning 寧

I return to consciousness with my body sprawled on the hard stone floor, the scream still choking my throat. My mouth tastes like copper coins. The shadow of the serpent remains above me. Its head large enough to blot out the heavens, the entire world. I throw my hands up, trying to defend myself, to fight back . . .

It takes me a few moments of struggle to realize it's Zhen. She's calling my name, her grip tight around my wrists, holding my clawing hands away from her face.

My head throbs with pain. When I stop struggling, she lets me go, but I crawl on my hands and knees toward Elder Tai. I have to see what happened for myself. I place my fingers at her throat, desperately looking for a flicker, something to tell me it was all just a terrible dream.

But it's real. She's left this world behind.

I sit back heavily, feeling all the strength draining from my limbs.

"I'm sorry," I tell her. To the keeper who dedicated her life to the pursuit of wisdom and the offering of counsel. To the young girl I met in her memories who lost everything. The girl whose diverted path somehow led her to me. "I wasn't strong enough."

"You tried." Zhen attempts to reassure me, but I don't want to hear it. I stand up and brush by her. There is no place to go where I can find a reprieve. I am crushed under the weight of self-loathing. The helplessness that enveloped me when Mother died, and then the constant worry when I sat by Shu's bed night after night.

I thought if I embraced the magic, then the way would be clear. I would have all the answers, the solutions in my grasp. But now I realize it is still not enough. I will never be enough.

I kick a pot against the wall, sending up a cloud of dust. I pick up and throw a basket into a shelf. Scrolls are sent flying, and I kick at them, too. Someone catches my arm, and I snarl at whoever is foolish enough to grab me. It's Shu, looking up at me with eyes so much like Mother's.

"I thought I told you to stay outside!" I yell at her, because it's easier to yell at her than to fall to my knees, crying. When everything else is broken around me, it means I'm not the only one who is broken.

"You saved *me*," she tries to remind me. "You did your best."

"My best isn't *enough*." I snatch my arm away from her. I rest my head against the wall, taking deep breaths until the rush of my anger fades and leaves only embarrassment behind. I know I am no longer a child; I cannot run into the woods to scream and cry any longer.

When I return to a clearer state of mind, I find myself alone in the chamber. Zhen and Ruyi are deep in conversation when I return to the main room of the temple, Shu and the children listening to them attentively.

Zhen waves me over when she notices me, and they all behave as if they did not see me lose my composure.

"We have to continue north, see if we can follow the trail of the commander," Ruyi says. "We will see if we can find those who are still loyal to the Emperor of Benevolence in Kallah."

"Agreed." Zhen nods. "We'll sleep here tonight and gather supplies in the morning before going through the pass. Do we have a map of this area?"

"Yes," Fei says. Her eyes are red-rimmed from crying. My heart constricts again. I want to apologize for not saving the elder's life, but my words are stuck in my throat.

Ruyi pulls me aside after we are given instructions to prepare for the night.

"I remember the loss of those I have not been able to save," she says, voice gruff. "Remember them. It will help you when you need to keep going, even when you feel there is nothing left for you to give."

I nod, not trusting myself with words. If I start crying, I may not be able to stop. Out of everyone, perhaps it is Ruyi who would understand best. From what Lian told me, she was taken from her home at a young age. What happened to her family? Whom did she lose?

I touch my side. In my sash, I still have Wenyi's letter. I have my promise made to him in the dungeons beneath the palace. I will bring his family his message and tell them what happened to him. There is work I have yet to complete.

I commit Ruyi's words to memory, the names of those I've lost or had to leave behind.

Mother. Father. Wenyi. Steward Yang. Small Wu. Qing'er. Elder Tai.

Those I've lost to Governor Wang, to the chancellor, to the General of Kǎiláng.

I will make sure they pay for what they did.

I fall into an exhausted sleep, and Shu has to shake me awake the following morning. We fill our flasks with well water and stuff the ponies' packs with more provisions. I wish we could move the bodies and prepare them for the fire or earth rites, settle them finally so that a part of their souls would return to their families. But all I can offer is a murmured apology, letting them know someday I will return to help gather whatever remains and lay them to rest.

Hongbo finds us some maps from the library to help us navigate the mountains. The path to Kallah should be relatively easy to follow, but we must be vigilant. Those who are responsible for the massacre at Yěliŭ may be lying in wait in the forest, or the governor's soldiers may be on our trail. The sooner we leave Yěliŭ far behind us, the better.

As the sun continues its course above our heads, Yěliŭ slowly disappears into the trees until we are deep in the forest. Along this path are multiple small shrines. Some are only stacks of rocks or a carved stone plaque on which the figure of a bird is etched. It seems the White Lady still has influence up north, even as we recognize her as our patron in the south. It is as Lian says—she is the same goddess who watches over us all. Having a different name doesn't change that. Seeing these tributes to her means we are walking in her domain, and I can find a little comfort in it.

It is here I know I must speak with Shu about what happened while she was in the grasp of the poison. I brood to myself while Shu and Fei walk up ahead, the young girl having attached herself to Shu's side since last night. I have avoided speaking to my sister about it, thinking it would force her to relive those bad memories, but I realize it was more about protecting myself instead. I didn't want to know what she had to endure while I was gone. Now, if I do not want to risk losing someone else I care about, I have to face those fears.

I walk up to Shu so we are side by side and ask if Fei could give us some privacy. The little girl bounds away to join Hongbo up ahead, and then only an expectant quiet remains between us.

"I . . . I'm sorry for what I said yesterday," I begin slowly. "I shouldn't have yelled at you." Even speaking those words eases the heaviness in my chest slightly.

Shu gives me a slight smile, shaking her head. "You've been through a lot," she tells me, voice soft. "I would have been more worried if you pretended everything is fine."

I laugh, despite myself. "You're telling me I'm not a very good liar." She gives me nothing in response save for a toothy grin.

It is then I know I am forgiven. My sister's love for me is simple. Father would have pointed out how my behavior embarrassed our family, but Shu accepts me just as I am, asking for nothing in return. Without her, I will always be lost; I see that now. She wants me to rely on her in turn, not only as someone I need to protect.

"I do need your help," I say to her then. "I need you to tell me what you remember when you were trapped in the forest with the serpent."

"The forest . . . ," she begins, hesitant. "The forest seemed familiar, yet it was not quite like our forest. It was eerily quiet. There was never any sound of animals, which was how I sensed I may be dreaming. Sometimes I could hear whispers, someone talking in the distance. Other times I could hear . . . a whistling, right behind me. But whenever I turned around, no one was there." She rubs her arms as if she is cold. A whistling, just like what I experienced with Elder Tai.

"What did the voices say?"

"They kept saying I had to . . . go to it, that they had what I was looking for."

"Where did they want you to go?" I ask.

"The voices just said to come closer," she whispers. "Sometimes I would see a deer in the woods. Other times, it was a bird. The last few times . . . it sounded like Mother." Her voice cracks.

My heart aches. She shouldn't have had to experience that terror, the poison altering her mind.

"Sometimes I would wake up, and I would still be in the forest. But it would be the forest I knew, and I didn't know how I got there. My feet would be muddy, and I would be alone and scared. Father would find me sometimes and bring me back. There are times I remember him carrying me; other times I would wake up back in my bed. It became harder to tell what was real and what wasn't. I would see things I know shouldn't exist, and yet . . . there they were."

I put my arm around her and squeeze her shoulders, to remind her that I am here and that she is no longer alone.

The climb up the mountain changes from a gradual slope to a series of switchbacks as the terrain becomes steeper. We walk for most of the day, but when the light starts to fade, Zhen decides to stop for the night rather than continue. It is too dangerous to risk a miscalculated step on the mountainside—if one of us were to slip, we could tumble into the forest below and break every bone in our body. We set up camp in a small clearing and share our rations. I wince as we settle down on the ground, rubbing my sore feet.

Fei and Hongbo keep up lively chatter around the campfire,

their initial shyness gone. We munch on dried fruit and pastries while Zhen asks them questions about the duke. It is through their conversation I learn how the duke followed the tenets of the Ascended Emperor, who united the divided empire through food from his own granaries.

Zhen laughs and speaks with them freely, not with the formal language of the court, and her warmth surprises me. I didn't realize how much she held herself apart until now. Here she was relaxed and open, her knees pulled up, gesturing with a winter-melon pastry in hand. Even Ruyi, usually alert and serious, manages to crack a smile at Fei's antics.

Lying in my bedroll, I see the night sky beyond the forest canopy. The stars are especially brilliant in the sky tonight. I stare up at them for a while, even after Shu's breathing deepens beside me and the forest is still. I wish I could read their patterns, know what is coming for us, if we are on the right path. But their secrets continue to elude me.

Sleep offers no comfort. I dream I'm chased by deer with too many eyes, shadows that slither after me, calling my name.

Chapter Nine

Kang 康

When Kang enters the Hall of Celestial Harmony, the conversation quiets. The unpleasant feeling of too many eyes on him prickles his skin. It is only for a moment, but he feels the lingering effects of their scrutiny like a stain.

The general has kept his promise, and other public punishments of various severities have followed. Until even Kang, who is used to the standard military disciplines of whipping and caning, finds these trials—no, these *spectacles*—excessively cruel. This morning, the steward of the kitchens was trampled to death by horses for her role in the escape of the princess. Kang petitioned his father for mercy for her daughter, a handmaiden to the former emperor, because there was insufficient evidence she contributed to the revolt in the kitchens. His appeal failed even with the support of a handful of officials, and the woman was hanged before the court.

Forms of torture and execution previously banned by the Ministry of Justice under the direction of the dowager empress and the Benevolent Emperor have been brought back for a time. The ministry insists it is only for as long as this period of transition. The general has shown he will uphold his promise of justice, of rooting out the rot. That there will be *order*.

Kang walks down the middle of the hall toward his father, seated on the throne at the dais at the very end of the room. He climbs the steps and takes his position to the right of the throne, as befitting his status. A fleeting thought intrudes as the herald calls for the commencement of the council: He hopes there will not be too much blood spilled tonight.

A procession is led into the room by two servants. Leading the group are four white-haired men and one regal-looking woman, appearing as the leaders of those who follow. They wear pale blue robes etched with silver thread. Blue-green pendants of jade dangling on white strings hang from their sashes.

Behind them, looking nervous, one figure stands alone. He is younger than the rest. Kang recognizes him: Shao, the shénnóng-tú who won the competition, whose magic he experienced once. These must be the shénnóng-shī who have been called to the capital for the ceremony. Other practitioners follow, also dressed in variations of blue, dressed in their finest to present themselves to the court.

Just like the variations in their outfits, from embroidered silk to coarse hemp, their expressions also differ. Some look around in interest at their surroundings, while others appear nervous as they survey the room and the waiting officials. Others are perfectly stoic, betraying nothing on their faces.

"We recognize the Prince of Dài, emperor-regent of this great empire," the herald calls out when the procession stops ten paces before the throne. With a rustle of robes, the shénnóng-shī kneel, then bow, touching their foreheads to the ground.

Kang's father gestures. "Rise."

Grand Chancellor Zhou stands from his seat. "Elder Guo, approach the throne."

The elder, the leader of Hánxiá, stands from her place along the perimeter, already appearing as if she is part of the court. It seems like his father and the chancellor have already made progress on their assurances to the Ministry of Rites. They will sway the hearts of the people and win the support of the gods.

Elder Guo motions with her sleeve, and the servant standing behind her seat also approaches, wooden tray in hand. The two of them kneel before the throne. The chancellor meets the servant before the steps and takes the tray. The court watches with rapt attention as the chancellor ascends the steps and offers the tray for the general to view.

Kang sees a round disc of pale white jade, with veins of light green and specks of gray. Even with his limited knowledge, he knows this jade is not the highly coveted variety that the wealthy collect: It does not glow with a milky hue or a rich, deep green. It is also not beautifully sculpted, such as the treasured carving of the bok choy by a famous artist, with its dark leaves of green, locked away in the palace vaults. The disc is thin, imperfect, and therefore close to worthless.

The general picks it up and examines it with a critical eye. This puzzles Kang—his father has never shown interest in material treasures. He prefers sparse, minimalist surroundings for clarity of mind.

"This relic belongs to Hánxiá?" the general asks.

"Yes, Your Highness, Hánxiá offers it as tribute, a demonstration of our loyalty to the throne," Elder Guo speaks, still kneeling. "Legend says it was worn by Shénnóng himself."

The gasps around the room are genuine, just as Kang could not hide the hiss that is expelled from his lips. Here is one of the treasures once held by the First Emperor rumored to contain part of the magic that allowed him to unite the clans.

"As you can see, ministers and officials of the court," the chancellor pronounces with a grin, "we are grateful for Hánxiá's offering in these desperate times. Take the relic to the vault for its protection."

Another servant approaches, ready to receive it.

"Wait!" One of the shénnóng-shī raises his voice in protest, hurrying forward and dropping to his knees beside Elder Guo. "If I may speak!"

"How dare you address the emperor-regent in such an insolent manner?" one of the officials cries out. A member of which ministry? Kang cannot be sure.

Two guards immediately step forward on either side of the dais, hands on their swords. The man touches his forehead to the ground.

"I mean no disrespect to the emperor-regent," he says. "Please."

"I will hear you," the general says, rising from the throne, his purple robe cascading behind him. "Stand and address the court."

"Thank you, Your Highness." The elderly man slowly gets to his knees and then to his feet, wincing slightly. He clears his throat and then bows from the waist to the court as well. "Honored ministers, I beg of you. Permit this relic to be returned to Hánxiá after the completion of tonight's ceremony. It was decreed by the dowager empress that it would remain there as a symbol that the monasteries and the academies were to be separate from the capital. Let Elder Guo remain to speak for Hánxiá before the court. She will be our representative; I believe that should be sufficient."

There are nods of agreement and murmurs of acknowledgment from the other shénnóng-shī, and also some among the court as well.

Other voices join the fray. "It is tradition!" someone cries.

Elder Guo leaps to her feet, appearing alarmed. "I did not know of Esteemed Wan's plan to speak before the court, Honored One!" Her plea seems to be directed at the chancellor.

"What say you, Minister Song?" the general asks. Kang is close enough to see the slight twitch in his father's cheek, knowing he is displeased.

"Er . . ." The usually composed minister seems to balk at the question; Kang sees that the man is struggling to find the most respectful answer that will not offend the emperor-to-be. "Yes, I do believe the Esteemed Wan is correct, Your Highness. The dowager empress did decree that in times of peace, the monasteries and the academies would govern themselves."

"Exactly!" The general claps then, making more than a few of the officials jump. "In times of peace. Then we can continue to follow the decrees of the brilliant empress, long may my mother's wisdom be remembered. But these are troubled times . . ."

He clasps his hands behind his back and begins to pace before the throne. "This was before we uncovered treacherous schemes within the court. An emperor was poisoned, before all your eyes!" He casts his gaze intently over the court officials, and they shrink from it. "A poisoner lurking in your midst, brought here under the guise of a competition.

"Have you forgotten that she murdered the Esteemed Qian?" he roars. "One of your own?"

With a gasp, the shénnóng-shī drop to their knees. The court follows, all of them offering their subservience.

For a moment, Kang feels that fear targeted at himself, and inside, he feels a sliver of shame.

Do not confuse fear with respect, he hears his mother's words whisper in his mind. *They will follow both, but you will see how easily one will falter.*

"You speak of rites and tradition," Kang's father's voice lashes out like a whip. "One of your own died, and you protest about how things used to be. You do not understand; we are once again upon the brink of war, where brothers will fight against sisters, mothers against sons."

"Minister Hu!" the chancellor calls out. "Bring the proclamation!"

"Rise to receive the decree of the emperor-regent!" the herald calls out, and everyone scrambles to their feet.

The Minister of Justice steps forth, his hands around a scroll. Behind him is another official, who unfurls a portrait for all to see. To Kang's shock, he recognizes that face. The wave in her hair, the curve of her lips. The one whose presence lingers at the back of his mind always.

Ning, the girl from Sù, stares out from the black-and-white portrait. At the corner of the portrait is the red stamp of the official seal of the Ministry of Justice. Wanted.

Kang forces his face to still, even as inside, he is screaming. He knows the court will regard his every movement, his every expression, and judge him for it.

"Zhang Ning of Sù has been declared an enemy of the realm," the minister reads from his own scroll. "Instructed to join the competition for court shénnóng-shī under false pretenses, and recruited by the former princess, Li Ying-Zhen, to carry out her shameful plot."

The urge to protest bubbles up in Kang's chest. He wants to speak in Ning's behalf, tell them none of that is true. He spoke with her, felt her thoughts as intimately as his own, in that other place where all secrets are revealed. He knows the sharp pain she feels over the loss of her mother. He felt her shock at discovering her parents' complicated histories, as complex as his own.

Wait, and watch, his mother's cool voice whispers. *Now is not the time. You will lose your head.*

"I have been assured it is impossible for a lone shénnóng-tú to perform such a feat." The general's voice booms over the cowering crowd before him. "She would have been taught by a shénnóng-shī to develop this type of poison. Who among you was that traitor? Who among you is an enemy to Dàxī?"

Some of them raise their hands and deny all accusations, while others fall prostrate and beg for mercy.

"No matter," the general says with a dismissive wave. "You will be subject to the attentions of the Ministry of Justice. Cooperate and your lives may be spared."

"You cannot do this!" cries Esteemed Wan, one of a few shénnóng-shī who still stands, outraged. He spins around and regards the people of the court, who flinch at his gaze. "Which of you will still recognize the gods? Which of you will step forward and speak up against this grab for power? Yěliŭ, Wŭlín, the other monasteries, they will all hear of this!"

But no one speaks.

"You haven't heard, Esteemed Wan?" Chancellor Zhou tells him with barely contained glee. "You're too late. Wŭlín has already sworn allegiance."

Kang earlier noted the absence of the Wŭlín warriors in the room, but now when they enter from the side door, he realizes the chancellor hid them for maximum effect, to be deployed at this particular time. They have grown in number, from three now to a group of ten. Their metal bracelets gleam in the light, their arms rippling with muscle, and their bare legs as strong as trees. But it is not their appearance that shocks the court, it is what four of them carry between them.

With a thud, it lands on the floor before the stunned audience. A cracked stone pillar on which the characters for Yĕliŭ have been chiseled. At the base, a carved tortoise with its head broken off, a desecration of the representation of Bìxì.

The Minister of Justice steps forward and with a grave voice states: "Yĕliŭ has fallen. Adviser Liang was found guilty of treason. He counseled the princess on how to remove her father from power, and so he has been executed."

"Where is your proof? Where is your evidence? I will not believe it!" The Esteemed Wan's voice is raised high, on the verge of hysterics. The officials of the court look at one another, uncertain, but they seem to have been stunned into silence. There is only the rustling of robes, the sound of someone weeping.

"This traitor does not speak for Hánxiá." Elder Guo is quick to defend herself. "I do. Hánxiá has no part in the plot. We will subject ourselves to the Ministry of Justice. You will find us innocent."

"The court will bear witness!" Chancellor Zhou calls out. "Wŭlín is devoted to our cause. Yĕliŭ is no more. Now, Hánxiá has surrendered. Take them all away."

Soldiers stream from the open doors and surround the gathered shénnóng-shī in a dark tide, assisted by the wŭlín-shī. Kang watches the resulting chaos with a sick, sinking feeling inside him. He could not believe this was what his father meant when he said he would gain the support of the monasteries and the academies. Force them to submit by coercion and by threats. The pillars of the empire are *gone*. The fabled warriors are assisting him in his plan, and it seems so contrary to their tenets. But perhaps the academy has changed in the years since he was a child.

Kang's eyes land on the face of one particular wŭlín-shī. He stands out from among the throng, face contorted in a ferocious scowl as he grapples with one of the wailing practitioners of Shén-nóng. He probably wouldn't have recognized him if it hadn't been for a distinct, memorable scar along his jaw.

Qi Meng-Fu. His former teacher.

He will have the answers for him. He *must*.

Chapter Ten

Ning 寧

The next morning, we emerge from the pine forest into rockier terrain. Since we want to put as much distance between us and Yěliǔ as possible, we travel even when the morning fog is still present, making it difficult to discern which path we are on.

At a split in the road, we decide upon the shorter route to the northwestern province, even if it may place us at greater risk. Time is ever against us.

It is only when we begin our climb over the first rise that the sun breaks through the mist. At the summit, it dissipates, revealing a glorious view of the jagged gray peaks and the stretch of green in the valley below. Guòwū Pass, pointing the way toward Kallah.

A river weaves through the canyon toward the distant horizon like a silver eel. It's as if we are standing above the entire world. Ruyi points out Heaven's Peak and Heaven's Gate, two of the most fabled mountains, in the distance beyond Kallah's plateau and past the borders of Dàxī. Past those mountains are other empires, other kingdoms. Travelers tell stories of glittering caves and beautiful temples. Standing here makes my dream of seeing these other places seem not so impossible as I once thought.

The beauty of the scenery invigorates us, and for the first time we are in good spirits as we continue our journey. The fresh mountain air fills my lungs, waking me up.

Ruyi joins me in this stretch of the walk, swinging her arms and rolling her shoulders. "Beautiful, isn't it?" she says. "Reminds me of home."

I have never seen her look so free, but then I realize I have hardly ever seen her outside the walls of the palace.

"Where is home for you?" I ask her.

"The mountains of Yún, not so far from Hánxiá," she says, and then after a pause, "I've not been back for a long time."

"Thank you," I tell her. "For the other day."

"For what?" She squints against the sunlight.

"For reminding me what is important: the people who are still alive."

"Ah." She sighs. "The dead can't come back, but we can carry on their legacy."

"Wise words," I say.

"When the dowager empress saved me from the unrest, I was the only one left of my clan. I was full of rage and half wild and didn't behave like a companion to the princess should," Ruyi says. "But she trusted me, fought for me to stay, and said we would be good for each other, Zhen and me. She was right."

They found each other, despite it all. In a way, they were opposites. An orphan with nothing left, and a princess who had everything. A connection that developed into love. They put their own safety in jeopardy to save each other, just like when my mother and father fled the palace.

The palace forces you to hide your true self for survival; I understand that now. The suffocating rules and traditions, intrigues and deceptions. The princess I first met in the palace is very different from the person I know now. Same with the fiercely protective bodyguard climbing the mountain next to me. I've held a knife to one of their throats, shared meals and drank with them, and together we've narrowly escaped being murdered. We've encountered enough dangers for one lifetime and more, sufficient for this commoner at least.

"Up ahead!" Zhen calls out.

Over the next rise, we see a small group of figures, all dressed in black, coming toward us. If the fog didn't lift, we might have stumbled right into one another.

They've noticed us, too. And their pace has quickened.

I should have known our reprieve would not last long, remembering the slaughter we've left behind. I should have guessed we might encounter the killers on our way up the pilgrim's path from Xìngyuán.

Shu gathers the children while I handle the ponies. Ruyi watches the figures approach. We don't have much time before they will reach us.

"Retreat or fight?" Zhen asks quietly.

"With the small ones, they will catch up quickly," Ruyi says. Then after a pause, she adds, "If I advise you to flee, will you listen?"

Zhen gives her a look that indicates exactly what she thinks of that suggestion. Her bodyguard sighs. "A fight it shall be."

"If the map is correct, once we cross over that ridge, we will soon be in Kallah," Zhen says grimly. "There is an outpost there that welcomes travelers during this season on the edge of Tiānxiáng Lake. I think the outpost is occupied—that could be why they turned back . . . I hope."

"Ning," Ruyi says, assuming the role of commander. "Take Shu and the children back down the path. Tie up the ponies and then go deep into the brush. Stay out of sight. Zhen and I will figure out a way to break through their ranks, make a run for the outpost, and see if we can call for help."

It seems a desperate strategy. I turn and lead the ponies to Shu, already formulating my own plan. I put both sets of reins in her hands. She looks at me, uncertain.

"Tie up the ponies," I tell her. "Then get Hongbo and Fei into the trees as fast as you can run."

Shu hesitates.

"Their lives are in your hands," I say. "I need to help Zhen and Ruyi. We'll all get through this. Together."

Shu nods, then sets her shoulders, accepting her task. She turns away to the children, and I return my attention to the princess. By making sure they make it to the outpost, I can save Shu. Getting to Kallah is our best chance at survival. By keeping Zhen alive, I have a hope of clearing my name and ensuring my father's safety back home, instead of living my life on the run as the fugitive accused of poisoning the Court of Officials and escaping from the imperial dungeons.

I can now see the glints of silver off the blades of those advancing toward us. Certainly not pilgrims, and we are outnumbered. I may not have my usual tools, but I've seen Mother put together make-shift tonics when she didn't have a fire at hand. She's used poultices like Father before, and there are variations, other approximations of the magic-enhancing dān that I could make. Even though I run the risk of being vulnerable when in the Shift, that is preferable to being slaughtered directly on the mountainside without trying.

Desperation allows for innovation.

I pull out several paper packets from my pouch, skimming the scribbled characters until I find the ingredients I need. My water flask in hand, I slip in the thin black strands of treated goldentip tea. This type of tea doesn't mind the cold—its essence will still slowly seep out. I break open the dried goji berries until their flesh is revealed and place them into the flask as well. I'm perfectly aware of what happened the last time I used goji, and I know to be careful with how many I add.

I swirl the water. Once, twice. *First, the dream.* Mother's familiar words echoing in mind. *Then heaven and earth followed. But what came after was water, and with it, life itself.*

Water inside us and surrounding us, sky and sea. The tea strengthens the connection with the gods, but the water is the link. I close my eyes and imagine my mother sitting by the creek. The water running through her fingers, glittering in the sunlight like stars spilling from her palms.

Zhen and Ruyi are on a narrow ridge, below a grove of trees that cling to life on this terrain. On the other side of the path is a rocky slope, which ends in a sharp drop off the mountain. I clamber up the rocks to join them. I expect Ruyi to rebuke me, but she doesn't. She only regards me with a nod.

I offer her the flask first. "I'll help however I can. I won't leave the two of you to face them alone."

Zhen hesitates, but Ruyi reaches over and takes a healthy swig of the brew.

"Princess?" She offers the flask to the other girl, and there is a hint of a challenge in her tone. Zhen looks back at her, surprised, and they have a silent conversation between them.

"I know this is not your intention, but I still have to be careful of anyone who may have the ability to exert influence over me. Do you swear you mean me no harm?" Zhen asks, turning to me.

Of course I know she has to be cautious, but her words sting all the same. She still does not trust me.

"If I wanted to poison you, I could have done so ten times over," I say to her. Remembering all the times we've shared our food, nights we've slept in the same room.

Ruyi arcs her brow. "She's right. She's saved my life, and I have experienced her magic. I know she has been touched by the gods, and that other place reveals her true self in turn. If she has ill intentions for us, after all this time, then she has far greater powers than we could possibly overcome. Ning has helped us time and time again; now is not the time to doubt her."

Zhen holds her gaze for a moment longer and then says, wryly, "You mean, we need all the help we can get."

The corner of Ruyi's lip quirks. "You could say that."

"There is a time for caution, and there is a time for trust." The princess acquiesces.

She takes the flask and drinks from it, meeting my eyes in acknowledgment, accepting my help. It seems momentous, her decision, standing at this precipice between sky and earth.

I take the flask back and drink, the goldentip tea leaving a sweetness on my tongue. The magic awakens inside me, waiting for direction. I touch Zhen's arm through the thin fabric of her tunic, then reach for Ruyi's arm as well. The magic sighs, connecting the three of us.

I am not Lian; this is not my specialty. I'm unable to gift them with uncanny speed or unbelievable strength, but I can make sure their steps are true and their movements swift.

"We'll make our stand up there," Zhen decides. "It will be hard for them to surround us with the path so narrow. They'll have to resort to fighting us one on one. We'll have the rock behind us as an advantage." Ruyi agrees with her with a simple nod.

"I'll go into the trees," I say. "Then I won't be in your way."

I climb up the rocky ledge, finding footholds and handholds easily. I crouch and place a palm on the tree next to me. The prickly needles weave their way into my hair, but the bark is warm underneath my skin. Through it, I feel the pulse of the earth. The trees drink in the sun on this windy patch of soil, clinging to the rock, continuing to survive. I steady myself on that feeling.

I close my eyes and reach out, connecting with Ruyi and Zhen. I sense the anticipation in their bodies, their focus on the menacing figures advancing toward us.

Then the first attacker is there, swinging their sword in a wide arc. Ruyi brings up her weapon to meet it, taking the blow. Her essence is red, just like when I saw her in the Shift. She glows with it. Zhen is bathed in silver light. As the attacker falls back, the next one comes up. Ruyi's sword flashes, moving like it has a light of its own. Zhen sweeps them back as well with her dao. They fight side to side, one attacking, the other defending, then the other way around.

These attackers are armored. Not simple bandits. They fight with the discipline of those with combat training. *Soldiers.*

I catch a flash of memory, Ruyi and Zhen running drills, learning how to fight together in tight spaces. The two of them sparred almost daily, lunging and countering, and also with the other guards. Until they could move as one. The black figures try to break them apart, but they continue to be repelled by their twin blades.

There's a shout to my left, breaking my attention. Something slashes through the trees, stomping on their roots. The trees yell out a warning, but it's too late. Rough hands grab my shoulders and pull me back. The branches try to hold on to me; they leave red marks on my arms when I'm torn from their grasp. I'm thrown to the rocky ground, and I scramble backward, shards of rock digging into my palms.

I look up at another figure swathed in black, dark armor polished to a shine. He wears a helmet with horns jutting out from the top of his head. The bottom of his face is obscured by black fabric so that only his dark eyes are visible.

"Found you," the shadow soldier utters with glee, and brings his sword straight down toward my head.

Chapter Eleven

Ning 寧

I am at once outside myself and within. A part of me is still caught in the fierce battle being fought by Zhen and Ruyi, and another part of me looks up at the sight of my death. Fleetingly, I recall a strand of melody, a song we used to sing about the goddess. *Grant me your swiftness of wing, descend upon me your blessing now...*

Even though my magic is supposed to belong to Shénnóng, she is the one I think of, and she is the one who heeds my call. The One of Many Names, the All-Encompassing... who some believe may be a remnant of the Great Goddess herself.

The world shivers, and the sword stops above my head.

The Shift is abrupt. It is no longer a subtle parting—I'm violently shoved to the other side. The light drops, taking all color with it. I am standing beside my body, but everything is black and white. Not quite like the in-between world of the Shift after all. This is... some other place.

I raise my hand before my face and notice my gray skin. Looking down, I see myself frozen in place, cowering, hands up to protect myself from the blade. I see the shape of the soldier, his arm raised, about to cut me in two, but there is something peculiar about his form. Black dust streams from his figure, creating a trail into the distance, and I sense I have to follow it. It is a feeling just like the strands of magic that led me through Elder Tai's memories to find her. I know I have to see where this leads.

I walk, and I keep walking, until I lose sense of time. Or am I somewhere out of time? Have only a few moments passed? Years? Until I find my way to the end of the black dust. To see a man waiting for me at the end of the trail.

He is gray as well, dressed in a black tunic. Vague shapes surround us in the mist. Like mountain peaks, but I can't be sure. He makes his way through the paces of a martial arts series. Thrust, foot spin, sweep the air, jump back. Even in this dull and lifeless place, his sword shines like a beacon.

"Stop!" I cry out, and the sword falters, coming to rest at his side.

He regards me with suspicion. From here, I see black marks around his wrists, a black line encircling his throat. Marks also run up his arms, crisscross lines. A series of scars.

"What are you doing here?" he barks at me. "Trainees should never interrupt the afternoon exercises. Go back to your classroom!"

He believes he is somewhere else, going through his daily routine. Still lost in whatever memory this realm has trapped him in.

"You're dreaming," I tell him.

Confusion flickers across his brow. "Dreaming?" He rebukes me with a scoff. "That's a new one. I'll have you running buckets of water up and down the Thousand Steps for that insolence!"

"Listen—" I step forward, but he raises his sword, bringing it up between us.

"Do not come any closer," he warns.

I brace myself and reach out to grasp the blade. I don't know the rules of this world, if weapons here can hurt me. But he is a threat to me in the real world, and I have to stop him from cutting me down. My hand passes through his sword, with only a brief sensation of cold. Different rules operate here, it seems.

I step closer and reach out to grasp his arm. My hand passes through him like smoke, but through that connection, I catch a glimpse of something. A memory. *I am scouting through the woods near Wŭlín. A shadow falls over the moon. Something descends from the treetops. It forces itself down my throat, and I choke on it. It tastes like smoke. I feel its tendrils sinking into my brain, and slowly, I begin to slip away…*

"What is this?" he gasps, and I realize he sees the same memory through the connection between our minds. "Dreaming," he mutters again, stumbling back. "I must be." He wipes his hand across his brow, trying to ascertain if he is awake.

"What is your name?" I ask.

"I am an instructor at the renowned Wŭlín Academy, a famed wŭlín-shī." The sword is again pointed at my face. "I will bow to no one. Begone, demon!"

"You should wake up," I tell him, more insistent this time.

Around us the fog begins to swirl. I see movement, shifting forms out of the corner of my eye. I turn, suddenly afraid of what is coming.

A darkness approaches. At first, it is only a slight shadow, but the closer it gets, the larger it grows, until it forms a hooded shape, tapering down to a slender form.

The serpent. The one that followed me through my dreams. The one who stalked me on the other side of the Shift. Who has found me again, somehow, in this other realm.

The serpent approaches, and my arm begins to ache. I cradle it against my chest, where it throbs against me.

The man recoils. "What is *that*?! Is this your true form?"

"This is your dream," I mutter, and then turn to shout at him, "You have to wake up!"

The connection between us is as fragile as smoke, but I see a thin thread connecting me to him. I send my magic down that cord, reaching desperately to see if I can pull him back to the waking world—

But with horror I see the black marks on his wrists and around his neck come to life. He makes a sound, as if choking, and then he is lifted into the air, hauled up by strands of black. His feet kick frantically as he claws at his neck, trying to breathe, but his arms are contorted by that unseen force, pulled back and upward. The cord between us strains, then snaps. He looks like a puppet, except one made of flesh and blood.

The serpent laughs above him, the harsh sound echoing in the space around us. *You again. Interfering little fool.*

"Let him go," I demand, even though I have nothing to use as leverage. No magic for attacking. No weapons. The man continues to thrash above me, straining for air.

The serpent regards me with its cold red eyes. *This man represents all of humanity. Your pathetic, short lives. How you continue to flail and struggle in your pitiful human way.*

"What do you want?" I manage to choke out through my fear.

I've had to hide on the fringes of your world for so long. In the darkness of your hearts, at the edges of your nightmares. It's no longer enough, the serpent hisses. *I will gorge myself on your souls. I will take all your heart's desires for myself.*

"You're a demon," I tell it. "Yet you want to be human. The two are contrary to one another."

The wǔlín-shī twitches in the air above me and then hangs limply from his bindings. I'm not sure if he is still alive.

I cannot exist with your pain and your despair, your rage and your sorrow. I refuse to be contained any longer. The serpent's eyes gleam in a peculiar way. It tilts its head, a strangely human movement. *Why don't we speak of you, Zhang Ning? The girl from the poor, pitiful province of Sù? I sense your desire for power. I know you want to ruin the people who wronged you. If you help me, I will ensure you have more power than you could ever imagine. Allow me to feast upon your fellow humans, and I will give you the ability to destroy your enemies.*

That it knows my name, that it recognizes who I am, makes my insides quiver.

"I'm not like you," I say to it, even though my voice sounds small and petulant to my ears. "I am a daughter of Shénnóng. I heal, rather than hurt."

It chuckles. *Shénnóng is no longer walking on this earth, and what remains of his power grows ever weaker. Your people descend into darkness. You all lie, you cheat, you betray, just to get an advantage over another. You willingly tear yourselves apart.*

"*You* are the poison," I spit. "Without your corruption, our nature is to be good."

In the Hall of Reflection, I questioned the philosopher's dilemma, but I must *believe* we are inherently good. Or else why should we continue the futile struggle if evil is inevitable?

Are you so certain? It says, leering in an approximation of a grin. *You hate that the princess still does not trust you. You hate the men in power who have betrayed you. You hate that the boy you care for is the son of the man who killed your mother. You hate that you still have not avenged her, after all this time. You hate that you are so helpless, so weak, so afraid . . . Shall I go on?*

The words crush me slowly, reminding me of all my failures. But it is nothing I have not said to myself before, time and time again. Nothing that I do not already know.

"What kind of monster would I be if I stand aside to save myself?" I tell the serpent. "I'll fight you until my last breath."

If you will not join me . . . It flashes its fangs and rises over me, a nightmarish vision. *Then you will die.*

The serpent unhinges its jaw, the cavernous maw descending on me. I shut my eyes and wait for the slash of teeth, for the darkness to devour me.

But it doesn't come.

A mysterious force yanks me out of the Shadow Realm, and I land back in my body. Everything aches, and yet I am still breathing. I have yet to be torn apart. I recognize the face hovering above me—not the princess, but a man I once met in the private room of a teahouse. The astronomer who counseled Zhen and guided me to the antidote that saved my sister's life.

"Astronomer Wu . . . ," I manage to choke out. Then I roll onto my side, coughing and retching.

"You were very far away," he says to me, helping me up once my stomach settled. "So far I almost couldn't pull you back. In that place of shadows."

Something slides down the side of my face, and I wipe at my cheek. My fingers come away with the sticky sensation of a balm, and my nose is filled with the pungent scent of camphor. He passes me a handkerchief to wipe the residue off.

It is only then I remember whom I left behind in that other place.

"Wait!" I cry. "The one who attacked me—"

"We found him." Astronomer Wu turns and points to the distance. Two soldiers struggle to control a figure between them, spitting and yelling. The covering has slipped off his face, revealing the same man the serpent was torturing.

"He's trapped in his dreams," I tell him. "Somewhere inside his own mind. There's something else controlling his body."

Astronomer Wu beckons for them to bring the man closer. He fights the entire way, dragging his heels through the dirt. For a moment, as he snarls, his features distort into a silent scream and then contort back into the furious expression.

"Can you pull him out?" I ask the astronomer. "He's a teacher from Wŭlín."

"I can try." He stares at the man, assessing him. I notice then, in his hand, he holds a small flask, and from his other fist dangles a frayed, gray cord.

"*Pathetic.*" The voice that comes out of the man's mouth is grating. I recognize it as the voice of the serpent, the voice that thundered in my head.

The astronomer is on alert. He reaches for the opened flask, smearing his fingers in the balm.

"*All of you, fighting the inevitable,*" the man snarls in a voice that is not his own. "*Can you stop the avalanche from crashing down the mountain? Would you stand in the way of a mudslide? Continue your useless struggle and be devoured.*"

"You have no hold on Dàxī." The astronomer regards him steadily. "We will continue to fight your influence." He reaches for the man.

The wŭlín-shī stares back with too-bright eyes, and then his head snaps back. He suddenly drops to his knees, his weight pulling the soldiers downward. Darkness fills his eyes until no white remains. He makes a gurgling noise, and then his head flops to one side. Blood begins to trickle out of his lips, dripping onto the ground beside him. The soldiers slowly lower him until he is resting on his side.

"Careful!" Astronomer Wu warns. "This may yet be another attempt at deception."

One soldier restrains the man's arms, and the other places his fingers at his neck. He shakes his head, expression grim. "Gone."

Footsteps crunch on the stones beside me, and I look over to see Zhen and Ruyi come to stand next to us, regarding this horrible sight.

"The others, too," Ruyi says. Beside her, Zhen's mouth is set in a hard line. "They all bit their own tongues."

"What are they?" The soldier closest to the man's body looks shaken, while the other looks a bit pale, as if he is ready to throw up. They appear to be seasoned soldiers, not young recruits. For them to look so disturbed . . .

I approach and pull up the sleeve of the dead man, revealing the marks on his skin. Thin, undulating lines. Scars, showing his dedication to Wǔlín.

"This man was a wǔlín-shī," I say to all of them. "I saw him in the . . . Shadow Realm."

"How is that possible?" Zhen asks.

"His mind was elsewhere, while his body was manipulated." I carefully place his arm back on the ground, along his side. He was used, and then he was discarded. I do not want to dishonor the dead and his memory—he had no choice in the matter.

"Has Wǔlín fallen?" Ruyi asks softly.

"We have not had contact with them for months." Another soldier joins us, but from the style of his armor and the confidence in the way he speaks, I can tell he is of a higher rank than the others. "The last communication we received was word of the emperor's death. We are returning with reinforcements to Yěliŭ, at the request of the duke."

Zhen casts her eyes down, her sadness evident. "I'm sorry to say, Commander, Yěliŭ is no more. The two children who are with us are all who remain."

The commander's cheek twitches, and he blinks rapidly, as if at a loss for words.

"It looks like we have much to discuss," Astronomer Wu says gravely. "Come, we will talk."

Chapter Twelve

Ning 寧

The outpost at the edge of the lake is a cluster of buildings. Most of them are wooden shacks, weathered and worn by the wind and sun. The lake is even bluer up close. I suspect, at this elevation, the water will be cold. The snowcapped peaks in the distance are like watchful giants, and I am reminded of the stories in *Wondrous Tales from the Celestial Palace.*

The first gods eventually grew weary from forming the earth, the heavens, and the oceans. They lay down to rest, and their bodies became the mountain ranges. Once, these mountains were known by another name—Gǔlún, the Bone Ranges—but after the empire of Dàxī was formed, it was given a new name, the name of the First Emperor in remembrance: Kūnmíng, the Mountains of Brilliant Peace.

Shu and the children skip stones on the surface of the lake. The ponies dip their heads into the water, drinking their fill, not minding the cold. I am asked to join the council at one of the tents of the outpost, where the interior is warmed with a burning wood fire at the center.

This was a performance, a demonstration of the serpent's power. I can almost hear the horrible, ringing laughter in my ears.

"How is it possible for my uncle to harness such a power?"

Zhen asks, her voice trembling with barely contained rage. "He was always disdainful of magic and the old gods. He believed in discipline and strategy, not magic."

"I, for one, do not believe this is an example of magical influence," Commander Fan counters. He thinks my claim that a mysterious serpent can control the minds of Wŭlín warriors is complete and utter nonsense and believes that they were merely following orders from the general. That they killed themselves to prevent the secrets they kept from being discovered through torture. "Astronomer Wu, have you seen for yourself the sort of demon this girl speaks of?"

"That is not within the range of my abilities." The astronomer frowns. "But—"

"Then it is resolved," Commander Fan interrupts. "We should speak of strategy. Find those loyal to the Benevolent Emperor and have them join our cause to oppose the false prince and ensure he does not take the throne. The princess has a better claim. We should not speak of imaginary monsters."

He was not present when the shadow soldier spoke in his guttural tones or when his eyes flooded with black. He saw only what he wanted to see. My hand tightens into a fist at the familiar slight. When the other competitors dismissed me for being from a rural province, without a famous mentor. The ease with which I was manipulated as a pawn for the chancellor's gain. It seems to happen again and again, and I am sick of it. For a moment, I think about the serpent's promised power. How easy it would be if I could convince them with the strength of my magic. Force them to *see* what I see, believe what I believe.

I swallow all that down. There is always a price for that sort of power, however tempting it may be.

Before I can blurt out anything rash, the astronomer bows his head. "If you would like to converse about strategy with the commander, then will you permit me to speak with the shénnóng-tú and with your bodyguard?"

"Of course." Zhen nods, while the commander waves his hand dismissively, already turning to speak on another matter. Zhen quirks her brow in Ruyi's direction. Ruyi nods, and steps to my side.

We walk around the lakeshore with the astronomer, and when we are out of earshot, I spit out the words I was holding in. "How could he dismiss what I saw?! Those soldiers did not behave as soldiers should."

"There are those who refuse to see things even when the truth is right before them," Astronomer Wu says with a sigh. "Sometimes it is better to work around them than to try to convince them of a truth they cannot comprehend."

"Commander Fan holds great influence among the court of officials," Ruyi explains. "His family have always maintained their connections, and he supported the emperor during the last civil war. He knows of the risk to his own family if the general ascends to the throne. Sadly, we need his connections, his wealth, and his influence. He is not someone we can afford to slight."

Astronomer Wu nods. "The general is a man he can understand and counter. He cannot fight a threat he finds incomprehensible, and, therefore, he refuses to acknowledge it as reality."

I ponder this as the astronomer leads us up a winding path through the trees. There is so much I do not understand about magic, about my own capabilities. The more I learn, the more I realize I am only a speck on the beach, a single grain of sand at risk of being swept out into the waves.

And yet I have already experienced much of the same ignorance and prejudice, even when I was a child. Saw people who dismissed my mother's abilities, questioned her magic, but would still never share a cup of tea with her, thinking it would put them at risk of falling under her influence. I never understood it. How could they fear something they do not even believe exists in the first place? Our contrary, human natures.

The last part of the climb is challenging, the path overgrown. We hold on to roots and tree trunks to pull ourselves up the steep hillside. But when we are at the top, we find ourselves in a peculiar space, hidden from view of the lakeshore.

There is a tower, bleached white from the sun, its sides worn and pitted. The vegetation in this part of the forest is dense, yet around the tower, nothing seems to grow. My eyes follow it up to the sky, where it narrows to a sharp point. Someone built this in the middle of the forest, purposely hiding it from sight. Is it a tribute to something? A shrine?

Through the trees, I see just a glimmer of the lake in the distance. Around us, the forest is alive, the air sweet with the scent of growing green things. For a moment, we stand at the top of the world, far away from the concerns of the empire, the intrigue of the court. But we are burdened with our awareness: of the shadows, the serpent, the other realm.

I notice the astronomer is waiting for me to return my attention to him. I bow, gesturing for him to speak.

"What you have told me about the serpent is troubling," he says. "We spoke of the darkness foretold in the stars, and now I believe that time is here.

"I trust you are familiar with the legend of the Twin Gods? The dragon and the serpent?" Astronomer Wu continues. Ruyi and I nod. Elder Guo told the story to the shénnóng-tú during the competition, and fleetingly, I wonder what happened to her. If she returned to Hánxiá, or if she is still at the palace. If she was one of the people who fell victim to the poison at the court, a crime for which I was accused and nearly executed.

"The dragon was formed from the clouds by the Great Goddess, and as all things in creation have their balance, the serpent was formed from his shadow in the ocean. The Jade Dragon called down the rains and created the river that ensures the fertility of the Purple Valley. The people worshipped him, for it is because of the river we are able to survive. The serpent grew jealous of the humans and their admiration for his brother. He saw the humans as playthings for his own entertainment and amusement, as lesser creatures who should bow down and worship him. He shifted the earth underneath the mountains and brought down the flood, reveled in the destruction it created. He formed abominations that crawled out from the depths of the sea or swooped down from the sky, and he enjoyed the misery it brought upon the humans. Eventually, the gods said *enough*.

"But the serpent fed on the pain and fear of humans and grew powerful. It took all the gods to subdue him. With a flap of her wings, the White Lady blew him to the far reaches of the empire, where a trap was set. Bìxì gave up their shell to capture him, and Shénnóng shed a magic scale that would imprison the serpent in his weakened form. The Tiger cut him apart limb by limb, until his blood flowed in great streams across the earth, creating new rivers and lakes. The Jade Dragon ripped out the serpent's eye, the center of his magic, and flung it into the depths of the Eastern Sea . . ."

Astronomer Wu gestures at the mountains in the distance, their unyielding peaks, looking like they have stood there forever and will stand there long after we are all gone.

"You've heard of the old names of these mountain ranges and the legend behind them," he continues. "But some believe that instead of the resting place of the first gods, these mountains were formed from the body of the serpent. We pass down these stories in Kallah, while the rest of the realm have forgotten him. We remember that the serpent is asleep but could awaken once more. He will begin to whisper to those susceptible to his influence, and they will gather those who will help him."

"How could he possibly extend his influence trapped beneath the earth like the legends say?" Ruyi asks.

"We know him as the ruler of the Shadow Realm, the realm of dreams and nightmares," Astronomer Wu answers. "That is where he is the strongest, and that is where he feeds. When the prophecy about the princess arose, we knew there were ripples in the heavenly streams. Whispers in the dark, telling us something was coming. It was why I was originally sent to Jia to advise the emperor, but he believed he was targeted by an earthly threat. So he sent assassins to Lǜzhou to kill his brother, but they killed his brother's wife instead."

Kang's mother. The one he spoke of with great respect and emotion. Her death was the spark that began the unrest, events set in motion long before the poisoned tea was distributed. She may very well be the origin of all this.

Kang and I will cross paths again, someday. I am sure of it. Call it magic, fate, or prophecy, something pulls us together. I still remember that day in the cave, the way we kissed—I know I should rid myself of those thoughts and not allow them to linger. I may need to make a choice, in the end, that should not be complicated by my own emotions.

"The emperor dismissed my warnings," the astronomer

continues. "He thought by crushing his brother's spirit, he would also ruin his taste for rebellion. I remained in the capital to instruct the princess and watch the course of the stars change and collide, forming new paths."

The astronomer leads us close to the white tower. We duck our heads under the low entrance and step within. Inside, it is surprisingly bright. The tower is constructed from thin white stone, stacked together in a spiral that twists upward. Peering closer, I see the structure is composed of carved . . . swords. It must be thousands of daos, pressed against one another like bricks to form this space. Strange.

"There is one missing." Sharp-eyed as ever, Ruyi points. "Up there."

Following the line of her finger, I see a gap between the rows and rows of swords.

Astronomer Wu looks up at the missing piece. "Hidden in this tower was a treasure the people of Kallah have guarded for centuries. Someone took it from here. It was said to be a bone sword, carved from the femur of the serpent's human form."

He looks at both of us and says in a grave tone, a warning: "I fear he has already begun his plot to return to this world. He will complete what he started all those centuries ago. To make Dàxī his playground. To make this realm home to his nightmares."

"You believe someone serves as his messenger in this world?" Ruyi asks.

"Someone is his vessel, and through that person, he will whisper and influence until he walks on this earth as he once did."

It makes sense now. Elder Tai tried to warn me. She said he was coming. I am afraid of what Astronomer Wu's words mean for us. Not only for Shu and Father, but now for all of Dàxī.

Whenever the villagers spoke about prophecy, when they shared stories about banished princes and great hunts and destined fortunes, they were about someone else. A person with greater legacies than my simple country life and my commoner background. I was meant for the gardens, planting and growing things, assisting my father until it was time for me to take over his job.

Now my path has crossed with two figures of legend—the prophesied princess and the Banished Prince—fighting for the future of the empire. In this complicated tapestry, what is my thread meant to be?

Chapter Thirteen

Kang 康

Each morning at the Hour of the Rooster, Kang is dressed and ready to be at his father's side to oversee the morning drills of the palace guards. This, at least, remains the same. A routine impressed on him since he was old enough to hold a sword. Sometimes he still wakes with a gasp in the middle of the night, thinking he missed the gong and will now have to endure a caning as punishment.

His dream, not so long ago, was to gain the trust and support of the soldiers. Of carving out his own place within the ranks. Of leading his own troops one day, defending the realm from all who would seek to weaken it. But that seems far out of reach within the capital.

The general is always in the same uniform as his commanders. Ready to step in and adjust the positioning of a stance, correct a form, demonstrate if needed. He is never on a distant platform, leading the army but not a part of it. This was always his way, and it endeared him to his troops—one of many reasons his soldiers would follow him anywhere. Even into exile at the far reaches of the empire, and then return to march on the capital and take it in defiance of the emperor. Loyalty. Perhaps this is how he persuaded Wǔlín to help him. The confidence with which he devoted himself to his cause, his promise to fix the troubles of the empire.

In the light of the morning, the events of the previous night seem like a bad dream. The screams of the shénnóng-shī as they were dragged away. The broken statue of Bìxì on the gleaming wooden floor, so at odds with the elegant surroundings.

For the first time, the wǔlín-shī have joined the general for the training exercises, their presence now revealed to the court and the rest of the palace. The recruits, and even some of the guards, stare at them. At their black robes and red sashes, and their recognizable adornments. Just like the representative of the Black Tiger, the woman he fought in the final round of the shénnóng-shī trials. Just like the teacher he once had, back in Lǜzhou—who stands among them now.

It looks like the path he would have been set on would be the same if he remained at Lǜzhou or went to Wǔlín. Either way, he would have returned to serve at his father's side, and some part of that thought is comforting and strengthens his resolve. There is a purpose to his father's bloody path to rule. He knows it. He has to believe it.

"Marshal Li!" his father barks, and Kang snaps to attention, caught in a moment of distraction. "Demonstrate the forms for the trainees."

To be called out in such a way in front of all the commanders, as well as the wǔlín-shī . . . this must be another way for his father to prepare him for the role of prince. To be observed, scrutinized. Kang's heart jumps to his throat, choking him.

"Sir?" As soon as the question is out of his mouth, he realizes his mistake. He coughs and quickly attempts to salvage his position. "Yes, sir! Which form?"

The general looks at him with narrowed eyes, and Kang almost withers under that gaze. "All of them."

Kang stands before the rows of trainees, his thoughts chaotic, unsuitable for the task at hand. He would never admit it to anyone, but there was another reason he begged his father to let him leave Lǜzhou. He wanted to flee the stifling house that contained too many memories of his mother, the place of safety and refuge turned into a cage.

With a deep breath, Kang forces his mind to settle. He turns his focus inward until he becomes the surface of a still lake. A perfect reflection. Once he reaches his center, Kang begins the first form of the Wǔ Xíng.

There are five forms that flow through the breath, the body, and the mind. Ones that are as familiar to Kang as breathing, having been taught them since he could walk. The winding form of the dragon for settling the spirit. The ferocity of the tiger form for postural building. The panther form for explosive strength. The slippery snake form for endurance. And then finally the crane form for focus.

From one movement to the other, Kang finds himself slipping into that familiar, meditative state. A place where his mind is finally quiet. Where his heart does not ache when he thinks of his mother, where there are no suspicions about what his father is keeping from him, and where there are no reminders of a girl from Sù who forced him to question everything.

When he is done, his body feels languid and warm.

Kang opens his eyes. His father gives him a nod and directs the trainees to continue their drills. The wǔlín-shī are impassive, saying nothing. Something inside Kang releases with a sigh.

It is time.

After completing the morning practice, Kang strides toward the cluster of Wǔlín warriors with purpose. They are cleaning their weapons, focused on their tasks. Words run through his head, considering carefully how he will greet his teacher after all this time. He will plead his case and ask for his assistance, calling on their history as mentor and pupil.

"Teacher!" he calls. "Teacher Qi!"

Ten heads rise in sync, regarding him with similar, eerily blank expressions. Kang's step falters in response. A coincidence, that's all. He must have called out too loudly.

"It is good to see you again." He stops before the figure of his mentor. "It has been years since we spoke." He greets him with a clasped fist, touching his forehead to his knuckles, as he was once taught.

Teacher Qi regards him with silence, and the other wǔlín-shī step behind him. Kang feels the hairs rise at the back of his neck. The peculiar, unsettling focus in their gaze, like they have examined him and found him wanting. For a moment, he thinks he might have been wrong, perhaps recognized the wrong person. But the scar, the ink-black eyes, the deep brown shade of his skin . . . it *is* his teacher. He could never forget.

"Sir, with respect." The words sound pleading to his ears, like a begging child. "Please, I require a moment of your time. May we speak in private?"

Someone brushes against him, and it's one of the ministers, his hat askew, breathless in his rush to reach Kang's side. He bows deeply, forcing Kang to take a step back. "This servant apologizes for not reaching you in time, Highness. I should have stopped you."

"Why?" Kang snaps, irritated at the interruption.

"The wŭlín-shī have pledged a vow of silence," the minister tells him. "They will not speak to anyone until there is an emperor on the throne."

Kang is taken aback. A vow of silence? For a moment, he doesn't know what to say.

"It shows their commitment and devotion to the emperor-regent's cause," a voice sounds behind them. Kang turns to see Chancellor Zhou. "I would ask that you respect their space."

Something inside him bristles. "Fine," Kang says tightly. He turns back to the group of wŭlín-shī and bows again. "I apologize for intruding."

His teacher is already turning away, dismissing him. It feels like a punch to the gut. There was no spark of recognition. Kang is a stranger to him, even though their lessons changed his life. To his beloved teacher, he is only a brief moment, lost to the winds of time.

Kang broods over this encounter the rest of the day. It seems like the wŭlín-shī are now everywhere, reminding him of his embarrassment. Following his father, standing guard at the doors of the council chambers, on the perimeter of the banquet hall. He picks at his dinner, not able to stomach the rich food. Usually, he would enjoy the stewed pork and thick noodles, but his mind continues to remind him of his blunder. Which he is sure the chancellor has brought to the attention of his father.

When dessert comes, Kang is barely paying attention to the trilling sounds of the bamboo flute and the guăn. Dancers flit by with their fans, but they are a blur of motion. He picks up a pastry with a red dot on the surface and bites into it. The layers crumble in his mouth, sweetness on his tongue. There is a strange taste to this pastry. Something dry. He peers down to see what it could be.

There is a slip of paper inside, tucked into the crevice beside the yellow yolk. His heart starts to beat faster. He glances around the room, to see if anyone is waiting for his response. The attention of the court is on the dancers or conversing among themselves. No one is looking in his direction.

He pulls it out, and it lands on his plate. It's only the length of half his finger, the width of a fingernail. Tiny characters written in red ink, but the meaning is clear. Four on one side and four on the other.

小心武林
装神弄鬼
Beware Wŭlín
It's a deception

Kang stares at it for a moment more before realizing where he is and the danger he is in. Someone has risked much to gain his attention. Who? Or is this a ruse to draw him out? Test his sympathies?

He puts the paper back into the pastry and shoves the entire thing into his mouth. Chewing and swallowing, trying not to gag, until the evidence is gone.

It tastes as dry as ashes. It tastes like a different sort of bitter disappointment.

Chapter Fourteen

Kang 康

For the rest of the evening, his senses are on high alert. The sound of the pipes has become discordant and wrong, the movements of the dancers stilted and awkward. Every time someone's attention lands on him, he wonders: Is this the person who put the note in his food? Are there others? From this point on, he knows he will have to operate as carefully as possible. Away from the chancellor's scrutiny and his father's attention.

On the way back to his residence, Kang decides to go to the kitchens. He has to know who, or at least get an idea of who, may be behind the secret message. His guards seem hesitant, but because it is within the palace, there is no reason for them to stop him, even with the chancellor's instructions regarding his "personal safety."

Before entering the kitchens, he already hears the sound of people talking. The sound of clinking spoons against bowls and comfortable conversation. So different from the stilted, formal banquets of the court. Kang didn't know he missed that until this moment; it reminded him of the meals he shared with fellow soldiers around campfires.

"Stay outside the kitchens," he tells the guards. "I'll be fine in there." Even as they protest, he waves them away. He's a prince, right? Supposedly.

When he enters, the conversation stops. One of the servants recognizes him and jumps to her feet, the others following.

"Your Highness," she says, bowing low. "We did not expect you. Was something not to your liking?" Behind her, he senses the nervousness of the staff. They shuffle on their feet, looking as if they already expect punishment.

He doesn't know who could be watching, listening. He doesn't know if there is anyone in the court he can trust enough to discuss his suspicions, and the chancellor is determined to keep him away from his father. All the people he would call friends are back in Lǜzhou, which suddenly feels very far away.

"I would like to give my thanks to the chef who made the delicious pastries for tonight," Kang says, keeping his voice flat and emotionless. "I'd like to speak to them."

"That is high praise!" She beams with obvious relief that he is not here to complain about tonight's meal. "I will look for him now."

She disappears through the doors, then returns soon after with a burly man. The woman ushers the rest of the kitchen staff out of the way with a tsk, leaving them alone in the kitchen courtyard.

The pastry chef is a head taller than Kang and broad-shouldered. He did not seem like someone who could make the delicate treats that come out of the kitchens, with their detailed folds and careful carvings.

Kang's thoughts about the man's striking figure must have shown on his face, because the man chuckles.

"You are not the first and will not be the last to react like this, Highness." The man bows. "My name is Wu Zhong-Chang, but everyone calls me Small Wu."

There is a brashness to his speech, a roughness in his demeanor, that Kang quite likes. He is more used to that than the polite distance of the noble and officials he is supposed to associate with.

"I enjoyed your pastries at the banquet tonight," Kang continues, choosing his words carefully, aware there may be others listening just around the corner. Small Wu smiles, a pleasant mask he is unable to read. "Please take this as a token of my appreciation." Kang holds out a small pouch, which contains a few coins. Small Wu receives it with two hands and an even deeper bow.

"Please wait just a moment, Highness," he says, after straightening. "I cannot have you leave empty-handed."

Kang tries to protest, but the man is gone and comes back with a covered basket in hand.

"This is all I can offer for your kindness. As your humble servant, I beg for you to accept," the man says gruffly. Kang takes it because he does not know how to say no to that. After a pause, Small Wu adds, "And thank you for speaking up in behalf of Chunhua yesterday."

Kang is taken aback at this—he did not think anyone noticed his attempt to spare the former kitchen steward's daughter from his father's brutal punishment.

"I wish I could have saved her," Kang says quietly. But he cannot dwell on his latest failure right now. There are more questions he needs to ask. "Are there any others I should thank . . . for the pastries?"

"No, it was just me. We have been short-staffed of late, since the recent, um . . ." Small Wu shakes his head. Kang knows what he is referring to. The recent purges. The servants who were implicated, confessions tortured out of them before being executed. "Please, Highness. Enjoy the treats."

Kang then realizes Small Wu's uncomfortable demeanor, the

nervous clutching of his hands. Even with this simple conversation, he may be risking the kitchen staff further. He's forgotten his place yet again. With another mumbled thanks, he takes his leave.

When Kang returns to his residence, he places the lacquered basket on the table. He thinks about the words on the hidden slip of paper again. Someone is warning him about Wǔlín, using the kitchens as their messenger, but why? And the literal translation of that particular phrase: *masquerading as gods, acting as ghosts.*

装神弄鬼

In common usage, the line is calling out a deception, pointing to someone as a charlatan. But it seems like a hint. Is someone pretending to be a god, with malevolent intent?

He looks down at the basket again, lifting up the lid. Three pastries. A golden one sprinkled with black sesame seeds, a pale white one dotted with red—just like the pastry at the banquet—and one that is light green.

Kang picks up the pastry with a red dot and splits it open, revealing the yolk inside—and finds yet another slip of paper.

With trembling hands, he pulls it out, unraveling it. He sees the small red characters, written in the same careful hand as the characters in the previous note. Someone ensured that he would receive the pastry with the note. Someone knew he would follow up with the kitchen staff and could provide him with the next clue. He rips open the other pastries, but they only have the usual fillings contained within.

Peering at the words, he studies them more closely. Whoever

this mysterious provider of notes is, they are well educated, for the phrases they chose seem to be selected for a specific purpose, but he cannot decipher it as of yet. Perhaps an official who opposes his father's rule, but why contact him? He is the prince, after all. His loyalty should be, first and foremost, to the general. And yet this faceless person wants him to doubt.

> 荼毒生靈
> 春生秋殺
> *A slaughter of innocents.*
> *What spring brings to life, autumn kills.*

Ominous words for an ominous time. Each phrase is accusatory, especially written as they are in red ink, the color of bad omens. Someone wants to know who is responsible for the deaths of so many in Dàxī, whether at the hand of the uprisings or poisoned by tea.

Kang feels the guilt of it. In some ways, he is complicit. But he realizes it is time now to step into the role he told his father he was ready for.

He will not stand by idly while the people suffer. Not anymore.

Chapter Fifteen

Ning 寧

Before we descend the path and return to the outpost, Astronomer Wu tells us there are other messages he must impart, away from prying ears. One for me, and one for Ruyi.

"You will inform the princess of the information I have passed on?" he asks Ruyi first. "This information is . . . delicate, and as you have seen from our conversations with Commander Fan, there is an appropriate audience for such knowledge, and then there are those who would hinder our way forward."

"I understand." She nods. "We will proceed accordingly with this counsel."

The astronomer turns to me then with a respectful bow, and I know in that moment he is going to tell me something I do not want to hear.

"I will warn you, with my deepest apologies, that you will not gain admittance to Kallah at this time," the astronomer says. Even though his voice is soft, I still feel the rejection like a physical blow. "I tell you this so that you will be prepared for what I will reveal to the council tonight when we convene with the princess."

"Why?" I manage to choke out. I went to the capital to save Shu and became embroiled in the mess of the court. Now we are on the run, and the one place I know that can offer us refuge will not permit me entrance?

"The serpent called you by name," he says. "There is a connection between you and him that I cannot ignore. Until we can be certain that your connection is severed, your presence will place the people of Kallah, and the princess, at risk."

"There is nothing you can do about this?" Ruyi asks. I'm grateful that at least someone would speak up in my behalf, that our bond is not something I've imagined.

"I cannot." He shakes his head. "Not until we discover how to stop the serpent, and that is beyond my power. I see the movement of the future through the stars and perform small, protective magics—like the ward I used to break the serpent's enchantment on Ning previously. But that is the limit of my abilities."

He turns back to me. "I know this is not what you wanted to hear, but I promise you I will find a way to resolve this predicament."

The astronomer begins to bow again, but I put a hand on his shoulder to stop him from continuing. He has to protect his people, that much I understand. I cannot fault him for it.

"But if I may offer an alternative option," he tells me. "You do have a part to play in the princess's prophecy. Albeit a different part than what you may have expected."

"I'm not sure what you mean," I say.

"There is a shénnóng-shī who resides in a gorge near Wǔlín Academy. She is said to be a being of great power. She was the one who provided the emperor with his prophecy."

"The one who spoke about the princess?" I ask.

That familiar line, given to the Emperor of Benevolence long ago: *Your child will bring you great sorrow and great joy. They will walk a path of starlight, but shadows will follow.*

He nods. "The very same. She may have knowledge of the serpent. She may be able to tell us about his weaknesses, whether there is a way for us to fight his influence and perhaps stop him from returning to the human world."

"You think she will listen to me?"

"It is said that sometimes she is willing to take on a pupil—someone who can demonstrate a gift for Shénnóng magic. I believe you will be able to convince her to join our cause."

We leave the bone tower just as the sun is setting over the lake. The encampment around the outpost has grown even larger. Additional caravans and tents have been set up while we were gone, and yet another group of travelers approaches on ponies.

"There is someone you may be interested in seeing again," Astronomer Wu tells me cryptically as we draw closer to the newcomers.

I hear a joyful cry, and then Lian comes running toward me, braids swinging, embracing me with the enthusiasm that comes when reuniting with a dearly missed friend. I hug her back, laughing, feeling a little lighter for the moment. Glad for the fondness and warmth she exudes, and glad for a distraction so I do not have to dwell on what awaits me tonight at the council.

"I'm so happy you're here!" I pull back and look at her fully.

She is dressed in the traditional clothing of Kallah—a red vest embroidered with flowers on top of a white undershirt with billowing sleeves. Her skirt is also white, embroidered with more flowers, and the pants underneath are red as well. On her feet are beautiful slippers, stitched with flying birds.

"And you, my friend." She holds my hands, beaming, and then her expression shifts to a considering one. "I was so worried when I heard about what happened in the capital and the chancellor's horrible lies. I always thought he was an honorable man, but it turns out even he would stoop to treason. And to pin his schemes on you!" She tsks.

I can only smile at her, realizing I was worried about Lian, too, since she left the competition. I wished she had stayed with me for the final challenge, but it was better for her to stay away, especially so she could protect Ruyi as she recovered.

"Come, I brought you lots of snacks from Kallah, and gifts." She hooks her arm with mine.

"And I shall introduce you to my sister," I tell her.

We spend the rest of the evening around the fire in her tent, drinking tea and eating the promised treats. She called them "snacks," but it is more like a feast. Pork roasted over the fire, dipped into slightly sour chili sauce. The sauce is made from various types of chilis and peppercorns, raw garlic and ginger mixed with soy sauce. Another dish contains dried plums cut into shapes of flowers, dusted with sugar. All this to be eaten with warm walnut bread, bursting with sweet and nutty filling in each bite. The heat from the tea and the spice from the food make my hands and feet warm, even though every time the tent flap opens, I feel the slight chill from the evening winds.

"I have a present for you," Lian tells me after we have drunk and eaten our fill. Digging through her packs, she finds and then passes me a small, embroidered pouch. The Kallah style of embroidery is different from the Sù style—their threads glitter in the light, wound with some sort of material that makes it sparkle, and the ends of the pouch are woven with small beads. It is of similar make to the details on her outfit and her shoes. I admire the design of a river landscape, but Lian encourages me to open the pouch and see what is inside.

Three balls lie within. I bring them up to my nose and sniff, finding a slightly medicinal fragrance.

"I spent some time with my teacher," she tells me. "He was working on a way to craft dān, a way for us to use our magic without requiring the full ceremony. These are among the few remaining in his stores, and he asked me to pass them on to you."

I look down at the dān with surprise, aware of their potent power. "You want to give these to me?" I ask. "Why not keep some for yourself?"

She shakes her head. "I am going to continue to learn and work on replicating his process. He told me you may need them." Even though shénnóng-shī do not see the strands that shape and unravel empires as the astronomers do, they might be able to catch a glimpse of a person's future. I was connected to Lian, through our chance meeting, our time spent at the palace, and her mentor saw me through her somehow. It is a priceless gift.

I give her my thanks, tucking the embroidered pouch into my sash. I will use them to the best of my abilities.

One of the guards lifts the panel to the tent not long after that and asks for us to join the princess in her own tent. When we are admitted inside, we see a council of people sitting around the lit brazier in the center. An opening at the top lets the smoke out, and I see a sprinkling of stars above. Somehow it makes me feel more comforted even knowing the challenges ahead, because I know the stars are watching over us.

There is Ruyi, Commander Fan, Astronomer Wu, and some other people I do not recognize dressed in Kallah's colors. Zhen sits on a chair, as befitting her status, while everyone else rests on cushions.

"Good." Zhen gestures for us to sit beside her on two empty cushions. "We can begin."

When all the council is settled in, she speaks. "The commander has offered to escort us into Kallah, knowing that dangers may continue to follow. I believe those soldiers who attacked us were only the first wave. We will leave tomorrow after clearing out the encampment."

Murmurs of agreement, accompanied by nods, are heard and seen all around.

"The ambassador has agreed to provide us with refuge among his people and will personally offer his home to us. We are deeply appreciative of this offer, and we accept. We owe you a debt, Ambassador." Zhen places her hand over her heart.

One of the men from Kallah, the one with a head of salt-and-pepper hair and similar gray in his full beard, inclines his head in acknowledgment. I realize this must be Lian's father, Ambassador Luo.

"Even though I am loath to say this, I must offer a word of counsel," Astronomer Wu says quietly, but firmly. "I do not believe the shénnóng-tú should gain admittance to Kallah."

All eyes in the tent turn to me, and even though I am prepared for it, it doesn't make it any easier to hear.

Lian jumps to her feet in protest. "What?! How can you say that?"

"Lian," her father cautions her. Reluctantly, my friend sits down, still grumbling to herself.

"Ning has shown herself able to make difficult choices under duress, and she has put herself in harm's way to save others. She risked her life for me, for Ruyi, many times over," Zhen says to the astronomer, a hint of challenge in her voice. "Why would you not permit her entrance to Kallah?"

I did not know how Zhen would react to the news, and it eases the rejection slightly knowing that she does think somewhat fondly of me. Despite her hesitation to accept my magic on the mountainside.

"I have sensed a darkness upon her," the astronomer explains. "A malevolent influence that may place you or the people of Kallah at risk. Although she may be pure of heart, that is a risk I am not willing to take."

For one commoner, he does not have to say the rest of his sentence out loud. I hear it all the same.

"You cannot help her get rid of this darkness that you sense?" Zhen continues to press him. Something about her words sparks a feeling of shame, knowing what the serpent saw in me. Those dark and twisted thoughts he thought he could use to his advantage, pull me to his side. Perhaps he was right.

"I cannot," the astronomer says.

"I know my daughter would speak for the integrity of this shénnóng-tú, call her a friend," Lian's father says with great authority. "I trust my daughter's word. But I have spent the past year building strongholds for my people, in preparation for the war that will eventually cross my borders. We know these mountains and hills because they belong to us, and if there is even the slightest risk she will lead the enemy to our doorsteps, even unintentionally, I cannot allow her entry."

"If I may present an alternate proposal," Astronomer Wu says. "To ensure the shénnóng-tú's safety, for it is clear from our brief encounter that she is a target of that dark force."

Zhen nods. "Continue."

"I propose sending her on another task, one that is just as important to our cause," Astronomer Wu offers. "We need someone to deliver the message to Wŭlín that Yĕliŭ has fallen."

"And you need someone to act as bait," Zhen says flatly. "You will use her as a diversion, to lead the enemy's attention away from us."

"It is a strategic plan," Commander Fan says. Of course he would approve of sending me away, and Astronomer Wu does not deny it. Ambassador Luo also nods.

I listen to them discuss my fate. Make plans for my future. Even Astronomer Wu's belief in me earlier does not ease this ache inside of me. The reminder I am not worthy.

"What sort of protection will you offer her?" Ruyi asks.

"Two of my best soldiers can accompany her," Commander Fan says. "She will be well protected."

Zhen's eyes fall on me again, and she addresses me directly, cutting through the discussions of the others. "I would never send someone who is unwilling. If you would rather go elsewhere, we will find another way."

I consider this. But where would I go? Back to Sù and bring the danger to my father and the village instead? Go into Yún and the wilderness and try to survive in the north?

Or I can see where this path takes me. I remember the mission Astronomer Wu has given me, to find the shénnóng-shī who wove Zhen's prophecy. If this is what it takes, then I will do it.

"I am willing," I finally say. "If you take Shu with you into Kallah." That is the only thing I want, the only thing I am willing to bargain my own life for. If Shu will be safe, then it will be worth it.

"Of course." Ambassador Luo bows his head. "We will ensure her safety. My own daughter will be her companion."

"I promise to keep her safe," Lian leans over and whispers in my ear, and it is only her promise that convinces me. I nod at the princess, accepting my fate.

Chapter Sixteen

Ning 寧

I RETURN TO OUR TENT, TRYING TO BE AS QUIET AS POSSIBLE. The council lasted late into the night, and fatigue tugs at the edges of my consciousness, begging me to sleep. But thoughts still race through my mind. Although I know the leaders of Kallah are protecting their own, a part of me still smarts at not being permitted to enter the province. Of being a threat to their existence, hidden as they are behind their mountainous borders. At least Shu will be safe.

As I get ready for bed, my sister sits up in the dark, having waited for me all this time.

"What happened at the council?" she asks, and then after a pause, "I want to know."

She wants to be involved, to be consulted. But I hope she can understand the choice I had to make. She cannot go with me, and I know she will be angry at me for making the decision without her.

I tell her of my conversations with the astronomer at the bone tower, of being sent on to Wǔlín, and then my new mission to see the shénnóng-shī there. Finally, I tell her, dreading her reaction, "You will have to go to Kallah with Lian. I will return for you when it's safe."

The flash of fury across my usually calm sister's face takes me aback. "You would leave me behind?!" she snaps.

"You can't come with me; it's too dangerous."

"You will *not* leave me behind!" she presses. "You can't!"

"It's not *safe*," I stress, willing her to see reason. "We'll be trekking up and down mountains. Sleeping on the ground. You saw those shadow soldiers who attacked us. We will be chased. They may want to kill us, or worse."

"The only reason I left Sù was to be with you," she tells me hotly. "I know you're hiding things from me. I know you saw things in the palace and you had to rely on yourself to survive. But you don't have to do it alone anymore! I was too weak to help you then, but I'm stronger now! Have you forgotten what Mother said? We're a family. We're stronger together."

It's unfair of her to bring up Mother. I do not want to be apart from her again, but I also could not bear it if anything were to happen to her.

I sigh. "We'll speak of it again tomorrow morning."

Turning away from her, I lie down and allow sleep to overtake me, wondering how I'll persuade her to let me go.

When I wake up in the morning, Shu is gone. Her belongings are packed neatly, ready for travel. I emerge from the tent to see her speaking with Astronomer Wu, nodding. A rush of fierce protectiveness overcomes me, and I quickly walk over to join them, my heart already beating rapidly in my chest, worrying over what I will hear them say.

"We had come to an agreement last night in the council," Astronomer Wu says to me, eyes sad. "But your sister has just informed me that she has also experienced a connection with the serpent. For the same reason, I must advise the ambassador that we cannot welcome her into Kallah."

"You . . . you did *what*?" I turn on her, furious. That she dared to do this without asking me, that she pronounced herself as touched by the serpent. Something far too dangerous to share with the wrong people.

Shu regards me steadily, with no remorse. "I'll come with you, then." She shrugs. "Isn't it as simple as that?"

I grab her arm and pull her away, not wanting the astronomer to witness our family argument.

"I cannot believe you've done such a foolish thing!" I yell at her. "You have no idea what sort of danger you've placed yourself in. This is not a game! This is not an adventure, either! You nearly died from the poison, and now you want to throw your life away!"

Shu stands there, allowing me to yell at her, but she says with infuriating calm, "It's done. You can't change anything. If you won't let me come with you, then I'll try to make my way alone. If I fall off a cliff on the way there, you can blame yourself."

"You . . . you . . ." I think I may just strangle her where she stands. Instead, I turn and stomp away, cursing myself, cursing her impulsiveness, her immaturity, her senselessness—

I find myself at the edge of the lake, and I kick a stone into the water, watch it splash. I shouldn't react in such a way. I'm the older sister. I've always been told to set an example, to do what's right. In so many ways, I do not match up to those expectations . . .

"Ning!"

"What?" I turn with a snarl, only to see Zhen and Ruyi approaching. I try to swallow my anger, but it still simmers there under the surface, ready to erupt.

"We wanted to see you off . . . say goodbye," Zhen says gently.

"Oh," I say. "We'll meet again after . . . all this." I gesture vaguely at the sky and the water, unable to form coherent words through my roiling emotions.

"You will be able to travel swiftly to Wŭlín with the assistance of the commander's soldiers," Ruyi says. "They know the forest. They will keep you and Shu safe."

"You have an important task ahead," Zhen tells me. "I recognize this. After this is over, you will be rewarded."

"I just want all this to end," I say bitterly. I don't care about a title. I don't care about the riches, the palanquin filled with treasure, the status. I only want to survive, keep Shu safe, without adding more names to my list of deaths to avenge.

"It will. I promise you I will do everything in my power to stop him." The princess grabs my hand, holding it in her own. I stare down at it in surprise. "Take care, Ning. Be careful."

We each carry our own pack and begin the trek up the mountain, heading to the east. Shu gives me space, knowing I am still seething about what she did. Commander Fan did send us with companions, as promised. Captain Tsai is an older woman who does not make much conversation, speaking only to provide us with curt instructions. Lieutenant Huang is a jovial man, who tells us to call him Brother Huang, even though he is about ten years older than us. Shu converses with Brother Huang, while I find Captain Tsai's silence just as companionable.

I said goodbye to Lian on the lakeshore, embracing my friend one last time. She promised she would see me later, and I certainly hope so. By then, we will know whether all our efforts have succeeded.

Initially, the trees are sparse along the path we take up a rocky mountainside, much like our previous travels through Guòwū Pass. It makes me miss the ponies, even if they had a faintly sour smell from the grass they loved to chew. Their steady presence helped me keep my balance, and without them, my boots constantly slip on the small stones. But ponies would slow us down, the captain told us, that we would be quicker on foot. She also informed us it would take half a day to reach the Bamboo Sea, and then a six-to-seven-day trek through it to get to Wǔlín.

As the heat of the day slowly rises, we arrive at the edge of the bamboo forest. The bamboo grows so dense here that being in the grove feels as if we are passing through twilight. The trees sway overhead, sounding like the whispers of a thousand voices. It does not take long until it is all we see. We're enveloped, surrounded by greenery, a marvel to behold. The path meanders through the endless, swaying stalks.

It would be easy to lose one's sense of direction here. If it wasn't for Captain Tsai's ability to navigate, I'm sure Shu and I would be easily lost. But Brother Huang is good company, and he regales us with funny stories about his training with the Yěliŭ regiment. Like getting pelted with apples by monkeys while on patrol in the woods or sneaking into the kitchens trying to get second rations.

His expression only darkens slightly when he remembers how some of his fellow guards died at the massacre, letting out a heavy sigh. "I . . . I just can't believe I won't see them again." Captain Tsai glances back at this but says nothing, only quickens her pace, as if she is worried the enemy soldiers who attacked Yěliŭ are already on our heels.

I continue to marvel at the bamboo as we walk. The air is filled with a bright scent, making the journey not altogether unpleasant.

I've heard of these bamboo forests, but the groves I've seen have always been compact, transported to the gardens of wealthy merchants or scholar families and contained to small plots.

The first day passes without much fanfare, and a hush falls over the forest too quickly. Without a crier to set the time here, it is easy to lose track of the course of the sun. We quickly set up camp for the night under a small rock overhang.

As we sit around the fire, Brother Huang pulls out a carving made of wood and starts to whittle it in the light of the flames.

"What is that?" Shu asks.

Brother Huang passes it over to her, and I lean over to see. It's a delicate figure of a woman. He's captured the details of her hair, swept back from her face in a half knot, and the folds of her dress.

"That's beautiful," she says softly. "You're talented."

"Just a hobby." Brother Huang ducks his head, looking bashful in the firelight. "A way to pass the time."

"Is this someone close to you?" She turns the carving in her hand.

"My betrothed," he tells us. "She promised to wait for me until I return from this assignment. I will finally have the coin to ask for her hand."

"I wish you success on this journey." Shu gives him a smile. "To make it back to the happiness waiting for you at home."

"Thank you." Brother Huang returns her smile with a grin. "I'll return a hero, having met the princess. All the exciting tales I will be able to tell my girl!"

Shu's ease with forming connections with others is something I've always envied. I feel like I usually stumble on my words or run out of things to say, and then the right words come to me when they are already gone.

Captain Tsai tells us to sleep soon after, that we will set out again at first light. The sooner we make it to Wŭlín, the sooner we can sleep in a real bed.

When I close my eyes, I am somehow back in that place. The Shadow Realm, where everything is devoid of color. The serpent's domain. There are so many questions I never had a chance to ask Astronomer Wu. Like if the Shadow Realm is the same as the Shift or if it is somewhere else entirely.

I am dreaming, I tell myself, as if that will make it easier to understand.

The dark shapes around me form themselves into trees—my family's orchards as they used to be. Fire falls around me like rain, lighting up the brush. The air smells acrid, black smoke billowing in thick clouds, forming menacing shapes.

I squeeze my eyes shut. *I'm not here. I'm in the bamboo forest. I'm lying down beside Shu.*

Then I hear whispers, something indiscernible, a malevolent chant. Until it turns into . . .

Ning . . .

My name.

Ning . . .

They beckon.

The fire continues to burn around me, and I fight my way through the trees. I think I see the sloped rooftops of my village in the distance, and I run toward it. A tree falls in front of me, landing with a burst of sparks.

"Ning! Ning'er!"

I recognize that voice: my grandmother. My mother's mother,

who tried to help with the fire in the orchards and caught a rasping cough that lasted until she passed a year later. My uncle used that to convince everyone I was a curse on the family, a disgrace.

"Ning!"

My head turns. It sounds like . . . Mingwen? The kitchen maid sentenced to sixty strikes with the cane for helping me. Did they ever carry out her punishment? Is she still alive, or . . .

My name continues to be called out by different voices. Begging for my help. Crying out for me to come closer.

And then, through it all, I hear Mother calling out to me.

They begin stepping out from among the burning trees, their faces lit up by the flames. Grandmother. Mingwen. Wenyi. The Esteemed Qian. The marquis. Steward Yang. Small Wu. A'bing. Mother.

I clap my hands over my ears, dropping to the ground. Surrounded by the voices of everyone for whom I carry guilt, all the lives ruined through my influence. They reach for me through the fire, even as it consumes them. They advance in jerky movements, the fire licking up their limbs, toward their faces, until their features begin to melt like wax, until the fire burns them all.

I weep for them, wishing I had the power to bring them back.

There comes another rustle through the trees—a long, serpentine shape, moving behind them.

The taste of your guilt, your shame, so sweet . . .

I wake up, thrashing. Shu's hands are on my shoulders, shaking me awake. I touch my face, and my fingers come away damp.

"You were screaming in your sleep," she tells me, holding up a flask. "I had to splash you to wake you up."

"I'm sorry, I was . . . dreaming," I mutter.

I turn away and put on a new tunic, spreading the wet one out to dry. The others are also concerned, having been woken by my cries as well, but Shu tells them I'm all right. I wanted so much to return home to my family; I thought if I found the antidote, everything would go back to the way it was. But I've returned as someone else, haunted by things I never want Shu to carry. I want her to remain innocent and hopeful, but now we are on the run from evil forces.

I don't say any of that to her. I try to fall asleep instead.

After what felt like the blink of an eye, the light seeps in through the bamboo. Morning is here. Even though my head still feels heavy, I know it's time to get up. Following a light breakfast of boiled millet with pickled vegetables, we continue our journey.

Which involves walking. Endless walking.

We have been swallowed by bamboo, and I understand why they call it the Bamboo Sea. In the forests near my home, each tree has their own voice. They occupy their own space, distinct from one another. Their roots may cross, their branches overlapping, but they stand alone. When I try to listen to the bamboo, they are . . . a chorus of voices, all speaking together. A vast, spreading thing. I try to ignore them and focus on walking instead, putting one foot in front of the other.

Captain Tsai draws a map for us in the dirt during our midday break.

"Here is Tiānxiáng Lake," she says. "And here is Guòwū Pass, to Yěliŭ. We are north of there. In the Forgetting Sea is a place we call Broken Earth. Here only a specific type of bamboo thrives: thorny bamboo. It is hard enough that it can be used as a weapon or as a barrier against wild animals. We have to be careful around it." Pointing with her dao down the path ahead, we see in the distance a place where the bamboo parts to reveal the sky.

I never thought I would be so grateful to see the sky.

When we reach Broken Earth, the bamboo grows in smaller groves, more like the type of bamboo I am familiar with. Here there is a clearer path laid out in the forest, covered by long grass that has been cut down. Where the bamboo has overgrown onto the path, Captain Tsai carefully uses her blade to bend back the stalks. She shows us the thin, protruding spines that poke out from the sides. We manage to avoid walking too close or stepping directly on the stalks that have fallen, or else it would be easy for those hard spines to snag on our clothes or puncture the soles of our boots. Because the path is wide, it is easy for us to walk quickly, and the afternoon passes until we encounter a house in the middle of the forest.

It is a strange, otherworldly sight. A house constructed entirely of bamboo, far away from any sign of civilization. It's a place that should exist only in folktales; I can't help but feel like a wise seer should come out to greet us, providing us with our fortunes. But when we go inside, the building is empty.

"How does such a place exist?" I ask. "Who cares for it?" Having lived close to the forest, I know how easy it is for a place to become overgrown and fall into ruin. But this house almost seems newly built.

"There are people who travel through the Forgetting Sea to maintain it," Captain Tsai explains. "Some of them have lost those they care for to this place and use it as a shrine to preserve the memory of their loved ones. Others pass through here to collect bamboo shoots, which are good to eat and can be sold at other villages, and they stay here for a night if they have ventured too far."

When we ascend the steps, I see markings along the doorframe of the house. Drawing closer, I realize they are names etched into the bamboo. A way to remember those who are lost. It makes me feel uneasy, thinking of all the people who have disappeared into these green depths, but Captain Tsai touches the markings fondly, with a smile.

That night we have a proper place to cook, and we have a filling dinner of earthy mushrooms, slices of smoked boar, and chopped tubers, along with some mysterious greens that Brother Huang gathered that have a sweet taste. I go to bed with my stomach full, and I finally have a night of restful sleep. There must be something powerful this deep in the Bamboo Sea, something that shields me from the notice of the serpent. He does not visit me, and instead, I dream I stand on a cliff of stars.

Here, I feel at peace.

Chapter Seventeen

Kang 康

The Hall of Eternal Light is brilliantly lit with burning braziers and swaying lanterns. The general sits on the dragon throne. He has yet to don the emperor's full regalia, but he wears an embroidered robe of phoenixes and dragons.

It has been a few days since Kang received the messages in the pastries, and he is not any closer to deciphering the riddle hidden in the phrases. He stares at that tiny slip of paper as often as he dares, but only when he is certain he is alone. He watches the members of the court more closely, trying to determine their thoughts. If there are any furtive glances in his direction or if there is a gesture that would give someone away. Yet, as hard as he tries to notice the slightest subtlety, nothing is out of sorts.

The court appears to function as it always does. The councils still continue, with his father or the chancellor presiding, meeting to address issues of the realm. Kang does as he is told. He goes where he is scheduled to be. He sits where he is instructed to sit.

The reports of the various ministers and governors and lesser officials of Dàxī all speak of difficult times. The people beg for relief from the various disasters that have occurred over the past year. Walking past a group of officials after the latest council, Kang hears one of them say: "It seems as if the very earth is crying out for help . . ."

The princess continues to elude the Ministry of Justice, and each time Kang sees Minister Hu, he seems more beaten down. He's seen him berated by the Minister of War, treated dismissively by the Finance Minister. He suspects the minister may not be in that role for long if he cannot capture the princess or the rogue shénnóng-tú. Kang still finds himself paying attention when she is named. There is so much he hid from her, so little he could tell her. He wants so desperately to one day remove that look of betrayal on her face, and yet he may not get the chance to. He should have known it was doomed from the start. He shouldn't have returned to her, again and again, trying to change what could not be changed.

The strike of a gong releases him from his reverie. Minister Song stands. "It is time for the people of Dàxī to present their tributes," he announces to the court. "We honor the emperor of Dàxī like we honor the gods, for he will lead us to glory." He bows, gesturing for the procession to begin.

Huá prefecture presents a gold sculpture in the shape of an ox—that wealthy region contains the most productive mines in the empire. Yún province is famous for their embroidery, and they bring forth rolls of the finest fabrics, embroidered with gold and silver threads. Ānhé submits scrolls of calligraphy crafted by a famous scholar once praised by the Ascended Emperor for the fluidity of her strokes.

The representatives drone on in flowery language about the beauty and rarity of the offerings, and Kang sips at his wine.

When the minister announces the offering from Sù, Kang

cannot help but turn his head toward the doorway, reminded once again of that girl who has found her way inside his head too many times to count. Governor Wang approaches, holding something in both arms. It is draped in red cloth, hidden from view.

The chancellor rises from his seat and joins the governor in the center of the room. They both bow to the emperor-regent. Governor Wang sets the item on the offering table, and the general, who has listened to the presentations half-reclined, leans forward slightly. It is a small movement, but Kang knows, because he is his father, that weapons appeal more to him than gold or jewels.

The governor pulls away the cloth with a flourish, revealing a simple wooden stand on which rests a sword. One with a carved white hilt, slightly yellowed with age. The blade is curved, wrapped with rope—a hastily constructed scabbard. It looks shoddy, out of place among the other treasures on the table.

Murmurs rise from the audience, questioning why such a battered thing would be worthy of presentation.

"You found it!" The general stands, his robe flowing around him in a dark pool. Kang notices he is speaking to the chancellor, who looks pleased with himself.

"Yes, Your Highness." The governor bows. "When the chancellor bid us to locate it, Sù spared no expense in searching for this relic."

"My son!" the general calls out, and Kang startles before lurching to his feet. He dislikes the feel of all these eyes on him. He bows before his father, waiting for instruction.

"Bring it to me," the general commands.

Kang obeys, lifting the sword off the stand with both hands. It feels warm to the touch, the parts of it that are exposed and not covered by the rough rope. There's a sparkle to the material, as if it is lit from within. He unravels the bindings, and pieces of it fall onto the table. The blade itself is also pale, the length of a forearm, with a slight curve. It's lighter than he expected. He turns and approaches the throne. Dropping to one knee, he offers the sword up to his father.

"You must be wondering about the origins of this relic." The general picks it up reverently, with a look of satisfaction. He grabs the hilt and checks its balance before taking one finger and gliding it along the flat side of the blade. "In the time of the Ascended Emperor, he encountered a clan that eluded his troops in his attempts to quell the unrest of the western highlands. That clan was led by the warlord Han Qi, who led a violent campaign against the emperor, believing himself to be a destined ruler, a king. His people were ferocious, fought like each battle was their last. Even when he was captured, he refused to surrender, and he died on his own sword. But the Ascended Emperor admired that ferocity, and eventually one of Han Qi's children became a great general, following his father's legacy.

"Legend has it, the sword is cursed with the ghost of the warlord. Wielding it meant certain victory, but at the cost of your own life." Kang's father scoffs at this. "I don't believe in such superstitions, but I do like the feel of this sword. The symbolism of it. I shall wear it as a reminder to myself, for the battles to come."

The chancellor approaches and bows. "We shall have a scabbard made so that you can do so, Highness."

The general places the sword in the chancellor's uplifted hands. It gleams in the light.

The emperor-regent nods. "See to it that you do."

With the tributes done, the court rises, Kang standing among them. They bow, echoing the words of the herald:

"Long live the Prince of Dài, Honored Regent of Dàxī. Long live the Prince of Dài, ruler of the realm."

Chapter Eighteen

Kang 康

In the inner wing of the palace, there is a strict adherence to schedule. Since he moved into the prince's quarters, Kang has come to believe there are servants who exist solely to keep time. The water clock runs in a steady stream at all hours of the day, and the incense coils continue to burn throughout the night. Servants arrive in the morning and read off the day's events from a scroll, assist him with dressing and undressing throughout the day, switching outfits and hairstyles and shoes to what would be appropriate for whatever event he was to attend.

Morning, afternoon, evening, and night. Household restrictions and court rites his father never bothered with in their house in Lüzhou. Now he is nudged into place at all times. Steered away from taking the wrong turn into another courtyard or picking up one dish on his plate that is not intended for consumption yet. So many rules, so many intricacies of behavior, his head hurts from attempting to remember them all.

Even as time moves slowly within the palace, the days are drawing longer as the summer solstice approaches. He wakes early in the mornings for training, followed by long afternoons of councils and meetings, then stays up late into the night staring at the mysterious riddles until his head hurts and sleep defeats him yet again.

On one evening, as soon as his meetings are complete, he writes out the first phrase in his passable calligraphy, making sure to take note of every stroke, and takes it to the library pagoda. There must be something in the words that he is not seeing, something that he is missing from the clues. When the first scholar greets him—nearly falling over himself in recognition—and Kang requests a consult with someone who has an understanding of ancient texts, he is led to the head scholar herself.

Mistress Bao greets him with a smile as the other scholar scurries away. "To what do I owe this honor, Highness? We have yet to see you set foot in our humble pavilion."

"Er, yes . . ." Kang shuffles his feet. He is not at ease within these stacks, having never been much of an academic. He remembers being terrified of the former imperial tutor, who has since passed on, but he can still feel the ghostly pain of lashes across his knuckles for falling asleep during lessons.

But he regains his composure and offers the explanation for his presence here. "I found myself studying a few classic texts lately, in an effort to improve my education, which I am discovering is sadly lacking. I found a phrase I have not seen before, and I hoped you might be able to provide me its context."

"I will endeavor to do so to the best of my ability." Mistress Bao inclines her head. "Please, follow me."

She takes him to an alcove containing a stone table and benches. Scrolls are stacked on the surface, and she calls for a servant to carry them away. Numerous windows are set high into the wall where they would not shine directly on the shelves in the center of the library. The light is slanted into the alcoves, where the scholars could review their texts without need of candlelight until dark. A clever architectural design.

When they are seated, Kang passes his rolled sheet of parchment to her. She examines his calligraphy with a critical eye, until he can almost feel himself shriveling as he prepares for the criticism.

"You are missing a stroke here." Using the end of a brush, she taps the middle of the first character.

Kang leans over, frowning. He had checked and double-checked his work, and yet—

"It is a common enough mistake," she says. "One many students would miss. See? The character you wrote is one that is frequently used, the one for tea. But here, see the next one."

She draws carefully on another piece of paper, until he sees that in the original phrase there is an extra line in the center of the character.

茶荼

"Ah." Kang can hardly believe it. One simple, little stroke, and yet it means everything.

Mistress Bao nods. "Such is the beauty of our written language. In the correct phrase, this character represents a type of bitter vegetable and is followed by a character for venom. It means to kill. The second part of the phrase represents the soul, the lives of innocent commoners, ones that those in power have vowed to protect."

The realization strikes Kang like a flash of lightning, so clear that he hates himself for not seeing it right away.

"Mistress, would you be able to find me a text that explains this? I would like to reference it for myself," he says, trying to emanate indifference. He has to ensure that this meeting is not reported to his father, for he is not sure where this information will lead him.

As she leaves to retrieve the texts, Kang forces himself to

breathe in and out deeply. In his mind, he moves through the winding dragon form of the Wǔ Xíng, attempting to find some sort of peace. But there is little to be found.

With a slim volume in hand, lent to him by Mistress Bao, Kang steps out into the garden from the dim depths of the library pagoda. The accusation is as stark as the red marks on the paper: The mysterious note-leaver is referring specifically to the tea poisonings and the senseless murders of the common people. Surely deciphering the second phrase will allow him to know the true meaning of that accusation. Is this a threat to reveal the truth of who ordered the poisoning, or are they merely trying to determine where his loyalties lie?

Kang notices the stones of the philosopher's path and hopes walking it will provide him with some sort of revelation. Dusk settles around him as servants light the lanterns that illuminate the stones. The path meanders behind the library, through groves of green bamboo and beautiful rose blooms. His guards trail behind him, giving him the space he requested. The path curves past the garden, and then in the distance, he sees the gate to the west wing. Beyond it is his former residence.

His heart starts to beat fast as the characters of the second phrase loom before him in his mind. Each residence is associated with a particular season, and the phrase references two seasons. Spring and autumn.

春生秋殺

Spring is where life originates. But what if life refers as well to . . . birth, the origin of the poison, the slaughter? And autumn . . .

autumn carried out the killings? Kang gestures for his guards to approach.

"Tell me," he says. "Who lives now in the Residence of Autumnal Longing?"

"The wŭlín-shī have been staying there," the guards report.

And Kang knows who resides in the Residence of Harmonious Spring.

Grand Chancellor Zhou.

Late at night, while the rest of the palace is asleep, Kang makes his way through the tunnels connecting the inner palace to the west wing. This is the only way he could think of to travel undetected. Moving through the damp and the dark, he is reminded of the times he would play in these tunnels as a child, with the princess and her shadow. The latest reports have her moving west, and it is suspected she will travel toward Kallah, where she may be able to appeal to those loyal to the dowager empress and the Benevolent Emperor.

He is a false prince. What prince is not well versed in the politics of the court? What prince has not been educated on the history texts and the usage of certain phrases by the scholarly officials? What prince feels like a failure, to have a suspicion in his gut, but no way to determine what is real and what is a lie?

He hurries through the tunnels and finds the particular ring he is looking for, easing the door open to slip into the wall of the Residence of Autumnal Longing.

There is only a single lantern in the courtyard, swaying slightly in the wind. The shadows cast by the trees are long, sinister shapes on the wall. From Kang's memories, there are three private rooms in this residence. He slips in through the opened window of the first room and finds it empty. The opulent furnishings, the expensive treasures, all indicate a person of higher rank used to reside here. It must all belong to the previous resident of this place—the marquis of Ānhé, who met his unfortunate end at the banquet. The next room Kang also finds empty. This one, more sparsely decorated, looks to be used as a study.

Through the window screen, Kang sees light in the final bedchamber. This must be where some of the wŭlín-shī are staying. He carefully makes his way along the side of the residence, keeping himself low. This, at least, he is good at. Years of training how to be light on his feet, to make himself small, like a good scout needs to.

He hears a low voice speaking. Someone is still up. He will see for himself how far the vow of silence extends, if they will speak freely when they believe they are alone. Whatever he gleans from their conversations and their behavior will help him understand how they are linked to the chancellor—if their connection is as tight as the note-leaver believes.

Easing the window open a crack, he peers in. There is only a brazier in the corner, from which the dim light emanates. A figure stands in front of a bronze mirror inset into a wooden frame, positioned so Kang sees only his profile. One of the practitioners of Wŭlín he recognizes by face and not by name.

"The Minister of Rites has kept the same schedule as predicted. Nothing appears to be out of sorts." The voice is deep and flat, almost a growl. It looks like he is speaking into the mirror, but then Kang notices other figures standing around the room.

A perfect row of three. Standing with their hands clasped behind their backs, posture erect. Staring forward at the man before the mirror, like stone statues. Kang marvels at how, even when they are alone, they do not seem to let up on their training. There is not so much as a twitch, not a single muscle out of place. He frowns, looking closer. Even disciplined as they are, how can four people stand so still, like they've fallen asleep with their eyes open?

"You will do the same tomorrow."

Kang bites back the gasp he almost lets out. His tooth pierces his lip, flooding his mouth with the taste of blood. That voice... it's the chancellor's. But how can he give orders to the wŭlín-shī? For all intents and purposes, they are the general's loyal warriors, answering only to him. Three of them follow the general's every movement as his devoted bodyguards, and three more stand guard outside whatever hall or room the general occupies.

But the others... Kang could not account for all of them at every moment of the day. They must be spies, but not for his father.

The conversation in the room continues while Kang puzzles over this new knowledge. None of this makes sense. His father's sudden obsession with the power of the gods, his interest in the relics of days past, and his trust in the chancellor... None of that is aligned with the father Kang knows. The general is notorious for his strategy on the battlefield, the adeptness of his siege warfare, the prowess of his fighting ability. He does not believe in superstition, in magic; he has always been disdainful of it.

Rubbing his eyes, Kang returns his attention back to the strangeness of that room. To look for where the chancellor is hiding, but there is a peculiar resonance to his voice...

And then Kang sees it. What he thought was the warped reflection on the curved surface of the mirror is another face. The chancellor, speaking to the wŭlín-shī through the mirror.

Kang's hand slips off the windowsill, and he sidesteps slightly off-balance. A branch snaps under his heel.

"Someone's there!"

With horror, Kang sees four heads turn toward him in unison. Four pairs of black eyes, filled with darkness. No whites to be seen. Inhuman eyes.

He drops below the window, his heart hammering a frantic beat as he runs along the back garden. He hears them in pursuit, moving quietly and steadily after him. Footsteps eerily in sync on the stones.

He slides his body through the gap and then shuts the door behind him as quietly as possible. Reaching up with fumbling hands, he blows out the torch, leaving him alone in darkness, his breathing too loud and harsh. He hears them scuttling on the roof, moving into the distance, in search of their prey.

Standing in the dark, Kang trembles, all his suspicions confirmed.

Something is terribly wrong in the palace.

Chapter Nineteen

Ning 寧

I wake in the morning, feeling rested and refreshed. Then I notice Shu's bedroll is already gone. A brief surge of panic erupts in my chest, thinking that she is wandering through the forest because of all those terrible things I said to her.

When I burst through the door, I see her sitting on the front steps of the hut. I stand there and look at her slight form, conflicting feelings stirring within me, and I know once again I must set aside my own anger and fear.

I sit down next to her on the steps. She somehow already has a cup of tea and thrusts it into my hands, like she knew I would wake up and come looking for her. She's fifteen years old now, but I still remember her as a child, toddling after me in the back garden. I always took my responsibilities seriously, to make sure she didn't fall into the kiln or prick herself on thorns. She was always so eager to help. She still is.

"We should talk about what happened while you were away," she says.

It seems like I am not the only one who has been thinking about our fight.

"I . . . ," she begins, but stops.

I'm surprised by her hesitation, because I don't feel like she has done anything wrong. All along it's been me yelling at her about putting herself in danger, despite hypocritically heading into danger myself.

"I didn't tell you everything," she finally says.

I look at her, hunched over her teacup, her obvious worry about whatever she is struggling with present all over her expression. Something clenches inside my chest.

"The poison made me weaker and more confused," she tells me. "But I kept ingesting the poison. I had to try to find the antidote as soon as possible, because I knew that with each day, my connection to Shénnóng was growing weaker."

"What do you mean?" I manage to choke out. How is this possible? I saved her from the poison with the right combination of herbs and ingredients, the pearl powder. She should be the same as she was before. Healthy. Whole.

"After you came back, I tried a few times. Again and again. I followed Mother's instructions. I poured the tea, I added the things that should have enhanced my connection to the magic, yuǎnzhì, bānjǐtiān... But nothing worked." She looks to me then, tears streaming down her face. "I couldn't feel anything at all. There is nothing left. No magic."

I set aside my cup of tea and hold her, even though I'm stunned by this revelation. Her tears soak into my shoulder, creating a wet spot. This is everything I've been afraid of. Before I left home in the middle of the night, before each and every round, even in the moment before I would pour the tea, I always hesitated. Afraid that when I reached for the magic, it would deny me. But why would Shénnóng take it away from her?

As we set forth for the day, Shu is unusually quiet, but she tells our companions she just had a poor night of sleep. Meanwhile, I continue to worry over what she told me. Why did the poison affect her connection to Shénnóng? She fears she has been tainted by it, and I am afraid she will be susceptible to the serpent's influence, just as I was. Could this place her at risk of being possessed, trapped in the Shadow Realm like the wǔlín-shī?

"You mentioned travelers in the woods," I ask Captain Tsai, eager to distract myself from the constant loop of questions in my mind, finding myself getting nowhere. "They maintained the shrines. Do you know if they were praying to a specific god?"

"It's not to any god," she says. "It's to the bamboo itself."

"There are tales about the Bamboo Sea." Brother Huang inserts himself into our conversation. "Disturbing stories." He attempts to make a fearsome face at me, but I laugh instead.

He feigns insult, puffing up with indignation. "I used to be trained as a performer! How dare you not appreciate this rare demonstration of my skills?" Beside me, I see Shu trying to hide a smile as well.

"Why do you refer to it sometimes as the Bamboo Sea and other times as the Forgetting Sea?" I ask. "Why does this bamboo forest have different names?"

"Captain Tsai's family is from a village on the edge of the Bamboo Sea," Brother Huang says. "She will know more about the legends."

The captain pauses at the side of the path. She presses her hands together, touches her fingers to her lips, and bows her head. "Please permit me to share your story with these travelers," she says, and a shiver passes down the back of my neck. What sort of entity lives here that warrants such recognition?

"I mentioned people who have been lost in the forest. That is why they call it the Forgetting Sea," the captain says, her tone reverent, acknowledging the power of the forest. "Every once in a while, people familiar with these paths, who have grown up foraging and cutting down the bamboo, will disappear. The families will think they've died somewhere in the forest, fallen into a ravine or taken by a wild beast, but they come out twenty years later, appearing the same age they were when they disappeared. Others tell of being chased by a predator, only for it to be repelled by something in the forest. Like there is a barrier they are unable to cross . . ."

"What do you think it is, then?" Shu asks. "Have you ever seen something in this forest?"

"I've never seen it for myself, but I am careful about where I place my feet. I respect whatever lives in here, and I ask for it to grant me a way in and a way out." Captain Tsai looks at me. "You asked me what sort of god lives here. I think it is a wild sort of magic, something that was never given a name."

I consider this. No wonder I have not felt the White Lady's presence since we entered this place, but it still provided me protection for the night from the dreams that have haunted me. Perhaps at least some part of it is benevolent.

It is then I know I must call on Shénnóng's counsel. I have to reach for my own magic, to see for myself what is preventing Shu from reaching through the Shift. When we stop for lunch, I ask Captain Tsai to light a fire and request some hot water to make tea.

She regards me with suspicion. I'm not sure what she knows of Shénnóng magic, but she does acknowledge the existence of something beyond this world. "Why?"

"I'm going to perform a ritual," I tell her honestly. "There are some personal questions I would like answered."

She looks uneasy at this. "What do you expect us to do?"

"You do not have to participate," I say. "All I ask is for your help in building the fire."

After a moment of hesitation, she nods and directs Brother Huang to gather water for us from a nearby creek while I build the fire with her.

When we are ready, Shu sits cross-legged beside me, facing the fire. She looks unhappy, the corners of her lips and eyes pulled down. I know how proud she was of being a shénnóng-tú, how happy she was when Mother named her as her apprentice. She had already devoted herself to learning about the growing and treatment of tea, to understanding the leaves and the water and the various ingredients. I wish I could give it all to her, and then a sharp thought rises up: *No, you wouldn't give up your own magic. You would be nothing without it. Worthless. Don't lie to yourself.*

I shove that thought back into whatever dark corner of my mind it came from.

Kneeling, I pour the bubbling water into the pot. The water spins in a vortex, and I find my magic following, unwinding itself within. All I want to do is see, and therefore, I've chosen the white chrysanthemum, a common enough brew for its mild sweetness. It does not require tea leaves—even though it is typically a flower for funerals and my mother had a distaste for it, I know its use in strengthening the connection between minds. I pass the cup to Shu, who breathes in the steam with a sigh, then drinks.

The tea burns down my throat, my worry for my sister as hot as the liquid. It is a different, unfamiliar flavor from what I am used to. I reach for Shu's hand, and it meets mine. She looks at me, hopeful, but a little lost. We step through the Shift together, until we are in that other place. Here, our surroundings are awash in silvery twilight, but the color still remains.

I stand alone at the edge of the forest close to our home. I've returned to a memory when we were sent to pick herbs from the garden and I was told to keep an eye on Shu. I'm so focused on picking the right flowers that I don't realize Shu has disappeared until Mother comes out asking me where she is. Spinning around, I remember vividly how the flowers looked as they fell from my hands that day. How loud my heart sounded—it felt as if it would burst out of my chest. How thunderous my footsteps were as I ran, calling her name.

Now, as I stand in the forest, the wind picks up a spiral of leaves and gives me a subtle push from behind. I know the leaves will lead me in the right direction, and I see her only a moment later, sitting at the foot of a tree. I taste the relief on my tongue, as sweet as chrysanthemum.

I approach her. She looks up at me and grows older before my eyes. From the child she was to the girl she is now. I peer inside her eyes and allow myself to fall into them, asking the magic to show me where her own magic should exist. *Like recognizing like.*

I feel myself falling, falling, falling forward into a great, deep hole. Into a cavernous space that is frighteningly empty but should contain the reserves of her magic. I sense a disturbance in this place, as if something has been forcibly pulled up and away, leaving only emptiness behind. A tree uprooted.

I return to my body with a gasp, and the expression on Shu's face shows me that she already knows what I have discovered. That I am afraid of what this may mean for her.

But before I can open my mouth to speak, a sharp pain rips into my arm, as if someone has taken a blade and slashed open my skin. I cry out, grabbing my wrist. Shu is somewhere beside me, but all I sense is the pain. Like something is burrowing itself through my skin, clawing its way out.

They're coming.

"We have to go," I force myself to gasp through the pain.

Shu helps me stand. I sway a little and then get to my feet.

"We have to go!" I yell this time, gesturing to our companions with my good hand.

We quickly gather our things, Captain Tsai and Brother Huang having picked up on my panic. The bamboo sways frantically above us, rocked by a sudden breeze.

"What is it?" the captain asks me, pulling on her pack. Shu just shakes her head.

I step off the path and into the bamboo, placing my hand on its hard surface.

"Who's coming?" I ask it. Perhaps the chrysanthemum tea has opened my mind, because I hear its quiet response.

He sees you.

I look down at my arm. The glow is back, along the jagged scar of the serpent's bite. Every time I use my magic, it draws the serpent to me. I thought it was coincidence, perhaps foolishly. The astronomer said the serpent and I are linked somehow. Now I see for myself it is true. I should have known better, seen it earlier.

"Who are you talking to?" Brother Huang regards me from the path, his voice a little high and nervous.

"I don't have time to explain," I say quickly. "It's the bamboo. I'm going to ask them where we should go."

Captain Tsai nods, accepting this with greater ease than I

expected. "There have always been those who can speak to them. I've taken care of the fire. Let's go."

I appreciate her levelheadedness, that she chooses to believe me. Like I am someone to be trusted. Closing my eyes, I inhale the scent of the forest around me. The bamboo seems to see forever. Each stalk connected to the other, all related, a great family that protects its own. They recognize one another, and they quickly converse, telling one another where the danger originates and where they believe it would be safest to travel.

"Follow me," I say to the rest of my party, and we head down the path. The walk is no longer peaceful, but propelled by urgency. I listen to the bamboo as they tell us to head deeper into the brush. Sometimes we stray off the path, but somehow they know where to lead us through until we return to the path again.

"Look!" Captain Tsai whispers.

Behind us, there are figures in the distance. The bamboo is right. Something is after us, something that wishes us harm. I stop beside one of the green stalks again. "Can you lead us to safety?"

The bamboo shivers around us, and then we hear the tumbling of rocks up ahead. Brother Huang runs forward and then gestures for us to see what the forest has unveiled. A statue of a monkey, its hands clasped over its mouth.

"A guardian!" Captain Tsai breathes, then points ahead. "Look! There's a path!"

It is barely perceptible, but it's there. I step onto it and follow, hoping my mistake did not cost us our mission or our lives.

Chapter Twenty

Ning 寧

We stay quiet, not daring to speak. The bamboo continues their swaying beside us, undulating waves of green. I can feel, walking through them, that the bamboo senses things. They have an awareness, just like Peng-ge, just like the trees near my village. They know who is respectful and who is not.

They lean out of the way, creating a path that leads us to a different part of the forest. Every once in a while, we would feel like we have been walking for hours, that perhaps we are lost, but another monkey statue would appear, its covered mouth a warning. They continue to lead us away from those dark figures until they are no longer behind us.

The air grows misty then, and a chill settles around us. We shiver but continue to walk, blowing on our hands and stomping our feet to keep warm. Strangely, the light doesn't seem to change here. It continues to fall through the canopy, slanted and weird, impossible for us to tell if dusk has fallen. Was the moon supposed to be full tonight?

"Up ahead!" Brother Huang finally breaks the silence, pointing forward to a flash of red through the trees. Red banners, hanging from the bamboo. Past them is a break in the green. We've made it to another part of the forest.

The captain reaches up and touches one of the banners, looking confused. "I don't understand," she says slowly.

"These look quite festive, like a celebration," Shu comments.

"They're meant to be a warning," Captain Tsai replies, pointing to the characters scrawled across the banners. Writing I do not understand.

"Wǔlín?" Brother Huang ponders, puzzled. "But you said it would take us at least six days to cross the Bamboo Sea."

"I did say that," the captain mutters.

When we pass the break in the trees, it is clear there is some sort of structure in the distance. A fortress. With brick walls, looming high.

Captain Tsai turns at the edge of the clearing and bows reverently toward the forest, and we follow her lead.

"The Forgetting Sea has carried us out," she whispers, putting her hands together at her chest in prayer, and bows again. "Thank you."

Captain Tsai warns us to stay behind her as we approach the building. It seems impossible for such a structure to be built among the trees. The gate is high and wide enough for two carriages to enter side by side, but it's shut. One part of Wǔlín is a monastery for the worship of the Black Tiger, but the other part is the academy for military strategy and combat. Looking up, it appears it could be a palace or a prison.

Still disoriented from the sudden appearance of our destination, I regard one of the stone lions that border the path leading to the fortress. I place one hand on its head, just to make sure it is real. To tell myself this is not a vision, that I am not somehow dreaming. The stone is cool to the touch and rough under my fingers.

A shrill whistle sounds from above, and then an arrow quivers in the ground before me. The captain whirls, yelling at us to get back. Brother Huang steps in front of me and Shu, sword in hand.

"Do not come any closer!" A head peers out over the top of the wall. "Wŭlín is closed to visitors."

Captain Tsai steps forward and raises her voice. "We bear a message from Yĕliŭ."

Besides the message Astronomer Wu asked us to pass on, there was also a letter that Duke Liang wrote and gave to Commander Fan. Slowly, the captain slides her dao back into its sheath. She pulls the scroll from her sack and then also raises the letter above her head for the inhabitants of Wŭlín to see. Then she sets both down carefully before the gate and backs away.

After a moment, a small door set into the gate opens. A guard dressed in full armor comes out and bows, his face hidden behind the helmet.

Shu grabs my arm. She trembles a little beside me, and I know she is remembering the soldiers who attacked us on the mountain. I pull her closer, making sure that whatever happens, I can get in front of her.

"Apologies, Captain," the guard calls out in a younger voice than I expected. "We are on lockdown on the instructions of Commander Hao. No one is permitted to enter or leave. We've experienced several attacks recently and must remain vigilant."

Captain Tsai raises her voice and calls back in turn. "We bring sad news from the west: Yĕliŭ has fallen. The missive was written by Duke Liang before his murder at the hands of assailants unknown."

"That is tragic news," the guard says, picking up the scroll and the letter, then bows to the captain again. "The commander will review your messages, and then someone will return with a response."

We stand outside and wait while they convene behind the fortress walls. No voices can be heard. There is no movement for a long while, until finally, the door opens again. This time, three people come out. Two armored guards and a woman who stands in front of them. Dressed in loose black robes, she wears metal cuffs on her wrists of a spiral design. The design continues up her arms in a crisscross of scars. Her dark hair is tied back, with a streak of gray at her temple. She reminds me of the Black Tiger dedicant who fought Kang in the final round of the competition.

"My name is Yu Jingyun." She salutes us with her hands clasped in front of her face. "I am one of the wŭlín-shī of this academy. I have read the messages that you carry. These are troubling times indeed."

"Elder Yu." Captain Tsai bows, and the rest of us do the same. "It is unfortunate we have to meet in such a manner."

"Apologies for our lack of hospitality. We have encountered threats to the safety of our inhabitants, and to protect them, we are not admitting anyone through our gates until we have come to a consensus on how to proceed," Elder Yu states. "However, Commander Hao and the leaders of Wŭlín have sent me to meet with you to discuss the contents of the scroll and letter. Everything they outline has occurred? Yěliŭ has fallen, and the princess has fled the capital?"

Captain Tsai looks in my direction. "My companion was present during both events and can tell you more. Go ahead, Ning."

The wŭlín-shī regards me steadily, waiting for me to continue.

I tell her about the competition and what has transpired since. About the General of Kăiláng marching on the capital with his soldiers, smuggled in by the shifting loyalties of the Governor of Sù. I speak of the chancellor and his role in my near execution. I tell them, too, about the devastation I saw at Yěliŭ and what happened after. The shadow soldiers. The serpent who trapped them in their dreams. With a chill, I suddenly realize how it was similar to Wenyi manipulating that snake in the third round of the competition. *Animation... nothing more*, he reassured the judges.

Except now there is a power with the capability to manipulate a human mind, to the point where it can overcome our instinct for survival.

Elder Yu looks unnerved at the thought. "If what you say is real, then I fear our scouts may have met the same fate. We've had a rash of disappearances in the past few weeks. We have already lost a full battalion."

Fifteen wŭlín-shī, fully trained, can take on a hundred soldiers. How much more damage can a full battalion be capable of? Only my magic gave Zhen and Ruyi the ability to defend themselves against the five who attacked us, and it wasn't until they were overwhelmed by Commander Fan's troops that there was a hope of capturing them.

"Knowing now the truth of our words, will we be able to gain admittance to Wŭlín?" Captain Tsai asks. "Will you lend the princess aid in the battle that is coming?"

Elder Yu exchanges looks with the soldiers next to her before slowly shaking her head. "Although we sympathize with the princess and her cause, we have lost too many already. If we can, indeed, be possessed and used as weapons against the people of Dàxī... that is against the entirety of our tenets, our greatest fear. But recently we have received another missive from the capital, which tells a different story."

She nods at the guard next to her, and he unfurls a scroll. With a start, I see myself staring back. They've captured my likeness in ink. I appear like a rabbit, ready to take flight. Beside my portrait is a red seal: *Wanted.*

"The girl you have brought as witness has been accused of poisoning the court officials, of being a danger to Dàxī. The shénnóng-shī of the realm have been called in to court. Hánxiá is closed, pending further investigation. We do not know whether the General of Kǎiláng can be fully trusted, either, and that is why we have turned away representatives of the court as well. We will wait to see who reveals themselves to be protectors of the citizens of Dàxī and who are merely hungry for power."

"Those are lies!" I burst out, unable to contain myself any longer. "I told you, the competition was rigged from the start. They wanted a way to gather all the shénnóng-shī into the palace—to poison the court and to accuse the princess of being a murderer. This is all a scheme created at the hands of Chancellor Zhou and the General of Kǎiláng!"

"So far all we have are accusations," Elder Yu says to me. "We do not know what is truth and what is lies. We will provide you with supplies for the evening, but you will leave the grounds tomorrow. Wǔlín will take your information into consideration, and we will proceed when we've made a decision."

I turn and walk away then, even though it is rude of me. The words about to come out of my mouth will certainly not be polite anyway. I sit down on a rock on the side of the path and contemplate what I have waiting for me.

Murderer. Thief. Fraud. Failure. All these names and descriptors I have been given. I'm hunted by the shadow soldiers and by the Ministry of Justice. If a bounty notice with my face on it is to be found everywhere the ministry has reach, then Shu will continue to be in danger wherever I go.

When I look up from my brooding, the captain, Brother Huang, and Shu stand beside me again. The people from Wǔlín are gone.

Captain Tsai regards me, meeting my eyes directly. "I know this may not be much comfort to you, but you have shown me things beyond my understanding. A full week has passed in real time, but as all of us know, we have not walked for so long. I believe you, Ning, everything that you have said about what happened in the palace and at Yěliǔ."

"Thank you," I tell her, appreciative of her support. If I can convince one person, then perhaps I will have a chance to convince others as well.

"What will you do now?" she asks.

Where else am I able to go, but onward to Yún?

"I have another task given to me by Astronomer Wu," I inform them. "I have to travel to a gorge near here, where a famed shénnóngshī is rumored to live."

Brother Huang looks at me, puzzled. "There is only one gorge in Yún, and that is the Bǎiniǎo Gorge, by the town of Ràohé."

Ràohé. My ears perk up at that familiar name. That is where Wenyi's family is from. For a moment, it seems as if the stars are aligning, that perhaps this is the direction the fates intended for me to follow. I have not forgotten my promise to Wenyi, and heading toward the gorge will bring me closer to his family.

"I will take you there," Brother Huang offers. "I know the place. I can be your guide."

"You heard what the elder said," I tell him. "I am wanted by the ministry. I'm a poisoner, remember? I've murdered ten officials. Are you sure you want to consort with such a monster?"

But instead of the reaction I expected, Brother Huang only laughs. "I promised that I would follow through on my mission before I return home, and part of that mission is to keep you and your sister safe. You will not keep my Xin'er waiting for too long, will you?"

"Then it's decided," Captain Tsai says, without allowing me a word of protest. "Brother Huang will assist you with getting to Ràohé. I have another mission I have to complete for the commander in a village close to here."

Wŭlín provides us with the supplies they promised, including thicker blankets for the evening and some hot soup with bamboo shoots and slivers of meat to warm us. Under the long shadow of the fortress, I have another night free of nightmares. No shadows leering from a distance, no watchful serpent whistling in the dark.

I dream instead of a boy who sits with me on the rooftops, overlooking the lights of the city. I wake up in the morning with his name still on my lips. Wondering if he ever found the answers he was looking for.

Chapter Twenty-One

Kang 康

"The regent requires your presence in his study."

The request comes from one of the palace guards as Kang is attended to by his servants. The robe settles over his shoulders, and this morning Kang feels like he is donning armor in preparation for a battle. A fight he is not adequately prepared for.

How will he tell his father the absurdity of what he witnessed last night, if his father will even believe him? A voice coming from the wrong reflection.

After passing through the maze of corridors in the inner palace that connects his quarters to the emperor's, Kang stands before a set of open doors. The study is a library in itself—a variety of treasures on display on the shelves, scrolls and books along another wall. All maintained by yet another retinue of servants whose sole task is to keep this room tidy for the emperor. But on the far wall, he sees a painting hanging in the corner, and in front of it is a carved tablet of rich ebony and an incense holder resting on a small table. Etched on the tablet is the name of his mother, and she smiles down at him serenely from her portrait.

Kang quickly calculates the time in his mind. Is it close to the anniversary of her death? Has he missed it already? He can't help but be drawn into the room, regarding her face with a familiar ache in his body. He misses her like nothing else.

"She was taken from us too soon," a voice says behind him.

Kang whirls around to see his father. The general stands with his hands clasped behind his back, looking up at the portrait of his wife. Using one of the braziers, he lights a few sticks of incense and passes one to his son. With the smoke curling above the bright spot of each stick, they bow in unison, in remembrance, in shared love. Kang places the incense in the stand before the plaque, hoping that their message will find her. That some part of her will know she has not been forgotten.

"You brought her here," Kang says quietly. He always thought her plaque would remain at Lǜzhou, in their house by the sea. His mother never expressed a desire to visit the palace; she wasn't much for the city. She liked the peninsula and shared with him her love for that place until he, too, saw it as his home, eventually.

"I could never leave her behind," the general replies, still gazing up at the portrait. "Just as she made me promise to always keep you safe."

Kang stays silent. If his mother were here, things would certainly be different, but long ago his uncle decided their mere existence was a threat. The sharp reminder of her murder is like a knife slipping into his side.

Now Kang sleeps in the former residence of the princess. Even with her furnishings replaced, her decorations removed, it still does not feel like his. None of this does. He rid himself of that entitlement a long time ago. He touches that place on his chest where he can almost feel the edges of the brand through his clothes.

No. They *burned* it out of him.

He walks away from the watchful eyes of his mother. She would not have approved of this. She would not have permitted the general to send Kang into the palace as a spy and, as he now knows, a distraction. She would not have allowed him to desecrate Yěliŭ, would have advised him to pursue other options. Where once his mother might have guided his father, Kang recognizes the chancellor now seeks to bind himself with the general, to ensure that their ascensions are tied as intimately as possible.

Kang looks over the treasures on the shelves, to distract himself from his chaotic thoughts. His father prefers bronze sculptures, galloping horses and ceremonial vessels, stained and pitted with age. A bow hangs on the wall above, along with a collection of arrows, each holding a particular memory. Of a battle, a hunt, a competition.

It is the white sword, however, that catches Kang's eye. The cursed sword that accompanied the warlord, who caused so much death and destruction. Yet, depending on how the story is told, he was either a rebel who fought senselessly or the heroic protector of his clan who defended them until his last breath. Kang wonders how historians will describe this time period. How *he* will be remembered in the records of history.

The carved hilt beckons to him. The blade is hidden in a new sheath, leather decorated with two bands of mother-of-pearl. How sharp is that edge? He's struck with an urge to grab it, pull it free, test it for himself . . .

"Take it," his father commands him.

Kang's hand snaps to the side, away from the sword. Even as a prince, he is not permitted a weapon in the inner palace. This is not a military camp in the countryside. This is not the battlefield, and yet his heart races as if it were.

The general gives him a knowing smile. "You held it once. If you are curious about the way it is wielded, now is your chance."

Kang turns back to the sword again, at the insistent pull he can still feel. From a young age, he'd been taught to assess each weapon available to him in every room he steps into. To prepare himself. He reaches for the blade and lifts it from the stand. Examines it sheathed, first. It's small. A secondary weapon, meant for stabbing someone if they get too close in hand-to-hand combat. He pulls it free and places the scabbard on the shelf.

His father steps back, giving him room. Sweeping his right arm and leg back, he tosses the sword into the air, grabs the hilt, and pulls it back, resting against his forearm. He then steps forward, spinning the sword in his hand, feeling it glide and shift against his palm.

It brings up memories.

Being pushed to the dirt and taunted by the older soldiers of his battalion.

Falling from a tree as a scout, breaking his arm in two places.

Thinking someone was a friend, only to overhear them talking about him as a tool to gain favor with the general.

The blade whirls, faster and faster, as he slices at an unseen threat. It moves in his hand, almost as if it is guiding him, encouraging him to use it on his enemies. It thirsts . . . he thirsts . . . for blood, for vengeance.

To cut down everyone who has ever wronged him.

His head spinning, he snatches the scabbard from the shelf and slides the sword back into its place. Beads of sweat gather at his brow.

Kang bows and offers the sword back to his father.

"Your thoughts?" The general plucks it out of his hands, weighing it in his palm.

"It's a finely made weapon for such a peculiar choice of material. Well taken care of," Kang says. He wipes his hand surreptitiously on his robe. He feels the remnant of an odd substance on the surface. *Something is terribly wrong in the palace.*

"You must be wondering why I brought you here." His father sets the sword back on its stand and regards him again. "I need you to complete a mission for me."

"A mission?" Kang perks up a little at the thought. To finally have a break from all the routines and structures of the palace, and yet . . . all his unanswered questions still hover around him.

"I've heard rumors of a treasure that has resurfaced in the northern region," his father continues. "There is a gorge in the mountains of Yún. Something of great value that was stolen from the First Emperor and then hidden."

More relics? There must be a purpose to all this. A master plan that Kang does not understand. The officials continue to come and talk with him about nothing of consequence, and he knows they are just as much in the dark about his father's plans as he is.

"You must be wondering why I have been in pursuit of all these items," his father says, reading Kang's expression easily.

"I know you must have a purpose for it."

Please, he begs him silently. *Tell me why. Give me a reason for all this so I do not have to fear how far you will go.*

"The academies and the monasteries have taken too much power from the throne," the general says, his fist clenching. "My brother ruined Dàxī with his benevolence. I will be seen as a vessel of the gods, their united strength."

So that's it then. The end goal of his father's ascendance to power. The First Emperor had always believed his rule to be given to him by the gods, and although the previous emperors had moved away from that belief, it seems that his father aims to return to it in his upcoming reign.

"I am not a man who believes in superstition, and yet I am aware of the strength of belief." The general picks up a disc on the shelf, and Kang recognizes it as the relic from Hánxiá. The one his father dismissed before the court, yet it made its way now to his personal study. "They will know me as the Divine Emperor once I control the three relics of Hánxiá, Yěliŭ, and Wŭlín, along with the three emblems of the First Emperor."

The sword. The seal. The throne.

"When I ascend, I will wield the cursed sword that has ruined men before me, and I will sit upon the throne with the sky-reaching miǎn guān upon my head."

The general picks up a seal from the shelf and holds it out for Kang to see. It is made of a wood so dark it almost looks black, like it could swallow the light that shines on it. Attached to the base is the carved head of a dragon, its elongated, curved mouth open in a ferocious roar. The sword is the representation of the emperor's military might, while the seal holds the official stamp that marks every proclamation that emerges from the palace.

"The First Emperor once had a crystal orb the size of a fist, so luminous it was said to glow in the night. It was looted from the palace many years ago, but it has since resurfaced in Yún province. They called it the Night-Illuminating Pearl, and it will rest upon my seal as another symbol of power."

The opened mouth of the dragon waits for that orb.

"They say it once belonged to the Jade Dragon himself," the

general says softly, gazing down at the seal. There is a hunger on his face, a fervent expression. "And soon . . . it will belong to me."

Kang is torn with the desire to go, but the danger of leaving his father in the grasp of the chancellor is too great; the general's next words resolve his conflict.

"You will assist the chancellor with the help of the gods, accompanied by Wǔlín and Hánxiá." His father blinks then, shaking his head. "I've forgotten. I suppose those academies are no longer."

This makes it easier for Kang to accept the mission. He can use this to keep an eye on the chancellor, to figure out his plans for his father.

The seal is returned to its place on the shelf, and Kang's father pulls out another item from his robe—a stone carving the size of his palm. Black tassels trail from the ends.

Kang inhales sharply when he sees it, recognizing it for what it is. The characters shine from within, set on a backing of pearl. The commander's talisman. The Blackwater Battalion will answer only to the one who holds this in their grasp. In his mind, it represents his father, his leadership, everything he has aspired to.

"My son, you will take over my role as leader of the Blackwater Battalion, as my trusted adviser and my personal representative," his father says, as emotional as Kang has ever seen him. A swell of feeling threatens to overwhelm Kang, to pull him under.

All his efforts for his father's recognition. The burning in his muscles after every drill, the relentless pursuit for perfection, the way he climbed up each and every rung of the ladder just so his father sees it.

Kang bows his head, holding out his hands reverently. His body fills with burning pride. He feels as if his chest may explode with the intensity of it.

"Thank you, Father," he manages to choke out. "I will not disappoint you."

Chapter Twenty-Two

Kang 康

Kang is given only two days to prepare to leave the palace. He knows he must reach out to the person who warned him about the chancellor. He needs to know whom he should look for, what sort of danger he should be prepared for on the road. But without a name or a face, there is only one person he can connect with, in the hopes that he could pass on the message for him. He does not want to show his face in the kitchens again, for fear that he may put others at risk. Instead, he sends a message to the Bakery Department expressing his intentions to hold a gathering in the gardens, and requests those particular pastries with the red dot on top, along with an assortment of other delicacies.

That evening, the pavilion in the Garden of Fragrant Reflection is lit up with lanterns. Their golden light casts a warm glow over the waters of the pond. A musician plays the zither, the mournful sound of the plucked strings weaving through the quiet conversations of the attendees.

"You have finally become more receptive to understanding the court," the chancellor says to him with a smile, complimenting him in front of the general.

Kang swallows his distaste, bowing to him and to his father

in turn. "I hope to receive more of your counsel on the road to Ràohé," he says, the words bitter on his tongue.

"See to it that you do." His father claps him on the back, in good spirits, and leaves him to entertain his other guests.

Kang moves through the gardens, hoping his discomfort is not too evident as he mingles. Much of the court is in attendance, not many daring to refuse an invitation from the son of the soon-to-be emperor. They wish him well for his trek tomorrow, some daring to probe further into the purpose of the foray to the north, but Kang repeats the same message as instructed: He is on an errand for the emperor-regent, and his findings will be presented before the court when he returns.

As the evening continues, Kang steps away from the conversations to clear his head. He pauses under a willow tree, its weeping branches reminding him of the day in the gardens of Língyǎ Monastery. The thrill of running away from the pursuing monks. The last time she looked up at him, trusting and open, before it all ended in betrayals and accusations.

"Your Highness," a voice says softly beside him.

Kang turns to see a man bow to him, and he nods in turn. The man seems familiar, wearing a pendant that indicates he is from the Ministry of Rites.

"I do not believe we have met," Kang says.

"I belong to the Department of the Palace," the man replies. "My family name is Qiu."

"Official Qiu," he says, and then he glances down at the pastry the official is holding.

One with a red dot.

It may be a sign, or it may be nothing. His pulse speeds up

slightly, and he struggles to keep his voice calm and unaffected. "I hope you are enjoying the treats. The filling of that particular pastry can be quite surprising to some."

The official nods. "I've heard it was the favorite of the . . . former princess."

Kang glances at him in surprise. So Official Qiu is here for Zhen. To appeal for her? To see where his sympathies lie? He glances around him, aware that there are too many eyes and ears in the palace.

"You are here on her behalf?" Kang steps closer, keeping his voice low.

"You've followed the clues I've left and pursued the information yourself," the older man tells him. "It confirmed for me that you are as she said."

"As she said?" He mentioned to Ning, not long ago, that officials had long memories. But to come to him so close to the time of ascension . . . perhaps the princess is more secure in her alliances than he originally thought.

"She spoke of you with respect," Official Qiu says. "You had convinced her with your conversations that you do care for the people. She cares for them as well, and she does not want to see them suffer."

"I believe my father will do what is best for the people of Dàxī," Kang says warily.

"Of that I have no doubt. I have heard how the general treats his people. But I am concerned that in his rise to power, he may have fallen under the influence of malevolent forces." His voice drops to a whisper as a few officials walk past them. "I hope you have seen it for yourself."

The chancellor. The face in the mirror.

"I have seen it, his . . . influence on the wǔlín-shī," Kang says. "But do you have evidence? Something I can bring to the court?"

Official Qiu shakes his head. "Only speculation. We have been investigating the chancellor since he turned on the princess. But his power only grows with each passing week, and the situation grows more dire with every one of his ploys. First, the poison tea, which we cannot prove definitively is due to his influence. Next, the bandits along the borders, paid with imperial silvers to cause unrest. Now the pillars crippled and their sacred relics unearthed. The astronomers have seen terrible signs of a great darkness approaching. We suspect he may have intentions other than placing a new emperor on the throne."

"And what do you want me to do?" His position in the court is tenuous at best. What does he have to offer besides being his father's adopted son?

"He may let his guard down while he is on the road, away from the comforts of the palace and the protections of his personal guard. You may be able to determine his end goal, or some sign of weakness, how he is influencing the wǔlín-shī. Anything that can help us."

"Us?"

"You and the princess both have allies in the court, do not forget that. Your interests may align closer than you believe." Official Qiu's eyes slide past Kang's shoulder, and then he drops into a deep bow as another official approaches. "All the best to you, Highness. I hope you find what you are looking for."

The rain in Ràohé is not like the drizzling, warm showers that Kang experienced on the coast. The rainy season involves downpours, until everything is soaked through.

Frustratingly, his ability to investigate what the chancellor has been up to in this journey has been hampered from the start. Even though he requested that he accompany the chancellor in his carriage for safety along the roads, Chancellor Zhou dismissed him, saying the wǔlín-shī are more than enough protection. Kang was told there are several more stops the chancellor must complete along the way, which means they will travel separately, and the chancellor will take longer than expected to get to Ràohé, where the Blackwater Battalion is stationed.

So, instead, Kang travels to Ràohé as fast as he can on horseback, determined to give himself as much time as possible in the camp before the chancellor's arrival. Some way of digging into the purpose behind this mission and finding the cracks that may lead him to what he is fishing for. He does not know whether to be comforted or disturbed by the thought of Official Qiu's revelations that potential allies are watching him, waiting to see what he will do.

At the camp, Kang is greeted by two captains, who welcome him as the new commander. As he settles into his new quarters, he is surprised by a visit from a grinning Ren, a soldier who took him under his wing when Kang was coming up in the Tiānguān Battalion. He's accompanied by another familiar face: Badu, whom Kang grew up alongside, both of them half-raised by the soldiers of Kǎiláng.

Even though he is tired and sore and chilled by the damp, Kang sees other familiar faces around the campfires and makeshift stables, and something inside him feels like he has returned home.

The next day he is shown around the camp and briefed on the

state of the battalion. Everything appears to be in order. Their supply stores are adequate, the armory well maintained.

But it is in the infirmary that Kang pauses, looking down at the occupants of one corner of the tent.

These people do not seem to be soldiers; he can tell from their smooth skin and delicate hands. They have not been weathered by travel or battle. One has his right leg set in a cast. Another is restrained, his face contorted as if in pain, mumbling nonsense to himself. The third lies still, eyes open and staring up at nothing.

With shock, Kang recognizes the second man. It is Shao, the winner of the competition. Once, confident in his magic. Then, hesitant and quiet before the court. Now, lost somewhere inside his mind.

"What happened to them?" he asks.

A medic approaches with a bow. "Commander. These are shénnóng-shī and shénnóng-tú sent by the chancellor to find the seer who resides in Bǎiniǎo Gorge. We accompanied them as they attempted to use their magic, but the few who returned came back like . . . this."

So this is where the practitioners of Shénnóng went after they were rounded up by the palace guards. No doubt some wanted to prove themselves after Hánxiá appeared divided, when one of their elders openly challenged the emperor-regent.

"What is this place you speak of? Bǎiniǎo Gorge?" Kang asks, feigning ignorance. His father had informed him only a select few are aware of the value of the treasure they are seeking. The battalion only knows they are looking for a particular person in the area who is protected by magical influence.

"Bǎiniǎo Gorge is the length of a hundred lǐ, Commander," a soldier responds. "The town of Ràohé overlooks the gorge, which carries a branch of the Clearwater River, the Fúróng, between the cliffs of Resounding Thunder on the Ràohé side and Silent Lightning on the other.

"Locals speak of a hermit who lives there, but we have been unsuccessful in our attempts to contact them," the soldier continues. "They have been rather . . . guarded to our presence."

Kang looks down at the woman who stares up, unseeing. He waves his hand over her face. Nothing, not even a twitch to indicate she is aware of anything happening around her. It reminds him, disturbingly, of his teacher's face. The lack of expression.

"When I went to the local apothecary to gather medicines for her treatment, one of the townsfolk said to me: 'Sometimes the gorge swallows people whole. Sometimes the gorge spits people out,'" the medic shudders at the memory. The soldiers glance at one another, uneasy.

"We will go to Ràohé," Kang decides. "I would like to see the gorge for myself."

Chapter Twenty-Three

Ning 寧

In the morning we leave the fortress behind. As we set off toward the forest, we pass more red banners that indicate to travelers they are approaching Wŭlín. Shu reaches up and touches one, then shivers slightly.

"Do you see it?" she asks.

"See what?" A soft rain has started to fall around us, the curve of the road leading into the trees.

"Something protects Wŭlín, I think," she says. "A boundary."

I look over at Brother Huang, who shakes his head as well.

Perhaps some part of the magic still remains with Shu, something unaffected by the poison. Maybe the shénnóng-shī that Astronomer Wu sent us to find will have answers. Maybe they can tell us how to return Shu's magic to her. A renewed purpose. My steps grow lighter.

"We'll see what we encounter on the other side," I say.

She nods with determination. "I'm ready."

I take her hand, and we cross over that boundary together. Toward whatever awaits us next.

With Brother Huang's knowledge of this area and our map, we determine it will be two or three days to reach the two potential ways to Ràohé, depending on how kind the summer storms have been to the roads. One path is on the edge of the gorge, prone to mudslides. The other is a more traveled road to the town, winding through a forest. Brother Huang regards the sky, not liking its appearance. There is a scent on the wind, and the temperature is dropping. At least we have the cloaks and the walking staffs gifted to us by Wǔlín.

"If we can outpace the storm, we may have a chance on the path along the gorge. But if this rain keeps up, we'll have to use the road," he cautions us.

The stones that line the path are slippery but manageable. Brother Huang's mood does not seem diminished at the long trek ahead. He even sings a duet with Shu during a brief reprieve from the rain. A folk song about a broken bridge that separates a boy and a girl from two different villages.

"Will you still remember me the next season?" Brother Huang asks.

"Will you come back and sing me your song?" Shu responds.

With their voices joined in the chorus, I think about Kang again. Everything is tangled up. The boy who flew in from the sky and then hid his intentions from me. The boy who raced with me through the marketplace, who I led through a sea of flowers. Then there is the knowledge of what happened to Wenyi's family, the atrocities committed in Ràohé. The chancellor who scoffed at my questions, who asked me how I could still believe in Kang's innocence when he was raised in Lǜzhou's camps. I cannot seem to reconcile all these variations of Kang in my mind.

"When you told me, time is fleeting, as we drank our share of autumn wine . . ." Brother Huang's voice carries through the trees, and then Shu's voice joins him for the final line: "I know, just like that summer, you'll never come back to me . . ."

I want to believe Kang is different, despite all the terrible things I've been told. I know the legacy of his father, and I know what the emperor did to him and his family. How he fought his own battle against his family's history, just like how hard I've strained against my parents' expectations.

By the time we reach a small temple, the rain is coming down again in earnest. We decide to seek shelter here for the night—at least it will offer a roof over our heads. We tidy up the space with a makeshift broom built of branches and straw, sweeping out the leaves that have been blown in throughout the season. There is some dry wood that a previous traveler had collected, and we build a small fire while the storm rages outside.

Over our dinner, Shu entertains us with a story. About a woman who found a tiger dying in the woods, choking on a bone. Instead of leaving it to die, she pulled the bone from its mouth and nursed it back to health. Months later, the woman met a ferocious-looking man in the woods. He had large golden eyes that reminded her of cymbals, and dark black whiskers. He told her she saved his life once and brought her up to his house in the mountains. He revealed himself as the Thunder God, the Black Tiger, and she became the Lightning Goddess.

This high in the mountains, the summers are not as warm as they would be lower in the valley. I wish we still had the warm blankets Wǔlín had shared with us, but they were too heavy to be taken on the road. Instead, I brew a cup of tea for my companions and sprinkle some herbs in with the leaves. Ginger, cinnamon, clove, and the strongest, most-aged tea I have in the form of a small brick

I brought from Yěliŭ's kitchens. I wish I could reach for my magic, to give us more energy and warmth. But I know it will just draw the serpent closer to us, and I cannot risk it.

Sipping at the tea, Brother Huang tells us the story of the Thunder God from his own village, up north, beyond the gorge. There, the Black Tiger is the god of travelers, and it is said he often wears a cloak with a hood to hide the stripes on his face. He bestows wisdom to travelers who provide him a seat beside their fires, and he would appear on a night much like tonight.

Just like I learned about the variations on regional cuisines in the imperial kitchens, I marvel at the versions of stories we also tell. How a facet of one god is common in one province, while another side of the god is revered in the other.

We fall asleep to the sound of the rain hitting the roof tiles and dripping from the rafters, almost like a song of its own.

I wake with a start in the dark. I hear Shu's deep breathing. Something has woken me. Branches tapping the side of the building? Or something else—

Movement, on the other side of the room. I turn my head. Brother Huang was supposed to keep watch, but I see he has drifted off, lying with his back to the wall, his chin almost to his chest.

I sit up slowly, my teeth chattering against one another. It's cold and dark, the chill having settled in as night deepened. There is a faint glow in the embers that still remain in the brazier. The light is just enough to illuminate the small space, throwing shadows against the wall. I hear a rustling sound and then . . . an unearthly whistle.

It must be a dream. I must be dreaming again. I feel the thud of my pulse against my throat, beating rapidly.

The whispers are back, building on one another. The shadows writhe in the corners and begin to take form, like a nest of snakes. Slowly, it grows on the wall, until it unwinds and the silhouette of a serpent appears. Its tongue darts out, tasting the air. We are so far away from the bamboo forest, from Wŭlín's protective boundaries. We are exposed here.

"*Found . . . sss . . . you . . . ,*" the serpent hisses.

My arm throbs. I thrust it closer to the paltry light of the embers, and my skin ripples and moves around my scars, something buried under the surface, squirming. Nausea rises in my throat.

I'm dreaming. I have to be dreaming.

I plead to the goddess to hear me. I beg her to pull me out of this nightmare.

I turn to shake Shu, to wake her, but her head lolls to one side. Putting my hands to the sides of her face, I realize her skin is cold. Her eyes look up, empty. The eyes of a dead girl.

I cry out and kick myself away, press my back against the wall. The serpent grows out of the wall, taking physical form as he rises over me.

"*I'll have you . . . your delightful, sweet magic . . . ,*" he sneers.

There's a sudden flash of light.

"Get back!" I hear Shu's voice cry out.

I see her. The outline of her body silhouetted by the light emitting from a torch in her hands. Above her head, I swear I could see the curve of white wings.

With a gasp, I break free of the bonds of the nightmare. A dream within a dream. The sound of those awful whispers . . .

Shu kneels on the floor before me. The two of us stare at each other. Wordlessly, she opens her hand, and resting in her blistered palm is a single white feather.

I help her clean and bandage her hand. Sleep is difficult to reach after what happened, so instead, we stay up talking about what she remembers. Shu tells me she woke up in the middle of the night. The fire had gone out, and the room was unbearably cold. She got the fire going again when she heard me cry out. She tried to shake me awake, but I was caught in the depths of my nightmare. The fire suddenly flared up beside us, a wall of flame, and she heard a woman's voice call out: "Reach into the fire, and save her."

She listened, and the fire leaped into her hand. She caught a glimpse of the serpent, recoiling from the light, and then the fire fell back to normal again. I was awake moments after that.

"Was this the same serpent that chased you through your dreams?" I ask.

"I . . . I'm not sure," she says, hesitant. "This serpent looks different. He was covered with scales. He seemed more . . . real somehow."

We don't speak of it to Brother Huang when he wakes up. We don't know if he will believe us. If he will think, like Astronomer Wu, that we are susceptible to evil influence. Or perhaps he will think we were merely dreaming.

The rain continued overnight, and the ground is soggy. Some water has begun to pool in low areas, and the force of the wind makes it a challenge for us to continue.

"The Tiger God is raging," Brother Huang mutters. "We may have to continue along the main road to Ràohé instead."

When we reach the fork in the path, we realize he's right. The upward path leading to the rise that overlooks the gorge is washed out. With torrents of mud streaming under our feet, walking up the steep path will be impossible. We have to continue the other way, but I do not like that it will put us at risk of encountering travelers who may recognize my face and want to capture me for the reward. At least with the rain, there is less chance of meeting others on the road. They are likely to stay inside their warm homes, where it is safe. Where we should be, instead of out here with our boots slipping in the mud. I feel myself winding tighter and tighter, like thread around a spool.

The next night passes with us huddled together, miserable in a cave. Everything is damp. I am too tired to dream.

As the drudgery of walking continues, our ascent reaches a flat portion of road, which is a relief to my aching limbs. In the late afternoon, we reach a bridge over a river, the water already spilling up over the wood. Carefully holding on to the railing, the three of us make our way over the planks. The rain is coming down so hard it feels as if we are being pummeled by tiny fists.

"Is it possible to go back where we came from? Wait out the rain?" I shout at Brother Huang over the din, but he shakes his head.

"I don't think it's a good idea," he shouts back. "It looks like the bridge is at risk of being washed out soon, and then we'll be trapped. We won't be able to make it to the main road until the water recedes again, and we'll be stuck on the mountainside without food."

We continue ahead, struggling against the wind. With the heavy rain and the poor visibility, we do not see the soldiers until we are almost upon them.

"Blackwater Battalion!" Brother Huang shouts over the noise of the rain, recognizing them. "Run!"

"Halt!" they call out as we turn to flee. My boot almost comes free as I struggle to run, tripping me to the ground. Brother Huang pulls me free from the mud. The three of us link arms and try to pull one another along, but the wind shifts. The rain blows down toward us now, cutting into our faces even under the hoods of our cloaks.

We see the river up ahead, but in the time it took us to struggle up the hillside and back down, the river has swelled, swallowing the bridge completely.

There's a yelp behind us, and I turn to see Shu struggling in the arms of a soldier. A hand clamps down on my shoulder.

We're caught.

Chapter Twenty-Four

Ning 寧

One of the soldiers brings coils of rope and binds our wrists. Then they lead us away, marching us back up the hill. They pull the hood off my head and peer at my face. I'm covered with mud, so I hope they do not recognize me as the wanted shénnóng-tú on the posters.

"If you get a chance," I whisper to Brother Huang as they examine our packs for illicit goods, "take Shu and run."

"Absolutely not," Brother Huang hisses back. "I will never give up those under my protection. It's against the code."

The camp we are taken to is a collection of tents. It seems they have been in the rain for a few days, the area a trampled mud pit. I inwardly curse our bad luck. These are not bandits who could be bargained with, who may have wavering loyalties. These are the monsters that Wenyi's family accused of poisoning or murdering those who opposed them.

We're led through the mud to the biggest tent in the center of the encampment. Inside the tent, it feels like we've stepped into a different world. There are braziers set around the room, warming the space within, which is larger than the entirety of my home in Xīnyì. As if someone had picked up a house and dropped it within this place. Under our feet is a platform made of wood, raised against the ground so that we do not have to walk in the mud. Copper censers hang from chains above our heads, wafting out the luxurious scent of tánxiāng, an expensive fragrance.

Several soldiers stand around a large wooden table at the center of the tent. I don't know how they would have traveled with such a huge piece of furniture. There are also a few people dressed in robes, who appear more like scholars, rather than seasoned warriors ready for battle. Strategists, perhaps? Regardless, they are arguing passionately about whatever is laid on the table before them.

"Captain!" one of the soldiers beside us calls out. "You'll want to see these prisoners."

The captain turns and strides toward us, scowling. "Why did you bring me a bunch of farmers? What use are they to the battalion?"

"See for yourself!" I'm shoved forward, and the soldier crows next to my ear, "This is Zhang Ning! The wanted girl! The disgraced shénnóng-tú." A scroll in one hand, my portrait unfurled for all to see; with his other hand, he yanks my head back, forcing me to look up. The commotion has drawn the attention of everyone in the tent.

"Stop!" Shu screams behind me. There is the sound of a struggle behind me, and I try to fight, but the man twists his hand in my hair, pulls until it is fire along my scalp.

A voice cuts through the noise. "Let her go."

"Commander?" the soldier beside me asks.

"I said, *let her go*." I stand still as the hand falls away from my hair and the soldier steps back. I straighten, turning my head, everything moving as if in slow motion. As if I am caught in one of my nightmares.

Kang stands there, his hair pulled back from his face. There are wings on the shoulders of his armor, and the head of a silver dragon snarls from his chest plate, indicating his rank in this battalion. *Commander*, the soldier had called him.

I want to look away from him, but I cannot. Those days I spent with him at the palace crash down around me. The last time I saw him, I left him in the chaotic space of the Hall of Eternal Light. Him, trying to follow, calling out my name. When I left all that finery behind. When I thought my sister was lost to me, and all my hopes were crushed beneath my feet. I crossed the empire and then traversed it again, but I did not, in all my wild imaginings, ever think I would meet him here in the wilderness.

But he does not speak to me. Instead, he turns and reprimands the soldier who grabbed me. "Did you think terrorizing young women would endear us to the people?" he growls.

The soldier looks taken aback and protests, "She is dangerous. She is an enemy of the realm!"

"And he is your commander!" the captain snarls. "Do you forget yourself?"

The soldier drops to one knee, sword to his forehead. "My apologies, Captain. Commander."

"Who are these people with you?" Kang's next question is directed at me. I force myself to look into his eyes. Should I lie? But I think he will know if I do not tell the truth.

"My sister and a guide," I tell him. Not the full truth, but partially.

His eyes widen in surprise, and I realize he remembers our conversation in Língyă, when I told him I would do anything to save my sister.

"Where are you going?" he asks, regaining his composure.

I can't tell him about our mission, certainly not surrounded by so many of the general's most loyal soldiers. So many of my enemies. He must sense my hesitation, because he gestures. "Leave us."

"But, sir!" someone protests.

Ignoring the others, Kang addresses the still-kneeling man beside me. "Have you checked them for weapons?"

"We found nothing of note," the soldier says. "There was a weapon we removed from the man, that is all."

"Take the man and the girl to the prisoners' tent," Kang commands. "I'd like to speak to the shénnóng-tú alone."

The captain steps forward again. "Is this wise, Commander? This is a wanted prisoner. Guilty of murder."

"I will take full responsibility," Kang says with authority.

I have never seen him like this before. Confident. Giving orders. A leader.

And then he adds wryly, a little more like the young man I know, "If she manages to murder me in the middle of a camp of sixty of my father's best soldiers, I think I am the only one to blame."

I look over at Shu, and she back at me. I don't want her to be separated from me, but I don't see any other choice. I give her a small nod.

"I would advise that you keep her hands bound," the captain says, before leaving through the lifted flap, and we are left alone.

The tent is suddenly both too large and too small to contain us, and I don't know where to look. I feel the mud caking the side of my face, the rain dripping down my body and pooling at my feet.

"I never thought I'd see you again," he says, sounding breathless. He immediately reaches for me, and I take a step back, but he gestures at my hands.

Oh.

I allow myself to look at him while he loosens the knots around my wrists, letting the rope fall to the ground. I drink him in, the familiar planes of his face, the set of his shoulders. Before, I asked him time and time again. Who is he? Who is he really?

The noble son. The soldier. The earnest boy who pulled me from the water, who stroked my hair and talked about his family. The warrior who stands before me, who speaks with authority, who commands an infamous battalion.

"We seem to say that to each other a lot," I tell him as a barrage of emotions fight inside me. Anger, regret, shock—and yet . . . I want to touch him, to see if he feels the same as I remember. The connection between us still pulses, trying to pull me back in.

"I see you saved your sister," he says, as if we are meeting somewhere else. Catching up over tea, a casual reunion. I cannot stand this softness. "You figured out the antidote."

In his opulent residence in the palace, I threw our intimate conversations back in his face. I told him our shared connection was all pretense, lies, and more. My face burns hot. I try to grab for that anger, hold it inside me, but it slips out of my grasp as easily as water.

"All I ask is that you let her go," I say. It's not in my nature to bend. I do not want to beg, but I must, if it means saving my sister.

Kang shakes his head. "I don't know what you believe of me, but I'm not a monster. I'll make sure you and your sister are safe." He takes a step closer to me. I know I should stop him. I should throw my hands up as a barrier. I should back away.

"I'm accused of murder." I keep my voice low. "They say I assisted in the death of the emperor at the direction of the princess."

A strange expression flits across his face. A reminder that he knew of the death of the emperor, that it occurred before I ever set foot in the palace. "I know that isn't true."

"You're so sure you know me that well?" I counter.

"I know you are not capable of murder," he says.

Something inside me stirs. If only I had that power. True power. If I could reach across dreams, distances, like the serpent can. I quickly smother the thought. It was offered to me once, but I know I cannot bear the consequences.

"How do you know?" I challenge him. "How do you know what I am capable of?"

He considers this. I notice shadows under his eyes, as if he has not slept for a while. As if something troubles him.

Kang sighs then. "Ning, I . . ."

The entry to the tent is thrown back, letting in a sharp wind. The flames in the braziers leap, and the censers swing on their chains, casting jumping shadows across the tent wall.

The captain enters. "Commander. There is an urgent message for you from the emperor-regent."

Kang rubs his eyes. "We'll continue this conversation after I'm done. Guards—"

"There's no need for that," Grand Chancellor Zhou says as he strides in. The one who accused me in front of the court, the one who sentenced me to death. The one whose name is on that order from the Ministry of Justice to track me down and bring me back dead or alive. "I will speak with her and take her to the other prisoners when I am done."

Kang regards him with an odd expression on his face, like he is the last person he expected to walk in. "Chancellor."

"My prince." The chancellor bows with a flourish that is almost mocking.

My eyes dance between the two of them. Kang winces visibly. There is a history between these two. One I do not understand.

Kang gives me one last look before marching out of the tent, leaving me alone with one of the men I despise the most in all the world.

Chapter Twenty-Five

Ning 寧

Prince. The reality of that title settles around me as the chancellor gives me the once-over. Only a few weeks have passed since I left the capital, and yet I see so much has changed. Commander of a battalion, soon to be prince. But even with all that, Kang still has to yield to the chancellor. It seems someone else has grown in power as well.

"Zhang Ning," Chancellor Zhou greets me, inclining his head.

"Chancellor," I murmur. I used to cower under his gaze. I used to regard him as kindly.

I used to believe a lot of things, most of them wrong.

"I would offer you some tea, but we know what you can accomplish with that." His smile is mocking. "Come, sit with me."

With a sweep of his cloak, the chancellor sits down on one of the chairs. I stand there, petulant. Remembering exactly how I felt when I was pulled into that courtyard by Governor Wang. When he looked down on me and passed his judgment. When I wielded the truth, the certainty that he brought the enemy soldiers into the palace, and when I found out the truth was not enough.

The chancellor watches me, amused. "Hold on to that anger. You will find it useful someday."

I still cannot control the emotions that run across my face, how easy I am to read. "You betrayed her," I spit at him.

The chancellor laughs, amused by my reaction. Like a cat batting at a fly, removing its wings and watching it struggle, flop around on the ground, useless.

"Power is everything, girl," he says. "Power, the sweetness of it. It is the lure, but very few are willing to give up everything to fully grasp it."

Perhaps it all aligned the way he wanted it to. We are pieces he pushes around the board. He tricked the princess into believing she had his support, even while he rallied the court against her. These grown-up games. I was, and still continue to be, a powerless child, filled with a mixture of annoyance and shame.

"Power calls to you, too," the chancellor continues. "The way you did not hesitate to use your power on that bird. Instead of pretty illusions, you saw the challenge for what it was: To see who could bend another to their will. Pity you lost. You would have been an interesting influence on the court."

I can't help but laugh. "You're a treacherous snake. Do you think I am a fool?"

He shrugs. "You were just a peasant in the wrong place at the wrong time. I could have picked any of those shénnóng-tú, any of those bright and shining stars of the empire, the most pliable. It was luck on my part that you made the choices you did, how the marquis was so easily goaded. But you . . . you did shine the brightest, the one destined to burn out before your time."

"What do you want with me?" I ask, even though I do not actually want to know. Whether he will drag me back to the capital and make an example of me yet. I know his capability for cruelty; he left

Wenyi on the floor of the dungeons, badly beaten. He can bloody my thumbprint and force a signed confession out of me and easily silence me with my death. What awful things has he planned for me?

"I have a task I require you to help me complete. If you help me gain what I am looking for, then I will ensure your name is cleared. You and your sister can scuttle back to whatever corner of the empire you crawled out of and live out the rest of your days in relative obscurity."

He regards me, pleased with himself. At this offer that is not quite an offer, at knowing how few options I have. It is a tactic I am familiar with, one that Governor Wang used quite often.

The offered hand becomes a backhanded slap. An illusion.

"And if I do not do as you say?" The words still make their way out of my mouth because it is the way I am. I must struggle with the futility of my position.

"I thought I would find your father." The chancellor taps his fingers on the table. "But it must be fate that our paths have crossed again, with your sister here. I suppose I will hold on to her and your friend until you return with what I seek. And if you do not, well . . . I think you know what will happen to them."

My fists clench at my side. I have played directly into his hands. I do not have anything to counter with, nothing I can offer. I've brought Shu directly into danger, and all I can hope for is that I will still get to the shénnóng-shī somehow once I've completed whatever challenge the chancellor has laid out for me.

"Tell me what it is you want."

"We are close to a town named Ràohé, known for its proximity to the Băiniăo Gorge. On the other side of the gorge is an old acquaintance of mine. They call her the Hermit. She has a certain item of great value in her possession. One that may very well affect the fate of the empire."

The Hermit. The shénnóng-shī. They must be one and the same—how many magical beings could possibly occupy one gorge in the north? But this is the first I've heard of this item. A treasure hunt seems like a foolish endeavor. What need does the chancellor, or the soon-to-be emperor for that matter, have for treasure?

"What is it?" I ask.

"It is a crystal orb," he says. "The rumor is, whoever possesses it can access an infinite store of magic. It is why she has been able to stay out of our reach." His voice is tinged with annoyance. When he turns away, I can't help but smile at his obvious irritation. How many times has this Hermit rebuked his attempts to get this treasure?

"The entrance to her realm is protected by magic; I suspect powered by this orb, and not one I have been able to cross," the chancellor continues, and I force my face back to blank compliance. "Nor my scouts, who end up getting lost in the forest, or the warriors from Wŭlín I have used to try to break through her defenses. I have heard she is only susceptible to Shénnóng magic, although the handful of shénnóng-tú and shénnóng-shī brought here have failed."

"And why do you think I can get through to her?" I ask.

"Sheer stubbornness got you through the competition. You were untrained, untested, and yet you made it to the final round. I did not lie to you, Ning of Sù. I truly believe you would have made a good shénnóng-shī." Chancellor Zhou smirks, knowing how little I want to hear his praise.

He shrugs. "Or we will find your body broken at the bottom of the gorge. Extinguished. Just like all the brightest stars that come to their eventual end."

I am returned to a small tent near the center of the encampment. Two soldiers stand guard at the entrance, and one of them lifts the flap to allow me through. Shu looks up at me, the relief evident on her face.

"They didn't hurt you, did they?" I ask, sitting down beside her.

She shakes her head. "And you?"

"I'm okay," I tell her. "Where is Brother Huang?"

"I am here," he calls out from the other side of the divider.

"Quiet!" the guard barks at us.

"I have to tell you something," I say, lowering my voice to a whisper.

She nods, making herself sit up taller, and because I can be read so easily, I know she can already sense my worry. "You can tell me," she says. "I will be brave."

She reminds me of Qing'er, trying so hard to hold himself together that day I said goodbye to him. I hope he is doing well, wherever he is.

"I have to leave for a while."

Her eyes widen. "Why?"

"I've been given a task," I tell her. I give her a brief explanation of what the chancellor told me about this treasure.

"The chancellor is not to be trusted," I finish. "He pretended to be loyal to the princess during the competition, only to betray her to the general in the end. You have to stay alert. Be vigilant. I will come back to you when I am done."

"I know." She gives me a small smile. "You always keep your promises."

I hug her as tight as I can, not wanting to let her go. "There is . . . something else I have to tell you as well." I do not tell her that it is because I am afraid I will not return from the gorge. Knowing Father, he will never share this information with her, and a part of her history will die with him.

I tell her about Mother and Father, what I uncovered about their relationship when I was in the palace. What they gave up to come home, to build our family. Shu listens to the entirety of the story, late into the night. She cries with me, remembering our mother. Something eases inside me, that I've come this far. I am able to hold her hand and share this story with her. She is still alive, and that is all that matters to me.

We fall asleep side by side, as we used to back in our room in Xīnyì. When life was the same, day in and day out. When we lived by the schedule of the tea trees and the orchards and our garden. When the events of the capital were a distant, faraway dream.

My fingers find the dān hidden in my sash, pressed against my skin. Is this the time to use them? There is one each for me, Shu, and Brother Huang. The three of us could flee into the night using the dān's power.

But something tells me to save them, to be patient. I will have need of the dān soon.

The Hermit. The shénnóng-shī in the gorge. It is fate that brings me here, but not in the way the chancellor believes it.

We all believe we are the center of the universe, but we forget we are merely specks among the stars. Moving through the streams of possible futures, sometimes colliding. Astronomer Wu showed me the way, told me where to go. Now all I have to do is follow.

Chapter Twenty-Six

Kang 康

By the time Kang returns to the main tent, Ning is gone, and instead, the chancellor sits inside waiting for him, drinking tea. Her presence has affected Kang, made him feel uncertain of himself. To face the chancellor, he needs to focus, so he forces himself to breathe.

He knows of the man's history after having taken the time to consult with the older soldiers of the battalion: passing the examinations as a commoner, accepted into Yěliŭ Academy at a young age. The top of his class each year, entering the palace via the Department of Defense. Rising through the ranks for his adept handling of various crises. Eventually coming to the attention of the Ascended Emperor, placed in charge of running the palace and then the entire court. Now it is obvious he will back the general to ascend the throne.

The rumor whispers at the back of Kang's mind again: *No one sits on the throne of Dàxī without the chancellor willing it so.*

Chancellor Zhou places his teacup on the table and pours Kang a cup as well, offering it to him. Knowing he could not politely refuse, Kang sits and takes a hurried sip.

"Somewhere to be?" the chancellor asks, amused. There's a clinking sound in his hand. Those orbs, spinning in his palm. The sight and sound of them cause a flare of annoyance inside Kang, one he cannot help but feel. They put him off-balance, even if there is no reason they should affect him like this.

"There are preparations to be made," Kang says stiffly. "I was told you received the same correspondence from my father this morning."

According to the missive from the capital, his mission was soon to be cut short: The princess is preparing to march on Jia with a force from Kallah, an army of allies still loyal to her and her father. A confrontation will happen in five days' time if the force she leads holds its steady pace.

His father's message is clear: Finish the mission. *Now.*

"I had hoped you would succeed where I have not," the chancellor says, sounding disappointed. "I thought three days would have been adequate time to prove yourself."

Kang sent soldiers to scour the entirety of the cliff, top and bottom, to find this alleged hoarder of treasure, but they have been elusive. The locals are suspicious of his soldiers and have given them less than welcoming treatment. Many inns have refused them hospitality, stating they are full of patrons, even though his scouts have reported they do not see many people entering and exiting the premises. Indeed, Ràohé seems to be a lively town, but the people are not particularly forthcoming. Kang has even seen the townspeople spit on the streets at their approach.

To see his father's battalion treated with such outright hostility is a new experience for Kang, and he finds himself weary of the poor treatment.

"Perhaps the thing you search for does not exist," Kang says through gritted teeth. "The sooner my father realizes this, the better, and we can stop wasting time and resources on this quest."

He's seen for himself that the gorge does not affect only the shénnóng-shī. Some among the battalion have refused to approach the gorge, stating they have seen strange visions. And then . . . there were the broken bodies they have carried out of the depths. Soldiers swept off the edge by a sudden wind or an unlucky slip on the rocky paths.

There have been other disturbing rumors as well, accusations against the Blackwater, that his father's battalion had disrespected the gods, and so have called down their wrath upon themselves. Not surprising, considering what the emperor-regent has done with the monasteries. Although Kang would never give voice to those doubts himself.

"You have only a few days left to ensure that your name is known among Dàxī." The chancellor smiles. "As the triumphant prince who returns carrying a great treasure back to the capital where it belongs, wielded by its rightful ruler."

Those spheres are still spinning in the other man's hand, strangely hypnotic.

"You believe, then, in the power of these relics?" Kang forces himself to look back up at the chancellor's face. "That they will assist my father in holding the throne?"

"They are but tools," Chancellor Zhou responds. "You are aware that an untrained person wielding the best weapon in the world can only go so far. Ambition, will, determination . . . that will carry you further."

"Then you have no use for Zhang Ning and her sister," Kang says, still not sure of the chancellor's intentions for his pursuit of the shénnóng-tú across the empire. There is no reason for him to be so intent on her capture, and only a fool would believe that the chancellor is devoted to the pursuit of justice. "You have used her for your purpose. You have ruined her good name and that of her family. If they are but tools that have fulfilled their usefulness, then what is the purpose in keeping them here?"

Chancellor Zhou sits back and smirks, setting the orbs back into their box. He picks up his own cup of tea, the image of indulgence. He speaks as if he relishes every single word. "Ah, yes, your dear shénnóng-tú. Your concern for her is precious. If you want to protect her, then complete your father's mission. She will make the next attempt at finding this treasure."

The missing shénnóng-shī were fully accredited. The dead soldiers were at the peak of their training. They all failed.

The chancellor will send her into the gorge next, and she will not refuse because he holds her sister as a pawn. Of course she will do it.

Fury suddenly floods Kang's gut, pinning him in place with the implication of those words. "You stay away from her," he growls. "There is another reason you are gathering these relics, and I will figure out why."

"You would do well to remember why you are here," Chancellor Zhou says, rising from his seat. "You are a mere boy, playing at command. Power that is given can be easily taken away. Blown into the annals of history like so many chaffs of wheat."

The chancellor sets down his cup on the table, his amusement clear. "Enjoy your tea."

Chapter Twenty-Seven

Ning 寧

In the morning we are given a hot breakfast, and then Shu and I wait in our tents for the soldiers to collect me. But it isn't until the midday meal has passed as well before I am told to prepare for travel. I'm given a change of clothes—a gray tunic with a roughly embroidered collar that smells faintly of horse and matching pants. But they do not give me my bag back, the one containing all my ingredients.

"Speak to the commander about it," the soldier tells me gruffly when I protest.

Commander. My chest tightens.

The chancellor is there to see us off. Brother Huang is brought to us with his wrists bound again, Shu standing pale-faced behind him. A clear reminder of what I have to lose if I do not succeed.

Kang stands at the entrance to the camp, wearing the same gray outfit as my own, flanked by two other men. They're obviously soldiers, by their build and their bearing, but for some reason they want to appear disguised as well. I do not understand what they mean to do until three saddled horses are brought forth, and I realize they will be traveling with me. To ensure that I carry out my task. A sudden rush of overwhelming hatred washes over me, so strong that my body trembles with it.

I despise the chancellor and all he represents. Kang is a reminder of that betrayal. Their connections to the murders at Yěliŭ, the attacks at Wŭlín. Elder Guo's obvious loyalty, the shifting alliances of Hánxiá. The poison hidden in the tea, these shadow soldiers under mind control, and old gods . . .

Everything we ever feared is coming to be. The Hermit may be our only hope.

"I wish you well on your quest," the chancellor says to me, as if I am still a participant in that competition and not a fugitive, a hostage. I ignore him and walk instead to Shu, to hold her close and say goodbye. I cautioned her last night to hide the feather and hide it well, for I do not know what Chancellor Zhou would do with her if he were to uncover whatever this new power may be. A different sort of magic, a talisman, or something else.

"Please, I ask that you protect her while I am gone." I make the request to Brother Huang with sincerity, even as the soldiers around him chuckle and exchange condescending glances.

He nods solemnly. "I will." I know he will take his role as protector seriously, and I am glad for it.

"Commander Li will ensure that you complete your task," Chancellor Zhou says. "If word returns that you have tried to escape, then . . ." He looks toward Shu and Brother Huang. "They will die."

With that ominous warning hanging over my head, Kang approaches my side on one of the horses. He holds out his hand, and I realize I'm supposed to ride behind him. With no choice but to take it, I allow him to pull me up.

As Kang turns the horse and nudges it into a trot, I look back at Shu.

I'm leaving her again. Leaving her, in order to save her.

Again.

I grit my teeth. I will come back alive.

At first, I try to hang on to the saddle as I am jostled up, down, and sideways. But after the horse sidesteps a rock on the road, I'm thrown against his back.

"Hold on!" I hear him call out as he pulls back on the reins. The horse's hooves slide in the mud as it struggles to climb the slippery path. I don't know where to put my hands, so I place them just under his ribs on either side. Until yet another jump throws me against him, and I yelp as the horse veers to right itself again. I resign myself to clinging to him for dear life as the three horses make their way up the road toward Ràohé.

Even with the heavy rains of the past few days and the occasional drizzle on our travels, this road is much better maintained than the mountain paths Brother Huang navigated with us. Some sections of the road are flattened with wooden planks where the earth is prone to sinking or set with stones so that whoever walks upon it can find purchase. But even with my new attire, I soon become one with the cold and damp.

It is impossible to talk while riding, so I just have to sit with my own churning thoughts about the challenge before me. The rest of the trek along the road is a miserable affair, and when we finally see the town ahead through the trees, I could cry with relief. My back, my legs, my neck—all ache from trying to hold myself upright.

Although we have not donned armor and are dressed plainly, like traveling merchants, we still look out of place. The townspeople stare at us when we pass. Children playing in the puddles are pulled inside by their families when we approach, shutting their doors behind them. They are distrustful of strangers, and . . . they're afraid.

When we finally reach an inn, the stablehand takes the reins of the horses. I would have tumbled off the horse and fallen face-first into the mud if it weren't for Kang, who catches me in his arms. The other soldiers avert their eyes, while Kang looks down at me in amusement. I push him off.

"It's something you get used to . . . riding," he says. Trying to make me feel better, but having the opposite effect.

"It's fine." I swallow my humiliation, even though my right leg twitches.

"Obtain rooms for us, and then we can rest for the evening," he directs the other men. They are off to engage with the innkeeper while I turn and look at my surroundings, pointedly ignoring the boy beside me.

This inn is much larger than the Hus' establishment, constructed entirely of bamboo, reminding me of the strange place in the Forgetting Sea where we rested our heads for the night. A large plaque above the doorway indicates this is the Fúróng Inn, sharing the same name as the river and the hibiscus flower. There is an open-air dining room on the main floor, with several tables, half of which are occupied. The second floor must be the guest rooms.

When the innkeeper leads us to the room to change out of our damp traveling clothes, I realize with horror I have to share a room with Kang.

Seeing my hesitation, he offers an apology. "We cannot permit you to sleep alone. Perhaps . . . you would like me to ask one of the others to stay with you?"

Both options seem equally terrible, so I shake my head, feeling my face grow hot with embarrassment again. I toss my pack onto the floor next to one of the beds. There is no time to be caught up in my delicate feelings or my disgraced reputation. I have to keep my wits about me. Find out where this shénnóng-shī is, if they are, indeed, the same Hermit that the chancellor referred to. And I have to find a way to get to Wenyi's family as well, to finally deliver his letter. I don't know if I will ever get a chance to return to Ràohé again.

But all this seems daunting to me at the moment.

Even though they took my ingredients, I still have the dān and the letter, wrapped in a separate pouch under my clothes. They gave me a quick pat down to check for weapons, but nothing more intrusive than that, and the pouch was not discovered. However, a medic did give my ingredients a once-over, removing two they determined to have negative qualities. The rest were given to Kang, who will control my access.

We take our evening meal in the dining room. This inn appears to be popular among the locals. Someone plays the flute, accompanying a young singer, for entertainment. On our table is cold sliced beef, pickled greens with bean curd. Hearty fare. Almost like my mother's cooking. I only half-listen to the conversation that swirls around me. They prefer to talk among themselves, ignoring my presence.

Kang refers to the older soldier as Ren-ge, and they seem to have a casual familiarity, for him to refer to someone as an older brother. The younger one is Badu, who always speaks with a joking tone and conveys an air of constant amusement.

When I reach for another serving of beef with my chopsticks, Badu stops me. "We'll need to serve you, miss." He looks sorry to say it, but he does it all the same. "Just . . . let me know what you want to eat."

Reminding me of my place.

Murderer. Poisoner.

My mood drops again as I regard the vegetables bobbing about in my bowl of soup. When I stir the soup with a spoon, I notice that the fúlíng mushroom is present in the dish, along with plump white lotus seeds. I chew on the tender pieces of chicken, surrounded by the sounds of enjoyment and slurps all around me.

It is then I realize I should have seen it all along. Soup is just another kind of tonic, ingredients simmered in water, increasing its potency. I already know my magic is not limited to tea; the leaves simply strengthen my ability to step into the Shift. Lotus seeds are a medicinal ingredient with calming properties. Mushrooms improve circulation and digestion. I have the only thing I need.

Water.

Reaching out, I grasp the ladle, then pull back again, apologizing. But not before a tendril of my magic escapes, sinking into the earthen pot. My magic settles into the bubbling surface of the soup, mixing among the various ingredients.

"The soup is really good," I murmur, and the others agree.

They will not sense the subtlety of my influence. The three of them will sleep well tonight.

When we retire to our rooms, I pray that Kang will not want to make conversation with me, but he seems content to be wrapped in his own thoughts. With only a brief good night, we lie on opposite sides of the room.

I wait for the sound of his breathing to deepen. In the palace, I was always waiting. Listening for the sound of the criers until the appropriate hour arrived. Waiting for the princess. Waiting for . . . him.

I tug on the connection I made during the evening's meal. My magic brushes against Kang's mind, checking to make sure he is sleeping. I catch a wisp of something like longing, like regret. My magic whispers, wanting to pull me closer, recognizing him as familiar. But I wave it away. I have no need for that feeling of sentimentality, I remind myself. It will only hinder me.

Satisfied that Kang is asleep, I quietly tiptoe out the door. When I pass by the room where the other soldiers are sleeping, I check in on them, too. Feel the subtle pull of their dreams. I catch only a few images from Ren, a rabbit running before him in the forest as he lets an arrow loose. Badu dreams he is flying above the ocean.

I tie my hair back and walk down the back stairwell. The bobbing light at the other end of the alley shows patrols walking through the town streets. I will have to avoid them—I do not know how many of Ràohé's guards are loyal to the Blackwater. How do I find Wenyi's family? All I have is a name and the knowledge that his mother runs a noodle shop.

But the princess told me how the letter outlined the townspeople's suffering since the Blackwater Battalion resurfaced in the area; that may be the connection I can use to my advantage. The innkeepers and teahouse owners of any town are certain to be the first to hear any news and to have the best awareness of the place in which they reside so they are better able to guide travelers. They are the ones I turn to first.

I enter the kitchen in the back and see three people sitting on low stools by the large wok. The fire underneath is only embers; they must be done for the evening, eating their own meal now that all the guests have been satisfied. The girl who served us looks up and sees me. She drops her chopsticks onto her plate with a clatter, and the man stands up in front of his family, obviously protective.

"Can I help you?" he asks warily. "Is something in the room not to your liking?"

I am regarded with a mix of fear and suspicion. It confirms everything that Wenyi wrote about the people here. I have to use this.

"I'm looking for the Lin family," I tell them. "Their son was dedicated to Yěliŭ and then sent to the palace for the shénnóng-tú competition."

The man still looks at me with hesitation. "Why are you asking?"

I debate how much to tell them. Whether they can be trusted or if they will sell me out to the soldiers, but I know I do not have time to play around with words. I still value the truth.

"I met Wenyi when he was at the palace. I have news for his family. News he wanted me to pass on. Please. He told me of . . . of how bad things have gotten in Ràohé."

The innkeeper looks back at his wife, suddenly afraid. I sense the change in the air. He quickly raises his hands in front of his face. "We don't know what you're talking about. Please. Leave us alone."

Instead of allowing myself to be pushed away, I stand firm. "This may be my only chance. I beg you. I will return before dawn. I swear, nothing will happen to you or your family."

The wife behind him seems to consider this and then places her hand on her husband's arm, coming to stand beside him.

"Those against the battalion are friends of ours, never forget," she says, voice tight. Then she looks at me. "You will find their noodle shop two streets over. Their name is written on a white lantern. If you truly do know Wenyi, then you will recognize it."

"Thank you." I bow to them and step out into the night. I keep to the shadows, away from the patrols and any movement I notice. I do not want to attract anyone's attention tonight.

The noodle shop is easy enough to find. A white lantern marked with the name Lin sways in the breeze. It's more a stall than a shop really, set in the open air with low wooden tables in front of it for customers to sit and enjoy a quick meal.

A woman stands there over two pots. One of hot water for the noodles, the other for broth. She lifts her chin in greeting. "Miss? Are you looking to buy some noodles?"

The scent of bubbling broth and steamed vegetables is, indeed, enticing, but it would only offer a brief distraction from what I must do.

I bow to her and ask, my throat tight with emotion, "Are you Wenyi's mother?"

A simple question, yet her expression tells me she can read everything in my face and voice.

The ladle drops from her hand with a clatter, hitting the wooden surface of the cart. I reach out and catch her before she falls, helping her to sit on a stool behind her.

She already knows what I am about to say.

Chapter Twenty-Eight

Ning 寧

"I'm sorry," I say to the older woman. Wenyi's mother just sits for a moment, and I stand there beside her. She stares into the distance, as if lost, before slowly coming back to herself with a few blinks.

"Yes, I am his mother," she finally says, turning to me. "And you are here to tell me he is never coming back."

I already have the letter in my hand. I pass it to her with another deep bow of condolence. She takes it from me and then slowly gets to her feet.

"Let us talk inside," she tells me. She places the lids over her pots and extinguishes the fire beneath. I help put the chairs up on the tables and push them against the wall beside the cart. Then she reaches up and blows out the candle inside the lantern.

"Please, come in." She pushes the doors of the gate open, and we step into a small courtyard. Stacks of split firewood are along one wall, fuel for the noodle stall. Jugs of various sizes line another wall.

I follow her to the receiving room of her residence. On one wall is a long table, on which rests several wooden plaques elaborately carved with names. This must be her family's memorial room, just like the one in the palace. A northern custom. She goes to stand directly in front of the plaques and bows, mumbling a quiet prayer before unfolding the letter and reading it silently.

In the air drifts the heavy scent of incense, a musk that gathers at the back of the throat. Around the room, on the walls and the shelves, I see talismans of Bìxì, devotions to the Emerald Tortoise in calligraphy and paintings. Clearly this family worships Bìxì—that would explain why Wenyi was dedicated to Yěliǔ at such a young age. But how did he come to be a shénnóng-tú? Why did Yěliǔ permit the diversion in his studies?

She reads the letter a second time, then dabs at the corners of her eyes with a handkerchief. Struggling to maintain her composure, she finally lets out a long sigh and gestures for me to sit on one of the chairs to the side of the room.

"How did you meet my son?" she asks.

I tell her about meeting him in the competition. I tell her how he was kind, respected by the other shénnóng-tú, about the confrontation during the last round of the competition, and how the chancellor punished him for it. How I was with him in the end.

We're both crying as I finish. "I told him not to go to the palace," she says, smiling despite her tears. "But he was adamant that he must serve both Bìxì and Shénnóng and that to do so he must go to the palace and attend the competition."

A part of me recognizes now that I am the same as Wenyi. Even though my magic is from Shénnóng, I have seen the White Lady, and it is she who watches over me. When I ask, both of them answer. Maybe he also did not have a choice.

"He thought of you and your family until the very end." Empty words to her ears, I'm sure, but I feel compelled to offer them all the same. I have many feelings about my village, about how they treated my family, about how much my father gave to them without anything in return. But when Mother died, they helped where they could, giving us whatever they could spare. Extra helpings of steamed rice, bundles of gathered greens and mushrooms. More than even my own uncle offered, and I've never forgotten that.

She gives me an odd look, as if she is seeing me for the first time. "You've grieved as well, haven't you?"

I stare back at her, wondering how she knows. If grief is draped over me now, like another mask I wear, or if it has become my true face.

There's a clatter in another room, the sound of something knocked over, disrupting our conversation. Wenyi's mother jumps up, and I follow. She pushes through the doors to the other room, leaving a gap wide enough for me to see through. Inside is a platform bed and a few tables on which there are a basin and some folded clothes.

She speaks urgently to someone in a low voice. The sound of other things falling. I creep closer to the door. Something inside me tugs, insistent, telling me I need to walk forward. Just like how I was guided through the bamboo forest, like the steps that led me here to Ràohé. I push past the door and into the room. A faint smell of sickness lingers under the incense, which drifts from a censer in the corner.

Wenyi's mother is holding down a thrashing figure on the bed. It's a young man, I realize, too young to be Wenyi's father, but older than Wenyi. His body arcs impossibly high, like a bow being pulled back, and then he falls. He turns toward me, face catching in the light from the lantern hanging from the wall. It reflects off the shine of the drool running from his slack lips and off another line of tears running from the corners of his eyes. In the darkness, it almost looks as if he is crying blood.

I step closer to them. My eyes already assessing, cataloging, comparing his signs with the symptoms Father made me memorize time and time again through his impatient instructions. *Don't you see it, Ning? Pay attention!* But the answer comes to me through the cracked lips, the dark tinge under his glazed eyes. As if someone dipped their fingers in ash and brushed them against his skin. Poison.

Wenyi's mother looks up at me, sadness emanating from her in waves. I don't need magic to know she pleads for someone, anyone, to help him.

"He was poisoned by the tea bricks?" I ask. She nods, dabbing his forehead with a damp cloth, hovering over him protectively.

"Will you allow me to examine him?" I ask.

"What can you do?" she replies, voice hollow. "The physicians have already been consulted. They have no answers."

"This is why Wenyi went to Jia," I say, finally realizing. How similar our paths were, how familiar our troubles, but I never knew it when he was alive.

"Wenyi hurried back from Yěliŭ when we sent word," she says. "He said he would seek out the Hermit in the gorge, ask for her aid. He disappeared for a month in the mountains and came back . . . different."

"Different how?"

"He carried with him a letter that stated he was the chosen shénnóng-tú of the shénnóng-shī of Băiniăo Gorge and said he was going to be called to the competition. He said that was the price for the medicine he brought back."

"What medicine?" I quickly calculate the timeline in my mind. Ràohé must have been one of the first places hit by the poison. For that message to be sent to Yěliŭ, for Wenyi to travel back here, disappear for a month, and then leave again for the capital . . . this man would have been poisoned months ago, and yet still he lives. Shu only clung to life because of the various medicines she tried, so the components of what Wenyi brought back may be similar. Enough to control his symptoms, but not enough to bring him back from the other side.

"Wenyi said it was going to be temporary. To stabilize his body while he went in search of the antidote." Wenyi's mother brushes loose strands of hair away from the man's face.

I feel a spark of excitement inside me. It's a clue. She might know how to reach the Hermit—perhaps Wenyi had shared that knowledge with her.

It's all coming together. The reason I am here. Why I met Wenyi, and why the astronomer sent me to this place.

"They said she was once the shénnóng-shī who advised the emperor himself. Is that true? Did Wenyi ever speak about it?" I ask, a little too eagerly.

"We just know her as the Hermit. A teacher who went to live inside the gorge long ago," she says, a hint of suspicion entering her voice. "Even though I hate her for sending Wenyi onward to his death, I still owe her for Huayu's life."

An idea unravels in my mind, perhaps a solution that can give me the answers I need. But before I attempt the antidote, I must be certain I am correct about the poison—if I give him the wrong medicine, if I am wrong about what ails him, I could kill him just as surely or trap him forever within whatever nightmare the poison has cast on him. I cannot do that to Wenyi's mother, who has already lost one son in pursuit of the cure.

"I know you do not have cause to trust me, but I would like

to help you save Huayu, because I owe Wenyi a debt as well." He stood up for me against Shao, and he always regarded me as an equal. I would like to pay him back somehow. Wenyi has already given up his own life. I cannot allow the serpent's plot to claim his brother, too.

Wenyi's mother regards me for a long time. "And what do you want in return, for helping us?" she asks finally.

"If you will provide me with some tea leaves and hot water, and if you can spare a small slice of ginseng," I tell her. "If I am able to help him, all I ask is that you tell me how I can find the Hermit."

"Do you promise you mean her no ill?" she says.

I touch my heart. "I promise."

She gives me a tight nod, then leaves to bring me what I've requested.

I sit down next to Huayu. His lips are moving, mumbling nonsense words. It brings me back to those months of worry, when I wiped the sweat from Shu's brow, had to pour the tonics down her throat even as she tried to spit them back up. When she fought for her life.

Soon Wenyi's mother is back with the hot water, the cups, and the tea, all balanced on a bamboo tray. I pull a table closer to the bed and use the water to quickly scorch the cups. Using my fingernail, I pierce the ginseng, testing its pliancy. There's still enough of its essence left; I place it next to the tea leaves. The water seeps into the leaves, sending them tumbling, and the magic bubbles inside me as well, calling out for me to use it.

I know there is a risk to this. The use of the magic could very well bring the serpent down on my head yet again. But I have to try.

I blow on the surface of the tea to cool it and take a sip. With a clean handkerchief that Wenyi's mother provides, I dip it into the tea and brush it against Huayu's lips. As the tea sinks into his skin, so, too, does the Shift tilt the world and slide me toward him. To where he is trapped in battle with the poison.

Chapter Twenty-Nine

Ning 寧

I step through the mist. It's like taking a breath and plunging my face into water and finding an entirely new realm underneath. I wish I were entering the Jade Dragon's underwater palace, like in the fantastic stories, but instead, I am standing on the banks of a river. There are pebbles under my feet. The water courses by, its swiftly moving surface a few shades darker than the white of the sky. On the other side of the river are sharp cliffs, and when I turn, I see the forest behind me.

Everything is muted. Without color. This isn't the Shift. It's the Shadow Realm.

"Huayu!" a voice sounds to my left.

I turn and see a figure walk past me.

It can't be . . . My heart constricts, and I can't breathe.

That slow walk. It's Wenyi. The one who spoke up for me, regarded me as a peer. I was there for his final moments. I listened to his whispered words, made him a promise on his deathbed. A responsibility my father has never taken lightly as part of his role as a physician, something I always understood as his assistant.

I take a step forward, then another, following him. The stones crunch under my feet, and the river rumbles beside me, its rapids foaming white. He walks too fast and I struggle to keep up. I have to know, is he a ghost? Is it his spirit, returning for his brother?

The wind picks up, blowing the fog off the mountaintops and down to surround us. The trees rustle in the distance, as if in warning. Still, that figure continues to call in that mournful voice. Where is Huayu? And why is he not responding to this call?

Hanging on to a tendril of magic, I propel myself forward. Urge my feet to move faster, to be more certain on the stones. Closing the distance between me and that tall figure.

I reach out to him, to see if he is a spirit or if he is a remnant of Huayu's memories, a part of his imagination. His arm is solid under my hand. Bone and flesh. He turns, but instead of Wenyi's face, the eyes are inhuman slits. The mouth is open in a snarl, releasing a barbed, split tongue. He hisses at me, a spitting, angry sound.

I've disturbed his hunt.

This is the poison.

The creature lunges at me, but I am faster. I dodge and let myself fall backward, allow myself to break through the Shift, that channel that links me from the waking world to the space between gods. The ginseng gives me mental clarity, aiding my swift reaction. But the ginseng is not enough for me to find Huayu. I have to have the strength to grab his soul, release the grip of the poison, and provide him with enough strength to bring him back.

I need the full power of the true antidote.

I wake with a gasp, looking up into the eyes of Wenyi's mother.

"What did you see?" She looks at me, fearing the worst.

"I cannot promise that I will be able to save him for certain, but I have done it once before," I say to her. "I know this poison. I know its tricks."

But I cannot do it without the pearl powder—I learned that

lesson with Elder Tai back in Yěliŭ. I have to make sure I have my own tether to reality, enough to bind my soul together to his, to pull ourselves back.

She does have licorice root in her kitchen, and I know I have lí lú in my pouch. The pearl powder, well . . . Kang must carry some. I will just have to hope he is still asleep when I return to the inn.

The sounds of the town criers follow my urgent footsteps back to the inn. It is the Hour of the Thief. I am running out of time.

My hopes are dashed when I ease open the door to the room and find Kang sitting there, waiting for me.

"Where did you go?" he asks, his expression severe. Like he's a stern-faced judge about to pronounce a verdict. To sentence me to a terrible fate.

A surge of annoyance courses through me. The expectation of his look, like he is asking me to explain myself. As if I deserved the situation I'm in, a fate of my own making. I do not say anything, and he slams his hand on the table beside him.

"You *were* planning something! You used your magic on me and my men." He has the gall to look betrayed, half-rising out of the chair, looking to confront me.

I walk right up to him then, releasing the bitter torrent of words that have been waiting for me to unleash them. "Yes, Kang, this is what I have planned for all along. To be thrown out of the competition, even though I proved to them I was capable, when I passed all the trials. I was *forced* into that position by *your* father, by the horrible suffering *he* inflicted on Dàxī's people!"

I move closer to him, until our faces are almost touching, until he can probably feel the anger and desperation radiating off me. He backs down, sitting heavily back onto his chair.

I press in closer. "I finally saved my sister, only to find both of us chased away from the one place I thought could offer me refuge. My face on wanted posters, accusing me of terrible crimes I didn't commit."

He looks up at me, eyes wide. I see the rise and fall of his chest. This boy whom I have no claim to. The one I kissed and the one I pushed away in turn. Who kept coming up in my mind when I was on the run. The one I refuse to admit to myself that I was glad to see when I finally saw him again, even though I am constantly reminded we are on opposite sides. Just as we are now.

"The chancellor is adamant he needs you. For a purpose I am still trying to understand," he says to me, breath brushing against my cheek. "I have to do what he wants if I'm going to keep you safe."

I laugh in his face then, and he flinches. I turn away. I'm reminded of how we were at each other's throats in those final days in the palace. The way we cut each other with words, straight to the bone. He envisions himself as my protector, even though it is impossible for him to serve his father and help me, too. Even though I aim to help the princess regain her throne.

"What are you doing?" he snaps as I walk to his bed. I grab his pack and empty everything out of it, rummaging through the items until I find my pouch of ingredients.

"Hey!" He grabs for my arm, and I wrench myself out of his grasp.

"I don't have time for you to figure it out," I tell him. "Trust me or don't, it's up to you. I've found a way to uncover the location of the Hermit, and I will get that relic, with or without your help."

With my pouch in hand, I walk out the door, and I hear his footsteps following.

"Ning, wait!" he says behind me, but I do not answer as I walk down the street.

Time and time again. The Golden Key, the Silver Needle, the final round of the competition. All of it revealed our truest selves to each other, and yet he still questions whether I am capable of those terrible things. I could see it in his eyes. That doubt.

It feeds into what I already feel about myself. *Am* I capable? All these impossible tasks, saving Huayu, uncovering the location of the Hermit, figuring out Shu's lost magic, preventing that demon from returning to earth . . .

I feel the weight of it all on my shoulders. Tears prickle my eyes.

"Ning!" Kang finally catches up to me. With one hand on my shoulder, he spins me around to face him. "Wait, please."

I should just brush past him and keep walking. Push him away and continue on. But there's an earnestness about him that keeps me still, makes me stand there and listen.

"I believe you," he tells me. "I know you are not behind the poisonings in the court, that you are as much in the dark as I am."

I chuckle mirthlessly at that.

"They keep telling me that you exist in opposition to Shénnóng magic," he says. "That you are an abomination against the natural order, but I know none of that is true. I've felt your magic for myself."

Hearing those accusations spill from his lips, even though he denies them with his next breath, feels like a slap to the face. I thought if I embraced that side of myself, returned to Shénnóng, I would be accepted. But I continue to find spaces in which I do not belong. As always, more at home with plants than with people. An abomination.

He takes my right hand in his and presses his palm against mine. "You keep telling me to trust you, and I do. Tell me what you need me to do."

I want to hit him and kiss him in equal measure, but I know I don't have time for either.

"Give me your vial," I say to him, extracting my hand from his and extending it in front of me, palm up.

He looks confused. "My vial?"

"The pearl powder," I say to him. "You can either drag me back to the inn and stumble about the mountains tomorrow with your soldiers. Or you can give it to me, then follow me and see for yourself what the poison truly is."

Kang regards me again, then he pulls out the vial from his sash, placing it in my opened hand.

My hand closes around it.

"All I want is the truth," he says.

"Then come with me."

When I return to the residence, Wenyi's mother regards Kang with shock.

"You bring a soldier of Blackwater to us?" she cries. "You're working for them... You mean to kill us all! They are the ones who took Huayu and sent him back like this!"

"We have a... complicated history." I place my hand on her arm. "He will not harm your family, I promise. And... I need him to help me." Not quite the truth, but not quite a lie, either.

"You swear it, then." Her eyes flash as she grips my hand. "You swear on the gods you will not harm Huayu."

"I swear it," I tell her. "On behalf of the truth contained in Bìxì's shell and the knowledge shared by Shénnóng. I swear on the Tiger's fearsome roar and on the wings of the White Lady, I am trying to save Huayu."

She nods then and permits us to enter her home.

As I set up my tools and ingredients, I contemplate the unknowns of my magic. How far I can push myself before it begins to consume me in turn. I have the knowledge imparted to me from books and from my previous encounters with the poison. I've learned much from removing the poison from Ruyi, and in a way, I sense these poisons are linked, sharing a similar component.

The serpent is behind them both.

"Where do you need me?" Kang asks.

"Stand there," I say to him. Even though he is here, I cannot allow him to be a distraction. I sit down beside Huayu.

I place my ingredients on the tray. One dān. A small thing, capable of containing so much power. Even though I have only three, I know this will amplify my power, and I owe this to Wenyi. For giving a voice to those who have been ignored and forgotten, for trying to save those dear to him.

I brew the tea first, and then, when it is a perfect cup of bronze, I add the lí lú, then the licorice root. On top, I sprinkle half the vial of pearl powder. That was sufficient enough to ground me in the other realm to pull Shu out, and I don't want to risk using more. I permit the concoction to brew for a few minutes, then pour it all into one bowl.

I pass the bowl to Kang, and he drinks. I do the same when he passes it back to me.

"Be prepared," I say to him. "It's going to be different from the previous times we've stepped through the Shift."

I place the dān into my mouth. As soon as my lips close around it, the magic leaps up inside me. Energy writhes in my body, building up to an intensity I've never felt before. It needs to be released or I shall explode from the force of it. I fumble for Kang's hand and find it, my magic leaping from me to him, forming a bridge. I place my other hand on Huayu's bare chest.

There's a jolt like lightning, shooting through me, through both of them. Time and space bend, and we're thrown forward.

Chapter Thirty

Kang 康

Darkness falls across his vision just for a moment, and then, as though a cloth is pulled off his head, this other world appears. Shades of gray, everything in monotone. As if he's stepped through an ink painting, a landscape come to life.

A slight breeze stirs his hair. He takes a step forward, and pebbles crunch under his feet. He lifts his arm, opens and closes his fist. It feels like he is still in his body, still in himself. It feels so real, and yet he knows it isn't.

A moment ago, he stood in a house in the town of Ràohé, holding the hand of a shénnóng-tú. Within the span of a breath, he now stands before a river, breathing in the mountain air. Footsteps sound beside him, and he sees Ning walk determinedly down the riverbank.

He follows, knowing he should stay close to her. This is like no place he has seen before. She warned him it would be different from his previous encounters with magic, and yet he knows, however she might have described it, words would not have been sufficient. Even the last brush with magic, when they drank the Silver Needle together, it was marked only by a sudden appearance of fog. He still remained in the garden, in the hall, where it was familiar.

He never imagined he could be transported to an entirely different world.

"Keep your eyes open," Ning says urgently beside him, looking around. "Huayu will be here somewhere. I can *feel* him." Huayu must be the man lying on the bed. Kang feels a thread of unease, but he swallows it down. She said to trust her, and so he must.

He notices a figure sitting at the edge of the river first, and he tugs on her sleeve. A young man perches on top of a large rock, a fishing rod in hand, the line dangling in the water. The river curves slightly there, forming a small bay. Where the current is not as fast, and where fish may linger and be lured by bait.

"This is the place where they used to come when they didn't want to go to school," she whispers beside him. The magic must reveal more to her than he can see. He feels that small stab of fear again, when he first regarded her face on the Ministry of Justice posters. When the chancellor warned him about the type of person she is and the type of magic she practices.

Able to crush your mind, make you see impossible visions, read your every deep, dark, and cherished thought...

Chancellor Zhou stood in front of the council and warned them all about the type of magic certain shénnóng-shī who have strayed from the path are able to practice. With Elder Guo standing beside him, nodding at his every word, there was no reason for anyone to contradict him.

She and Kang quickly close the distance between them and the young man on the rock, until the wind carries over the sound of another voice.

"*Brother...where are you?*" the voice echoes through the canyon. Up ahead, Kang sees the young man's head turn, looking down the river for the source of the voice.

Kang cannot keep it in anymore. He has to ask. "What is this place? Who are they?"

"This must be Bǎiniǎo Gorge," Ning murmurs, and then she closes her eyes, pressing her finger to her temple, as if listening for something. A sound only she can hear. "The other figure . . . the one who looks like Wenyi. You cannot trust him. If he gets closer, keep him away." Her eyes snap open, and she holds his gaze intently. "At all costs."

"Wenyi . . . ," he says, feeling a bit slow in understanding. "He is the boy who slowed me down in the final trial. The one who died in the dungeons." A brief flare of pain, a hollow echo in his chest, confirms his own sense of guilt. He tried to speak up in the shénnóng-tú's behalf, but the chancellor refused to listen.

Kang, do you understand? her voice resounds in his head. He should be afraid of her intrusion. He should brush off the tendrils of influence. And yet all he senses is her urgency. Her concern for Huayu. She is afraid of what is coming, whatever he is supposed to keep away from them as she uses her magic. He nods, turning his attention in the direction of that mysterious voice.

This is what the others did not know or simply did not tell him. That when a follower of Shénnóng casts their magic, when she pulls him toward her with her mind, it means she can read him, true, but he can see her, too. The most hidden parts of him, she uncovers, and what she once tried to hide, he now sees.

Ning approaches the fisherman, calling out a greeting. Kang approaches the water instead, the rippling surface of the quieter pool. Something dark moves in the water. Something big . . . something that shouldn't be there. He shudders, stepping away. His instincts say he shouldn't get too close.

Tendrils of conversation float over to him. "You're scaring away the fish. Have you seen my brother? He's a head taller than you, maybe a little taller than your friend over there. Handsome fellow, if a little scrawny."

"You've been poisoned," Ning says.

Kang glances over to see how Huayu will take this revelation, but the man only laughs, hopping down off the rock.

"If I were poisoned, would I be here, fishing? Enjoying a rare day of peace?"

"Wenyi has not been home in years," Ning insists. "He was dedicated to Yěliŭ when he was sixteen. Do you remember?"

Huayu's brows furrow in confusion. "Yěliŭ?"

Above their heads, the wind starts to whistle. In the distance, the towering trees sway, disturbed by the sudden gusts that barrel down the canyon. A flutter in the water catches Kang's eyes.

A fish shoots out from the water with a splash. It lands with a heavy thud at Ning's feet. She looks down at it, confused. The fish gasps for air on the shore, but Kang still keeps his attention on the water. The ripples seem to be moving faster, the waves growing stronger, spilling over the shores of the river and onto the rocky bank.

He watches with disbelief as the flailing fish twists and throws itself at Huayu. Ning yelps and pulls him away. The fish's unnatural, large teeth clamp on to the edge of Huayu's tunic.

Kang leaps into action. He picks up the fishing rod where it has fallen onto the stones and hits the fish until it lets go, and then he uses the end to sweep it away.

There are more thuds. More fish bodies strike the ground around them. The fish jerk, snapping. Instead of fangs, their yellow, humanlike teeth glisten in the light. They gnash together, grinding, wanting to tear them apart. Their eyes pale white. Rotten. They latch on to the bamboo rod, the *scratch-scritch* sound of their teeth gnawing against the bamboo is an awful noise. The rod snaps in his hand, bent under the weight of so many fish.

"Get away from the water!" Kang yells, and runs toward the mountainside, ushering the girl and the man with him.

"My brother!" Huayu protests, pointing to the bridge.

The bridge is white in the distance, having somehow manifested out of thin air. A figure stands on top of it, gesturing frantically at the three of them, calling out for help.

Huayu suddenly spins out of Ning's grasp and runs toward the bridge.

"We have to save him!" he cries out. "We have to save him from these monsters!"

Kang lunges forward, and his fingers find the edge of his tunic; it's enough to slow the man down. Ning pulls him back as well, and it's a tug-of-war, two against one, as Huayu struggles against them.

One of the fish flies out of the water and latches on to Ning's arm. She yelps in pain, and Kang grabs it in his hand. Its cold and slippery body crunches in his fist. He wrenches it away from her, and it comes away with ripped fabric, blood, and skin in its mouth. The sight seems to snap Huayu out of his desperate trance, and he stares down at Ning's bloody wound in horror.

"That's not your brother!" Kang yells at him as the wind continues to pick up, churning the water into a frenzy, whipping droplets into their face and their hair.

"Your brother left at sixteen! You have to remember!" Ning pleads with him, wet strands of hair in front of her eyes.

Huayu stands there, panting. He looks down at his hands and then back up at them.

"What's happening?" he asks. Before their eyes, the plumpness, the shine of youth in his cheeks, grows gaunt. He looks taller, but thinner, stretched out—more like the man lying in the sickbed.

"You were poisoned." Ning reaches out for him again. "Your mother is waiting for you to return."

"Poisoned?" he repeats slowly. Unable to comprehend, unable to align his understanding of reality with this dreamscape around him.

Kang still hears wet, sloshing sounds behind them, and he turns to see the swarm of fish piling up on the water. Before his eyes, he watches the pile grow bigger and bigger, gathering itself into a larger form. It morphs into a grotesque, writhing shape, built of many eyes and fins and gills and moaning mouths . . .

Ning is still begging Huayu to come with them.

"Look at this!" Kang yells to get his attention. "You're poisoned! You're dreaming! You will be devoured if you do not come with us!"

The stench of decay and dead flesh wafts toward them on the wind.

"Huayu . . ." The voice is suddenly all around them. *"You abandoned me . . ."*

The great, writhing mass of fish grows into an elongated body, a diamond-shaped head . . . a serpent that unfolds before them.

"Time to go," Ning whispers, and she tows Huayu along with her. Kang follows, running after them into the forest. Branches break under their feet and hands as they struggle to pull themselves up the steep path. The trees shake and shudder around them.

They break out onto the side of the mountain, a flat part of the path that will lead them away. Kang spares a glance behind him, and all he sees are the quaking trees as the massive form of the serpent snaps the foliage under his body.

Before him, Ning and Huayu have stopped. Ning has her hands

against his forearms, and Kang sees black tendrils make their way up his shuddering form. Huayu's eyes have rolled to the back of his head, showing only the whites. He falls to his knees, taking Ning with him. Leaves cascade around them like rain.

"He's dying!" Ning cries out desperately. "I can't hold him together enough to use the antidote! Kang, I need your help!"

He reaches out for her. Their fingers close the distance, touch, and he feels the pull of her magic.

More lines appear on Huayu's skin, gray streaks spreading through his black hair. The tendrils tighten around his flesh, leave him gasping for air.

It doesn't . . . hurt, not really. The warmth of her magic pulls out whatever energy, whatever essence, he has within him, to join it with hers. Huayu and Ning begin to glow, then Kang realizes the glow is coming from him, too. From his chest and down his arm to meet Ning's, then to her heart, then from her arm down to Huayu. She's sharing that energy somehow, conducting it among them.

The serpent is almost on them, but he screeches, recoiling from the light. The black tendrils pull away, releasing Huayu, dropping back down into the earth. The world rumbles around them, cracks, and falls apart.

Kang shuts his eyes.

Chapter Thirty-One

Ning 寧

I return to the dim room. Sweat slicks my back, my breathing harsh. Kang gasps beside me, and when I look down, I see the remnants of magic still glowing between us. Linking me to both. I let my hands fall to my sides.

Beside us, Huayu lets out a weak, shaky gasp.

Wenyi's mother cries out. I stand up, stepping back to allow her to reunite with her son. I sway, almost fall, but Kang catches me. For a moment, I lean against him, feeling the solidity of his body, his heartbeat against my ear. Reminding me that I am back again. That the world is real and that we are no longer in that cold, colorless place.

Until I remember where I am, and I look up at him. He looks down at me with an unreadable expression. The magic pulses between us. It is no longer the draw of the Golden Key, no longer the soul-digging compulsion of the Silver Needle. It just . . . recognizes him.

I know you.

The sound of Huayu coughing disrupts that closeness, and I push myself away, even as the room spins. I steady myself on a table.

"The two of you . . . ," he says, voice hoarse, but eyes clear. His gaze sweeps to Kang and then back to me. "You were in my dream."

"This is the shénnóng-shī who said she would cure you of the poison," his mother says, giving me a grateful look.

"Let me check on you." I take a step toward him and then nod at Madam Lin, who does not seem to want to let her son go. "If I may."

"Yes, of course." She steps back but still hovers, not wanting to take her eyes off her son.

I help Huayu sit up on the bed, supporting himself with one arm. The other arm I gently take into my lap, and then I read his pulse. His heartbeat is strong and steady under my fingers, a regular rhythm. It will take time for the poison to be cleared from his body fully, but he is here. Sitting before me, breathing and talking. That is all I can ask for.

"I remember now. My brother was sent to Yěliŭ years ago, but did he return while I was . . . away? Is he here now? Can I see him?" Huayu looks around eagerly. I drop his hand and look toward his mother for help. It wouldn't be right for me to tell him. She sits down next to him, but her eyes beg me to say the words for her.

Huayu looks at us, bewildered. "What?"

"Your brother . . . your brother is dead," Madam Lin says gently.

"But . . . you said that wasn't him!" His gaze cuts into mine, wounded, accusatory. "In my dream. You said he was just away!"

"I did tell you the truth," I say to him. "He went away, but then he came back to try to save you, and now he is gone. That spirit in your dream was a component of the poison. It draws out the memories of those you care for. Feeds on your loss and your grief."

"Wenyi . . . ," Huayu barely manages to say before he starts to weep, shoulders shaking with his sobs.

"I think the two of you should leave now." Madam Lin looks toward us, a gentle request. "Huayu needs to rest."

"You said you would tell me how to get to the Hermit." I pause, then add softly, "Please."

She looks down at her son in her arms and back up at me again. I am reminded how my mother loved me and Shu. How she would have given anything to protect us.

"There is a single willow tree that grows on a protruding section of the cliff looking over Bǎiniǎo Gorge, just north of town. The legend is, if you seek the Hermit, you should go there and make your request. If she finds you worthy, she'll answer."

"Thank you." I bow my head, and we take our leave, giving mother and son space to grieve together.

Kang and I are quiet on the way back to the inn.

The serpent knew I was in Huayu's head. I sensed his draw to my magic while I was in the Shadow Realm. It's a sign of things to come, just as the astronomer said. It makes me a danger to those I am around.

When we step through the door to our room, fatigue rushes over me. There's not much time left until morning, and we will have to set out to find the Hermit.

Kang stops me. "Your arm."

I look down to where the serpent cut into me with his fangs. The skin is still closed, the scar jagged but whole.

"No, over here." He points to a hole in my sleeve, from which ragged threads dangle. "Here, let me help you."

He leads me to the set of bamboo chairs and table in the corner of the room, ignoring my protests. From his own pack he produces a box that contains bandages and various stoppered vials labeled with names of different tinctures. I watch him as he carefully cuts away the fabric with a knife, peeling it away from my skin. I hiss when the fabric grazes my open wound.

When it's revealed, I see the indentations of the teeth. The serpent hurt me again through the Shadow Realm. Astronomer Wu said he wanted to bring back his reign of darkness, to send monsters crawling over the earth. It would seem I've just met another of his abominations.

When the fish bit me, something connected in my mind, a flash of some other memory. One that didn't belong to me. *The chancellor kneels before me, emanating the intoxicating scent of fear. He will ensure my plan is complete. Black tendrils encircle his head, entering his ears and his eyes and his nose. He tries to scream, but no sound comes out…*

Kang grimaces, and he looks up, meeting my eyes. The connection still hums between us, and I know he also caught that fragment of memory. The confirmation that the chancellor is the messenger of the serpent.

"You already know," I say, surprised.

"I had my suspicions," he says. "In the palace, I followed the wǔlín-shī and saw that they had an unnatural connection to the chancellor, that they were under his control. But I did not know how he controlled them."

"Using the shadows," I whisper, knowing exactly what he means.

He holds my gaze for another moment, then turns his attention to my wound. "Be still," he tells me.

Around the teeth marks, my skin is bruised purple. The sight of the wound causes my arm to throb in response, and I wince at the pain.

I watch Kang pour the contents of one vial over the wound, cleaning it. Then from another vial, he taps out a powdered substance onto my arm. It must be some sort of numbing substance, because the pain fades to a dull ache.

"It looks like you've done this before," I comment.

"Part of being on the battlefield," he says, giving me a grin. "Done."

A fleeting thought brushes against my mind: *If only we had met at a different time. If we were different people.* His expression suddenly turns serious again, and I wonder if it is my thought or an echo of his.

He opens his mouth to speak, but I don't want to listen. "This treasure we must obtain from the Hermit," I say to him. "Do you know what it is?"

He hesitates, pulling away. I sense his obvious reluctance, and I am reminded again of my role and his. Him, the captor, and me, the prisoner.

"It's a relic from the time of the First Emperor," he says finally. "A crystal orb they call the Night-Illuminating Pearl."

Another folktale, a story that belonged in the pages of *Wondrous Tales from the Celestial Palace*. When the First Emperor united the various warlords that ruled over sections of the fragmented empire, it was said the Jade Dragon showed himself to the court. As the shimmering dragon encircled the hall, the orb descended from the sky, into the hands of the First Emperor. It was then that all the warlords and his officials bowed to him, touching their foreheads to the ground in awe, for anyone so touched by the gods must be the destined ruler of Dàxī. It was lost years later, after the First Emperor passed. There are legends, however, that if one emerges with the orb in hand, then they are the rightful ruler of Dàxī.

"You saw the reality of what was in the poison. The same poison that affected my sister. Those who consume it are trapped, wandering in a living nightmare," I say softly. "This is what your father has permitted the people to suffer in his pursuit of power."

"He would not be happy to hear he has been manipulated through magical influence," Kang insists. "I will find a way to ensure he listens. He will be outraged when he finds out the truth."

We regard each other, neither of us willing to give in. He believes the chancellor is the source of the corrupting influence, but I am uncertain if the general is already too far in his grasp.

It doesn't matter what Kang shared with me in the Shadow Realm, giving me some of his essence to strengthen my link with Huayu. It doesn't matter how often he tells me all he wants is the truth.

The distance between us is as vast as any gorge, and I don't know if it can even be mended.

Chapter Thirty-Two

Ning 寧

In the morning, I expect Ren and Badu to regard me with suspicion, either having sensed the magic I worked on them in the night or my late-night activities revealed to them by Kang. But both soldiers make small jokes at each other's expense over breakfast as though nothing is amiss.

Kang and I are mostly quiet as we eat our food. We blow on the surface of the steamed soup dumplings held up to our mouths with a spoon, then use our chopsticks to pierce the thin skin. The broth bubbles out, coating the bottom of the spoon in a rich golden hue. The filling is pork, chives, and finely chopped mushroom, which gives it an earthy fragrance.

When we set off for the gorge, Ren and Badu speculate about the existence of the Hermit. I sit behind Kang on the horse, again trying not to fall off as we head north out of town. Before leaving, I asked the innkeeper's daughter if there is a willow tree in the area. She gave me directions to a tree the locals refer to as the Wishing Tree, where the townspeople write their wishes on strips of paper and tie them to the branches. It seems like that is the best place to start.

"Could someone like that even exist?" Ren scoffs. "It's probably some old woman living in the woods that the children noticed and started attributing some strange stories to."

"Or she could be one of those practitioners of a lost magic, like in the tales told by traveling storytellers!" Badu seems eager to believe that such a person is real. "She's the only one left of her people, and so she vows to become the best practitioner of her art so she can avenge her clan."

Ren laughs. "You certainly have a wild imagination."

The trees continue to thin the higher we ascend. A light rain began to fall when we left the town, and as we approach the edge of the cliff, the air seems to get colder and the mist thickens. Tendrils of fog drape themselves over the branches of the trees like fabric.

We have to leave the horses here—if they were to step too close to the cliff's edge, we could all tumble down to the canyon below. Then there are only our footsteps on the path, and the creeping sinister fog, making it difficult to see.

"This mist . . . ," Badu whispers. "It's unnatural."

Unnatural. Like the chancellor's accusation against me. That I am no true follower of Shénnóng, that instead I practice a wicked deviation of his magic. But in his accusation, the chancellor had revealed a bit of himself, because I now know the poison is somehow related to the serpent. This means someone must have made a bargain with the god, accepted the promise of power to set him free. The answers to my questions seem to dangle just out of reach, lost in the depths of my mind's own fog. If the chancellor gave the poisoning scheme to the general, then . . . does the general know the evil he is working with? Or is he in the dark, as Kang seems to believe?

In the distance I see the shape of a great tree looming through the mist. It is taller than all the others surrounding it, with long, trailing branches like wisps of an old man's beard. Tied to its branches are fluttering strips of paper. The Wishing Tree.

"There," Kang whispers beside me, recognizing it as well. The knowledge Madam Lin exchanged with me for her son's life, but she did not say how to call the Hermit to me and how to let her know I am here. Only that I was to make my request and await the Hermit's judgment of my worthiness.

We are only ten paces from the tree when the fog deepens, obscuring it. We are wrapped in an opaque curtain of white and gray.

"Ning?" I hear Kang's voice, and I take a few tentative steps in his direction, but I don't find him. There's nothing but the swirling fog, even though I was certain there was a rock, waist high, somewhere nearby. I hear Badu and Ren shout each other's names, but they sound distant, far away.

"Kang?" I call out. I am careful where I place my feet because I know how close I am to the cliff's edge. But was it twenty paces? Or more? All I find is more dirt and rock. I lift my arm, stretching it out in front of my face. I can barely see the shape of my fingers. The shifting mist seems to take on strange, living shapes, like elderly women or water buffalo. Animals and figures, shadows and ghosts.

My fingers search for the pouch at my sash. Two dān left. Should I use one? If she is the shénnóng-shī of legend, if the chancellor sent other shénnóng-shī to try to speak with her, perhaps only with the use of my magic will she recognize me and respond to my call.

I don't hear anything anymore. Not the voices of the two

battalion soldiers or Kang. Not even the call of the animals who should be in the forest or the sound of the rain. There is only quiet, and my breathing suddenly sounds unbearably loud. I have to choose, and the more time Shu stays in the grasp of that power-hungry man, the greater the risk. He could have been lying to me all this time. The world spins, and I feel the onset of panic rising in my body.

I fumble for a dān, pulling it out. I place it under my tongue, and the moisture softens the outer shell. It crumbles, releasing the bitter taste of herbs and roots, and that sharp, almost painful, thrilling release of magic. I gather it, eyes closed, envisioning it taking shape around me, forming a ball of light between my hands. I'm surrounded by the calming scent of tea flowers, and I release the beacon upward, above my head and into the gorge. I hope she will see me.

Please, I need your help.

There is the sound of a flute, carried on the wind. For a moment, I'm filled with dread. Did I call the serpent to me again? I open my eyes and gasp. Without taking a step, without moving, somehow I have ended up under the willow tree. Its branches drape around me like strands of hair, brushing against my shoulders, tickling my ears. I reach out and touch the tree's bark, its trunk curved overhead like someone reaching down to embrace a child. My magic senses something inside, just out of reach. I draw out the power from the dān, sending it into the trunk: *Can you hear me?*

Suddenly there is a screech, the fluttering of wings. I look up to see a flock of birds darting out from the branches. Appropriate for the name of this place, Bǎiniǎo, the Gorge of One Hundred Birds. They fling themselves out toward the top of the gorge, and the fog parts to reveal a figure standing on the edge of the cliff. The sweet sound of the flute continues, played by this mysterious stranger. The birds swoop and dance in the air, dipping down and then leaping upward. Following the lead of the music.

I step away from the tree and toward the figure, wrapped in white, almost as if enrobed by the fog. Strands of white flow from her wide-brimmed hat, from the billowing sleeves and skirt, tangling around her legs. I chew the remnants of the dān, swallowing it, so I can speak.

"Are you the Hermit?" I ask, hesitantly approaching.

She turns, the veil obscuring her features. The flute drops from her lips, and yet its ghostly melody still plays. She reaches up and lifts the veil from her face, revealing dark, long-lashed eyes. A woman around my mother's age. Soft features, cool ivory skin, a full mouth. She's beautiful in a faded way, as if she belongs to a faraway time.

The woman examines me. I sense this is a being of great power. An echo of her is in the tree behind me, a web of her magic connecting her to each of those birds. She also controls the fog, causing part of the mountain to disappear.

I bow to her. "My name is Zhang Ning. I come from the province of Sù." I keep my head down as I speak, hoping she will see the importance of my appeal. "I've come to ask for your assistance in a serious matter."

I feel hands touch my arms, lifting me to stand upright.

"How peculiar, Ning of Sù." A familiar feeling—being watched, evaluated. "It looks like you have been touched by each of the gods . . ."

She lifts up my chin with her cold hand, tipping back my head, as if searching for a secret contained within. Inside her eyes, I see waves crashing onto the shore, the constant movement of the tides.

"Shénnóng's magic, that much is evident," she says, and once again the scent of flowers tickles my nose, the resultant tug of magic inside me flaring back to life. Like reacting to like.

"And yet . . ." Her hand goes to my hair, and then, when she pulls back, she's holding a feather in her grasp. "Her mark is on you as well. The Lady of the South." She lets the feather fall out of her hand, and the wind carries it away, tumbling into the distance.

"You've encountered those who bear the mark of the Black Tiger." Lines appear on her arms, the patterns similar to those who are Wŭlín-trained.

"Yĕliŭ as well. You were there." She seems to see everything. In her eyes, flames leap up. I recognize the brazier of the sacred fire. The one that is supposed to remain lit but has since fallen to ash since Yĕliŭ is no longer.

"I met your apprentice," I say to her. "Wenyi."

She casts her eyes down. The mist dampens my cheeks, as if the very air weeps with her. "I felt his presence depart from the earth, across a great distance. I sensed you were there as well, at the moment of his passing. I think you may have offered him some comfort in those final hours."

I choke back a sudden rise of sadness as the memory of the dungeons returns to me. The damp stone walls surrounding us, the bars that separated me from the young man I should have been able to save. A failure to the teachings of my father. One of many deaths that trail after me, never to be forgotten.

"Yes, death leaves a mark," she whispers, as if she hears my thoughts. "And you are still so young . . ."

"I'm here to save my sister," I tell her.

The Hermit turns then, her veil brushing delicately across my face. "Come with me."

She brings her flute back up to her lips, casting that sweet, sad sound across the gorge. The birds leap up from the canyon, too many to count. Their bodies form a bridge, crossing the gorge to the unknown, shrouded by mist. The path shifts and dances above the vast emptiness. One wrong step and I could easily fall through.

She steps off the rock and onto the bridge of birds, and I know I have to follow.

The birds shift under my feet but carry my weight so I am not dashed upon the rocks below. I am reminded of an old legend about an ill-fated love affair. A woman who lived among the stars, and the man who yearned for her on earth. They could reunite only once a year, when the stars aligned and a bridge of swallows brought them together.

"Ah, that was long ago," the Hermit says. Even though I see her up ahead, her voice sounds as if she is speaking clearly next to me. "Many of the legends had human forms once. Were human once . . ."

I don't quite know what she means. Perhaps she met the original cowherd and the weaver. I wonder if they have become gods, adrift somewhere in the endless, starry sea.

The shape of another cliff appears before us, and then we are off the swaying bridge and back onto solid rock. I look behind us and see only the empty gorge. The birds are gone. I turn around, and a stone pavilion has appeared in the mist. The fog is still thick, muting everything around us. A tree grows out of the center of the stone, its canopy the roof, its trunk old and gnarled. Beside it is a circular wooden table carved from a section of tree, its whorls and golden hues captured on its smoothed surface. The base still retains the pattern of bark. Four stone stools sit around it. On top of the table is a tea set.

My feet ascend the steps leading up to the pavilion, and to the right I hear the tinkling sound of water. Peering over the edge, I see stacked piles of rock. A cascading waterfall, spilling into a dark pool. Shapes swim underneath the water, a flash of red and white. Koi. But my stomach flutters, remembering the vicious fish that almost tore us apart in the Shadow Realm. I reach out and touch the stone railing hesitantly. It feels solid, the edges of the carved leaves and flowers rough against my palms.

"You'll drink with me?" her voice calls out, and I turn back to her. She lifts the hat off her head and sets it on the edge of the table. Her hair is pinned loosely away from her face, falling down her back in a dark stream. I sit across from her, watching her as she prepares the tea.

So much of our daily lives can be measured in cups of tea. It's how we wake up in the morning, how we greet our guests, how we accompany our meals. How my father's patients, my mother's patrons, thanked them for their work.

I bring the cup to my nose. The fragrance that reaches me is lightly green, like the smell of gathered tea leaves still wet with the morning dew. It tastes delicate and fruity on my tongue, wound with an essence of hope. The magic bursts inside me, and in response, a sharp pain, cutting down my forearm. The cup falls from my hand, landing on the table with a thud.

I gasp out an apology, but she is there beside me, too fast for me to see her move. She grips my wrist with an inhuman strength, running her fingertip down my arm. Where her touch grazes against the still-healing scar, it burns.

"I almost didn't see it," she murmurs. "An old magic, something I haven't encountered for a long, long time . . ."

She gazes down at the scar, and then in her hand, I see the flash of a blade.

"This is going to hurt," she warns me.

The knife parts my flesh before I even have a chance to scream.

Chapter Thirty-Three

Ning 寧

The scar is opened. But no blood wells up as I expect. Instead, there is only a gaping hole. The pain is still there, but through it, there is a sensation of something moving under my skin, that awful, squirming feeling I've experienced time and time again.

Her fingers plunge into the open wound, and I have to look away as bile rises in my throat, my vision darkening. I feel pulling, something still trying to cling to my arm, and I sense each and every tug of the struggle to get it to release from my body. Then, finally, I am free from it.

I force myself to turn back. Through my tears, I see a dark, wriggling shape. It's a centipede, venomous, its many legs moving in the air. Its color is a deep, dark red, as if it has been feasting on my blood this whole time. Revulsion rises again at the back of my throat as the Hermit dangles its plump body from her fingertips.

"It feeds on the life force of the living," she says mildly, as if it were nothing more than a common household pest. "But it loves the taste of magic. It savors it."

"Is this what was in the poisoned tea bricks?" I ask her.

"Similar," she tells me. "All his abominations carry a part of him. A drop of the venom that drips from his fangs. You simply experienced it directly from the source."

A different type of magic. It thrashes in her hand, trying to curl in on itself, writhing. I sense another flare of her magic, and red strands, like silk, unravel from the centipede's body, until it shrivels into a husk of itself and stops moving. With a wave of her other hand, the wind carries the husk away, scattering it into dust. The threads of red magic also dissipate into the wind.

"He won't be able to follow you any longer." She pours herself another cup of tea and drains it, then she makes a face, as if the taste has been affected.

"That was a piece of the serpent's magic *inside* me?" My skin crawls, as if I can still feel its presence. I was pierced by the serpent's fangs when I was in Shu's dream—that must have been when he infected me with his venom. It would be why the serpent could feel me every time I used my magic, how the shadow soldiers always knew where I was. The Hermit nods, confirming my suspicions as if I'd said them aloud.

"Thank you," I say to her, grateful. "Could I please have your name? So I may know how to address you."

"You can call me Lady An." She inclines her head. Reaching over, she places the hat back on her head, the veil once again falling over her face and her shoulders. "Come with me, and we'll get that wound cleaned and sealed."

I stand and follow. She leads me down a path that curves around the stone pavilion. A little down the path, we come to a lattice structure to the right, almost groaning under the weight of gourds of various sizes, covered with climbing vines. To the left is another dense tangle of greenery, something I wouldn't think possible to grow this high up in the mountains. The mist still drifts through here, trailing through the verdant growth. A wild place, like someone had lived here once and let nature reclaim it.

Bending over, Lady An picks up a large, curved sickle resting against a tree. She steps under the lattice and chops down a gourd, which she hands me to carry. She also chops off the green tops of a few vines, dropping them into a waiting basket at her feet. Picking up the basket, she wades into a lush herb garden that grows past the lattice. The herbs grow so densely that they brush her calves, reaching almost to her knees. With practiced hands, she pulls and tugs at what she needs, and the earth gives up the plants willingly.

There's another structure up ahead. A bamboo cabin, a make-shift kitchen built beside it. There is a shelf against the side of the cabin, a brick stove, and a large wooden table on the center of the platform. She lifts a slab of wood from where it was resting against the wall and places it on the table. She sharpens a cleaver against a stone and then uses it to chop the leaves on the block. The pieces are then thrown into a waiting stone bowl, and using a pestle, she mashes it into paste. She gestures for me to extend my arm, and I obey.

Carefully, she seals the wound with a thin layer of the green paste. Lowering her head, she blows onto the surface gently, and I feel that sensitive shift. The tingle running over my skin that tells me magic is being infused. Using a long strip of fabric, she wraps the poultice tight against my skin and ties it off in a knot. I wiggle my fingers. Everything is still working as it should.

"You know how to use a knife in the kitchen?" she asks. I respond in the affirmative. I was raised to always be another helping hand in the household. I was given tasks ever since I was young and able to walk, to gather firewood for the stove or prepare ingredients for the apothecary or assist with the evening's meal. She hands me another wooden block to use as a cutting board, instructing me to chop the gourd into pieces.

Splitting the gourd open, I recognize it as a winter melon by the pale green innards and the flat white seeds. I cut it into chunks as wide as silver pieces. Lady An returns with an earthen pot for me to place the pieces in and then scatters aromatics around it, smashed cloves of garlic and slices of ginger. Looking around, I see the signs of a well-used kitchen. Tools hung within reach on the walls. Dried cloves of garlic and chilis hanging from the roof, appearing like massive bouquets of white and red. I'm given green beans to peel as she works on the contents of another clay pot. When she lifts the lid after a while, I smell the strong scent of soy sauce, sesame oil, and basil. Three cup chicken.

My hands are kept busy as Lady An directs me to stir this or chop that, but my dread grows, knowing I have so many questions I need to ask her. Whether she is, indeed, the shénnóng-shī of legend, the one who advised the emperor that a darkness was coming. If she could lend her assistance to us in these dark times, to prevent an old god from awakening. But there never seems to be an appropriate time to say anything as the meal comes together around us.

The table is cleared, the place settings ready. The bubbling pots are set on the surface, and we eat. What I thought was three cup chicken is actually made with meaty chunks of oyster mushrooms, drenched in the salty, rich sauce. There is a sweetness to the soup, a nice counterbalance to the spiciness of the green beans. I eat some of the food, but as I am aware of the passing of time, I know I have to speak up, even if I may be seen as insolent and disrespectful.

"Begging your pardon, Lady An." I set my chopsticks down. "I am grateful for your hospitality, but I would like to speak to you about the reason I have disturbed your rest."

She sips at her sweetened wine, which I had declined because I wanted to keep my wits about me. I don't know what sort of challenge she could present in order for me to receive her assistance, and I have to be alert.

"Let me tell you a story about the one who marked you with his venom," she says. She takes another long drink of the plum wine, and looking up, I see the moon reflected in her eyes. With a start, I cast my eyes up to the sky as well. When did the moon rise? And how is it so bright and full? I feel a flash of alarm. How much time has passed? What if the chancellor has decided I've run away and is about to execute Shu and Brother Huang?

"Do not worry," she says to me, reading my agitation. "We have time yet, I promise you."

I force myself to sit still and listen. What is the flow of time to someone who can call down so much magic? I have to be patient.

"You know the story of the serpent, that it took the efforts of all the gods to subdue him." She continues when I nod. "Each of them offered a component of their power. From Shénnóng, a silver scale. From the crown of Bi-Fang, a feather. A claw from the God of Thunder, and the shell of Bìxì. The feather reached across a great distance and pulled him within the reach of the rest. The shell bound him so that he could not use his elemental powers to break free from their bindings. The scale landed on the seat of his magic, sealed it so that he is trapped in his human form. Finally, using the Tiger's claw, they cut out his left eye, and the Jade Dragon threw it into the Eastern Sea. They tore out his femur and shaped it into a sword, hid it in the mountains. And finally, they cut out his heart, which sank to the depths of a lake, where it lay undisturbed for many years."

A familiar story, but each time I hear it, different details emerge.

"Know and remember his name," she says. "Gongyu."

I repeat it, acknowledging the weight behind it.

"The bone sword was eventually found, and it spilled a river of blood across the empire before it was subdued and hidden again. The people of the north built a tower to contain its terrible power," Lady An goes on. "The crystal heart was found when humans began building their settlements, constructing dams and rerouting rivers. It was part of the founding of Dàxī, yes, but it also resulted in the massacre of innocents. Gongyu appeared as a corrupting vision, taking on the form of the Gold Serpent. He attempted to lure others into completing his plan. That is when I was called. I stole the heart from the court, and I was asked if I was willing to leave the human world behind. That is the price of becoming its guardian."

The ageless woman regards me with great seriousness. "But now, the winds have shifted yet again in his favor. The jade eye has been found, and Gongyu's insistent whispers have led the one who carries it to the bone sword. Now he needs the crystal heart to rise again and to consume a thousand human souls to return to his human form. The same vile magic he once cast to walk the earth."

I realize what this means. What I must ask of her. The cost of saving my sister.

Lady An smiles. "I was told to wait, until the time comes, until the right person asks the right questions.

"I've been waiting for you, Zhang Ning . . . for a long, long time."

Chapter Thirty-Four

Ning 寧

"Why would you welcome me?" I ask Lady An. I know she is aware of what I have come to ask of her. The very thing she protects, which could result in the ruin of the world.

She shakes her head, still smiling. "You do not understand. You are the one who will take it away."

"Why?" I ask her, horrified at the very thought. How could I possibly carry that burden with me? To be so selfish to take the heart and give it to the chancellor just to save my sister and myself, but to doom the rest of the world.

"You are someone who is not quite in this world but not quite out of it," she says. She speaks in riddles, and I cannot keep up.

"I suppose now that the gods have been away from the world for so long, their knowledge is quickly disappearing." Lady An sighs. "The monks sequester themselves in their monasteries, limiting those who would study in their academies. They hide behind their high gates, shutting themselves away from the rest of the empire. They believe themselves to be representatives of the gods, and yet neglect their duty to the people they are supposed to protect."

"You heard the calling of the gods and you responded to them . . . Are you a god then? An immortal?" I ask. "Could you return to the human world to fight Gongyu?"

"The gods shared with me only a fragment of their power, but when they fought Gongyu, they lost much of it." She turns her face up to the moon again; the corners of her lips pull down with sadness. "There is not much left. The crystal heart holds this place together, and when it is gone, I will be gone as well."

"But . . . I can't . . ." If saving one life means the death of another, how can I justify it? What is the worth of one life, even if willingly given?

"You must!" Her voice thrums with power. "When Yěliŭ fell, I felt it. When Hánxiá was corrupted, I felt it, too. A great pain. Each time the poison spreads, the land grows weaker and his hold grows stronger. He's been waiting for a long time . . ."

"What if . . . what if I am the one to stay here?" I throw out the only option that is available to me, the only alternative I can offer. "What if you return to the human world in my place? Let me guard the heart instead." With so much power inside her, she is stronger than me, and she can stop Gongyu.

Lady An throws back her head and laughs. "Oh, child . . . ," she says with amusement. "You do not know what precious thing you have offered me, but you are not meant to bear this burden. You may crave a life of isolation, believing it will bring you peace, but the magic that holds this place together is already unraveling. Even if I wish to pass this to you, I cannot, and I would not wish this fate upon anyone."

"But . . ." I cannot bear it. "All I want is to save my sister. I want her to be able to commune with Shénnóng, like she was once able to." Her missing magic, the unbearable void inside her. I want everything to return to the way it once was. I want the impossible.

Lady An shakes her head. "Do you not understand? Magic does not belong to Shénnóng. It is not unique to one god or the other.

Those are human terms, human rules. All magic is the same. It is only the vessel that shapes it."

I am reminded of the feather that appeared out of nowhere when we had need of it. The wings of fire.

"You will figure out a way to save her," Lady An says to me. "The bond of family is a kind of magic all its own."

She stands, swaying a little on her feet, cheeks flushed from the wine. "Follow me. The moon is bright tonight."

The ground dips as we walk the slightly slanted path that continues past the bamboo house. There's a pond back here, covered in water lilies. Their round leaves float serenely, blooms swaying in the breeze. Bending down, Lady An gently extracts a bloom from a lily pad, murmuring a word of thanks. The heads of the other blooms bow to her in turn. With the lily in hand, she walks to a small rock face dripping with ivy, and there, in the shadows, is the opening of a cave.

"I ask you, Ning of Sù." The way she pronounces my name seems to send a reverberation within me. Like she is asking me to make a choice that could alter the destiny of everyone in Dàxī. Like I am no longer responding to a question about my own fate, or even the fate of my family. It will touch everyone I know, everyone I've loved and lost, everyone I've saved and everyone I've failed. "Will you do what is required of you, even if the path ahead is uncertain?"

In her hand, she cups the flower.

Her words give me hope. She says there is a way ahead, where I may find what I am looking for.

"Yes," I breathe. If this is what the gods have asked of me, then I will do it. Lady An offered up her life as a sacrifice, years of waiting, while all the people she cared about faded away from her. I can do the same.

"The cave will try to speak to you, but ignore the voices, even if they sound familiar. You'll find a pool at the center, where the heart resides. Reach in." She blows a puff of magic into her hand. It turns into a ball, shining with unearthly light. Tipping her hand, she settles it into the fully opened bloom of the water lily, where it emanates a pink glow. "Call him by name, and his heart will answer."

Gongyu. Even the thought of his name seems to make the air around me tremble. She offers the flower to me, and I accept it into my cupped hands. It is warm but not unbearable. A pleasant heat.

I carry it with me toward the darkness of the cave, toward whatever is waiting for me in its depths.

I follow the path into the cave. It leads me deeper, the earth sloping downward. I spare a glimpse behind me, at the silhouette of Lady An framed by moonlight, and it gives me the strength to continue. It doesn't take long until the light from the opening reaches me no more, and only the glow of the flower in my hands illuminates the path ahead. The walls of the cave are wet with moisture, and the rocks under my feet are slippery. There is the sound of dripping water in the distance. Holding the flower up to the rocks, the light catches on something sparkling within the stone.

I continue the descent, and the path narrows until I feel as if I am being entombed, the earth heavy above me. My breath starts to frost in the air, and my tunic suddenly feels too thin for the chill that emanates from the walls. The stone around me seems to change in color, the sparkle more pronounced until it grows into shards of crystal embedded in the rock, some the size of my forearm, others the size of my fist. Many reflective surfaces, catching the light in strange ways.

Movement, out of the corner of my eye.

I spin around, and I see nothing but sparkling rock. I bite my lip and keep walking, faster.

I hear whispers then. More movement, skittering at eye level, but when I look, there is only my own face looking back, reflected in the crystal. The sound of weeping echoes through the tunnel, then . . . the chant of a prayer. The voices emerge from the stone, growing louder the farther I walk.

"Mother?"

"I'm so sorry . . ."

"I didn't know!"

". . . not my fault . . ."

"Forgive me!"

Someone recites a snippet of poetry. A woman hums a fragment of a song.

In this place there are only ghosts.

Who is trapped in here? Are they real or imaginary?

In my haste to get to the center of the cave, my foot slips on a protrusion of stone, and I steady myself against the wall. It's sharper than I expected. My hand comes away bloody.

"She's alive?"

"She's alive!"

"Save us!"

"Help us!"

The light reveals human shapes behind the shimmering, translucent crystals. Fists and splayed hands beat against the walls, the force of their blows causing the walls to rumble and shake. I start to run. The voices follow, pleading with me to listen, begging me to save them. I keep running, and I'm reminded of all that I am. Touched by many gods. Intended for something else. Ning. Sister. Daughter. Friend.

The tunnel before me widens into a cavern no bigger than my family's home. There is a pool at the center, as Lady An promised. I stop at the edge of the water, and the flower rises from my hands. I watch, marveling at the sight. The flower drifts over to the middle of the pool and descends until it rests on the surface of the water. The petals begin to fall, one by one, sinking into the dark. Until the light that remains sinks as well and disappears.

My turn now.

I tentatively put my hand into the pool and am rewarded with the feeling of *cold*. So unbearably cold. My hand grows numb with the chill. I force myself to push my arm deeper, and it feels as if it is peeling away my skin, until my arm feels like a raw nerve.

You're weak. You're not enough. Give in. The doubts return, nibbling at the corners of my mind. *Give up. Lie here. Let the walls consume you. Become one of the spirits. Just close your eyes. Let the rest of the empire burn. Let it all succumb to the serpent. The chancellor will smile behind the general on the dragon throne. He will force everyone to obey.*

The voices of everyone trapped in this cave rise to a cacophony. So much anger, desire, lust, pride. Neighbors killing neighbors. Brothers stealing from brothers. People cheating. Lying. In the shénnóng-shī trials, we extolled the virtues, but here . . . this place is an altar to all the vices.

I am filled with a deep, seething rage. I deserve to be accepted. Free of this realm of nightmares. They never remember me during their waking hours. They curse me, curse my name. While others obtain shrines, devotees, worshipped by their many followers. When is it my turn?

It takes all my strength not to pull myself away from that water, free myself from that painful longing, the so very human emotions exhibited by one of the gods. He wants to be celebrated. He wants to be loved. He wants to move through a world of color. He wants to feel, taste, smell, see. He is no longer sustained by so little of the human experience. What he wants most of all is to be fully and utterly and completely human, something just out of reach, and he is willing to take it by force if he must.

The orb glimmers under the surface. The water moves as if it has a life of its own, sliding up my arm, toward my shoulder, creeping up my hair. It remembers my fear of the water, having grown up far from the sea, and the time I fell into the spring—the suffocating pain when the water flooded my lungs and my mouth and my nose and choked me. But I cannot be afraid.

Reach in.

I take a deep breath and plunge my head into the water. The shock of the cold overwhelms me. I force my eyes to open wide, even as my whole body is racked with shivers. Under the water, the light is somehow brighter. The weight of the water pulls me down, and I spread my arms and legs out. I should float, but instead, I fall deeper into the pale blue. Above me, there is nothing but black.

Darkness above, bright below.

The petals float around me, suspended in the water.

"When the Gold Serpent finally fell from the sky, his blood dotted the lakes and ponds of Dàxī like rain," I murmur to myself, remembering that water lilies are born from the blood of the serpent. They are a part of him, and yet the water lilies speak to me, too. They all point toward where the light is falling, at the very bottom of the pool. Where the crystal orb rests, emitting a light of its own. I stretch out my hand, send out a tendril of magic, along with a name. *Gongyu.*

The water grows warm around me, rippling. The orb flares with a bright light and floats up toward me until I can grasp it in my hand.

The wŭlín-shī I've ensnared, puppets following my directions. They will ensure my plan is set.

The chancellor I've bent to my will. Through him I will achieve the peak of my human form. The pinnacle of existence.

I will achieve perfection.

Half human, half god.

I lift my head out of the water and find that I am kneeling on the bottom of the pool. It cannot be more than knee high. Around me, the shimmering walls of the cave are now dark. The shadows are no longer behind them.

"It's time . . . it's time . . ." I hear the faint cries of whatever spirits or memories were trapped in the cave fade away. The dreams and nightmares that held this place together are finally free.

When I emerge from the cave, it is snowing. Large flakes float from the sky, settling on my shoulders, on the rocks and plants around us. Lady An waits for me at the start of the path, by the bamboo house. The beautiful woman with still youthful features is now gone. She has grown gaunt and pale, her face lined and weary. But the smile she gives me is genuine and unburdened. White hair flows around her shoulders, soft and fine.

I do not want this. This heavy, glowing burden in my hands. I don't want any part of this treasure. I'm filled with the bitterest regret.

"It is not a bad thing to want," she says.

"How will we be able to defeat him if he has this? Once he comes back, once he returns fully into his power?" I ask her.

"He wants to be human. Let him . . . *indulge*," she says dreamily.

But I don't understand. Why would we *give* him his power?

Lady An grows paler, her hair silver now, as if lit up by the moon. Her skin grows translucent, until I see through her to the trees beyond.

"You were willing to give up your life for your sister, and I sense the power of your love held inside your beating heart. To be human is to be vulnerable. To be human is to have more power than the gods will ever wield, Ning. Never forget that."

"What?" I ask again. "How? I need you to teach me!"

"Use what the gods have left for you. Remember, the relics contained him once. Give him what he wants . . ."

She clasps my hands in hers, the barest brush of warmth, and then she's gone.

Chapter Thirty-Five

Kang 康

The fog swept in hard and fast, and they all disappeared into it. Ning. Badu. Ren. Until he is left wandering alone in a world of shifting shapes. It reminds him of that awful place, what Ning called the Shadow Realm. Where he saw an abomination that shouldn't have existed, and a man age before his eyes.

Kang continues to call out for his companions, but he is surrounded by trees and rock. He could not find the cliff's edge, which would lead him back to the road, and he could not find the horses. He is alone on the mountain, with only his thoughts, and he finds he is poor company.

There is too much time to doubt. Kang proved his worth to the people of Lǜzhou. He gained their respect. He left Lǜzhou believing in his father's cause—even if he didn't agree with his methods, he knew sacrifices had to be made for the people. Seeing the effects of those sacrifices for himself . . . he wasn't so sure any longer. How could he justify the use of a poison that not only destroyed the body but the mind as well?

Could he face his beloved teacher if he is able to release him from the chancellor's influence? Could he look into Teacher Qi's eyes and tell him he followed his tenets, made himself worthy of the Black Tiger?

Having lost all sense of time and direction, Kang is relieved when he finally sees the willow tree. He eagerly runs toward it.

A sudden gust almost blows him off his feet, and he watches with shock as the wind strips the branches bare. He's engulfed by hundreds of paper knots, carrying the wishes of everyone who came before him, like the wings of a thousand birds taking flight. A few of the pieces of paper slice across his forehead, and he throws his arm up to protect his eyes.

The paper knots are swept away by the wind, lost to the gorge, taking the fog with it. When Kang drops his arm, he sees a figure kneeling underneath the tree. The tree shivers, branches dark against the white of the sky. Before, it was covered in trailing tendrils of green. Now it is brittle, shedding curled brown leaves.

He takes a hesitant step forward, and a branch cracks under his foot. The figure looks up, and it's Ning. Her face covered in tears. He closes the distance between them. In her hands, she holds a luminous orb, the size of an egg.

"The Night-Illuminating Pearl," he whispers. "You found it."

She nods.

"How did you—" She struggles to her feet, and he steadies her. She looks lost and tired, like finding this treasure has taken a great toll on her body.

"How long was I gone?" she asks, voice hoarse.

"An hour, no more than two," he says. It is late afternoon, judging from the position of the sun in the sky.

"Good." Her shoulders sag with relief. She hands him the orb, as if she can't bear the sight of it. "Can you take this from me?"

Kang slips his pack off and unwinds a piece of fabric inside that was carrying the medicine flasks. He wraps the orb in the fabric until its shine disappears and puts it inside carefully.

"Leave the medicine out," Ning says to him. "You're bleeding."

"It's nothing," he says, touching his hand to his forehead. His fingers come away tinged with blood. "It was the wishes."

When the words leave his mouth, he realizes it is a peculiar thing to say, and when she looks at him, he knows she is thinking the same.

She smiles for a brief moment. "It's been a strange day indeed."

He sits down on a flat rock, and she crouches next to him so that they are looking at each other eye to eye. Sprinkling the pain-relieving powder into her hand, she dabs it onto the little paper cuts. It stings only a little. He watches her careful process and feels that sharp tug in his chest again. That unbearable, aching longing. But then she pulls away, and the connection is gone.

He has to ask. "You met the Hermit?"

"Yes, I did," she says, and that lost look returns to her expression. "On the other side of the gorge."

Kang looks out over the cliff's edge. The other side is a span of probably a quarter of a lǐ, an impossible distance for even a horse to jump. But he does not doubt her; she disappeared and reappeared before his eyes, carried away and returned by the fog.

"She's dead," she says. Kang doesn't know what to say to comfort her, if that is even what she wants. Instead, she looks up at him again, an undercurrent of emotion running through her voice. "You know what will happen when you give the Night-Illuminating Pearl to *him*."

It is not a question. It is a statement.

"It's a symbol," Kang says. "Of the reunification of the empire. When the First Emperor first made it so, and it will come to be again."

Ning laughs but it is a brittle sound. "Is that what Chancellor Zhou told you? This is no mere symbol. It's a great source of magic."

A symbol. A source of magic. It could be both. All he knows is that it will mean more people will die to secure the throne for his father.

Can you bear the weight of it?

"What if... we take it away? Hide it, find some other way to deceive him?" Kang asks.

"You would do that?" she asks. It stings, her questioning, but he has opposed her at every turn. It took him too long to believe her. Her own doubt is fair.

"You showed me what was on the other side. What happened to the people who are poisoned," he says. "Hundreds of people dead. Hundreds more living in that tormented state. I truly believe that my father is under the chancellor's influence, that he must be controlling his mind in some way as well. He has not been the same since my mother died, and the chancellor is too eager to fuel his desire for vengeance."

Her fingers suddenly grip his arm, so tight that it may bruise. She's so close.

"You want to save your father, and I want to stop the chancellor from completing his plan," she says. "You helped me before—I have to ask you to do it again. Because I have to believe that you want the best for the *people* of the empire, not only for the empire itself." Her words are fierce, uttered with an intensity that strikes him to his core.

"I want to help the people," he responds. "But I can't do that without knowing what you know. Will you tell me?"

His father has continually kept him in the dark. Trying to uncover the truth is like tangling himself further and further into a web, until there is no way to be free from it. He knows now that he must oppose his father's rule, even as Kang himself was tempted by the power offered to him. The ability to lead the battalion and gain the loyalty of all the soldiers, what he thought he should aspire to, but not at this price. So many dead, so many suffering. He realizes now: This future is not the one he wants.

Ning rocks back on her heels until she is sitting on the ground. Kang settles in, ready to hear her answer. Preparing himself to know the truth, if he can bear it.

"The prophesied darkness is here," she says, her voice grave. "Not long after the shaping of the world, there was the Jade Dragon and the Gold Serpent. The serpent rebelled against the other gods and wanted to rule over the humans, and for that he was punished. The serpent is returning to the world now. He wants to live again. The chancellor is the chancellor no longer. He has been possessed by the serpent. His soul may already be consumed."

"The magic in the orb . . . ," he says softly. "That will help him regain his power?"

Ning nods. "There are three treasures he must reclaim: his eye, his femur, and his heart. The jade eye, the bone sword, and the crystal orb."

Part of him wants to rebel against the thought that his father had a hand in this, the part that is still loyal to the general. The man who took him in, who raised him as his own. The realization brings him nothing but pain.

"You know something," she says sharply, noticing his reaction.

"I don't know if it is what you are speaking of, but . . . the chancellor carries two spheres of jade. He presented a sword made of bone to my father. Now . . ." He looks down at his pack, the orb contained within. "This must be the final piece. We cannot allow him to have it."

This is it, then. The destruction of Dàxī is at hand. The line has been drawn, and Kang must decide on which side he will stand. But Ning's next words surprise him.

"We have to bring it back to him," she says. "And it's not only because of my sister—"

"We can find some other way to save your sister. I promise you," he says, and he means it with every part of his body.

Ning gives him a soft look and shakes her head. "Lady An, the Hermit, said we must let him have it. It is only when he reaches his full power that he can be contained."

He senses the way she is torn about this, just as he is. He doesn't understand. "But, why? Did she give a reason?"

Ning pulls her lips into a grim line. "I don't understand it, either. Only that it is what we must do."

"Commander Li!" The voices of Ren and Badu erupt from the trees, getting closer.

Kang looks toward Ning with a question: *Ready?*

She gives him a decisive nod in return.

They will do this together.

Chapter Thirty-Six

Ning 寧

We find Badu and Ren and return to where we tethered our horses. They have been contentedly grazing on what little grass there is. I ride behind Kang as before, holding on to him as we return to town. I can still feel the eyes of the townspeople on us as we make our way past them. Fearful. Afraid. Distrustful of the empire's authority. I had hoped—before, in my ignorance—that the problems affecting my village were only because of my father's position and the governor's influence. Now I see how the rot has continued to grow, the darkness spreading.

Torches burn in the distance, illuminating the tents through the trees. The horses were pushed to ride in the remaining daylight, arriving just when it would have been too dark and dangerous to travel the mountain roads. Kang helps me down, beckoning for me to follow him as he leads the horse into the makeshift stables constructed on the edge of the camp. We keep our voices low so we cannot be heard over the animals' snorts and nickers.

"There is one more thing I should tell you before we go to the chancellor," he says. "I received word from my father that Zhen is marching on Jia with her forces. They will reach the capital soon. My father and the chancellor are preparing for something, but I don't know what."

I consider this. "I'm not sure how long it will take the serpent to fully come into his power once he has the three parts of his body. You said the general has the bone sword, so if the chancellor has the eye and the heart in his possession, then he has to join your father before the serpent can be made whole."

"You said he has to come into his power before he can be contained," Kang says. "But there is a way to stop him then?"

I walk a knife's edge. If I give him too much information, and he turns against me, then all of Dàxī will be thrown into darkness. And yet . . . I look at his earnest expression. I think about what Lady An said about being human. To want. To trust. To not have to do this alone.

I see Ren approaching. We've taken too long to talk.

"We'll speak of this soon," he says, and I remember his promise. The importance of his word.

I almost reach out to touch him, to catch his hand in my own. To tell him that I know what it costs him to believe me. Still, my hand remains at my side.

If we survive this, there is so much more I want to tell him. But not yet.

Ren leads me away from Kang and to the tent where we were held prisoner previously. He lifts up the flap, and I practically throw myself through, looking for that one figure I most wish to see, the one person who means more to me than all the world.

Shu looks up at me, startled, and with a cry, she flings herself against me.

"Are you all right?" I ask, looking her over to make sure they had not done anything to her while I was gone.

"I'm fine. They kept me in the tent, letting me out only to relieve myself," she says. "I haven't seen Brother Huang, though. They have not permitted us to talk with each other."

I let my breath out in a rush. I've made it back, even if I have brought back a terrible thing. I have kept up my end of the bargain, and now we will see if the chancellor will keep up his.

"You found it then, the treasure the chancellor is looking for." Shu looks at me, fearful. "What does this mean for us?"

"I don't know," I tell her. The truth from now on. To Shu, to Kang. I will not have my suspicions and doubts hold me back. I was distrustful of so many, put up walls, pushed people away. It got me nothing in return but pain.

I tell her all of what I encountered in the gorge. The wisdom Lady An imparted to me. The mission that will be fulfilled. I suspect we will soon be on the road to Jia as the chancellor's prisoners. At least we will be together.

"It sounds as if we still have a chance," Shu says, her continued optimism buoying me up. "We just have to figure out where the power of the gods is contained, like the challenges you solved during the shénnóng-shī trials."

It seems a lifetime ago when I survived those challenges. When Lian and I put our heads together and came up with answers to the puzzles. I have to believe Shu and I can do the same.

"You're right," I say. "Lady An told me to give him what he wants, which is to reunite him with the pieces of his previous human form, so he can . . . create a new body?"

"You said the wǔlín-shī he has under his influence are like his puppets, that he is animating their bodies and trapping their minds in the Shadow Realm," Shu muses out loud. "He is using the chancellor to direct and influence the others around him. Could those contain pieces of him, too?"

I ponder this. "But it doesn't sound like his true form. Some part of him must still be trapped in the Shadow Realm—that is why he could follow me. Perhaps that is what Lady An meant. All of him must join the chancellor so that he can step fully into his body, become the true amalgamation of his forms. Human and god." Shu shudders at the thought.

"If what Kang says is true and the princess is marching on the capital, then that must be when he is going to reveal himself. When he'll use the full might of his power to crush her once and for all."

All my words are speculation. We can only guess at what the serpent's intentions are, and even if we did know his plans, we are powerless. Especially if we remain his prisoners.

"While you were gone, the goddess visited me," Shu says in a quiet voice.

I start at this. "What? What happened?"

"I was sleeping," she tells me. "I woke up, heard her say my name. There was a . . . a crane in the tent."

The representation of the goddess. It makes sense. "What did she say?" I lean forward. "What did she tell you?"

"She told me to be ready. Something is coming." Shu shows me the feather in her hand. "She said if I needed her help, I can call her with fire."

"This must be what Lady An referred to!" I say, the excitement filling me. "What the gods have left us! We have the feather from Bi-Fang. Now we must gather Shénnóng's scale, the Tiger's claw, and Bìxì's shell."

My enthusiasm deflates as the impossibility of our mission crashes around me. Where would we ever find this lost magic? It is as difficult as finding a needle in the sea.

"Well, we have one, at least," Shu says. "Even though we do not know how to use it."

I squeeze her arm. "We have to believe the gods will reveal the path to us in time."

The flap to our tent is lifted, and the feather quickly disappears inside Shu's sleeve. A Blackwater soldier thrusts his head in, surveying the space to ensure there is no suspicious behavior.

"The chancellor and the commander request your presence," he says, and the flap falls closed again.

Shu and I look at each other. I thought we would be spared from confrontation this evening, but it seems like the chancellor has plans of his own. On our way to the main tent, I see that other tents have been taken down. Posts gathered, rolled up. The camp is preparing for travel. The chancellor will join the general soon and achieve the ultimate cumulation of the serpent's power.

I walk into the tent next to Shu, hand in hand, ready for whatever awaits us. I still have one remaining dān, and she has the feather. We will use our magic, if required.

Inside the tent are a handful of armored guards and Brother Huang, trapped between two soldiers. He has a bandage on his head and a bruise on his face that I can see even from here.

I round on the chancellor, who stands beside the great table at the center, his two Wǔlín bodyguards standing behind him. "What did you do to him? You said they would both be safe while I got you what you were looking for."

Chancellor Zhou greets me with a slow smile. "That was

dependent on whether they behaved themselves. Your companion tried to break free."

"Liar!" Shu snaps before Brother Huang even speaks a word in his own defense.

"Shut her up," the chancellor commands. Two guards grab her, twisting her arms behind her back. Another comes forward, striking her across the mouth. I hiss and lunge at him, but a guard blocks my path, a smirk on his face, daring me to challenge him.

"This is how you treat children?" I snarl at the chancellor. "I did not think even you would stoop so low."

It is then that Kang enters the tent. The soldiers snap to attention. He surveys the scene, scowling.

"Stand down!" he barks.

"But—" the guard protests.

"I am your commander as long as I hold the talisman," Kang growls.

The soldier drops to one knee. "Commander."

"Release the prisoners," Kang orders the rest of the soldiers.

I quickly go to Brother Huang's side, pull him close to me with Shu at my side. We retreat to the other end of the tent, as far away as we can get. Brother Huang gives me a weak grin. We are stronger together, and it looks like Kang will speak for us.

In his hand is the bundle of fabric. "She has done what you asked, Chancellor."

"Bring it here." Chancellor Zhou gestures eagerly, eyes shining in the firelight. Kang does not look at me as he advances toward the man, depositing the bundle into his outstretched hands. The chancellor pulls away at the fabric, dropping it to the ground. The orb glows in his hand, beautiful and shimmering. It is easy to see why it is called the Night-Illuminating Pearl. Easy to see why people would kill to possess it.

"Your regret is plain on your face," the chancellor says to me. I tear my eyes away from the pearl and meet his gaze, the echo of the serpent's laughter still in my ears. That is all I see now behind those eyes. The chancellor no longer. I don't know if the serpent claimed him after I first met him during the competition or if he was always there since I've known him.

"You said you would let us go if I brought the orb to you," I say to him, trying to keep my voice steady. "I want to believe you are a man of your word."

Even though I know what he truly is—a man no longer.

"Somehow she has severed my connection to you. Still a thorn in my side after all these years. But I cannot sense her spirit, so she must have passed. Yet another reminder of how frail, how brief, the human existence is." He smiles at me, holding up the orb in one hand. "Pity you will not be around to see Dàxī come into its full glory."

He turns to the Wǔlín warriors behind him.

"Kill them."

Chapter Thirty-Seven

Ning 寧

Two figures leap from behind the smug chancellor, their sinister blades already drawn. One wields a two-handed long-sword while the other holds a pair of butterfly swords. Their eyes are intent, burning into the three of us as their targets.

"Stop them!" Kang bellows.

"Stand down," the chancellor retorts.

The conflicting calls result in a flurry of confusion. The soldiers look among themselves, uncertain whose orders to follow. Kang tries to cross the length of the tent to save us. But he will be too late.

The longsword cuts in front of us first, sweeping through air. Brother Huang pushes us back, face determined. The butterfly swords follow soon after, slashing in the air, while we grasp at whatever we have in our reach. Shu and I fling bamboo scrolls at their heads, and Brother Huang kicks a chair in their direction, sending it spinning. The longsword warrior responds quickly with a kick, and the chair smashes into pieces under the force.

The butterfly swords slice toward us. With no more bamboo scrolls, all I have left to hold up is a book. The blades cut through it easily, the pages reduced to ribbons at our feet. I jump back, but we are cornered in the back of the tent. Blocked from the entrance. Nowhere to go.

The warrior with the longsword advances, and next to him, the butterfly swords cross before the grinning face of the other wŭlín-shī.

"Here!" Kang yells, and pulls a dagger from his boot, tossing it in an arc. Brother Huang catches it in his hands, and then the attack is on. Metal strikes against metal, the small blade looking like it could not possibly withstand the brutal force of the longsword, and yet it holds. The sound of ringing steel fills the air, piercing our ears, and then Brother Huang has to fend off a flurry of attacks from the other direction. His shoulder knocks against the brazier, sending it to the ground. The flames quickly find the books, and the dried papers immediately ignite.

Shu slips out of my grasp, kneeling before the fire. I stumble after her, realizing she is trying to call on the goddess. She looks up at the sky, the feather clenched in one fist, and thrusts her hands into the flames.

I scream as a blinding flash bursts around us. When the light fades, all I see is Shu, gazing with wonder at her hand. While everyone around us stumbles about, stunned, she flings her arm skyward. A fan opens in her hand, revealing the image hidden inside: a bird on a white background. Long beak, spindly legs, outstretched white wings.

"The princess!" I call out, sending a desperate plea up to the goddess. "We have to get to the princess somehow!"

"Get under the wings!" Shu yells as a burst of sparks erupts from the fire. I hear the swoop of wings, see a red glow. I throw myself forward and pull on the back of Brother Huang's tunic, yanking him toward us, even as he is still trying to fend off the attacks of the Wŭlín warriors. We are swept upward, our feet in the air. We look down at the head of the chancellor, who gazes up at us with hatred in his eyes.

I see, too slow, that he pulls out a dagger from his robe. I can only watch, horrified, as he pulls his arm back and flings it toward us.

The dagger flies through the air. Brother Huang bumps into me. I feel wind flowing through my hair, rushing past my face and my body. We tumble through darkness. I see nothing. Only feel my hand holding on to Shu's arm, my fingers clutching Brother Huang's tunic. Gripping them as tightly as I am able, until my hands grow numb.

We fall onto hard, packed earth, the breath knocked out of us. I don't know which way is sky and which way is earth. Someone's elbow is in my side, and I cough, unable to take a full breath. Around us I hear shouting. The clomping of boots, shaking the ground. But there is no longer the tent above us or the smell of smoke and fire. There is only the night sky, then faces appear above us, all of them in a blur. I'm pulled to my feet, questions coming from all directions. They demand to know who we are, but I don't recognize them.

Rough hands pull my arms back until I am forced to kneel.

"Shu!" I cry out. "Shu!"

"Ning?" I hear a familiar voice, and I look up to see Princess Zhen. She is clad in armor, a helmet under one arm. Beside her stands Ruyi, wearing an incredulous expression.

"They fell out of the sky," one of the soldiers reports behind me.

"Another! Over here!"

I turn, knees in the dirt, to see them pull Shu off a prone figure. She is crying, hands reaching out for the body.

Oh no.

"Let them go," Zhen commands. The soldiers release me, and I rush over. Brother Huang is lying on his side. I roll him onto his back. His eyes are open, pointing skyward, but seeing nothing. There is a red stain on his chest, a dagger protruding from it. I fumble for it, pressing down on the wound, feeling the warmth of the blood seep into my skin. Maybe, maybe I can still save him . . . My finger goes up to his neck, checks for a pulse. But there is nothing. Nothing at all.

He will never return to his village, to be reunited with his betrothed. His carving will remain unfinished. He will always stand on the other side of the broken bridge, forever separated from his lover, just like in the song. We no longer have his stories.

Death, trailing me again at each step. He must have thrown himself in front of us when he saw the dagger.

"He promised to protect us," Shu chokes on a sob.

I sense Zhen behind me, and I whirl around, looking up at her, not caring how I must appear—smudged with dirt, hair matted around my shoulders.

"Do you believe me now?" I spit. "Something is coming. Something that must be stopped! Something worse than your uncle!"

"We'll speak of this in private," she says, not reacting to my outburst. She bids one of the guards to help us clean ourselves up.

Shu weeps next to me, inconsolable. Ruyi gives me one last look before turning away to follow the princess. I put my arm around my sister, who continues to cry while they take away Brother Huang's body. I hold her up as the soldiers lead us away. She shakes beneath my touch, and I feel a familiar rise of anger. The general and his soldiers, the princess and her commander, the court officials, the noble families. All of them the same. Squabbling over territory, fighting over gold, their rank in the court, their reputations . . .

Soon there will no longer be an empire to rule, and we'll all reside in the serpent's realm of nightmares.

Soon none of it will matter at all.

We are given tubs of lukewarm water to wash ourselves with, as well as a change of clothes—simple, but clean, unrestricting and meant for traveling. We are not being kept as prisoners, but the soldiers who assist us avert their eyes, keep their distance. Whispers spread about us. The girls who fell from the sky.

Shu and I are left to sleep. No one will question us for now, a brief reprieve that Zhen is able to give us at least. I hold on to Shu like we used to when we were children, bonded together by our shared grief, having lost someone who became close to us in that brief period of time. Who promised to protect us until the end, and kept that promise, even as his journey ended before our own. Outside the tent, the crier calls out the Hour of the Thief, and I drift off into the darkness.

When I wake, the tent is already filled with light. My limbs feel relaxed and languid, my head clear. I must have slept for quite a while. Shu is still curled beside me. I pull the bedroll up over her, to make sure she does not catch a chill. She must have needed the rest after all we've been through. There is a small bowl of water with fresh towels set out for me in the main area of the tent, and I use it to tidy my appearance.

A familiar face appears at the entrance, letting in the sunlight. "Are you dressed?"

I greet Lian with surprise, stepping outside the tent in order not to disturb Shu's rest. To see a friendly face is a relief.

"I accompanied my father. He believes now that I have also

begun my medical training, I can be of assistance. Away from the front lines, of course." She grins at me. "I told him of my plans to specialize in healing, like you. He's pleased I've finally chosen a path to follow."

I embrace her again, so happy that she is here.

It is then I look around us. I realize the tent is in the middle of the camp and feel watchful eyes on us. Guards stand close. They keep a careful distance, but I know we will be easily eliminated if we provide any semblance of a threat.

"The princess requests your presence when you and your sister are ready," Lian says. "I want to hear about all that you have experienced. All your adventures."

I can't help but flinch at that term. If only it was as innocent as a romp across the empire.

Lian notices my changed expression and immediately looks contrite. "That was a poor choice of words. I did not mean to offend. I know you have been through a lot."

"It is not your fault." I shake my head. She is ignorant of what I have seen, what we have been through. Where before I may have reacted with anger, all I feel now is resignation. "I will go and wake Shu. We must speak to the princess as soon as possible."

I prepare Shu for our meeting with Zhen, and not long after, we are welcomed into her tent. I had passed along my request of a private audience, and it seems to have been respected. There is only the princess, reviewing documents, Ruyi standing next to her. Lian takes the lead as we enter. She bows; Shu and I do the same.

"Ning." Zhen greets me with a cool smile. A little tentative. My face burns at the thought of yelling at her last night before the entirety of the camp.

"I apologize for my behavior last night," I say to her, my head still bowed. "I was . . . not quite myself."

"You gave my soldiers quite a scare," she says, inclining her head. "Please. There is no need for apology. You can speak freely to me, as I have always requested of you. Tell me what you have seen on your travels. Were you successful in your quest? Did Wǔlín hear of our appeal?"

Ruyi steps forward then. "They look starved, Princess," she comments dryly. "Perhaps they should eat something first, to ensure their memories are clear."

"You are, of course, correct, my love." Zhen sighs. "Forgive my eagerness."

We sit at Zhen's table, where servants bring us bowls of millet congee with beans, served with preserved cabbage and slices of brined and smoked pork. There are also round pieces of sesame bread filled with salted egg. We eat eagerly, washing it all down with cups of hot tea.

But with our stomachs full and the tables clear, Zhen sits expectantly, waiting for my report. I requested that Astronomer Wu join us—perhaps he can help us with the puzzle Lady An presented. He now sits in a chair next to Zhen's desk.

I tell them about our trek through the bamboo forest, how we lost the shadow soldiers with the assistance of the Forgetting Sea. How we pleaded for Wǔlín to give us aid, but they turned us away. Our eventual capture by the Blackwater Battalion, and then the appearance of the chancellor. Saving Wenyi's brother. My meeting with Lady An, the crystal heart I pulled out of the pool, and . . . how I provided Gongyu with what he so desired. Now time is against us.

Zhen listens to it all with a focused expression. Ruyi, with her usual intensity. Astronomer Wu mutters to himself, recording things on paper, apparently working on some calculations that make sense only to his mind. Lian's reactions are the most natural, occasionally gasping and barely able to contain her desire to ask a thousand questions. Shu assists me with certain details, observations that I have missed. Until finally, the two of us fall silent.

We wait to see if the princess will believe me. If the astronomer will dismiss our warnings.

But the princess nods at me after I complete my story. She does not hesitate. "Astronomer Wu? How do you propose we address this threat?"

The astronomer bows his head, setting his ink brush on its stand. "The darkness is progressing faster than we anticipated," he says. "It is troubling to know the role Gongyu must have played in the founding of the empire and how he hid the magic contained in those items from us. I thought we would have more time to prepare, but . . . no matter. We will do what we can to stop the serpent. I will consult the ancient texts, find out what we can learn from the old stories."

They are finally understanding the urgency. The darkness is not the coup. It is not the general ascending the throne. The darkness threatens the souls of everyone in the empire.

"You have experienced more than most would in a hundred lifetimes. I promise we will return Lin Wenyi's remains to his mother and ensure your family is protected." Zhen places her hand over mine. "Thank you, Ning."

It doesn't feel like a princess addressing her inferior. It feels like an acknowledgment from a friend.

Chapter Thirty-Eight

Kang 康

The fire burns through the tent, consuming everything in its path. But nothing burns as bright as the chancellor's fury. Chancellor Zhou grabs one of the soldiers closest to him by the arm and brings his hand down into the coals of the still burning brazier, holding it in the flames while the man screams.

"Go find them!" the chancellor demands, with the fire reflected in his eyes. The soldiers scatter, following his instructions. "Or else the next thing that burns will be his head!"

He can be heard in the camp throughout the night. Accusations and threats of torture, grievous punishments if the three prisoners are not found: Limbs will be severed; heads will roll.

Kang pulls the weeping man away from the chancellor and directs one of the scouts to lead him to the infirmary. He oversees the control of the fire, making sure it doesn't spread to everything else. But soon he is summoned to the chancellor's tent. The once imposing man looks disheveled, his hair covered with ashes, his clothes stained with soot. Where he previously moved with energetic purpose, now he seems consumed by a frantic need.

"You knew about their magic! Their plots!" The insults are hurled at Kang as soon as he enters. But Kang allows them to wash over him. He knows what Chancellor Zhou is now.

He is aware the chancellor is more dangerous than he expected, if he is on the verge of coming fully into his power. To his eyes, at the moment, he seems like a petulant child, angry that he did not get his way.

"The emperor-regent will hear of this," the chancellor spits. "Your father will see your lapse in judgment, your worthlessness."

"I look forward to that discussion," Kang says, keeping his voice bland. "Your carriage has been prepared."

Chancellor Zhou bristles at his insolence, and Kang knows the man would love nothing more than to tear his head off his body.

"Your father once thought he could protect the woman he loved. Now, she is but a memory," the man says coldly, his hatred evident. "Soon I will have the girl you care for in my grasp, and I will snap her neck before your eyes, and there is nothing you will be able to do to stop me."

Kang turns on his heel and walks away before he pulls his sword and cuts a clean line across the chancellor's throat.

He may never know the true answer to this, but he wonders how long the chancellor has been the vessel. If it was the chancellor or if it was the god who whispered in the ears of the emperor and had him send the assassins to Lùzhou.

If he ever finds out the truth, he will kill him. God or not.

He leads his horse down the mountain, preparing how he will present his argument to his father, who is usually disdainful and dismissive of all magic, even if he has since been more receptive to acknowledging its existence in the past year. Even so, the probable result of telling him the chancellor is possessed by an old god would be banishment from the inner palace. For how could such a thing be possible if the general has never seen it with his own eyes?

Under his father's understanding, Wŭlín's warriors draw from their devotion to their practice, an innate talent. Just as the shénnóng-shī have an understanding of entertainment. Sleight of hand, practiced illusions, a performance relegated to the teahouses that disciplined soldiers would not waste their time frequenting. But what Ning has told him is the hidden potential in everyone's body, and magic is the expression of those who have greater affinity than others. Magic to call, to shape, to express. Except his choice to join Wŭlín was taken away long ago, and he will never obtain that sort of knowledge, that type of devotion.

He rides toward Jia, to his father, who waits to hear whether he's accomplished his mission. Who does not know the terrible cost of this achievement. He will protect his father, and he will protect Ning.

And most of all he hopes he will not have to one day choose between which one to save and which one to lose.

Jia appears to be a different city compared with the one he left. The city guards receive them at the massive gate, which has never been closed in Kang's memory except for that one year. The year of the coup. The marketplace is empty, the stalls covered with fabric. Patrols comb the streets. The criers call for the citizens to seek refuge in the palace and Língyă Monastery, to prepare themselves for what is coming.

The siege. The rebel princess. The promise that the emperor-regent, the city and palace guards, will protect them.

On his horse, Kang watches the stream of commoners as they are herded toward the center of the city. At least they will be taken care of if the battle for Jia does occur. He is hopeful that the lives lost in the conflict will be minimal. Or that the battle will not come to be, if they can stop Gongyu, and his father will see sense.

When he enters the palace, Kang is escorted through its winding halls, past the doorways to courtyards filled with the press of human bodies. Babies crying, a multitude of voices, the din of so many people contained in the palace grounds.

He is received into the council chamber, where his father consults with his other advisers over a map of the territories of Dàxī. Chancellor Zhou is already there and welcomes him with another hateful look.

"Father," he greets the emperor-regent, who is dressed in a dragon robe.

"My son." His father bestows a smile on him. "The chancellor reports you were essential in the quest to obtain the treasure. I knew you would not disappoint me." The Night-Illuminating Pearl sits at the center of the table, emanating its own light upon the spill of fabric, covering a portion of Ānhé.

The officials around them murmur their congratulations. His father's words do not conjure the usual rush of pride. Instead, he swallows the bile that rises in his mouth.

"Soon, all of Jia will see that I am the most fit to rule." The general gestures toward the map. "The loyalties of the provinces. The support of the army. The treasures of the First Emperor."

"Father, I have important information I must share with you," Kang interrupts, for he may not be given another chance to speak. He clasps his hands, bows, hoping his father will hear the urgency in his voice. But the general waves his hand, dismissing him. He doesn't see him, for all he sees is the map, the spread of Dàxī. All the things that were taken from him, now within reach.

"Tomorrow, you will see," his father says. "You will stand at my side on the city walls, and you will look over the empire you will one day rule. This is my legacy for you, the one your mother always wanted. Our armies will take our stand on the battlefield before Jia, where the First Emperor conquered those who would oppose him."

Tomorrow on the city walls, Kang decides. That will be his opportunity to make his plea. To make him finally listen. He is not only his father's son. He will also become the prince his mother always taught him to be.

Chapter Thirty-Nine

Ning 寧

The astronomer travels with only a few bound volumes, but he brings the texts into the tent for us to read them and discuss our findings. It is a familiar activity to me and Lian. I pore over the volumes eagerly, hoping they will provide us with answers. In the meantime, Astronomer Wu examines the feather that has turned into a fan, which Shu was reluctant to part with. But it is returned to her after he determines he cannot sense any magic contained within.

"The relics answer to only those whom the gods have deemed worthy," he says. "It appears Bi-Fang has determined you are the one to wield it."

We speak of the existence of the other relics. After some convincing, and with great reluctance, Commander Fan provided the princess with the relic that he carried with him away from Yěliŭ at the duke's request. A stone bowl, etched with patterns on both the inside and outside, ancient characters that no scholar alive can understand.

"There are rumors that most of the empire's shénnóng-shī are in the imperial dungeons," Ruyi tells us. "They were welcomed to the palace under the guise of instating the new court shénnóng-shī and then captured."

I can't help but wonder about Shao. I feel an initial twisted sense of satisfaction that he had fought so hard for that position, only to find out it was a farce. But I know it is only my bitterness speaking.

"The reports from the capital said that a relic was among Hánxiá's tributes. It will be presented at the emperor's ascendance ceremony along with Wǔlín's relic. A dagger."

So the Tiger Claw is in the general's grasp as well. If the chancellor can take over the minds of the Wǔlín warriors, then it is no surprise he can infiltrate them and take the relic for himself.

"The planning for the ceremony still continues then?" Zhen asks, expression dark.

"That's what the scouts have told us," Ambassador Luo confirms, having joined our council. "He has informed the citizens of Jia that he will crush the uprising on the banks of the Jade River, similar to the battle that won the city of Jia for the First Emperor."

The Purple Valley burned in that battle. It took years for the land around the capital to recover. People had to be displaced, moved to the south, in search of more fertile land.

The general has already mobilized his troops and set up Jia's defenses in preparation for a siege, and his army from Lǜzhou is marching to join him as reinforcements. The princess's forces are also prepared to move at her command, ready to attack if the general continues his plans to ascend the throne.

But the movement of armies is not my concern. I have proposed to Astronomer Wu and the princess a different task.

"He does not come fully into his power until he consumes a thousand souls, and it is at that point when he may be the weakest," I explain to them. "I believe that is what Lady An was trying to tell me. He now has his leg, his heart, and his eye. He is in the process of fully coming into his human form, to walk this earth again as an immortal. But before he consumes those souls . . . he is vulnerable."

"That is our chance, then," Astronomer Wu says. "We will not give him the battle he wants. He will not get those souls."

"He will be well protected," I add. "We have to get someone close to him when he is weak. Provide a distraction, and then . . ."

"Hurt him, perhaps even kill him." Ruyi nods. "A sensible plan, but how do you propose we communicate with Kang?"

"I'll use my—I mean, our—magics," I say to her. "Shu was able to transport three people across the empire. I believe I will be able to reach him with her help."

"Li Kang . . . do you think we can trust him?" the astronomer asks, the question heavy on my mind. I've asked myself the same over and over again, even after all this time. The boy whose mind has touched my own.

"Yes, I trust him," I say softly.

I have to.

Time, as ever, is against us. With the swiftest carriage, riding throughout the day and the evening, the chancellor can cut the travel time in half from Ràohé to Jia. Two days. That is all that we have, and so the princess has an envoy deliver a message.

Terms of negotiation of possible surrender and a peace offering to demonstrate her sincerity. She has heard that the general is looking for the relics of the gods, and so, she will provide them with Bìxì's shell, which she has in her possession.

The envoy returns from Jia with two demands.

One: The princess must be seen on the battlefield. To show she is truly the one behind the message.

Two: The relic must be hand-delivered by the shénnóng-tú wanted across the realm.

Me.

It works in our favor—I will ensure the relics are not lost. Gods willing, I will be able to gather them and confront Gongyu if our plan fails. I am hopeful that the relics are not needed, that our initial plan will be sufficient enough for the gods to bless us with success. Otherwise, there will be war, and thousands will die, in addition to Gongyu's harvested thousand souls.

On the second day, the ambassador's spies deliver a message back to us: The chancellor and the prince have entered Jia.

Kang is within reach. I must speak with him.

It is my final dān that I will use for this. I believe I have used the generous gift Lian has provided in the best way I know how. Now it is time to see if Kang will provide me with his promised aid. I have shown him the truth of what I know of the poison, of what Gongyu is. I hope that it is enough and that in returning to his father's side, he will not be once again swayed by their family ties. I know how tight those ties can bind us, even if we may not agree with their decisions. Still, we follow, despite their flaws, because we love and care for them.

I am given access to the tallest building in the camp—the drum tower—because I believe if I can see the palace, I can make the connection from a distance. Then tomorrow at midday, when the sun is at its highest, I will take a horse and deliver the relic of Bìxì to the chancellor.

The crier calls out the Hour of the Ghost. It seems appropriate, as this is the time when he used to visit me, back when we were in the palace and I was a competitor. It feels like an eternity ago. The fire burns hot in the brazier next to me, the kettle at a steady boil that I pour into my teapot. In the camp, there is only the potent tea brick, but I find an older one, which has a more fermented scent. I need its age, its history.

The availability of ingredients in the camp is limited. I have been given access to the medics' stores, and they brought with them treatments for common ailments. I pick the língzhī mushroom once again, for mental acuity. The dried bulb of the long chive from the kitchens, for opening a channel. Brown strands of yuǎnzhì, for concentration, for it will take all my power and focus to hold myself together. At the edge of the camp, I regard the walls of Jia in the distance, the lights that dance on top of the city walls.

Shu is with me, as she always should have been. We will perform this ritual together. I look down into the camp, and Ruyi is sitting before a fire below us. She will watch over us, make sure we are safe. I am glad for her presence, even if I would never admit it to her.

In the shadow of the drum, I slice the tea and place the piece of it into the teapot. I lost the painted teapot I purchased from Ho-yi on the road, but this plain, unadorned one will do. Its roughness comforting, familiar. I place the piece of língzhī mushroom on top of the leaves, then the chive bulb and the peeled strands of yuǎnzhì root. The water is poured. I inhale the aroma of camellia flowers, tea, and magic. The tea leaves and the herbs soften, steeping, flavors releasing into the water.

The magic flares into being, bright and strong within me.

"Shénnóng, Bi-Fang," I whisper, knowing now that the magic is all around me, knowing that I carry the touch of all of them. "Black Tiger. Bìxì . . . and Lady An." I refuse to believe she is not somewhere out there, that some part of her does not still remain, waiting to see if we succeed. "Hear my call. Help me with what I need to do."

On the table next to my tea set, I have Kang's blade, the one he pulled out of his boot and threw to Brother Huang to defend us. The wavelike pattern on the dagger catches the light, and the mother-of-pearl inlay sparkles in the hilt.

I recognize it—it is the dagger he gifted me in the palace. The one I returned to him in the Residence of Winter's Dreaming. He carried it all this time, kept it close to him. Even though it was a spurned gift, even though it carried unpleasant memories.

Something warm fills my chest. A fondness, coupled with an uncertainty. Similar to my fear of the gods taking away my magic. Afraid he will spurn me and turn away. That he will refuse me.

I am afraid, and yet I still continue. I have Shu beside me. She is a reminder that magic is never entirely lost, that it can change to something else. She will always be there for me, even if everything else falls away.

I place the dān in my mouth. I pour the tea. The lid burns my fingertips as the tea flows into the cups. We drink, following the ritual. Allowing its warmth to fill my body, the magic to spread through my mind like lightning and, in turn, connect me to my sister. She gives up her essence willingly, eager to help. My tongue breaks through the outer shell of the dān, and the tea dissolves it.

I lift the dagger with both hands and send our magic out toward that bright city, call him by name.

Kang.

Chapter Forty

Kang 康

He dreams of the fire that burned down the doors of the palace. His mother's bodyguard bursts into his chamber and pulls him out of his bed. He is surrounded by the stench of smoke and metal. Screams. Crying. He is nine years old again, shorter than everyone else, thrust from person to person in the chaos. His mother, eyes as sharp as the curved blade at her side, directs people to leave out the back gate.

Go with them, Kang! she orders, turning to throw herself back into the fight.

No! he protests, but arms lift him up and away—

He wakes thrashing in his bed, sweat drenching his brow and body. He is in the palace again. Choking on the scent of incense. Surrounded by wood and paper. All of it so easy to burn.

"Kang?"

Someone calls his name in the night. It sounds like Ning.

"Kang!"

The voice beckons to him, more urgent this time.

His feet touch the floor. He has to follow.

She waits for him in the moonlit garden, where the princess once had him kneel, calling him a traitor. The garden is his now, but he has never lingered. He prefers to walk through it as quickly as possible, as not to be reminded of that night. It is too easy to recall his cousin's accusations, and yet all of it is coming to fruition now.

A gentle breeze stirs Ning's hair. She is dressed as he remembers her best: that day in the market, in her competitor's robes. Is this a dream? He's not certain. They've met, time and time again. Fate pulling them close, their threads tangling with each other, until their destinies were inevitably tied.

"Are you actually here?" he asks her.

She smiles and gestures for him to sit down. "It's all a dream."

He sits on the stone bench. It feels real underneath him, solid. The bench where the princess held a knife to his throat. When he remembered the pain of being branded by the emperor's soldiers, being taken from the only home he ever knew. Watching them do the same to his father and his mother. He meets her eyes, and he knows she feels the weight of that memory. The anger and the shame. But she does not judge him. She knows what it is like to love someone and lose them. She knows what it is like to love someone and have them disappoint you.

She pours him a cup of tea, the movements as graceful as he remembers. Each gesture meeting the other, a practiced flow.

"Tomorrow I will bring the remaining relic to your father," she informs him, voice light and unburdened. Like she is telling him she will visit him at his residence, and she will bring gifts. As his intended would, if she were to become his bride. If they had met at any other time. If they were two very different people.

"Gongyu asked for this," he says through gritted teeth. The chancellor is doing this because she embarrassed him, and he is doing this to hurt Kang. "He is obsessed with you. This will be giving in to him. Don't go."

She doesn't disagree. "You sound just like the princess." She smiles, and there's a fondness to her words. "She's also tried to convince me otherwise, but don't you see? Whatever connects me to you also connects me to him. It is where I am meant to be."

Ning pushes the cup toward him across the table, and with her other hand, she reaches for his clenched fist. Runs her thumb over his knuckles, tenderly, the lightest touch. He allows her to open his grip, to linger over each line and groove of his palm, skim over his calluses, sending a shiver up through his body. Until he almost forgets she isn't here, not really.

"A warrior's hand," she says, her brows furrowed. "I hate that I have to ask you to do this."

He looks up and meets her eyes, senses the hesitation there. The regret. As familiar to him as his own thoughts.

"You can tell me," he says.

"You'd better drink the tea," she tells him, frowning, and pulls her hand away.

The tea goes down smooth. Clean, sweet, slightly floral. He marvels at how it could taste, even in the dream. Almost as real as reality.

"The princess and the general will bring their forces to the field before Jia," Ning says. "The princess has requested a meeting with the general, presented it as a possible surrender, and as a show of good faith, will provide him with a relic."

Kang already knows. The shell of Bìxì. How his father's advisers had crowed when they heard the message, convinced Zhen is weak and afraid. But from what he understands of his cousin, he knows it cannot be so simple. He knows the chancellor prepared a response. He did not know it would involve Ning herself.

"These are the relics that Lady An told me may be required to stop him, as they once did before," she says. "Shénnóng's scale. Bìxì's shell. Bi-Fang's feather. The Black Tiger's claw."

Something shivers in the very air around them when she utters those words, as if this dream realm bows before the power and recognition of the old gods.

"And she is in agreement you will give it to him? Does the princess believe a truce is possible?" he asks. "That my father can be persuaded to stop without blood being spilled?" Even he knows it is a foolish endeavor. His father did not obtain his reputation for nothing. He pushes to succeed, no matter the cost, exploiting every possible weakness.

Ning shakes her head. "That does not matter to me. I wish to prevent Dàxī's people from falling to a fate that is worse than death."

Abominations coming to life. Crawling out of the bowels of the earth. Kang sees it all in his mind's eye, images, each one more horrible than the last, being shown to him through their connection.

"What are his other terms?" Kang asks. He knows the chancellor is capable of great trickery, and there must be something about his strategy. Something he does not quite understand.

"Only the timeline. The exchange must be made tomorrow."

Why accept a meeting when there is no real advantage? When Jia's granaries are full, when it has an easily defendable position on the highest point of the valley. When there are the palace guards, the city guards, the soldiers from Sù and Lǜzhou. Jia can withstand a siege. His father can ascend as emperor at the auspicious time, safely sequestered behind the walls of Jia. He has the benefit of time, to wait for further reinforcements from Lǜzhou, and for the unrest within Ānhé to settle itself, because while there are factions loyal to the former emperor, there are factions vocal in support of the general's ascendance as well.

"What is so special about tomorrow?" he murmurs, trying to make the calculations from a military perspective, trying to see it from his father's eyes.

"She warned me about his magic," Ning says. "He will require sacrifice in order to bind himself to his human form. He has no blood of his own, no life force. He can only hold the human form for a time, an illusion in itself. He will have to use the darkest magic to take over the chancellor's body fully, to walk on earth again. Not as a parasite, not as a puppet wielder, but to take a true human body for his own."

He does not want to ask the next question: "What does he require?"

"A thousand souls. He needs to consume a thousand souls for him to walk this earth again."

Kang shudders at the thought.

"Once he uses the power of the eye, the leg, the heart, it will wear away at his human vessel. We believe he has a limited time to consume those souls to live, and that is the reason for the timeline."

"How will he be able to devour so many at once?"

"A ritual of some sort." She rubs her forehead.

"Wait . . . ," he says. "The exchange. How many are to be on the field?"

Ning ponders this, and then they come to the realization at the same time. She slaps her hand on the table.

"He intends to flood the plains. Kill everyone in the corridor between Jia and Huadu. No wonder he agreed to the terms of the surrender, why he wanted to see Zhen from the city walls. She would not stand there alone. She would have the protection of her battalions around her." She stands then, pacing. "When he is able to reach for a portion of his magic, it wouldn't take much. The rivers are already swollen with rain, the floods that have begun since even late winter, the early spring... the rain that has been unlike any they have seen for a hundred years. It was him. Preparing."

"The old name for the Clearwater is the Gold," he says slowly. "For the river sometimes ran clear and sometimes ran in yellow torrents, and brought rockslides that destroyed everything in their path, spilling into the Jade, rendering it undrinkable for a time..."

The Jade and the Gold. The Dragon and the Serpent.

"Now we know what we must do, and this is what I must ask of you." She steps close to him, takes his hands in hers.

But he already understands. "You would have me kill him."

"Take the bone sword and plunge it into his heart when he is most vulnerable. Before he has the chance to consume the thousand souls he needs to seal his magic," she says with certainty.

He understands this. All paths lead to the inevitable. They must ensure that he falls.

Fight poison with poison, he catches her fleeting thought.

"The bone sword is our greatest chance at hurting him, for it contains a part of him. We will use his own magic against him," she says quickly, her mind already calculating the possibilities.

Kang will have his revenge upon the chancellor, for bringing this evil to the empire, for involving his father with these schemes.

"Be safe," Ning whispers, looking up at him. She cups his cheek in her hand. He places his hand on hers, sharing her warmth.

"I'll see you tomorrow," he whispers back. Around them, this dream begins to crumble. The walls disappearing into nothing. The garden shrinks, smaller and smaller. Until she is gone.

Chapter Forty-One

Ning 寧

In the morning I am dressed in finery, as befitting an envoy of the realm. A robe of silver, on which there is the lightest outline of green bamboo. A pattern of embroidered flowers decorates the sleeves and the collar. A circlet around my neck, rings upon my fingers. My hair is gathered in a style befitting an unmarried noblewoman, secured with a pin dripping with jewels. I will ride, bearing a message from the princess. But instead of bringing riches and honor to my village, I may very well be carried to my doom.

Before my departure, I am given time to prepare for the most important cup of tea I may brew in my life. Shu acts as my assistant, bringing me the ingredients I need. I sense her emotions beside me, her worry and her frustration. Even though I hate to see her go, I embrace her and send her off with Lian; I need to focus for the task ahead.

In the *Book of Tea*, it is said this drink will permit the wielder to see through illusions. I hope it will assist me with what I need to do. When I open the package, the mixture of aromas wafts up to me. The scent of earth. The scent of the garden. The scent of my heritage.

Ruyi enters the tent, greeting me with a bow. She always looks as a warrior should, with her sun-bronzed skin and lithe body clad in armor, a sword at her side. I envy her for her confidence.

"Join me for a drink?" I offer. She sits before me, and I carry on my ritual.

I speak the steps aloud, for I know she will want to know what she is ingesting.

"Dāncān," I whisper as I crumble the ingredient into the water. "For tapping into the inner life force.

"Chénxiāng." I take a long whiff, drawing that fragrance into my lungs. "For clarity of mind, to light the way.

"And shārén, for steady hands." I grind down the dried seeds and then sprinkle the pieces into the pot.

It takes only a few moments to steep, for me to feel the pull of the magic. Leaving the ingredients, entering the water, changing into something new and wonderful. We drink together, the flavor both sweet and bitter.

I regard her, the princess's handmaiden. I had once tracked Ruyi through the palace, intending to kill her to exact my revenge. And yet, she has become something else to me. Someone I trust, whom I can confide in, whom I can even call a friend. Like Lian. Ruyi is willing to speak up for me, even in opposition to the one she loves.

"She would never wish for me to lie and say only what she wants to hear," Ruyi says to me, and I realize with the connection of the tea, she can catch the edges of my thoughts. As if I need another way for someone to read my expressions that are so easily revealed on my face.

Ruyi laughs at my thought, a throaty sound. Inside my chest, there is a twinge of longing. She is beautiful, and if only someone would look at me the way she looks at Zhen.

And then, the remnant of another memory surges before I can

stop it. A boy looking at me while my touch lingered against his hand, who looks like there is much he wants to say but does not know how to say it.

"I think someone already does," she says softly.

Heat rushes to my face, and I turn red with embarrassment, scrambling to my feet.

"Never you mind," I say, and her laugh follows me all the way out of the tent.

We stand on the field where the battle was fought hundreds of years ago. Beside me is the Jade River, its waters having carved a path out of what existed before Dàxī and what will remain after Dàxī crumbles into the dust.

The princess sits mounted on her warhorse, Commander Fan at her side. Around her, the battalion stands in formation. I warned her about the rockslides in the mountains near the Clearwater, about Gongyu's plan to call down the water and drown everyone in its path. She brought a force of only two hundred, all mounted riders. I hope it is enough to thwart his plans.

I walk in front of the princess and bow to her, carrying the relic of Bìxì in my hands. She also bows in turn, acknowledging the danger I am walking myself into. Beside me, Ruyi brings the horse. This, I know, pains Zhen more than anything. She did not want to send her beloved into danger, and yet she is the only one who knows and accepts my magic. Who will allow me to use her essence, her body, her mind, if there is ever a need.

This is where Shénnóng is powerful and Gongyu is not. For he only knows how to take by force, but Shénnóng asks for you to yield. A give and a take. A question and an answer.

I feel the fierce connection between me and Ruyi. My awareness of her presence as she closes the distance. For a moment, I am myself, and I am also her. In preparation for what is to come.

Do you trust me?

Yes is the echoing answer. The resounding response. Beside us, the drum towers begin to beat. I hear a horn coming from somewhere in the distance.

We fly down the road, heading toward Jia. Toward the waiting general, toward Gongyu.

I am myself, and yet I am not. I feel the thundering hooves under me; I feel Ruyi's strength in my hands and my legs, urging the horse to go faster. She is thinking about Zhen. She is thinking about their moment this morning, in their sleeping chamber in the boat. When everything was quiet around them, when it was just the two of them together, her fingers trailing through Zhen's hair. Ruyi opened her mouth to speak, but the princess only pressed her finger against her lips. *Shh ... let me have this for a moment longer ...*

I pull myself away from that intimate memory. It is not for me.

The distance closes. I see the rows of soldiers standing before the city's gates. I see figures up on the city walls, archers pointing their arrows in our direction. I smell camellia flowers, and in my mouth, I taste the fragrance of chénxiāng still lingering. The dark presence is up ahead, for that sort of magic is something that cannot be hidden, cannot be contained. The dark entity that lies coiled behind the eyes of the second-most important man in the realm. There is so much to be afraid of.

Falling into the abyss, losing yourself to the darkness that creeps beyond the edge of the forest, falling under the influence of the whispers of your nightmares. Losing yourself. Losing those you love.

I give strength to Ruyi as she steadies herself and stands straight in the saddle. In the saddlebag, she hid a quiver of arrows.

We are almost at that row of soldiers. We are close enough to see the face of the general, the chancellor, and close enough to see... Kang. He drank the tea I told him to drink, placed in it a common enough ingredient that I told him about in the night. One that eases headaches but also strengthens my connection with him as well. That pulls me to him when my magic reaches for him across the distance, because my magic knows him, recognizes him, sees him for who he is.

Ruyi draws the bow and sends an arrow, straight and true, toward the general's heart.

Chapter Forty-Two

Kang 康

Kang feels the brush of Ning's magic against his mind. A signal to prepare for what is to come. His hand finds the hilt of his sword, and as he sees Ruyi rise out of the saddle, the sword is in his hand. He throws himself forward as the arrow spins toward them.

"Father!" he cries out, sounding every bit like the devoted son.

The sword knocks the arrow down to the ground. His father looks at him in shock. Below them there are shouts as the commanders order the archers to unleash arrows toward the envoy.

The general smiles, but his approval no longer has the same effect on Kang. "My son! You saved me."

"I'm sorry," Kang says, reaching for the other sword at his side. He pulls it out of its sheath, and then spinning around, pushes the general back.

Chancellor Zhou stands at the edge of the city walls, looking down at the chaos with satisfaction.

Kang puts his hand on the man's shoulder and then plunges the bone sword into his back, into where his heart should be.

The sword sinks into his body, striking true. The chancellor jerks forward, spitting a bloody stream into the air. Kang stands there, panting, as the body slides down to the stones at his feet. He did it. What was asked of him.

"What have you *done*?!" the general's voice erupts behind him, in shock and disbelief.

He turns to face his father, the chancellor's blood on his hands. "Father, please, you must understand." Now he will know the truth. He will see everything happened as it should.

But suddenly a blade is at his throat, an arm around his body, and hot breath against his ear. Chancellor Zhou stands beside him, his chest a gory ruin. Blood trickles down onto the stones. His father looks at the chancellor in horror.

And there it is. The truth. No man could withstand a sword through the back. Kang felt the twist, the crunch of bone, and knew his father heard it, too. He felt skin and muscles parting, felt the blade tear into the flesh and come out the other side. He should not have lived, and Kang would die to show his father the truth of the monster that lurks beside him, guiding his actions.

The general's face ripples before him. Kang blinks. It must be sweat, or the light playing tricks on his eyes. He feels Ning's desperation, her fear, amplifying his own.

Something... something is not right... Were they her words, or his?

"I have given you what you asked for," Gongyu says. "I have killed your enemies, the ones who murdered your beloved. I have brought vengeance to their doorstep and ripped from them what has been taken from you. Now it is time for you to give me what you have promised in exchange."

He sees it now, clearly before him. *The general, fishing a jade orb out of the water of the Eastern Sea. A voice, ringing in his head.*

Promising him everything if he is willing to follow, to do as he is asked to do. But the final price is his body.

"I have your son, your hope, the one you have accepted as your own," the chancellor's oily voice says into his ear. "You want the protection for him that I promised? Then finish what you've started!"

Kang does not understand. He does not understand why his father holds up his hands. He does not understand why his father kneels before him, asking the chancellor not to hurt his son. He does not understand why his father closes his eyes and nods.

Suddenly arms pull him back, Wŭlín warriors with their dead expressions restraining him. He yells for someone, anyone to stop this, but there is no one else on the city walls to help them.

"Kang!" He hears Ning scream from the battlefield below. No . . . he hears her clearly in his mind.

The chancellor is in front of his father. His skin is peeling, falling off him like black dust. He is disintegrating into shadows before their very eyes. His hands are placed on the general's shoulders. Carefully, as a lover would, he pulls him close. His father is engulfed in the shadows, his eyes darkening. His arms are pulled back, pulled taut. He shudders.

The crystal orb that was in the chancellor's body glows through the darkness and then enters his father's chest, sinking into his skin. The bone sword descends into his leg. The jade eye forms itself above him, and with a crack, the general's head is pulled back, his mouth pulled outward in a silent scream.

The shadows descend through his open mouth and stream into his body, convulsing, trembling, until the man falls forward, catching himself with his outstretched hands. Kang struggles against the iron grip of the Wŭlín soldiers, but it is useless. They will not let him go.

The god within his father throws his head back and laughs. He slowly straightens until he is on his feet. He rolls his shoulders back. He turns his head. One way, then the other.

"Did you think it would be so easy?" The voice is low, breathy. Kang feels Ning's fear, her recognition of that voice from her nightmares. "Once, you may have been able to kill me with my own sword, but I am too strong now. All my magic has returned to me." He opens and closes his hand, marveling at the movement.

"My eye, which your father pulled from the deep. My heart, returned to me by the girl you love. And now, Li Kang, you tried to kill me. All it tells me is that I am right: Humans are pitiful and weak and easily influenced. All I have to do is threaten those you love, then watch you desperately try to save those who would not even save themselves. You will crawl before me like the wretched creatures you are."

His face ripples again, and then lines appear on the surface of his skin. Cracks. His form contorts, changes, his body bulging, swelling as no one ever should. Pieces of his armor fall to the ground, his helmet striking the stones with a clang. His skin peels off, revealing black scales the size of a human head. The serpent continues to elongate toward the sky as the ground underneath the wall shakes and rumbles.

Kang knows through their connection that Ning senses the sudden outpouring of magic that is pulled from under the earth, something that was lying there in wait for this moment. For the reemergence of a god.

Screams sound in the distance as the soldiers of Jia begin to see the dark shape of the serpent above the city. The stones breaking underneath as it grows, crumpling part of the city wall. It is taller than even the bell tower, the highest point in Jia.

Kang tries to yell at Ning and Ruyi to run, but one of the Wǔlín warriors strikes him in the stomach, causing him to fall to his knees.

Arrows fly, striking the thick scales, only to harmlessly ping off.

The serpent laughs again, a terrible, booming noise that pierces Kang's skull.

"You thought you were so clever. You thought you could fool me, but I was prepared. For what pathetic humans could stand before a god?"

The creature comes for him, its body sliding in coils around him. Kang tries to push it away, to resist, but it squeezes. It wraps itself around his legs, his body, until he is enveloped all the way up to his neck. Until he finds it difficult to breathe.

"Bring them to me. Bring them all. They will witness my plans for the great Dàxī," the serpent orders.

It is the last thing Kang remembers before darkness closes over his head.

Chapter Forty-Three

Ning 寧

The serpent looks down at me with his red eyes. He sees me as I pull the threads connecting this world and the next. He sends a message directly into my head.

I should have killed you when I had the chance, and now I will have no regrets. Devouring all your pathetic dreams and desires. Your foolish belief that you can still save the princess, save this empire from ruin.

The earth continues to rumble underneath me, the drums still sounding around us. There are cries within the city, of all those people trapped inside.

I feel the pressure of the serpent's coils on Kang's body. That crushing force, overwhelming him, until it is difficult to breathe. I felt every part of that pain, as if it were on my own body, and from the way Ruyi falls next to me, I know she feels it, too. As the breath is pushed out of Kang's lungs, we also lose consciousness. As my awareness fades, I see the shadow soldiers above us. They carry us away.

I wake with a gasp. I am being carried in the arms of an impassive soldier. Even though I try to reach out with a tendril of my magic, a desperate attempt at persuasion, it runs up against a blank wall.

He is somewhere, lost and out of reach. I have no dān. I have only two relics, half of what is required to break Gongyu's power. But he is close to ascension to his true form. He did not flood the valley, and I have no idea what his plan is. Ruyi also takes in a shuddering breath beside me and then struggles in the grasp of the soldier who carries her. She fights, but he is too strong, and she is easily subdued by the others. Her hands and feet are bound for her efforts.

I send a tentative strand of magic out toward Kang, try to feel him through my connection. It is weak, but the connection is there. He is moving away from me, unconscious.

We are transported through the city streets, which are quiet. There is no one else but us. No figures peering at us from the shuttered windows. No people watching us from the alleys. It is silent. Eerie. Like moving through a city of ghosts. The sense of unease inside me grows stronger. Where is everyone? Tens of thousands of people should inhabit Jia. They could not all have fled during the commotion.

We enter the palace through one of the side gates. We are brought through hallways and past courtyards where many people appear to be lining up in an orderly fashion. It is still quiet. Too quiet. I don't know why they are standing docile. I try to scream at them, to tell them to get away, but a piece of fabric is quickly shoved into my mouth, silencing me before I can even make a sound.

This is the Courtyard of Promising Future, one I am familiar with. Its looming walls have witnessed my many trials in the palace. We are carried up the white marble steps, like a prized pig bound for slaughter, bound for a feast, toward the great open doors of the Hall of Eternal Light. Behind us, there is a throng. So many people filling up the space. Soldiers and commoners and merchants. So many people, and yet they are silent. They are so quiet, and I am afraid.

It is when we enter the doors that I see what is happening. The great body of the serpent fills the entirety of the back wall, curved around the throne, where the emperor would have sat to receive dignitaries and tributes. But where the tables would have been lined up for the officials, the beautiful redwood furniture is splintered into pieces and stacked in a pile in the corner. Vases lie shattered on the floor, while the soldiers lead people up to the serpent.

The great head of the serpent descends on the first of the humans in line. It is a woman with a placid smile, who lowers herself in a sloppy curtsy. The serpent's head pauses above her. Magic lashes out of him, like a whip, but she does not flinch at its touch, even as it sinks into her skin. Then, strands of her essence are drawn out from her eyes, her nose, her throat . . . pulled into his open mouth. He is feeding.

The woman's face grows gaunt and pale before our eyes. Her eyes grow sunken, her flesh drawing tightly over bone, until she collapses into dust. As the final strands of her life force enter the serpent's body, a single perfect scale forms on the serpent's back, glowing gold. All that remains of her is a pile of ashes, to be crushed under the heels of the next victim who is beckoned forward. The glittering remnants of what I thought was sand on the floor is the remnants of the people he has already killed.

The once beautiful hall, the glory of Dàxī, has become a graveyard.

The shadow soldiers bring us forward, and we are thrust to our knees before him. The cloths are pulled out of our mouths. The serpent pauses in his consumption of souls to leer at us, gloating in his power and the success of his plan.

"Witness me!" he cries out, the sound of his voice horrible and echoing in the chamber. Bouncing off the walls and the floors. "I will consume the citizens of Jia and reach my full power. I will show you the futility of your struggle."

One of the shadow soldiers approaches, holding items on a tray. I recognize what they are with a gasp.

"Yes, your pathetic treasures," he says. "What remains of your once glorious gods."

Rough hands fumble at the bag at my side, pulling out the shell of Bìxì, and I can do nothing but watch it be carried away. It's placed on the tray next to the other treasures.

"A bowl. A dagger. A disc," the serpent sneers. They are all here. Everything we've been searching for. The feather that has turned into a fan is tucked against my body. Perhaps, if I can . . .

But my hope is quickly shattered in the next breath. One of the shadow soldiers picks up the disc and breaks it in half, throwing its pieces against the wall. The bowl, he crushes in his hands, and the dagger, he snaps cleanly in half, severing the metal from the handle. I cry out in despair.

"Join your gods and your prince." The serpent laughs as the shadow soldiers lift me up by my arms and throw me against the wall. I hit with a thud and then fall to the ground. A bundle of cloth that rests in the shadows moves slightly, and I realize it's a person.

Kang. He wheezes with each breath he takes. I sense his broken ribs, his punctured lung.

"Break her legs," the serpent instructs, and one of the soldiers holds the struggling Ruyi back as another soldier beats her with a staff until she screams. I feel the bones snapping as if they are my own, and I scream with her. They dump her next to us as well, and my legs burn with her pain.

"I will savor the three of you when I am ready," the serpent smirks.

The relics are scattered around us in pieces. Innocent souls are devoured before us, one after another. We can only lie there and watch with our broken, pitiful human bodies. I am once again helpless before the inevitability of my failure.

I manage to crawl toward Ruyi, pain shooting through my body with every jarring movement. I listen to her shallow breathing, brush her hair away from her eyes. I draw from that pool of magic inside myself, the remnants of the healing powers of the mushroom and the tea. Share my own essence with hers.

"That is all I am able to do," I whisper to her. With my limited power. She nods at me, and I feel her thanks.

Next, I check on Kang. He tries to give me a smile, but then he winces when he draws another breath. I send him a bit of my magic, too, to ease the pressure on his side. To dull the edge of his pain. As I lean my weary body against the wall next to him, ready to accept my eventual death, something jabs against my palm.

The half of the jade disc. Shénnóng's scale. It is broken and its sharp edge is enough to pierce my skin. I glance over at the serpent and the shadow soldiers. Their attention is not on me, at least for the moment. I begin to cut away at our bonds, using the jagged edges.

When my hands are free, I go to Ruyi and help her, too, free her arms and legs, even though she is unable to walk. The serpent continues to feed. I try to gather the broken pieces of the relics, to see what I can salvage. Everything is beyond repair.

I look up. The serpent's body is almost too brilliant to look at—only a smattering of black scales remains. I understand now why they once regarded him as a god. Gongyu, brother to the Jade

Dragon, a god of dreams and nightmares. But something flares hot against my side, and I quickly stifle a yelp. The fan. I pull it out from where I hid it. It lies in my hand, pristine and white.

Kang's hand tightens on my leg.

Look!

The pieces of the relics begin to tremble.

Chapter Forty-Four

Ning 寧

Before me, Shénnóng's disc fuses back into a circle. Bìxì's shell moves like it is made of soft clay, shaping itself once again into a bowl. The Tiger Claw snaps together, spinning on its side, until it returns to its full form.

An ornamental disc. A stone bowl. A metal dagger. A paper fan.

Simple, everyday items. Easy to dismiss. Easy to disregard.

But they hum with power, with magic, and I feel myself react to it. It rushes in through me, and I send it outward to the two bodies beside me, making that connection. Shénnóng's power flows through Kang and Ruyi, fusing broken bones together, mending holes, stopping the bleeding, until we are all whole and ourselves again.

We are bound by the magic, our minds connected, moving as if we are one. I pick up the disc and take the fan along with it. Ruyi scoops up the bowl. Kang wields the dagger.

Fire cleanses. I hear the whisper of the White Lady's voice inside my mind, and I know my companions hear her, too.

I open the fan and sweep it before me. Fire flows out, leaping onto the stack of furniture, which bursts into flame.

The serpent whirls around, dropping a body from his grasp, his meal interrupted, and advances on us. His eyes spin in their sockets as his tail whips around and lashes in our direction. I sense Ruyi's movement as my own, moving in accordance. We leap and roll out of the way.

The fire quickly catches the wood panels, which I know are regularly oiled to maintain their shine. The whole place is a tinderbox, and it quickly ignites. The main buildings of the palace are constructed not from a base of stone, but from wood, demonstrating the architectural marvels of Dàxī—and the arrogance of being able to maintain the wooden frame, the type of heavy timber that must be pulled from the deep forests of Yún. It is this that causes the whole place to go up easily, the fire leaping up the thick timbers, desperate for fuel.

The serpent quickly lunges between us as shadow soldiers cut off our paths for escape. Ruyi and I stay back to back, separating from Kang. Because he has the dagger, he leaps into action, sending the shadow soldiers sprawling. The room rapidly fills with smoke around us. Ducking under the sweep of the tail, Ruyi rushes forward and presses the bowl into the serpent's side. Green rings explode from it when it touches his body, forming symbols of Bìxì. The rings wrap themselves around the serpent, binding him. They quickly move up the length of him, constricting him in segments, glowing with a peculiar flame.

"*What is this?!*" His body begins to thrash, his tongue darting forward and back.

Ruyi picks up a blade that had fallen at her feet. She tries to strike at the gold scales, producing a shrill, keening sound that is painful to the ears. Then the tip of her blade catches the edge of a black scale, finding a soft spot, and she slices it open. Black blood splashes out, but wherever it touches skin, it burns like acid. Ruyi hisses, spots smoking on her arms. She readjusts her grip and bites her lip, edges forward again and causes another scale to fall.

He will be bound again. This time, a chorus of voices echoes around us.

The serpent roars, turning away, and slashes at us with the tip of his tail. Bìxì's green rings tighten around his body, pulling him taut. She continues her bloody task, prying each scale with the dao as a lever. The blood gushes forth, but Ruyi is aware of how the splatter will happen this time and sidesteps it. Where it eats into the floor with a sizzle. The blood burns strange patterns into the wood... almost like flowers.

Behind me, screams erupt. Bìxì is the god of truth—under their influence, the serpent's illusions no longer take hold. The shadow soldiers clutch their heads, screaming, as Gongyu's hold on their minds slackens. They start to remember who they are.

Go! I call out to Kang.

He springs into action, now that the shadow soldiers are no longer on him. Tiger Claw in hand, with one sure stroke, he slices the entirety of the snake's belly from bottom to neck.

A flood of black blood rushes out as the serpent's body convulses. The green rings slowly shrink, and a man crawls out from the carcass, coughing and choking. Green chains bind his throat and arms and legs; he stares at us with hateful eyes, kneeling but not subdued. Still recognizable as the general. Still recognizable as Kang's father. He gives us a bitter, wide-mouthed smile.

"You think that you can hold me with these simple toys, these echoes of the power that the gods used to hold? I fought them all, and a part of me still remained." He spits black blood onto the floor and laughs. "My physical body is weakened, but I have healed. I cannot starve, I cannot thirst. I can wait. Wait until one of you foolish mortals wishes to break me out again, until someone finds a way to finish what I started."

From the ground, Shénnóng's relic shimmers. It rises from the floor, turning from the disc into a scale, its true form, and centers itself above Gongyu's head. Even as the man thrashes and tries to move away, the chains hold him in place. It shrinks until it settles into his forehead. Branding him.

Ruyi and Kang drag him out of the dripping body of the beast, then force him to his feet. The rest of the great hall burns around us like a pyre. I see Small Wu at the door, ushering people out. There is A'bing, standing beside him, and more people from the kitchens. They look at me, in shock and surprise, as I follow Ruyi and Kang down the steps.

"Help them!" I tell them. "There are more people in there!" They nod, and they return to the doorway of the burning building, calling out to those who still remain. The general falls to his knees, and his son pulls him up.

Smoke billows above the Courtyard of Promising Future. Above the entirety of Jia.

Chapter Forty-Five

Kang 康

Kang carries his father through the palace grounds. Around them, there is chaos and destruction. There is the scent of smoke, burning, and death. Ruyi leads them through the tunnels to Língyǎ Monastery, where a smaller force of soldiers loyal to the princess will wait for them. When they emerge from the tunnel, they are greeted by the abbess, by a group of monks, and also by the princess, who wears her own suit of armor, gleaming red. At least, Kang thinks fleetingly, she is not clad in black and gold, his father's preferred colors. The soldiers come and quickly restrain the general. They pull a white tunic over his head, then bind his hands and feet with rope. The green rings of Bìxì's bindings have disappeared.

The three of them drop to the ground before Princess Zhen, in accord, bound by their connection to one another.

Zhen goes to Ruyi first, embracing her tightly.

"My love," she whispers into her hair. Kang could hear it, almost as if it were spoken beside his ear. He feels a surge of love rising from Ruyi. A love that is almost like pain. For she almost lost her.

Then she lifts Ning to stand, expressing her gratitude with a warm embrace as well, before coming to Kang, lifting him up to his feet.

"Cousin," she says. "You have my thanks."

"Please, let me speak to him," Kang pleads, neglecting all niceties. "Before you proceed with whatever punishment you deem appropriate."

The princess nods. "You have my word." She turns then and calls out a command. "Begin preparations!"

The general is led through the gardens of Língyă Monastery. Kang sees from Ning's expression that it hurts her that the flowers have been disturbed. The once tranquil garden is now partially a mud pit, due to the stomp of so many boots breaking through them. The palace still burns behind them, lighting up the sky with an ominous orange glow.

The abbess leads the way, and they see what the monks have prepared for the past few hours while the battle raged in the palace. The earth has been opened, the side of the stone mountain cut away, and a slope leads down into the earth. Shénnóng's sacred spring. Ning places her hand on his arm, and he knows she senses his feelings. Rage. Uncertainty. Frustration. He wanted so much to redeem his father, and yet . . .

The soldiers stop with the general before the pool. They are surrounded by torches, casting everyone's face in ghostly shadows. Zhen gestures for them to step aside, and Kang is now able to approach.

"This is what waits you!" he calls out, pushing Gongyu forward until he looks over the waters of the spring. "Surrounded by rock and submerged in water. Chained to the wall. Is this how you want to live the rest of your immortal life? Is this how you want to suffer? Leave him. Return to whatever rock you crawled out from under."

Gongyu's head spins toward him as he gurgles, mockingly. One jade eye spinning in its socket, Shénnóng's seal burning on his forehead. "Everything I experience, your father will experience, princeling. Every choking, desperate attempt at a breath. He will drown, again and again, with every dying gasp, every prayer to end it. He will be there, living alongside me. He will be there. What do you think about that?" He resumes his harsh, barking laughter, the sound echoing in the stone chamber.

Kang points his dagger at his throat, intending to silence that horrible laugh, but Gongyu just grabs it and grins, blood dripping from his fingers.

"Kang!" Zhen calls out in warning. Ning is there again, pulling him away. He pushes her off and walks toward the wall, footsteps crunching on the pebble beach. He knows the futility of arguing with a god, and yet he had to try that one final time.

They force the general to kneel. The soldiers replace the ropes with shackles. They bring thick chains, meant for horses and heavy labor, and fasten them to his wrists and ankles and neck.

"One last chance," Zhen pronounces. "Will you leave him?"

Gongyu spits at her feet. "No." He's still grinning that mad, unhinged smile. "What will the history books say about you? Who made her uncle disappear? Will they call her ruthless? Wise?"

"Do it," Zhen cuts him off.

Ning's hand finds his, and from that, he can at least find a small bit of comfort.

The process is bloody and violent. They cut out the pieces of him that are eternal. The eye, the heart, the leg. Kang forces himself to watch. Every last bit of it. Every moment he commits to memory, for he is the reason behind his father's terrible bargain.

When it is done, the general falls forward, catching himself with his hands.

"My son . . . ," he says weakly, lifting his head slightly. Kang witnesses his hideous visage, the gaping hole where his eye should be. "Make sure those pieces are sent to the edges of the earth. Make sure to bury them where they can never be found."

"I'll make sure of it," Kang chokes out. He does not falter, even though his knees want to give way. Ning does not make a sound next to him, even as he crushes her fingers in his grasp. She feels like the only thing tethering him to the world.

With a nod from the princess, the chains are dragged, pulled up, and passed to waiting hands. The chains are connected to four iron rings embedded deep into the stone. The prisoner is placed on a platform, the chains pooling at his feet. Four men push the floating platform away into the center of the lake, and then, one by one, they cut away the barrels, and the figure in white slowly sinks into the water. Until nothing of him remains.

Chapter Forty-Six

Ning 寧

It takes hours for the fire to be extinguished, and afterward, the Hall of Eternal Light is a smoldering ruin. The empire's architectural marvel gone, but so is the menace that threatened the entirety of Dàxī. I am reunited with Shu in the gardens after the fire is contained. She is covered with soot, and so am I. Shu throws herself into my arms at the sight of me, sobbing with relief.

"It's over now," I whisper, and she nods through her tears.

Later, I stand next to Lian in the infirmary tents set up in the courtyard of the physicians, making ourselves useful. I fill pails with water, wring out cloths, cut up bandages, everything I could do to escape the memory of the writhing serpent that loomed over our heads. Mourn the many souls that were taken before we could save them. Of the ones Gongyu consumed, there are no bodies to bury.

I am glad to see Zhen herself walking among the wounded, offering words of encouragement, assisting where she is able. I wondered, before, if she would be a capable ruler, and knowing her now, I believe she will prove herself to the court and clean up the discord that Gongyu sowed throughout it.

Beds are set up in the residences and the library pagoda to accommodate those who remained in the palace, even though most have been sent out to the monastery and the rest of Jia. Many will be needed to help with the healing that is required, the rebuilding of the capital.

Even though the bed calls to me, promising me the rest I need, I feel a slight tug in my chest. That insistent cord, that connection. Calling to me, now that my body is still. He is out there somewhere, alone.

The receiver must be willing. I didn't really understand it when the White Lady first said it to me. But now I know. He is open to me of his own volition. He hears me, and I hear him in return. I am no longer afraid of our connection and of what the magic has to offer. Our strange, shared intimacy. A bond that is solely our own.

I step out into the Garden of Fragrant Reflection. The air still smells of smoke. The moon is a sliver in the sky. But I do not need the light. I follow the connection between us, sense the chaos of his thoughts keeping him from sleep as well.

It brings me all the way across the palace, from the west to the east. I climb up the wall and make my way along the rooftop, sitting down beside him. This was my former residence, when he came to find me that fateful evening.

"Yes," he says softly, turning toward me in the dark. "When you tried to kill me. I remember."

I chuckle. "I am not the one always skulking in the shadows."

"I think that may be where I belong," Kang says. His mood quickly darkens, like the moon obscured by clouds on a windy night.

"You blame yourself," I tell him, and also nudge the almost empty jar of millet wine at his feet. "So you're going to drink yourself into a stupor."

"Isn't that how the poets do it? How they reach enlightenment?"

He laughs, but it is not a happy sound. I've only caught a glimpse of this Kang before, consumed by his guilt and shame.

I know there is more to him under the surface. He's not just the joking boy or the serious almost-prince. There is a part of him that he always tried to hide from me, even though the Golden Key, the Silver Needle, attempted to coax it out of him.

"Most of them end up drowned, trying to scoop up the moon. They'll find your body in a rain barrel, with your legs sticking out," I say to him, trying to lighten the mood. He does reward me with a more sincere chuckle.

"A fitting end for a failed prince," he says, trying to reach for his wine jar. I am faster than him, my mind not muddled by the alcohol. I snatch it out of his hand and throw my head back, drink it all, even as some of it dribbles down the front of my tunic.

Kang gapes at me. I wipe the back of my mouth with my hand and roll the jar down the roof tiles, where it disappears into the bushes with a clatter.

"You told me beside the sacred spring not to blame myself," I challenge him, the wine making my face and my body burn with heat, giving me courage to say the things I am going to say. "I couldn't have known, and it was true. It wasn't my fault my mother died. It was that . . . that scheming rat, Gongyu."

He stares at me for a moment and then falls sideways laughing. He almost loses his footing, and I yank him back by his sleeve, certain he is going to roll off the roof and break his head open just like his jar.

"Only you . . . only you . . . ," he wheezes. "Only you would call the god of nightmares . . . a *scheming rat*."

"I couldn't think of the phrase," I mumble.

I should be embarrassed. I should shove him off the roof myself, but I am glad he is laughing. I feel him shaking through my hands, and then, when he tries to turn and hide his face, I notice the wet streaks of tears on his cheeks. Shining in the dim light of the moon.

I pull him close, even as he tries to push me away. In the end, he lets me hold him, just as he held me on the shores of that pebbled beach.

"It's not your fault," I whisper to the boy who was taken from his home over and over again, whose loneliness reflects my own.

In my arms, he weeps for his mother, who died senselessly. He weeps for his father, who avenged her and almost ruined the world. The father who gave his life to save him, like my mother once did for me.

Epilogue

Winter has come late to Jia. The gates of the city are adorned with scrolls of calligraphy, and the citizens of Jia are dressed in their finest. This year, the decree from the new empress has been to announce that the city be draped with brilliant colors. She has requested dyes of rich hues, previously banned as too extravagant by the old court, but now, available for all to wear.

The temples are filled with the presence of well-wishers. Those there to pay tribute to the gods, for they have seen with their own eyes what would have happened if they were not there to protect them.

Official Qiu, representing the Ministry of Rites, offered me a palanquin to carry me through the streets of Jia, like I always envisioned in my daydreams. But I declined his offer. I would rather be on the ground, mingling with the happy crowds. I want to see for myself how Jia has rebuilt itself from the devastation I left behind months prior, when I set off as part of the convoy responsible for making sure the pieces of Gongyu will never be found. It took many months, but our task concluded at the beginning of winter, and I was able to return home.

I went to the pomelo grove with Father and Shu to speak to Mother at the one-year anniversary of her passing. We brought her a plate with three white fluffy manto and three plump oranges. I made sure to peel them, because she hated the feeling of the rind under her fingernails. In the grove, I lit her favorite incense, letting the smoke carry my thoughts to her.

She made it clear throughout her life that she didn't want to be remembered with a plaque inside the house. She wanted to be found in the trees, for us to remember her when we were outside. I wondered once if there exists a shénnóng-shī who has the ability to speak to the dead. To whatever remains of my mother here. I dismissed it as foolishness then, but now I would never say that such a thing is not possible, for I have seen and experienced too much of the impossible.

Shu and I traveled back to Jia from Sù up the Jade River, and it was an experience different from the first time I boarded the ferry. With the seal from the empress, we were able to charter a small vessel and have a private room.

For Dōngzhì, the shortest day of the year, the realm celebrates the end of the harvest, the granaries filled. Happy that the year is nearing the end, the new year approaching. Time for the officials to pay respects to the empress, wrap up the remaining days of the year before returning home to our families.

But this year, even while we celebrate, I know the capital is still mourning. When we enter the palace gates, I see the ruined structure of the Hall of Eternal Light up ahead. Only the base remains, the grand staircase ascending to nothing.

Minister Song assured us through letters they performed the funeral rites not long after we left. The souls of all those people. I hope whatever remained of them found their way back to their families and on to the stars.

At least the living in the palace can now be free of the fear of investigation and punishment. I saw Qing'er in the kitchens earlier. We lit sticks of incense for his grandmother and his mother. Small Wu and A'bing took him in, made sure he still had a family to call his own. I left Shu with Lian in her residence, playing games from Kallah. The two of them struck up a friendship as well, as I thought they would. I was glad to see Fei and Hongbo there, too—they were adopted by the Kallah people.

But there is somewhere else I need to go on this shortest day, the darkest night. Someone else I have to meet.

I walk through the gates of the monastery, and the guards let me pass when they see the pendant I wear.

Everything is covered with a light dusting of frost. The snow is beautiful, but I know how fervently the flowers will bloom in the spring, and I miss them. The revelry in the streets behind me seems a quiet contrast to the icy lake, and in the center, a mound of earth. Four stone stelae stand before it, taller than two men, each bearing a carving of one of the gods.

There is a stairwell carved into the rock, curved around the eastern side, chiseled into the earth. At the top, a stone column points up at the sky. There, a familiar figure stands, surveying what is carved into the column. His fingers trace the characters, lingering over them.

永誌不忘

Never forget.

Sealed under that mound there is a spring and an almost-god buried in chains.

He hears me approach, and he turns to greet me with a smile.

This will be the last time we will see each other in person for a while. Soon, he will be the newly appointed Marquis of Lǜzhou, and I will be tasked with maintaining the *Book of Tea* in Hánxiá.

Although he will not be too far away. Only a few hours by boat down the Clearwater. But his absence will take getting used to, considering the time we spent together every day when we journeyed through the empire, fulfilling his father's final wish.

"How are you?" I ask him, knowing this is his first Dōngzhì without his family.

"Thinking about how easily it could have all gone to ruin," he says, shoulders heavy with the weight of it.

"He made a choice," I tell him, even though I know my words do not take away the pain.

Kang rests his palm against the stone. "Thinking about everything that was lost."

I place my hand over his, and he turns to me again, pulling me close. "And everything that I've gained," he says, lips against my hair.

He holds me for a while, until the bell tolls in the distance, reminding us of the time. We've been invited to the feast, even though I know neither of us enjoy these grand celebrations.

"Before we have to don our court costumes, I may have persuaded Small Wu to give us something from his personal stores," he tells me, pulling out a flask.

I pull out the stopper and sniff it, nose tingling at the scent. "Osmanthus wine!" I exclaim. "You must have given him something spectacular for him to part with this!"

"Let's not speak of it." He grins, pulling out two cups as well. Mine is still warm from being tucked under his cloak.

We clink our cups and drink. The chill dissipated for now; we speak of lighter, sweeter things, like the tangyuan he promised to make for me later, rolled by his own hands.

Once, someone spoke of a new dawn rising over Dàxī. But not too long ago, a great serpent almost obliterated us all. I send a prayer of thanks up to the White Lady, if she is watching.

Grateful to be alive and beside someone I love, watching the sun set over Jia as it sends streaks of color across the sky.

Acknowledgments

First, thank you to my readers for picking up the sequel and finishing the Book of Tea duology with me. Thank you for coming along with me on this journey. I appreciate all your messages, reviews, and comments. Many thanks as well to the booksellers and librarians who have shared your enthusiasm and support for Ning's story.

A special thank-you to the reviewers who made my debut experience so much fun: those who participated in the TBR and Beyond Book Tour, especially Melanie and Heather for organizing. Also to Bri and the members of the B2Weird Book Club, for your wonderful photos and posts on Bookstagram.

Thank you to my editor, Emily Settle, for taking the very rough draft and seeing something worth salvaging in there; for your patience and encouragement in helping me figure out the story. I would not have survived the process without your guidance!

Thank you to my agent, Rachel Brooks, for being there each step of the way, and for your enthusiasm when I want to try something new.

So many thanks to Sija Hong for your gorgeous illustration in bringing Kang to life, and to Rich Deas for designing yet another beautiful cover. Thank you to production editor Avia Perez and copyeditor Tracy Koontz for your careful attention to make sure my manuscript is in the best shape it could be. As well as the rest of the Feiwel and Friends imprint for your continued support of this duology. Also much appreciation to the amazing marketing and publicity team: Gabriella Salpeter, Leigh Ann Higgins, Morgan Rath, Sara Elroubi, Nicole Schaefer, and Cynthia Lliguichuzhca, along with Fernanda Viveiros at Raincoast.

To my good friends, Nafiza and Roselle: Our group chat has gotten me through some tough times, and I appreciate you both so much.

To Kat Cho and Axie Oh, for being among my first author connections and continuing to be funny and fabulous friends years later.

To the members of Our Writer's Room: Thank you, Lana, for running this group, and for everyone in it. You are all so generous with your time and support for new authors.

Thank you to Joan He, Xiran Jay Zhao, and Juliet Marillier, for taking the time to read the work of a debut author.

To my junior high teacher, Mrs. Wees, who was the first to encourage me to pursue publication and who planted that initial dream in my mind. So amazing to connect with you years later!

To Mimi, who taught me about sisterhood. Can't wait to celebrate with you finally in person.

As always, thank you to my husband and Lyra. I love our beautiful family.

Glossary

Terms

Term	Chinese	Pronunciation	Meaning
Blackwater (Battalion)	黑江(營)	hēi jiāng (yíng)	A rebel force operating near the Clearwater River
dān	丹	dān	Medicine contained in pill or powder form, usually associated with enhancement of magical properties
Dōngzhì	冬至	dōng zhì	Winter Solstice (holiday)
guǎn	管	guǎn	A double-reed pipe instrument
miǎn guān	冕冠	miǎn guān	The Chinese equivalent of a crown, worn by the ruling emperor
shénnóng-shī	神農師	shén nóng shī	Master of Shénnóng magic

shénnóng-tú	神農徒	shén nóng tú	Apprentice of Shénnóng magic
wŭ xíng	五形功夫	wŭ xíng gōng fū	The five forms of martial arts
wŭlín-shī	武林師	wŭ lín shī	Master of the martial arts of the Black Tiger
zhīcáng-sī	知藏司	zhī cáng sī	The Keeper of Secrets, an Elder of Yĕliŭ

Character Name Pronunciation Guide

Name	Chinese Name	Pronunciation
Badu	巴渡	Bā Dù
Bìxì	贔屭	Bì Xì
Chen Shao	陳邵	Chén Shào
Fei	霏	Fēi
Gao Ruyi	高如意	Gāo Rú Yì
Gongyu	龔禹	Gōng Yŭ
Hongbo	宏博	Hóng Bó
Ho-yi and Ho-buo	何姨, 何伯	Hó Yí, Hó Bó

Huang (Brother / Lieutenant)	黃(師兄/上尉)	Huáng (shī xiōng / shàng wèi)
Li (Xu) Kang	李(許)康	Lǐ (Xǔ) Kāng
Li Ying-Zhen	李瑩貞	Lǐ Yíng Zhēn
Lin Huayu	林華宇	Lin Huá Yǔ
Lin Wenyi	林文義	Lin Wén Yì
Luo Lian	羅蓮	Luó Lián
Qi Meng-Fu (Teacher)	齊夢福(師尊)	Qí Mèng Fú (shī zūn)
Ren (Ge)	仁(哥)	Rén (gē)
Small Wu (Wu Zhong-Chang)	小吳(吳忠昌)	Xiǎo Wú (Wú Zhōng Chāng)
Tai (Elder)	泰(師尊)	Tài (shī zūn)
Zhang Ning	張寧	Zhāng Níng
Zhang Shu	張舒	Zhāng Shū

Place Names of Note

Place Name	Chinese Name	Pronunciation	Location
Ānhé (Province)	安和(省)	ān hé (shěng)	Southeastern agricultural and coastal province

Băiniăo (Gorge)	百鳥(峡)	băi niăo (xiá)	The Gorge of One Hundred Birds; the town of Ràohé overlooks it.
Clearwater (River)	清水(河)	Qīng shuǐ (hé)	River that separates Yún province from the Emerald Isles
Dàxī	大熙	dà xī	The Great and Brilliant Empire
Forgetting Sea (Bamboo Sea)	忘憂竹海	wàng yōu zhú hăi	Bamboo forest that is on the border between Kallah and Yún
Fúróng (River)	芙蓉(河)	fúróng (hé)	A branch of the Clearwater River, runs through the Băiniăo Gorge
Guòwū (Pass)	過巫(關)	guò wū (guān)	Mountain pass leading to Yĕliŭ
Hánxiá (Academy)	函霞(寺)	hán xiá (sì)	Academy dedicated to the Blue Carp (studies of agriculture, animal husbandry, and tea)

Huá (Prefecture)	華(州)	huá (zhōu)	Prefecture to the west of the capital city
Jia (City)	佳(都)	Jiā (dū)	The capital city
Kallah (Province)	佧㺶(省)	kǎ lā (shěng)	Northwestern grassland province
Língyǎ (Monastery)	陵雅(寺)	líng yǎ (sì)	Monastery, tomb of former emperors. Located within Jia.
Lǜzhou (Prefecture)	綠(洲)	lǜ (zhōu)	Northeastern prefecture composed of a peninsula and a group of islands, also known as the Emerald Isles
Ràohé (Town)	遶和(鎮)	rào hé (zhèn)	Town along the Clearwater on the eastern edge of Yún
Sù (Province)	溯(省)	sù (shěng)	Southwestern agricultural province

Tai Shan Zhuang (Residence)	泰山(莊)	tài shān (zhuāng)	The former residence of Elder Tai
Tiānxiáng (Lake)	天祥(湖)	tiān xiáng (hú)	Lake on Kallah border
Wǔlín (Academy)	武林(寺)	wǔ lín (sì)	Academy dedicated to the Black Tiger (studies of military strategy and martial arts)
Xīnyì (Village)	辛藝(村)	xīn yì (cūn)	Ning's home village
Xìngyuán (Village)	興元(村)	xìng yuán (cūn)	Village at base of mountain pass leading to Yěliǔ
Yěliǔ (Academy)	野柳(寺)	yě liǔ (sì)	Academy dedicated to Bìxì, the Emerald Tortoise (studies of justice and rites)
Yún (Province)	雲(省)	yún (shěng)	Northern mountainous province

Chinese Medicinal Ingredients Mentioned

Name of Ingredient	Chinese Name	Chinese Pronunciation	Scientific or Common Name
bānjǐtiān	巴戟天	bā jǐ tiān	Root of *Morinda officinalis*
benzoin	安息香	ān xí xiāng	A resin obtained from bark and used as incense and perfume
chénxiāng	沉香	chén xiāng	Resin of agarwood
dāncān	丹參	dān cān	Root of *Salvia miltiorrhiza*
fúlíng (Mushroom)	茯靈	fú líng	*Wolfiporia extensa*, a fungus
hú huáng lián	胡黃連	hú huáng lián	Root of *Picrorhiza scrophulariiflora*
kūnbù	昆布	kūn bù	Seaweed
licorice root	甘草	gān cǎo	Root of *Glycyrrhiza uralensis*
lí lú	藜蘆	lí lú	Root of *Veratrum nigrum*

língzhī (Mushroom)	靈芝	líng zhī	*Ganoderma lingzhi*, a fungus
pearl powder	珍珠粉	zhēn zhū fěn	Ground from pearl or shell of *Pteria martensii* (Oyster)
shārén	砂仁	shā rén	Dried fruit of *Wurfbainia villosa*
white peony root	白芍	bái sháo	Root of *Paeonia sterniana*
yuǎnzhì	遠志	yuǎn zhì	Root of *Polygala tenuifolia*
zheěrgēn	折耳根	zhé ěr gēn	Tuber of *Houttuynia cordata*

Thank you for reading this Feiwel & Friends book. The friends who made *A Venom Dark and Sweet* possible are:

Jean Feiwel, Publisher
Liz Szabla, Associate Publisher
Rich Deas, Senior Creative Director
Holly West, Senior Editor
Anna Roberto, Senior Editor
Kat Brzozowski, Senior Editor
Dawn Ryan, Executive Managing Editor
Kim Waymer, Senior Production Manager
Emily Settle, Editor
Foyinsi Adegbonmire, Associate Editor
Rachel Diebel, Associate Editor
Avia Perez, Production Editor